PENGUIN BOOKS

Tempest-Tost

Robertson Davies was born in Ontario and educated in Canada and at Oxford. A much-produced playwright in Canada, he once studied acting at the Old Vic—where he was Sir Tyrone Guthrie's literary assistant and where Mr. Davies met and married his wife, Brenda. Robertson Davies was for twenty years the editor of the *Peterborough Examiner,* during which time he wrote a number of novels and books of criticism and also served as principal book reviewer for the weekly *Saturday Night.* One of Canada's most distinguished men of letters, he has written more than twenty-six books—among which are the celebrated novels *Fifth Business, The Manticore,* and *World of Wonders*—and many plays, the most recent being *Question Time.* Until the spring of 1981 Mr. Davies also taught at the University of Toronto, where he was Master of Massey College. Penguin Books also publishes Mr. Davies's *Deptford Trilogy, Fifth Business, High Spirits, Leaven of Malice, The Manticore, A Mixture of Frailties, One Half of Robertson Davies, The Rebel Angels,* and *World of Wonders.*

ROBERTSON DAVIES

TEMPEST·TOST

Penguin Books

Penguin Books Canada Ltd., 2801 John Street, Markham, Ontario, Canada L3R 1B4
Penguin Books Ltd., 27 Wrights Lane, London W8 5TZ (Publishing & Editorial)
and Harmondsworth, Middlesex, England (Distribution & Warehouse)
Penguin Books, 40 West 23rd Street, New York, New York 10010, U.S.A.
Penguin Books Australia Ltd., Ringwood, Victoria, Australia
Penguin Books (N.Z.) Ltd., 182-190 Wairau Road, Auckland 10, New Zealand

First published in Canada by Clarke, Irwin & Company Limited 1951
First published in Penguin Books 1980
7 9 11 13 15 14 12 10 8

Copyright © Clarke, Irwin & Company Limited 1951
Published by arrangement with Irwin Publishing Inc.
All rights reserved.

Manufactured in Canada by
Webcom Limited

Canadian Cataloguing in Publication Data

Davies, Robertson, 1913-
Tempest-tost

ISBN 0-14-005431-6

I. Title.

PS8507.A95T45 1980   C813'.54   C80-005130-0
PR9199.3.D3T45 1980

I'll drain him dry as hay:
Sleep shall neither night nor day
Hang upon his pent-house lid;
He shall live a man forbid.
Weary se'nnights nine times nine
Shall he dwindle, peak and pine:
Though his bark cannot be lost,
Yet it shall be tempest-tost.

MACBETH I. 3

CHAPTER

1

"IT'S GOING to be a great nuisance for both of us," said Freddy. "Couldn't you make a fuss about it, Tom?"

"If your father said they could use the place, it's no good for me to make a fuss," said Tom.

"Yes, but Daddy just said that they could use the place in a large, general way. He didn't specially say that they could use this shed. Anyway he only said it because Griselda is probably going to have a big part. It seems to me that I remember him saying that he didn't want them in the house."

"Now Miss Freddy, you'd better be sure about that. You've got a way of remembering your Dad said just whatever you wanted him to say."

When Tom called her Miss Freddy she knew that he had temporarily ceased to be a friend and had become that incalculable, treacherous thing, an adult. At fourteen she had no defence against such sudden shifts. People treated her as a child or an equal, whichever suited them at the moment. But she had thought that she could rely on Tom. Still, had Daddy really said that he didn't want the Little Theatre people trampling through his house? She could hear the words spoken in his voice, quite clearly, but had he really said them? Solly had once told her that she interpreted Daddy as priests interpret their gods, for her own ends. This was a moment for discretion. She would achieve little without Tom's help.

"I didn't mean that you should refuse to let them in here, or anything silly like that. I just meant that you could make it rather difficult. You don't want them snooping around in

3

here, poking into all your drawers and using your tools, and getting everything all mixed up. That's just what Larry Pye will do. There won't be a thing left in its place by the time he gets through. You know that, Tom."

Tom's expression showed that he knew it very well. He didn't want strangers in his workshop, messing about, dulling all his carefully sharpened edges, snarling his tidy coils of twine, using his pruning shears for cutting wire, as like as not. What might not happen if they began nosing into his special pride, the cabinet where all his seeds were kept, labelled and tucked away in tidy brown envelopes? Be just like them, to go rooting into what was none of their business. In his heart he was on Freddy's side, but he wanted to enjoy the luxury of being persuaded. Anyway, he shouldn't give way to a child too easily. Bad for the child's character.

"Maybe I don't want 'em," he said, slyly; "but you want 'em even less. I've got my things to keep neat. But I've got nothing to hide."

"It's beneath you to say a mean thing like that, Tom," said Freddy.

"Bad enough if they get larkin' around with my seed, but suppose they get hold of those bottles of yours? I don't want anybody poisoned in here, and police on the job, and you put away for anything up to forty years." Tom guffawed, relishing his flight of fancy.

"Oh, Tom!" Freddy was disgusted. How stupid adults could be! Even a nice man like Tom.

"They'd let you off easy for murdering Larry Pye. But bootlegging! That's where they'd get you. Brewing and distilling, and thereby cheating the Government out of its taxes on alcoholic liquors! That's real crime, Freddy."

"Tom, I'm not a bootlegger! I'm a scientist, really. I'm only a bootlegger if I offer it for sale. And I give it away. As you certainly ought to know, for I gave you a bottle of my blackberry wine last Christmas, and you drank it and said it was good."

"And so it was good. But you put quite a bit of your

Dad's brandy in that blackberry before you put it down to mature."

"Of course. All those dessert wines have to be fortified. But it wasn't just the brandy that made it good; it was good wine, and I made it with the greatest care, and I think it's downright miserable of you to make fun of it."

"I was just coddin' you, Freddy. It was real good wine. But I don't know what your father would say if he knew how much stuff like that you've got hidden away in here."

"You'll know what he says in a few weeks. His birthday is coming, and I've got a dozen—a whole beautiful dozen —of champagne cider to give him. It's wonderful stuff, Tom. A year old—just right—and if he likes it, I'm going to ask him to let me study in France, and learn everything about wine, and then come back here and revolutionize the wine industry in Canada. He's got a lot of stock in a winery, and he could ask them to give me a job. Just think, Tom, maybe I'll end up as the Veuve Cliquot of Canada!"

"Can't say that I know what that is."

"It's the name of a woman. 'Veuve' means widow. Madame Cliquot's champagne is one of the most famous in the world. She's dead, of course, but her name lives."

"Well, anything can happen," said Tom, considering. "Widow Webster's Wines; that's what yours would have to be called. Sounds like something you'd take for your health. But that's a long way off, Freddy. I'd give it a rest, now, if I was you."

"I couldn't be Widow Webster if I'd married," said Freddy, practically; "I'd be Widow Something Else. Tom, you don't understand how serious I am. I really mean it. I'm not just playing. I really have a very professional attitude about the whole thing. I've read books about wine chemistry, and books about vintages, and everything about wine I can get my hands on. I know I'm young, but I'm not being silly, really I'm not. And if you let me down I don't know what I'll do, for there isn't another soul I can really trust. Griselda wouldn't understand; she hasn't any brains anyway, and when it comes to wine she simply hasn't a clue. And Daddy will have to be shown. Please be a sport, Tom, and don't go all grown-up on me."

Tom was not the man to withstand such an appeal. He was fifty, he had an excellent wife, he had two sons in the Navy, he was the best gardener within fifty miles, he was a respected member of the Sergeant's Club, and he was bass soloist—unpaid, but highly regarded—in the choir of St. Clement's; but age and honours could not change the fact that Freddy—Miss Fredegonde Webster, his employer's younger daughter—was a very special friend of his. As he often said to the wife, Freddy had no mother. But if he was to give in, he'd have to give some advice, as well. That was only fair; if a kid gets her way, she has to take some advice. That is part of the unwritten code which governs the dealings between generations.

"Well, Freddy," he said, speaking her name on the low D which was so much admired at St. Clement's, "I know you're serious, right enough, but you've got to remember that you're only fourteen, and if most people knew what you was up to, they'd be shocked. They'd never believe that you could make it and not drink it. Now wait a minute; I know you just test it, because you've got to keep your palate sharp. I know you just gargle it and spit it out and smack your lips like the real wine-tasters. But they'd never believe it. They'd misunderstand. I've seen a good deal of life and a good deal of war, and I tell you, Freddy, it's a shocker how people can be misunderstood. I'll say nothing, but you be careful. You've got to keep your nose clean, as they say. If your Dad found out, and knew I knew, it'd be as good as my position is worth. And I don't want to leave this garden because you've been found tight under a lilac and I'm an accomplice. See?"

Tom was a Welshman, and the native taste for preaching was plainly strong within him this afternoon, so Freddy struck in hastily.

"Oh yes, Tom dear, I do see, and I'll be very discreet. And I do think you're being simply marvellous and big-souled about the whole thing. And I won't take to drink; I swear I won't. That isn't what interests me in wine at all. I'm really very professional. I'll say special prayers against the temptation."

This was not a happy inspiration. Freddy had, within the last year, become rather High Church in her views; St. Clement's was Broad, with a tendency to become Low under stress. Tom took breath for another lecture, but Freddy hurried on.

"It won't be a secret from Daddy after his birthday, you see. I'll give him the champagne cider, and explain everything, and I'm sure it will be all right from then on. He might even let me set up a little lab in the house—maybe even a tiny still—"

"I can see your Dad letting his daughter set up a still in his house," said Tom, using his low D again to achieve an effect of irony. But Freddy was not to be checked. She liked to talk as well as he.

"It's sure to be a success. It's good; I can see that. Not a hint of acetification or rope to be seen in a single bottle of the dozen. I took care of sediment before I bottled. And I bottled just at the psychological moment. I bet if Veuve Cliquot had been there she would have been pleased. And now it's been ten months in bottle and should be quite fit to drink. Of course another year would do no harm, but it's ready now."

"I shouldn't think your Dad was just the man for cider," said Tom.

"But it isn't just old common cider. It's champagne cider. And Morgan O'Doherty says in *Life through the Neck of a Bottle* that he has tasted champagne ciders which were superior to all but the finest champagnes! And you know that ache Daddy gets in his back on cold days? Well, the doctor says it's just an ache, but I suspect it's gravel. And do you know what's the very best thing for gravel? Cider! It says so in the *Encyclopaedia Britannica*. It says, 'The malic acid of cider is regarded as a powerful diuretic which stimulates the kidneys and prevents the accumulation of uric acid within the system.'"

"I told you it was medicine," said Tom, who was not a man to let a joke perish half-savoured. "Try the Widow Websters Wines for what ails you."

"Tom," said Freddy, in a cold voice, "was your Christmas bottle of my blackberry like medicine? Your wife told me she didn't know where you got it, but that you never let it alone till it was all gone, and you sang Gounod's *Nazareth* four times without stopping and embarrassed her before company. Let's not hear quite so much about the Widow Webster."

Tom did not receive this well. But Freddy had reached an age where she no longer felt called upon to submit without protest to the impudence of her elders, even in the case of such a valued friend and ally as Tom. There was a silence, during which Tom continued to do mysterious things with some wilted bits of green stuff which he called 'slips'. Freddy, having made her point, was willing to risk a snub by starting up the conversation again.

"Do you think we can keep them out of here?"

"We can try."

"Daddy said they could do their play in the garden. They don't really have to come in here."

"My experience with people who do plays is they have to go everyplace that isn't locked and they have to move everything that isn't fastened down," said Tom, with bitterness. "This'll be the nearest place for them to get their electric power from, and they'll have a lot of tack they'll want to store here between practices and the like. What your Dad said to me was, 'Give 'em whatever help they need, and if it gets past bearing, come to me.' Well, I can't go to him first off and say I don't want 'em to use the workshop and toolshed. That'd mean they have to use the garage or part of the cellar, and he won't want that. They mustn't get into the house. That is, unless we all want a row with them Laplanders."

Tom's grammar was variable. Speaking officially to his employer, it was careful. But for emphasis he relapsed into forms which he found easier and more eloquent. He never spoke of the admirable Swedish couple who headed the indoor staff except as "them Laplanders".

"But we'll do our best, won't we?"

"Yes, Freddy, but I got a hunch that our best isn't going to be good enough."

And with that Freddy had to be content.

In her daydreams Freddy sometimes fancied that her native city would be known to history chiefly as her birthplace, and this as much as anything shows the extent of her ambition. Salterton had seen more of history than most Canadian cities, and its tranquillity was not easily disturbed. Like Quebec and Halifax, it is a city which provides unusual opportunities for gush, for it has abundant superficial charm. But the real character of Salterton is beneath the surface, and beyond the powers of gush to disclose.

People who do not know Salterton repeat a number of half-truths about it. They call it dreamy and old-world; they say that it is at anchor in the stream of time. They say that it is still regretful for those few years when it appeared that Salterton would be the capital of Canada. They say that it is the place where Anglican clergymen go when they die. And, sooner or later, they speak of it as "quaint".

It is not hard to discover why the word "quaint" is so often applied to Salterton by the unthinking or the imperceptive; people or cities who follow their own bent without much regard for what the world thinks are frequently so described; there is an implied patronage about the word. But the people who call Salterton "quaint" are not the real Saltertonians, who know that there is nothing quaint—in the sense of the word which means wilfully eccentric—about the place. Salterton is itself. It seems quaint to those whose own personalities are not strongly marked and whose intellects are infrequently replenished.

Though not a large place it is truly describable as a city. That word is now used of any large settlement, and Salterton is big enough to qualify; but a city used to be the seat of a bishop, and Salterton was a city in that sense long be-

fore it became one in the latter. It is, indeed, the seat of
two bishoprics, one Anglican and one Roman Catholic. As
one approaches it from the water the two cathedrals, which
are in appearance so strongly characteristic of the faiths
they embody, seem to admonish the city. The Catholic
cathedral points a vehement and ornate Gothic finger toward Heaven; the Anglican cathedral has a dome which,
with offhand Anglican suavity, does the same thing. St.
Michael's cries, "Look aloft and pray!"; St. Nicholas' says,
"If I may trouble you, it might be as well to lift your eyes
in this direction." The manner is different; the import is
the same.

In the environs of the cathedrals the things of this world
are not neglected. Salterton is an excellent commercial
city, and far enough from other large centres of trade to
have gained, and kept, a good opinion of itself. To name
all its industries here would be merely dull, but they are
many and important. However, they do not completely
dominate the city and engross the attention of its people,
as industries are apt to do in less favoured places. One of
the happy things about Salterton is that it is possible to
work well and profitably there without having to carry one's
work into the remotest crannies of social life. To the outsiders, who call Salterton "quaint", this sometimes looks
like snobbishness. But the Saltertonians do not care. They
know that a little snobbery, like a little politeness, oils the
wheels of daily life. Salterton enjoys a satisfying consciousness of past glories and, in a modest way, makes its own
rules.

More than is usual in Canada, Salterton's physical appearance reveals its spirit. As well as its two cathedrals it
has a handsome Court House (with a deceptive appearance
of a dome but not, perhaps, a true dome) and one of His
Majesty's largest and most forbidding prisons (with an
unmistakable dome). And it is the seat of Waverley University. To say that the architecture of Waverley revealed
its spirit would be a gross libel upon a centre of learning
which has dignity and, in its high moments, nobility. The

university had the misfortune to do most of its building during that long Victorian period when architects strove like Titans to reverse all laws of seemliness and probability and when what had been done in England was repeated, clumsily and a quarter of a century later, in Canada. Its buildings are of two kinds: in the first the builders have disregarded the character of the local stone and permitted themselves an orgy of campaniles, baroque staircases, Norman arches, Moorish peepholes and bits of grisly Scottish *chinoiserie* and *bondieuserie*, if such terms may be allowed; in the second kind the local stone has so intimidated the builders that they have erected durable stone warehouses, suitable perhaps for the study of the sciences but markedly unfriendly toward humanism. The sons and daughters of Waverley love their Alma Mater as the disciples of Socrates loved their master, for a beauty of wisdom which luckily transcends mere physical appearance.

At an earlier date than the establishment of Waverley four houses of real beauty were built in Salterton by the eccentric Prebendary Bedlam, one of those Englishmen who sought to build a bigger and better England in the colonies. By a lucky chance one of these, known as Old Bedlam, is upon the present university grounds, and houses the Provost of Waverley.

While upon this theme it may be as well to state that, among the good architecture of Salterton, there is much that is mediocre and some which is downright bad. The untutored fancy of evangelical religion has raised many a wart upon that fair face. Commerce, too, has blotched it. But upon the whole the effect is pleasing and, in some quarters of the town, genuinely beautiful. There are stone houses in Salterton, large and small, which show a justness of proportion, and an intelligent consideration of the material used, which are not surpassed anywhere in Canada. These houses appear to have faces—intelligent, well-bred faces; the knack of building houses which have faces, as opposed to grimaces, is retained by few builders.

It was in one of these, though not the best, that Freddy

11

lived with her sister Griselda and her father, George Alexander Webster. The house was called St. Agnes' and it was very nearly a genuine Bedlamite dwelling. But when St. Agnes' was three-quarters finished Prebendary Bedlam had run out of money, and had not completed his plan. He had not died bankrupt or in poverty, for in his day it was almost impossible for a dignitary of the Church of England to descend to such vulgarities, but it had been an uncommonly narrow squeak. After his death the house had been completed, but not according to the original plans, by an owner whose taste had not been as pure as that of Bedlam, whose mania for building had been guided by a genuine knowledge of what can be done with stone and plaster. In a later stage St. Agnes' had suffered a fire, and some rebuilding had been done around 1900 in the taste of that era. Since that time St. Agnes' had been little altered. George Alexander Webster had made it a little more comfortable inside; the basement kitchen had been replaced by a modern one, and arrangements had been made to heat the house in winter by a system which did not combine all the draughtiness of England with the bitter cold of Canada, but otherwise he had not touched it.

His contribution to the place was made in the grounds. St. Agnes' stood in ten or twelve acres of its own, and Webster's taste for gardening had brought them to a pitch which would surely have delighted Prebendary Bedlam. Under the owner's direction, and with the sure hand of Tom to assist, the gardens had become beautiful, and as always happens with beautiful things, many people wanted them.

Mr. Webster did not like lending his gardens. He knew what the people thought who wanted to borrow them. They thought that a man with such gardens ought to be proud to show them off. They thought that a rich man should not be so selfish as to keep his beautiful gardens to himself. They thought that common decency positively demanded that he make his gardens available for a large variety of causes, and that he should not mind if a cause which had borrowed his gardens should thereupon charge other people admission to see them. He was, it was argued, "in a position to entertain"; most of the people who "gave of their time and effort" in order to advance causes "were not in a position to entertain"; the least that he could do to minimize the offence of being better off than these good people was to assume the entertaining position upon demand. But he did not like to have other people taking their pleasure with his gardens any more than he would have liked to have other people take their pleasure with his wife, if that lady had been living.

He was ready to admit that he was well off. (Rich men never say that they are rich; they think it unlucky.) He was ready to contribute generously to good causes, even when the goodness was somewhat inexplicable. But he did not want strangers trampling through the gardens which were his personal creation, and which he liked to keep for himself. The people who wanted his gardens did not, of course, know of his opinions in this matter, nor would they have believed that any man could seriously want such large gardens all to himself. Indeed, there were people of advanced political opinions in Salterton who could not imagine that one man with two daughters could really want so large a house as St. Agnes' all to himself, for any reason except to spite the workers and mock their less fortunate lot. These advanced people pointed out that a man could only be in one room at a time, sit in one chair at a time, and sleep in one bed at a time; therefore a man whose desires soared beyond one room with a chair and a bed in it was morally obliged to justify himself. An instructor at Waverley who was enjoying the delicious indignations of impecunious youth had once made a few remarks to a class in elementary philosophy on the iniquity of consuming seventy tons of coal each winter to warm one man; as Waverley had already drawn upon Mr. Webster's purse and hoped to give it many a good shake in the future, the instructor was instructed to find fuel for his own fires further from Salterton. But Mr. Webster, beneath the horny carapace which a rich man must

13

grow in order to protect himself against his natural enemies, the poor, had depths of feeling undreamed of by those who talked so much about him; he dearly loved his big, rather ugly old house and his big, beautiful garden; after his daughters he loved these best of all.

It was because of his daughter Griselda that he had agreed to lend his garden to the Salterton Little Theatre for an outdoor production or, as Mrs. Roscoe Forrester preferred to call it, "a pastoral". The particular pastoral which had been chosen was *The Tempest*, and Griselda, who had just been released from boarding-school, was named as a possible person to play Ariel. It had been Mrs. Forrester's intention from the beginning that the play should be done at St. Agnes', and at the meeting where the matter was discussed she began her campaign in these words:

"And now we come to the all-important question of site. There are several places in the city where a pastoral could be done. Bagot Park is just lovely, but it has been pointed out to me that there is baseball practically nightly. The Pauldrons have a lovely place, but Mrs. Pauldron points out that it is right on the river, and well, if one of the boats sounded its siren right in the middle of a scene, well, it would ruin the scene, wouldn't it?" (Laughter, led by Mrs. Pauldron in a manner which she later described to her husband as "laughing the idea out of court".) "Anyway, it gets damp after sundown." (Histrionic shudder by Mrs. Pauldron.) "The lawn in front of Old Bedlam is just perfect, but the Provost tells me that there are likely to be several theological conferences there this summer, and therefore he cannot be sure of anything. Mrs. Bumford has kindly offered her grounds, but the committee feels regretfully that even if we put a row of chairs on the street, we could not accommodate more than sixty people in the audience. So the matter is still up in the air."

Here a lady rose and asked if anyone had thought of approaching Mrs. S. P. Solleret? Mrs. Roscoe Forrester pursed her lips and closed her eyes in a manner which made it plain that she had spoken to Mrs. Solleret, and that she did not wish to go into the matter of Mrs. Solleret's reply.

It was at this point that Professor Vambrace, who had been primed by Mrs. Forrester before the meeting, rose hesitatingly to his feet.

"Has any thought been given to St. Agnes'?" said he.

Mrs. Forrester's eyes flew open, and she seemed to project beams of new hope from them at the audience. "I hadn't thought of it," said she. "I suppose it is because Miss Webster is likely to be a member of the cast, and we just never thought of looking among the cast for—er—um." Mrs. Forrester found these uncompleted sentences, the Greek rhetorical device of aposiopesis, very handy in her duties as president. She would drop a sentence in the middle, completing it with a speaking look, or a little laugh, thereby forcing other people to do her dirty work. Professor Vambrace, that bony and saturnine hatchet-man of the Salterton Little Theatre, obliged her now.

"May I suggest," he said, standing in the half-squatting, jackknife position of one who wishes to address a meeting without making a formal speech, "that Miss Griselda Webster be appointed a committee of one to approach her father regarding the performance of *The Tempest* in the gardens at St. Agnes'."

That was how it was done.

The approach which Griselda used might have surprised the meeting. It took this form.

"Daddy, have any sharks been after you for the garden this year?"

"Two or three. I said I'd think about it."

"The Little Theatre has put me up to asking you if you'd let them do the play here. They thought I didn't see through them, but I did. They asked a few first, and pretended there was no place to go unless you kicked through. You don't have to say yes because of me."

"Do you want to have it here?"

"Well, there's no denying that it would be nice."

"Was that why they hinted about giving you a leading part?"

"Probably. But they wrought better than they knew. I'm really quite a good actress. And I'm not what you'd call plain. At least, not what you'd call plain when you consider that the only other possible person is Pearl Vambrace, who has rather a moustache. I'll be quite good even if we do it on Old Ma Bumford's little hanky of a weedy lawn, with half the audience sitting in the road."

"It sounds like one of Nellie Forrester's sneaky tricks."

"Yes. But Daddy: if you let them have your garden you have a good excuse for refusing it to everybody else for the rest of this summer. Had you thought of that?"

"Yes; I suppose so. All right. Remind me in the morning to tell Tom."

Tom took it very well. Very well, that is to say, for a gardener. He pointed out that it was not the damage to the lawns that he minded; that could be repaired by a month or so of rolling. It was the way people got their feet into his borders that bothered him. However, he realized that his employer had to lend the garden sometimes, and from what he had heard, the Little Theatre performances did not draw very big crowds, so it might not be too bad.

Mr. Webster sympathized. Nevertheless, he said, if the thing was to be done, it must be done properly. Therefore Tom was to give the Little Theatre people any help they wanted. Mr. Webster did not intend to have anything to do with the business himself. It pained him to see people in his garden who did not appreciate it as much as he did, and he did not propose to give himself needless pain.

Tom accepted this direction with a mental reservation. If it was in any way possible, he meant to keep the intruders out of the part of his domain which was called The Shed. It was here that he kept his tools, neatly hung up in rows, and tidily arranged on his workbench. The sight of a rake or a hoe standing on the floor, however neatly, offended Tom's professional sense. He was the kind of gardener who sharpened hoes with a file. Mr. Webster had once remarked that he had been shaved with razors which were duller than Tom's hoes. In The Shed, Tom was in the capital of his kingdom. It is a measure of his affection for Freddy that he had permitted her to store her home-made wines in a corner of The Shed, in some racks which he built for her himself. They were covered by a folded tarpaulin. Insofar as a gardener's workshop can be neat, The Shed was neat.

The Shed was a misleading name for this workshop. It was in fact a conservatory, built by the Victorian owner of St. Agnes' who had bought it from Prebendary Bedlam's heirs. It was an elaborate and hideous erection; from the ground rose a stone foundation three feet high, and, above this, iron supports soared upward, to meet in an arch. Between the iron-work was glass, so that, inside and out, The Shed presented the appearance of an oblong birdcage. An elaborate system of canvas curtains had been devised to keep the sun from scorching the plants within, and these curtains were drawn up or let down by an intricate system of cording, like the rigging of a sailing-ship, which added to the birdcage a strong suggestion of a spider-web. The iron framework was ornamented at intervals with outbreaks of iron leafage and iron fruitage, which had grown rusty with time. There were no broken panes of glass in it, for Tom would not have permitted such an offence against neatness, but not all the panes matched, and some of them were discoloured by rust from the ironwork. In this conservatory Victorian lovers had doubtless flirted and whispered. And in its warmth, among displays of fern and large, opulent plants which were valued for their rarity rather than their beauty, rheumatisms long since at peace, and gouty toes which have ceased to twinge, were eagerly discussed and described by their owners. But the glory of the conservatory had fled. It was now The Shed, and the plants which served the garden and the house were grown in a modern greenhouse behind the garage. But The Shed was Tom's citadel, and he meant to defend it to the last.

As luck would have it, The Shed was the first thing to fall into the hands of the Little Theatre. It happened about a week after Griselda had spoken, as a committee of one, to her father; since then Freddy had allowed no day to pass without working upon Tom, heartening him for a vigorous resistance to any invasion of The Shed.

It was a Friday afternoon, and after a threatening morning a businesslike rain had begun to fall. Tom sat by his workbench, mixing some stuff which was related to the future welfare of begonias; Freddy sat on a pile of boxes, reading George Saintsbury's *Notes On A Cellar Book*, which was a favourite volume of hers. The door burst open without warning and Mrs. Roscoe Forrester, Professor Vambrace and Griselda ran in.

"You'll be dry here," said Griselda; "I'll go into the house and see if I can find some umbrellas."

She ran out into the rain again; the door which led from The Shed into the rest of the house had been locked for many years, and a heavy cupboard stood before it.

"You'll be Freddy," said Mrs. Forrester, who liked to use this Gaelic form of assertion jocosely. She was not a Scot herself, but she liked to enrich her conversation with what she believed to be Scottish and Irish idioms. "How sweet you look, sitting there with your wee bookie!"

"I am Fredegonde Webster," said Freddy rising. "Good afternoon. You are from the Little Theatre. This is Mr. Gwalchmai, the gardener: Tom—Mrs. Forrester and Professor Vambrace."

Tom touched his cap and said nothing. He had been a good soldier in his time—a first-rate sergeant—but he had never known what to do about surprise attacks, except to resent their sneakiness.

"We're going to be great friends, Mr. —uh—but perhaps I'd better call you Tom right away," said Mrs. Forrester, reaching for his hand. Tom's hand was covered with muck, and he would have dearly liked to give it to her, but he forebore. Professor Vambrace gave what he doubtless meant to be a friendly glance, but was really a baleful glare, at both

Tom and Freddy, to be shared between them.

"Wet," said he. Classics was his subject, and he sometimes affected a classical simplicity in social conversation.

Freddy was young in years, but old in certain sorts of wisdom; she had learned from her father, for instance, that nothing is so disconcerting as silence, and she was preparing to give Mrs. Forrester a lot of it. But Professor Vambrace's summing up of the weather had scarcely died upon the air before the door burst open again and Griselda rushed in with two more people under an umbrella. The first was Solly Bridgetower, a young man whom Freddy admired in a friendly sort of way; the other was an unknown woman.

"We can finish talking here," said Griselda. "We'll get wet if we try to make a dash for the front door."

Griselda did not recognize The Shed as Tom's special property. She thought of it simply as an extension of her father's house. Tom was not the big figure in her world that he was in Freddy's.

"What about Larry and Mr. Mackilwraith?" asked Mrs. Forrester.

"We'll keep an eye out for them," said Griselda. "Larry wanted to finish his little sketch of the lawn. Anyway, he's hanging about to look for What's His Name—the fellow who's going to play Ferdinand."

"Mackilwraith will not be here until after four," said Professor Vambrace. "School."

"Probably not until after half-past four," said Solly. "If old Hector hasn't changed his ways he'll have some wretched child under his eye for at least half an hour after closing-time. One of the really great detainers and keepers-in of our time, Old Hector."

"Mr. Mackilwraith is a schoolteacher," said Mrs. Forrester to the unknown woman. "I do hope he'll be able to take a look at the lawn; he's our business manager, and he can always tell how many it will seat, and what money that will mean, and all those things. A mathematical wizard."

"A creaking pedant," said Solly.

Professor Vambrace gave him a look which suggested

that while irreverent remarks about schoolteachers did not necessarily affect university professors, they were in questionable taste.

"I speak, of course, in a rich, Elizabethan manner," said Solly, with a rich, Elizabethan gesture which almost toppled a tower of small flower pots. "He's not a bad chap really— I suppose. Freddy, I greet you. You and Miss Rich haven't met, have you? Miss Rich is from New York and she is going to direct our play. This is Fredegonde Webster; she lives here, but splendour has not corrupted her. A pard-like spirit, beautiful and swift."

"How do you do, Miss Webster," said Miss Rich holding out her hand.

"I am very well, thank you," said Freddy, thinking that Miss Rich was a very well-mannered person, and nicely dressed. "Solly is a great tease, as I suppose you have found out."

"We only met about an hour ago," said Miss Rich.

"Aren't we dignified, though?" said Mrs. Forrester, with what she believed to be a laughing glance toward Freddy. "When one is just growing up—oh, the dignity of it! I remember when I was that age; do you remember, Val? Wasn't I just loaded with dignity?"

"I don't really remember, Nell," said Miss Rich.

"Well, I do." Mrs. Forrester was firm. "We were both absolutely bursting with dignity."

"But you got over all that, didn't you?" said Freddy, sweetly. "I suppose that's the fun of being grown up; one has shed so many things which seem desirable to somebody of my age."

"That will do, Freddy," said Griselda.

Freddy was happy to leave the matter there. Griselda's rebuke carried little weight, and she was pleasantly conscious of having choked off Old Ma Forrester.

"Well, have we made up our minds?" asked Professor Vambrace. "Will the lawn do? Will those trees give the background we want? If so, let us make our decision. What do you think, Miss Rich?"

"I think the setting is charming," said she; "if it is agreeable to you, I am quite happy about it. But won't Major Pye have something to say?"

"He's sure to have plenty of fault to find," said Solly, "but he wouldn't completely approve of any place. You know how technical men are; they love to face problems, and when there are none they create them. They're overcomers by nature; the way to please 'em is to give them lots to overcome. 'To him that o'ercometh, God giveth a crown.' That hymn was written especially to flatter stage managers."

"Now don't begin antagonizing Larry at this stage," said Mrs. Forrester; "his work will be hard enough, and we must let him get well into it before we offer any suggestions. So do be good, Solly, and jolly him along."

"What I love about amateur theatricals," said Solly to Miss Rich, "is the way everything is done by jollying everybody. You must miss that dreadfully in the professional theatre. Just a dull round of people giving orders and people obeying them; no jollying."

"You are quite mistaken," she replied; "there is really quite a lot of jollying to be done, though perhaps not quite so much as with amateurs."

"Solly, if you say amateur theatricals again I shall hit you," said Mrs. Forrester; "thank Heaven the Little Theatre left all that nonsense behind years ago. In fact, it may be said that we have a truly professional approach. Haven't we, Walter?"

"Quite," said the economical Vambrace.

"I'm sure it may be said, but is it true?" said Solly. "It certainly wasn't true when I went away; have two years made so much difference?"

"You're just conceited because you've been to Cambridge," said Mrs. Forrester. "But you can't shake off the fact that you got your start with the Salterton Little Theatre, and that it has made you what you are today, theatrically speaking—"

"Oh, God," interjected Solly.

"—if you are anything at all, theatrically speaking, which

has yet to be shown. And it is a great privilege for you to be working with Miss Rich, and don't you forget it, young man."

Mrs. Forrester laughed with a little too much emphasis, to show that this lecture was intended to be friendly. She always maintained that you could say literally anything to anybody, just so long as you said it with a smile, to show that there were no hard feelings. It was going to be necessary to keep Solly in hand, she could see that.

"Mrs. F., you are being grossly unfair," said Solly. "You want me to jolly Larry Pye, to keep him happy. Jolly Solly, that's what I'm to be. But do you jolly me? No, you jump down my throat. Why do you, if I may so express it, make flesh of Pye and fish of me?"

"You're too young to be jollied," she replied. "And don't you call me Mrs. F."

"Well, if you are going to badger me in that tone I certainly can't call you Nellie. If I'm too young to be jollied, you are certainly too old to be treated with friendly familiarity. What do you want to be called: Dame Nellie Forrester?"

"You can call me Nellie when you are a good boy."

"And you shall be called Nagging Nell when you are a bad old girl."

Mrs. Forrester never lost her temper. She prided herself upon this trait and frequently mentioned it to her friends. But sometimes, as upon the present occasion, she felt a burning in the pit of her stomach which would have been anger in anyone else. How stupid it was of Solly not to be able to take a rebuke without all this bickering! She groped for something crushing which could be said in a thoroughly good-natured way, but nothing came. Luckily the door opened at this moment and Major Larry Pye came in, followed by a young man in a raincoat, but without a hat.

"Well, we can do it, but it isn't going to be easy," said Larry, who liked to begin conversations in the middle.

"If anybody can do it, you can," said Solly, in an artificially hearty voice.

"It'll mean a lot of new cable; that's one thing," Larry continued, and he would have set out at once to explain the delightful difficulties he had discovered, and which he meant to overcome, if Mrs. Forrester had not pounced on his companion.

"Roger," she cried, "how sweet of you to come in all this rain! You don't know anyone here, do you?"

"Yes; I know the Major and I've met Professor Vambrace," said the young man.

"Twice," said the Professor.

"This is Miss Valentine Rich, of New York, who is going to direct the play; Roger Tasset, Val, who is to be your leading man. And Griselda Webster, who will probably be our Ariel; Lieutenant Tasset. And this is Solly Bridgetower; he will sort of dogsbody and stooge for Miss Rich; he's just back from Cambridge. Oh, and I almost forgot dear little Freddy, who lives here. And Tom who is going to be our very good friend, I'm sure. Larry, have you met Tom?"

"Hullo, Tom," said Larry.

Tom had a firm grip on the fact that Larry, at some distant time, had been a major, and was still addressed by his military title; this seemed to him to be the one truly creditable fact about the group of people who had come bursting into his Shed, tracking dirt everywhere, and talking silly. So he gave Larry something which was almost a salute.

"Good workshop you have here," said Larry. "Got a lathe?"

"No sir," said Tom.

"Too bad. But we can do most of our building right here," said the major. "It will save a lot of cartage. We might as well have everything as convenient as possible."

With these words Tom's last hope of saving The Shed was slain.

"The rain is growing worse," said Professor Vambrace.

"We shan't be able to do anything else this afternoon," said Mrs. Forrester. "I suppose we should think about ways of getting home. Now have we really decided that this is the place for the play? If there is an objection of any kind, now is the time to state it."

"I don't understand you, Mrs. F.," said Solly spitefully. "You know that we have had our hearts set on this place from the first. Now we've got it. Why fuss?"

"Solly!" cried Mrs. Forrester, and stamped her foot. But in an instant she was smiling. "He only does it to annoy, because he knows it teases," she said. Solly was always quoting; she could quote too.

"It's not as cut and dried as all that," said Larry Pye. "Where's your heavy duty cable to come from? I'd be glad if somebody would tell me that." He looked around at the company. All they thought about was strutting in fine clothes. But it was the old story of the grasshopper and the ant; when the practical business had to be done, they had to come to him. He knew very well where the heavy duty cable would be brought in; he had it all clear in his mind; but it would never do for them to know that.

"The lawn and the trees are quite lovely," said Valentine Rich, "and if you can solve your technical problems, Major Pye, I should like to use this setting very much. I've heard that you are a wonderful stage manager, and that you do miracles every year."

"Don't know about miracles," said Larry, looking like a little boy who has been given a six-bladed jack-knife, "but I'll do my best. Can't say any more than that."

"Then I haven't another worry," said Miss Rich, smiling at him, whereupon he giggled, and decided that it really took a professional to understand what he was up against.

"Did you see the upper lawn, Roger?" asked Mrs. Forrester.

"The Major showed it to me," said Roger Tasset; "jolly good."

"It's wonderful of Roger to act with us," the president continued. "He's terribly busy, taking a course, or giving a course, or something. But I know he's going to be simply wonderful."

"I don't guarantee it," said Roger. "Haven't done anything in this line since I was at school. Can't say I know the play awfully well, as a matter of fact. Is it the one where the chap turns into a donkey?"

"No, it's the one with the shipwreck," said Solly.

"Oh? Good show!"

"We hope it will be," Solly replied, with a courtesy which was a little overdone.

The door opened once more, and a man in a raincoat and a sober grey hat stepped inside, lowered his umbrella, and shook it carefully out of the door before bringing it in after him. Not a drop fell on Tom's floor.

"I'm sorry to be late," said he. "I had to oversee some detentions."

It was Hector Mackilwraith. He brought with him an air of calm command, developed during eighteen years in the schoolroom, which had its effect even upon Solly. He did not take charge, but in his presence Mrs. Forrester quickly established and ratified the already obvious fact that *The Tempest* would be performed six weeks hence on the upper lawn at St. Agnes'. Major Pye agreed that the problem of the heavy-duty cable, though vexing, could be solved. From measurements supplied by Major Pye it was soon decided by Hector Mackilwraith that a sufficient audience could be accommodated to pay the costs of the production and realize a useful profit. Then a silence descended, and when it was plain that there was nothing more to be said, Griselda suggested that she should fetch the big car and drive them all home. It was Hector Mackilwraith who held his umbrella over her as they walked to the garage; and as they drove about the city, dropping the Little Theatre enthusiasts at their widely separated dwellings, it was Hector Mackilwraith who sat by her side.

When they had gone, Freddy and Tom looked at one another in glum dismay. The coming six weeks stretched before them as a period of sheer Hell.

"Well, if you won't stay with us, I suppose you won't," said Mrs. Forrester, with a pout which had been rather attractive fifteen years earlier, "but we could have had a barrel of fun."

"It's not that I won't, Nell; it's that I can't," said Miss Rich patiently. They had covered this ground more than thoroughly during the evening meal. "I shall have to be busy every day, seeing lawyers and auctioneers and so forth. I'd be a nuisance."

"Well, then, let's not talk about it any more. We don't want to quarrel. Though I've been looking forward to having you just a little bit to myself. Haven't I, Roscoe?"

Roscoe nodded, with a smile which might have meant anything, but which probably meant goodwill, sympathy in his wife's disappointment, understanding of Valentine Rich's predicament, reluctance to let a friend of his wife's stop at a hotel, and pleasure that no guest would disturb the peaceful routine of his household. Roscoe Forrester was an admirable salesman; he made a very good income from selling insurance; one of his foremost assets in this highly competitive work was his ability to share with perfect sincerity in several opposed points of view.

They continued with their meal of spiced meat and salad from the delicatessen, ice-cream from the dairy, and cookies from the bakery. Mrs. Forrester believed in what she called "streamlining household work".

The Forresters, as they told everyone they met, had "neither chick nor child". Their failure to have a chick never provoked surprise, but it was odd that they were childless; they had not sought that condition. But they were not driven apart by it, as people of more intense feelings sometimes are; if anything, Roscoe Forrester was a little more attentive toward his wife for that reason, as if he reproached himself for having failed to provide something which might have given her pleasure. He helped her in any way he could with her amusements, which she called "activities", and he gave in to her in all matters of dispute. His attitude toward her was admiring and protective, and in his heart he believed that she was a remarkable woman.

She had, for instance, Taste. Their apartment showed it.

Many people would have sworn that only an interior decorator could have produced such an effect. In the living room, he would explain, there were just two Notes of Colour; one was a picture, a print framed in natural wood, of some red horses playing rather violently in a field; the other was a large bowl, of a deep green, which stood on the pickled oak coffee table. All else in the room was cleverly arranged to be of no colour at all. The suite of two armchairs and a sofa was upholstered in a dingy shade called mushroom; the walls were distempered in a colour which recalled, if anything, vomit. The carpet, a broadloom, was mushroom too, and the hardwood floor, where visible, repeated more firmly the walls' note of delicate nausea. There was one other chair, with no arms, which sat upon a springlike arrangement of bent wood. This was very modern indeed, and was avoided by all save the lightest guests.

An arch in one wall of the living-room gave upon the dining-room, which was smaller, but just as tasteful. Certain concessions to human frailty were permitted here; for instance, on the top of a cabinet sat an effigy in china of an old woman in a bonnet, offering for sale a bunch of rather solid-looking balloons. The furniture was of old pine, which Mrs. Forrester, and Roscoe under her direction, had rubbed down with pumice, and rubbed up with oil, and shellacked until it had a permanently wet look. It was old, and the table was so low that it was rather inconvenient for large guests, but everyone assured Mrs. Forrester that the effect was charming. The bedrooms, kitchen and bathroom of the flat were not carried through on this high level of Taste, but they bore many personal touches; the guest towels, for instance, were marked "Yours" (in contrast to "His" and "Hers" which were used by the owners) and by the bedside in the guest-room was a cigarette box with three very dry cigarettes in it, and two packets of matches, wittily printed with the words "Swiped from The Forresters". Their library was accommodated in a single case in their own bedroom. The most coherent part of it was what Mrs. Forrester called "her drama library"; it comprised three anthologies of plays, a curiously unhelpful manual called *Play Direction For Theatres Great and Small* (written by a professor who had never directed a play in any theatre which might be called great), and a handful of dog-eared acting copies of plays in which Mrs. Forrester had herself appeared. There was also a book about acting by Stanislavsky, which Mrs. Forrester had read to the end of the first chapter and marked intelligently in red pencil, and which she recommended to amateurs who did not know what to do with their hands when on the stage. There were also several books which instructed the reader that peace of mind of the sort possessed by great saints could be achieved by five minutes of daily contemplation, and two or three complementary books which explained that worry, heart disease, hardening of the arteries, *taedium cordis* and despair could all be avoided by relaxing the muscles. There was a book which explained how one could grow slim while eating three delicious, satisfying meals a day. There was a copy of the *Rubaiyat* bound in disagreeable limp suede (a wedding gift from Mrs. Forrester's aunt). And in addition there were twenty or more novels, some bound in cloth and some in paper covers.

"It's going to be a wonderful lift for our group to work with you, Val," said Mrs. Forrester as they took their coffee into the living-room; she switched on a tasteful lamp, which lit the ceiling very well, and in the increased light the red horses whinnied tastefully to the green bowl, which echoed tastefully again. "I mean, now that you've worked with professionals for so long. You've got an awful lot to *give*. Don't you feel that?"

"I wouldn't like to say so," replied Miss Rich; "I feel too often that there are large tracts of the job about which I know nothing at all."

"Ah, but that just *shows*," said Mrs. Forrester. "He that knows not and knows not that he knows not—avoid him; he that knows not and knows that he knows not—uh, wait a minute—uh, instruct him; he that knows and knows that he knows—cleave unto him. That's the way we feel about you."

"I don't quite see where I fit into that," said Valentine, "but I'll do what I can. I've done quite a few outdoor shows. They are always successful unless something absolutely awful happens. People aren't so critical outdoors."

"Oh, but that's just where you're wrong!" Mrs. Forrester caused her eyes to light up by bugging them slightly. "There'll be people here from other Little Theatre groups everywhere within a hundred miles. And they'll have their tomahawks with them. They'll be jealous, you see. They've never done a pastoral. They've never attempted Shakespeare. They'll be on the lookout for every little flaw. Won't they, Roscoe?"

"I guess that's right, hon," said Roscoe, smiling.

"The only thing that persuaded us to try it at all was that you would be here to give it a professional finish."

"But Nell, you wrote me in February that it had been decided, and it was then that you asked if I would help."

"Well, we were toying with the idea, but we would never have decided on it if you hadn't been willing. It was only decided at a full meeting of the members; the committee hadn't really made up their minds. I know that sounds undemocratic, but in these Little Theatres you have to use common sense as well as democracy, don't you?"

"One of the nicest things about the professional theatre is that it is utterly undemocratic. If you aren't any good, you go. Or maybe that's real democracy. I don't know. I'm not a bit political."

"If you let democracy run away with you in the Salterton Little Theatre you'd end in a fine mess," said Mrs. Forrester. "I don't mind telling you that Professor Vambrace and I have to do all the real deciding, and get it through the committee, somehow, and then the committee usually carries the meeting. Otherwise people like Larry Pye would come up with the queerest ideas; all he can talk about is doing a musical comedy, so that he can monkey with lights."

"I hope he doesn't want to monkey too much with the lights in *The Tempest*."

"Oh, you'll be able to deal with him. You must be used to cursing electricians."

29

"No, I've never cursed one that I can remember. You see too many movies about the theatre, Nell."

"Don't be afraid to speak your mind to our people. I've had one or two real knock-down-and-drag-out fights with Larry. Haven't I, Roscoe?"

"Sure have, hon."

"And he respects me for it. You'll find us fully professional in that way."

"I can usually find some other way," said Valentine, who did not wish to appear superior, but who was not going to promise to abuse the Salterton Little Theatre's electrician merely to gratify Nellie's desire for disagreeable frankness. She was already beginning to be uncomfortable with Nellie; after all, it was fully fifteen years since they had been on intimate terms. Not that the terms were so intimate even then as Nellie appeared to think. Curious that her memory could so distort a quite ordinary friendship. Valentine's own memory was excellent.

"I'm sorry about Solly Bridgetower," said Mrs. Forrester, "but you see how it was. When it looked as though you couldn't come to us, during that two weeks, we were desperate, and somebody thought that Solly might direct instead. He's at Cambridge, you know, only he's at home just at present because his mother has been so dreadfully ill. I was going to help him. In fact, I cast the play provisionally before we asked him to direct. Of course he accepted. Then, when you found that you could come after all, we had to ask him to step down, and told all the people who had been promised parts that the final decision would be yours. That was when he said that he would be your assistant. I was against it, but we couldn't very easily refuse. He says he'll just be your errand boy, because he wants to learn, but I'll believe that when I see it. He's conceited."

"I thought he seemed rather nice."

"He's a smart-alec. Education in England spoils so many Canadians—except Rhodes scholars, who come back and get Government jobs right away. There's a kind of nice simplicity about a Canadian that education abroad seems to destroy. Lots of boys go through our Canadian universities and come out with the bloom still on them, but when they go abroad they always come home spoiled. Isn't that so, Roscoe?"

"What I always say is," said Roscoe, "it takes all kinds to make a world. I like Solly. He's a nice boy."

"Oh Roscoe, you like everybody," said his wife.

"Well, that's pretty nearly true, hon."

The interior of St. Agnes' was, by Mrs. Forrester's standards, lacking in Taste. The personal preference shown in the matter of furniture and decoration was that of Mr. Webster, for his wife had been dead for more than ten years. He liked things that were heavy, and he liked dark wood, intricately patterned wallpaper, and an atmosphere of over-furnishing which Griselda called "clutter". He liked books and had a great many of them. He liked Persian and Chinese carpets, and his rooms were silent with them. He liked leather, and there was plenty of it in his house, on chairs, on fenders, on books and even on lampshades. The house was dark and somewhat oppressive in atmosphere, but it was as he desired it. Griselda had been permitted to decorate a combined bedroom and sitting-room for herself in her own taste. Freddy's bedroom was austere, for she had cleared the nursery pictures of kittens and rabbits out of it, and had added little save a bookcase which contained her favourite works on wine and the liturgy of the Church of England as it might be if the revision of the Prayer Book could be recalled. The only picture she hung in her room was a colour print of *The Feeding of the Infant Bacchus*, by Poussin; the podgy godling, swigging at his bowl, was not her ideal of a wine-taster; nevertheless, something in the picture appealed to her deeply. At the head of her bed hung a little ivory crucifix.

No, Mrs. Forrester would have found St. Agnes' sadly lacking in Taste, and she would have thought it a pity, for obviously a great deal of money had been spent to make it as it was.

Most of the people who thought about the matter at all

imagined that the Websters dined in great state every night. But on this evening, after the successful assault upon The Shed by the Little Theatre, Mr. Webster and his daughters were eating sandwiches and drinking coffee from a thermos in the large, gloomy dining-room. It was the servants' night out. Mr. Webster rather enjoyed these picnics.

"The Little Theatre people were here this afternoon, Daddy," said Griselda.

"Oh. Did they approve of my garden?"

"Mphm. They'd like to do the play on the upper lawn, against the background of big trees."

"Well, they'll do as little harm there as anywhere. What is this bloody stuff?"

"Some kind of fish goo."

"Aren't there any peanut butter sandwiches?"

"Yes, but I think they're meant for us. You aren't supposed to like peanut butter. It isn't a masculine taste."

"I like it. Give me one."

"Daddy," said Freddy; "don't you think you'd better say a word to Tom about keeping them out of The Shed? All the valuable tools are in there."

"I don't suppose they'll take them," said Mr. Webster.

"No, but they might spoil them, messing about. Anyhow, you know how Tom hates people in The Shed."

"Tom will have to get used to it."

"Freddy was rude to Mrs. Forrester this afternoon," said Griselda.

"Good," said her father.

"Don't encourage her, Daddy. She's above herself."

"She was rude to me first," said Freddy; "I get sick of being treated like a baby. I've got just as much brains as you, Gristle, and I ought to be treated with as much respect."

"When you are older, dear," said Griselda, with a maddening air of maturity.

"Nuts," retorted Freddy, rudely; "there's only four years between us. If I had a great big bosom like yours, and a fanny like a bumble-bee, people would smarm over me just the way they do over you."

"If you are waiting for that, I fear that you will wait indeed," said Griselda. "It's plain now that you are the stringy type. Your secondary sexual characteristics, if and when they come, will be poor things at best."

"Children, don't speak so coarsely," said Mr. Webster, who had a vague notion that some supervision should be exercised over his daughters' speech, and that a line should be drawn, but never knew quite when to draw it. He had allowed his daughters to use his library without restraint, and nothing is more fatal to maidenly delicacy of speech than the run of a good library.

"The play is going to be directed by a woman," said Griselda. "She looks very sensible and doesn't say much, which is odd, because she seems to be a friend of Mrs. Forrester's. A Miss Valentine Rich. Lived here ages ago. She's been working in professional theatre in the States. Do you know anything about her, Daddy?"

"If you ever looked inside a newspaper, Gristle," said Freddy, "you'd know that she is quite famous in a modest sort of way. She's a good actress. She doesn't often play leads, but she gets feature billing, if you know what that is, which I doubt. And she directs. She's directed some awfully good stuff. She did a performance of *The White Divell* two years ago, and the critics all said the direction was fine, even if the actors were rotten and it flopped."

"If she's so good, why weren't the actors good?"

"Perhaps she can't make a silk purse out of a sow's ear; we shall see on our own upper lawn, quite soon. Anyway Americans can't act that sort of thing. They are utterly without flair." Freddy grandly dismissed the American stage.

"I think I've heard of her," said Mr. Webster. "Her grandfather died about six weeks ago. Old Dr. Savage. He was quite a bigwig at Waverley a long time ago. He wasn't seen much during recent years."

"She's come back to sell up his things," said Freddy. "She

33

is his heir. There'll probably be an auction. Do you suppose it will bring in much, Daddy?"

"Impossible to tell. Not likely. Professors rarely have interesting furniture. She might get a few thousands, if the sale went well."

"He probably had a lot of interesting books," said Freddy; "if she has an auction may I go, Daddy? I mean, may I have a little money, just in case something interesting turned up?"

"You have the instincts of a packrat, Freddy," said Griselda. "What do you want with dirty old books out of a dead professor's house? Aren't there enough books here already? And how do you know so much about Miss Rich?"

"My eyes are turned outward, toward the world," said Freddy. "Yours are turned inward, toward yourself. In the innermost chamber of your spirit, Gristle, you kneel in constant adoration before a mirror."

Griselda smiled lazily, and threw a fish sandwich at her sister.

When this simple meal was finished, the Webster family dispersed to entertain itself. Mr. Webster went to his library, and sat down to rummage through some volumes of the Champlain Society's publications. This was his favourite reading. Unlike many men of wealth in Canada he had never sought gold in the wilderness or lived an explorer's life among guides and Indians; he did not like to hunt or fish. But exploration in an armchair was his pastime, and accounts of the hardships of others were full of interest to him.

For a time Freddy shared the room with him, quietly taking down one book after another until she had gleaned all the information the library contained about the late Dr. Adam Savage. It was not much; he was named in a *History of Waverley* as a professor of Greek, as a contemporary of a number of other professors who, in their turn, were named as contemporaries of his. It is a habit of the writers of such histories to list the names of dead pedagogues as Homer listed the ships, hoping for glory of sound rather than for the illumination of their audience. In the memoirs of a politician who had been a Waverley man, Dr. Savage was referred to as "grand", but this was unconvincing; to politicians any teacher whom they have subsequently surpassed in notoriety is likely to appear grand. Otherwise there was nothing. Dr. Savage was dead indeed. Freddy bade her father goodnight, and went to her own room.

She removed her clothes and surveyed herself in a mirror. Griselda's remark about her figure rankled in her memory. "I look just like a boy," she thought. This was untrue, and if she had been more intimately acquainted with boys she would have known it. "Gristle is right; I'm stringy," thought she. This also was untrue. Slim she undoubtedly was, and breastless and economical in the rear, but she was not stringy, and there was promise of better things to come. But Freddy was not in a mood to be satisfied with herself, and as she put on her pyjamas and jumped into bed she wondered what Daddy would say if she suggested that in a year or two she should become a postulant in an Anglican nunnery. Somewhat illogically she broke off this train of reflection to read the large illustrated Rabelais which she had abstracted from the library. She found it very good fun, and made a mental list of several abusive terms to use in her next quarrel with Griselda.

Her older sister was likewise preparing for bed. There were four young men in Salterton all of whom were wishing, that evening, that they could take Griselda Webster out. But as none of them knew her very well, and as her beauty and her father's wealth frightened them, and as they feared that they might be rebuffed if they called her, and as they were convinced that such a girl must have all her evenings spoken for months in advance, none of them had done anything about it, and Griselda, at eight o'clock, was in the bathtub.

Long baths were one of her indulgences. She liked to lie in a scented tub, refreshing the hot water from time to time, smoking cigarettes, eating chocolates, and reading. She liked romances of two kinds; if she were not reading Anthony Trollope, whose slow, common-sense stories, and whose staid, common-sense lovers she greatly admired, she liked spicy tales of the type which usually appear in paper-bound copies, in which bishops are forced to visit nudist camps in their underwear, in which men are changed into women, in which bachelors are surprised in innocent but compromising situations with beautiful girls. Hers was a simple but somewhat ribald mind.

She shifted her hips so that the warm water swept over her stomach, which had grown a little chilly. She prodded a chocolate clinically, and as it appeared to be a soft centre she popped it into her mouth. She turned a page of *The Vicar of Bullhampton*. Peace settled upon St Agnes' for the night.

At five minutes to six o'clock Hector Mackilwraith left the Y.M.C.A. and walked briskly toward the Snak Shak. This restaurant, in spite of its name, was pretentious, and appealed to the students of Waverley by a display of unnecessary electricity, unceasing popular music played by a machine which lit up like a baboon's rump with red, blue and green lights, and by quaintly scholarly touches in its decoration. One of these was a wall-painting of a goggle-eyed gnome, just identifiable as Shakespeare's Puck, which appeared over the soda fountain and food counter; from the mouth of the gnome emerged a balloon in which the words "Lord, what foods these morsels be" were written in Old English lettering. The Snak Shak was not elegant or restful, but it was fairly clean, and it was possible to eat a three-course dinner there for sixty-five cents if you bought meal tickets by the ten dollar book. Hector was one of its most faithful supporters.

A man enters a familiar building in quite a different manner from that which he shows when going to a new place. Hector's steps took him to the door of the Snak Shak so neatly that he was able to seize the handle and enter without losing momentum. He walked to his accustomed stall, at the farthest possible distance from the baboon-rump music-box, hung up his raincoat and hat, and sat down to read his newspaper. In time his accustomed waitress—she had been with the Snak Shak for almost three months—came to him and greeted him with the friendliness which she reserved for "regulars" who never "tried to get fresh".

"G'devening," said she. "Terrible out, eh?"

"Yes. A wet night."

"Yeah. Terrible. Juice or soup?"

"The mixed vegetable juice, please."

"Yeah. And then?"

"Hm. The chicken à la king?"

"I'll tell you—not so good tonight. The hamburger's good."

"All right."

"Heavy on the onions as usual, eh?"

"Thank you. Yes."

"What pie?"

"The coconut chiffon."

"I was bettin' with myself you'd say that. You got a sweet tooth, y'know that?"

"Do you think so?"

"Yeah. And why not? You're not so fat. What's your beverage?"

"Tea, please. With two teabags."

"O.K. Right away."

Hector turned once again to his paper. He was usually a methodical reader, taking in the world news, the local news, and the editorials, in that order, and then glancing briefly at the rest. He always finished by reading all the comic strips; he did not particularly enjoy them, and persuaded himself that he read them only in order to know what his pupils were reading; but the fact was that they had become an addiction, of which he was rather ashamed.

Tonight his reading progressed slowly. He read the same report twice without realizing it, for his mind was elsewhere. Hector was debating a weighty matter within himself. He was trying to make up his mind whether he should ask for a part in *The Tempest*.

To many people, such problems are simple. If they want something they set to work to get it, and if they do not want it they leave it alone. But Hector was a schoolteacher, and a teacher of mathematics at that, and he prided himself upon the orderliness of his thinking. He was as diligent as any Jesuit at arranging the arguments in every case under *Pro* and *Contra* and examining them thoroughly. When at last he recognized what was troubling him he folded his paper neatly and laid it in the seat by him, and drew out his black notebook, a book feared by hundreds of pupils. On a clean page he wrote his headings, P and C, and drew a line down the middle. Quickly, neatly—for this was his accustomed way of making up his mind, even upon such matters as the respective merits of two Chinese laundries—he wrote as follows:

P	C
HM Been treasurer Little Theatre 6 yrs—served LT well—deserves well of LT	*HM teacher—do nothing foolish*
HM Probably as gd an actor as most of LT crowd	*Couldn't take part of lover, clown or immoral person — plays full of these — Shakes often vulgar*
Feel need of augmented social life—all work no play, etc. have enough money to take place with best of LT	*Heavy demands on time —do nothing to forfeit respect of pupils, colleagues, etc. — not in position to entertain— Invading field of English Dept.?—remember specialist certificate in maths*
Be fun to wear costume, false whiskers, etc.—Shakes v. cultural	

He considered the page before him. The waitress brought his meal, all on one tray, and he drank his mixed vegetable juice absently, as he pondered. He was deep in his problem as he attacked his hamburger and vegetables, but he reflected momentarily that with onions he should have ordered a glass of milk, to kill the smell on his breath; still, he was not going anywhere that evening, and there was no need to consider himself; he liked the smell of onion. But he pulled himself up sharply: that was slovenly thinking and slovenly living; a gentleman, his mother had often said, was a man who used a butter knife even when alone. A slovenly action, thrice repeated, has become a habit. He called the waitress and ordered the milk. To thine own self be true, etc.; Shakes.

The problem gnawed. Usually either the *Pro* or the *Contra* column was markedly longer or weaker than the other; in this matter they were pretty evenly matched. From a folder in his inner pocket he drew a letter, and re-read it, as he had done twice before that day.

GOVERNMENT OF ONTARIO

DEPARTMENT OF EDUCATION

Dear Hec:

Just a line to let you know that you are going to be asked to be one of the Revision Board in Maths this summer—to head it up, in fact. The list has not been finalized by the Deputy, but it won't be changed now. You know what this means. You'll be Head Examiner in Maths next year, or the year after. And that means you can have a Department job if you want it, eh? Your friends here can fix it if you put up a good show on the Revision. Remember what Churchill says; Give us the tools and we'll finalize the commitment. So long Hec, old boy.

Russ

At any previous time in his life such a letter would have thrown Hector into a well-controlled ecstasy. Signal preferment was offered as an examiner in the provincial examination system, and the prospect of a job in the Department of Education, that Moslem Paradise of ambitious teachers! Here was his old friend, Russell McIlquham, himself a rising man with that most desirable of all departmental benefactions, "the ear of the Deputy", practically assuring him that it was only a matter of time before he, Hector, would revel in departmental authority with a good chance of imposing his pet schemes upon other, reluctant teachers. But as so often happens in an unsatisfactory world, this good news came at the wrong time. His cup of professional ambition was filled at a moment when he hankered after other, strange delights. What should he do? Should he act,—a course from which his common sense told him he was unlikely to derive any benefit except his own satisfaction—or should he put out his hand and pluck this plum which had ripened in his professional life? He was somewhat astonished at himself to find that he hesitated in making his choice.

He had worked his way almost to the end of his coconut chiffon pie. He ate methodically, devouring the cardboard-like crust at the back of his segment of pie (his trained eye told him that it was a reasonable, but not an exact, sixth of a pie ten inches in diameter) but leaving one last mouthful of cream and coconut, to be chomped voluptuously when the crust was done. It was as he was about to raise this tidbit to his mouth that he lifted his eyes and saw a vaguely familiar figure standing at the counter, some distance from him.

Hector had an excellent memory for names and faces. He sometimes amused his colleagues at teachers' entertainments by reciting the nominal roll of some class which he had taught ten or twelve years before; he never hesitated over a name. He knew that this young man was Lieutenant Roger Tasset, whom he had met briefly one hour and twenty-five minutes earlier in The Shed at St. Agnes'.

Tasset was talking to the waitress behind the counter. Hector could not hear what was said, but the girl leaned toward Roger, and her face was stripped of the suspicious, somewhat minatory expression which waitresses often wear when dealing with young male customers. She appeared to glow a little, and her lips parted moistly as she listened to what he said. He was, in fact, making some mention of the heavy tax on the box of cigarettes which he had bought. But to Hector's eye the girl seemed to be responding to the easy gallantry which was plain in Roger's figure and face, if not in his words.

Hector popped the gob of coconut cream into his mouth

with unaccustomed haste, seized his black notebook and drew a line under the two columns. But instead of writing, as was his custom, the name of the victorious column in capitals under this line, he wrote instead: "There are some decisions which cannot be made on a basis of reason."

In the glare of the lamp the small but distinct bald spot on Mrs. Bridgetower's head glowed dustily as she bent over her dish of oyster stew. It was an ugly lamp, but there was a solemnity, almost a grandeur, about its ugliness. Hanging from one of the false oak beams in the dining-room by an oxidized bronze chain which the passing of years had made even more rusty, it spread out like a canopy over the middle of the dining-table. The shade was of bronze strips, apparently held together by bronze rivets, and between the strips were pieces of glass so rough in texture, so shot with green and yellow and occasional flecks of red, that they seemed to be made of vitrified mucous. When she and the late Professor Bridgetower had built this house, before the First World War, it had been a beautiful lamp, for it accorded with the taste of the period. So did the rest of the room— the oak table and chairs which owed so much, but not perhaps enough, to William Morris; the "built-in" buffet at the end of the room, with its piece of cloudy mirror and its cabinets with leaded-glass windows, in which cups and saucers and the state china were imprisoned; the blue carpet upon the floor.

It was in the manner which had been current when her house was built that Mrs. Bridgetower ordered her meals and caused them to be served. The table at which she and Solly were seated was spread with a white linen cloth; she thought, quite rightly, that people who used mats did so to save washing, and she thought it unsuitable to save in that way. She did not approve of careless, quick meals, and although she did not care greatly for food herself she coursed Solly through soup, an entrée, a sweet and a savoury every night that she faced him at that table. She insisted, making a joke of it, that he wear at least a dark coat, and preferably a dark suit, to dinner. And she insisted that there be what she called "suitable conversation" with the meal. Suitable conversation involved a good many questions.

"And what have you been doing this afternoon?"

"I had to go to St. Agnes', mother, to look at the site for the play."

"Oh, and so we are to be vouchsafed a glimpse of the gardens at St. Agnes', are we? I'm sure the Little Theatre is privileged."

"Mr. Webster is lending the upper lawn."

"As Griselda is to play a leading role, I suppose he could not very well refuse."

"The play was provisionally cast before he was asked for the gardens, mother."

"That does not alter the position as much as you appear to think. Not that I care whether he lends his garden or why. He is not a man I care for greatly."

"I didn't know that you knew him."

"I don't."

Silence. The soup gave place to a pork tenderloin. Solly wondered what to talk about. He must keep his mother away from international politics. This had been her study —no, not her study, her preoccupation and her particular source of neurosis—for as long as he could remember. Before her marriage, as an alert college girl determined to show that women could benefit from higher education every bit as much as men, Mrs. Bridgetower had been greatly alarmed, in a highly intelligent and realistic manner, of course, by the Yellow Peril. The years of the War had been devoted, patriotically, to the Prussian Menace, but she had returned to her earlier love immediately afterward. The rise of totalitarianism had kept her busy during the 'thirties, but when the Second World War began, and Japan entered it, she brought dread of the Yellow Peril to a particularly fine flowering. Since the subjugation of Japan she had developed several terrors and menaces in Latin America and South Africa, and had, of course, given the Red Menace a great deal of attention; but, by determinedly regarding Russia as an Asiatic power she was able to make the Red Menace seem no more than a magnification of the old Yellow Peril. She was growing old and set in her ways, and old perils and dreads were dearer to her than latter-day innovations.

The trouble was that when Mrs. Bridgetower was talking about any subject less portentous than the Oriental plottings in the Kremlin, she was apt to be heavily ironical, and Solly did not like to expose anything in which he was truly interested to her ill-nature. However, he must say something now, or she would hint that he did not care for her company, and stage a long and humiliating scene in which he would have to protest his affection, his concern about her weak heart, and end by making it clear that so long as she lived, the outside world held no comparable charm for him. He plunged.

"I think the play may be rather good. We've got together quite a strong cast."

"Didn't you say that Professor Vambrace was playing a leading part?"

"Yes. Prospero."

"Hmph. He's thin enough. Who are your women?"

"Well, there's Pearl Vambrace, she will probably play Miranda, and Cora Fielding, who will be one of the goddesses."

Mrs. Bridgetower pounced. "But that leaves only the part of Ariel free; you don't mean to tell me that you have cast Griselda Webster for that? You are confident, I must say."

"I did not cast the play, mother; a tentative list of the cast has been drawn up, but Mrs. Forrester did that before I was asked to have anything to do with it."

"I suppose Mrs. Forrester cast her because of her looks. Well, I for one have never thought much of them; she looks a regular Dolly Varden, in my view." Just what Mrs. Bridgetower meant by this condemnation was not clear. But Solly knew it of old, as a phrase used by his mother to describe any girl to whom she thought he might be attracted.

Aha, so that was it? Mother thought he admired Griselda? No wonder she was being so ugly.

At this point the tenderloin gave place to a Floating Island. Gobbets of meringue sat motionless upon a chocolate sea.

He must be cautious. He must reveal no hint of feeling for Griselda, to whom, in fact, he was reasonably indifferent, nor must he hasten to agree with his mother. She would at once suspect agreement as a form of duplicity and be more than ever convinced of his attachment.

"There are not many girls available at present who would do at all," he said. "I don't suppose you would prefer to see Ariel played by Pearl Vambrace?"

This was an astute move. His mother's contempt for the Vambraces was one of her lesser intellectual amusements.

"It will be six of one and half-dozen of the other, I should say. Though the Vambrace girl would probably be a little more hesitant about showing her legs. And with good reason."

Once again Solly was compelled to admire the fire which his mother could rouse in herself by the mention of young women's legs. They were an iniquity which she attacked with the violence and vituperative strength of a Puritan divine. Not that she lacked reason in the present case; Griselda's legs were not a matter upon which anyone remained indifferent; those who did not condemn them as incitements to worldliness were lost in admiration. In her latest speech she had scored a double; she had condemned Griselda's legs because they were beautiful, and sneered at poor Pearl Vambrace's because they were not. Mrs. Bridgetower had indeed benefited from higher education.

"When do you begin rehearsals?"

"At once, mother."

"I suppose you have been busy preparing the play? A good many of your cast will find it coming quite freshly to them, I am sure."

"I've done a good deal of work. But I shan't really be directing."

"Oh? And why not?"

"Miss Valentine Rich has come back to Salterton for the

summer, and Mrs. Forrester has asked her to do it. When they asked me to step down I was glad enough to do so. After all, she's a professional. I shall work with her, and I hope to learn a good deal."

"Valentine Rich? That granddaughter of old Professor Savage who went on the stage?"

"She has made quite a reputation."

"So she ought. There was brains in the family. I see. And is she here now?"

"She arrived this afternoon. I think she has come home to settle up the old man's affairs."

"I presume she was his heir. Well, she might have come back sooner. He was entirely alone at the end."

"Not entirely, mother. He had many friends, and I heard that they were very good during his last years and his illness."

"They were no kin. I hope I shall not have to die with only strangers at hand. However, one must take whatever Fate has in store for one."

Solly recognized danger. When under stress of emotion it was his mother's habit to speak of herself as "one"; somehow it made her self-pity appear more truly pathetic. But by this time the Floating Island had been consumed, and prunes wrapped in fried bacon had also come and gone. His mother rose.

"Shall we have coffee now, or will you join me later?"

This was a survival from the days when, for a few months, the late Professor Bridgetower had sat at table for precisely five minutes after his wife, drinking a glass of invalid port which had been ordered as a tonic. The notion that men lingered over their wine had taken hold, and Mrs. Bridgetower still pretended that Solly might take it into his head to do so. There was no wine in the house, only the brandy kept against Mrs. Bridgetower's "spells" and Solly's own private bottle which he kept in his sitting-room cupboard. He did not trouble to answer his mother, but rose and followed her to the gloomy drawing-room, where a great many books lived in glass and leaden prisons, like the china in the dining-room. There, in the gloom, they took coffee ceremoniously and joylessly, as though it were for their health. And thus concluded what they would have been surprised to learn was the most ceremonious and ample dinner eaten that night in Salterton. It was Mrs. Bridgetower's notion that everyone lived as she did, except people like the Websters, who ate much more, and took longer to do it.

"Well," she said, as she put down her cup, "it will be a pleasure to see *The Tempest* once again. I have seen the Ben Greet Players perform it, and also Beerbohm Tree when I was a girl. Your father and I saw it at Stratford on our memorable trip of 1934. Whatever Miss Rich and Griselda Webster concoct between them, I shall have my rich memories."

As soon as he decently could, Solly composed his mother with a book about geopolitics, and retired to his own room in the attic, saying that he had work to do. His mother's enmity toward Griselda had produced the effect that anyone but Mrs. Bridgetower could have predicted; by nine o'clock, as Griselda was reheating her bath for the third time, and wishing vaguely that she had something more interesting to do than pursue the placid love of Mary Lawther, Solly was sitting in his attic, drinking rye and tap water, and wishing that he had the courage to call her, and suggest that they meet for—what? He could not have his mother's car; he knew of no place to go. His impotence and his fear of his mother saddened him, and he poured some more rye into his glass, and put a melancholy piece of Mozart on his gramophone.

It was at this time, also, that Valentine Rich, who had escaped from the Forresters', stood in her grandfather's deserted house, holding in her hand a bundle of letters which she had written to the old man during the past twelve years. Each was dated on its envelope; all were neatly bound together with a piece of ribbon. They were the first things which she found when she had opened his old-fashioned domestic safe. She had loved and honoured him, and although she did not wish him alive again, she missed him sorely. Before she continued her search she sat in his revolving desk chair, and wept for the passing of time, and the necessary death of the well-loved, wise old man.

CHAPTER

2

HAVING decided that he would ask for a part in the play, Hector Mackilwraith acted quickly, within the limits imposed by his temperament. He did nothing that Friday night. He returned to his room at the Y.M.C.A. and passed a pleasant evening marking a batch of algebra tests. To this work he brought a kind of mathematical elegance, and even a degree of wit. He was not the kind of schoolmaster who scribbles on exercise papers; with a red pencil as sharp as a needle he would put a little mark at the point where a problem had gone wrong, not in such a way as to assist the erring student, but merely in order to show him where he had fallen into mathematical sin. His assessment of marks was a miracle of even-handed justice; there were pupils, of course, who brought their papers back to him with complaints that they had not been given proper credit for their work, but they did it in a perfunctory manner, as a necessary ceremonial rather than with a hope of squeezing an extra mark out of Hector.

It was in dealing with stupid pupils that his wit was shown. A dunce, who had done nothing right, would not receive a mark of Zero from him, for Hector would geld the unhappy wretch of marks not only for arriving at a wrong solution, but for arriving at it by a wrong method. It was thus possible to announce to the class that the dunce had been awarded *minus* thirty-seven out of a possible hundred marks; such announcements could not be made more than two or three times a year, but they always brought a good laugh. And that laugh, it must be said, was not vaingloriously desired by Hector as a tribute to himself, but only in order that it might spur the dunce on to greater mathematical effort. That it never did so was one of the puzzles which life brought to Hector, for he was convinced of the effectiveness of ridicule in making stupid boys and girls intelligent.

If he had dealt in ridicule wholesale, and if he had joyed in it for its own sake, he would have been a detestable schoolroom tyrant, and his classes would have hated him. But he dealt out ridicule in a selfless, almost priestly, manner, and most of his pupils admired him. Mackilwraith, they said among themselves, knew his stuff and would stand no nonsense. There is a touch of the fascist in most adolescents; they admire the strong man who stands no nonsense; they have no objection to seeing the weak trampled underfoot; mercy in its more subtle forms is outside their understanding and has no meaning for them. Hector, with his minus awards for the stupid, suited them very well, insofar as they thought about him at all.

The class upon whose work he was engaged on this particular evening lacked any remarkable dunce, any girl with a hopelessly addled brain, or a boy who was incapable of recognizing even the simplest sets of factors. But there were certain papers upon which he put a cabbalistic word which he had taken over from a teacher of his own younger days. Written always in capitals, and flaming like the Tetragrammaton on the breastplate of the High Priest, the word was TOSASM, and it was formed from the initials of a teacher's heartcry—The Old Stupid and Silly Mistake.

The following morning, however, as soon as he had taken breakfast at the Snak Shak, he went to a bookshop and bought a copy of *The Tempest*. He then made his way to the Salterton Collegiate and Vocational Institute, for although there were no classes on Saturdays it was Hector's custom to enjoy the freedom of the empty building. He let himself in, nodded to a couple of janitors who were, as school janitors so often are, mopping at something invisible in the corridors, made his way to the Men Teachers' Room, and settled down to read the play, and to make up his mind which part he would request for himself.

Hector's acquaintance with the works of Shakespeare was not extensive. When himself at school he had been required to read and answer questions about *Julius Caesar, The Merchant of Venice* and *Henry V*; owing to some fold or tremor in the curriculum he had been compelled to spend two years upon this latter play. In his mind these plays were lumped together with *Hiawatha, The Lay of the Last Minstrel* and *Sohrab and Rustum*, as "literature"—that is to say, ambiguous and unsupported assertions by men of lax mind. But as he had grown older, he had grown more tolerant toward literature; there might be, he admitted to himself, "something in it". But it was not for him, and he had had no truck with it. He very rarely read a book which was not about mathematics, or about how to teach mathematics; he subscribed to *The American Mathematical Monthly*; he read newspapers and news magazines, and occasionally he relaxed with *The Reader's Digest*, for he had a taste for amateur doctoring, and liked to ponder over the miraculous drugs and therapeutic methods described there.

He found *The Tempest* somewhat baffling. He had supported the suggestion that the Little Theatre present a Shakespearean play, for he was strongly in favour of plays which were "worth while"; it was widely admitted that Shakespeare was worth while. But in what precise union of qualities this worthwhileness lay was unknown to him. His first encounter with *The Tempest* was like that of the man who bites a peach and breaks a tooth upon the stone.

In the very first scene, for instance, there was a coarse reference to the Female Functions. He read it again and again; he consulted the notes, but they were unhelpful; in spite of a conviction held over from school days that poets were people who hid their meaning, such as it was, in word puzzles it seemed clear enough that in this case Shakespeare meant to be Smutty. Obviously this was a play to be approached with the utmost caution. He might even have to change his mind about acting.

He read on. It was toilsome work, but by mid-afternoon he had finished *The Tempest*, he understood it, he had assessed the value of every part in it, and although he would not have gone so far as to say that he liked it, he admitted to himself that there was probably "something in it". He had decided, also, that the part for him was Gonzalo. This person was described as "an honest old counsellor", and he had no offensive lines to speak; he had fifty-two speeches, some of them quite long but none which would place an undue strain upon his memory; he was not required to do anything silly, and he would require a fairly impressive costume and almost certainly the desired false whiskers. This was the part for him. He would speak to Mrs. Forrester about it on Monday night.

He began memorizing the part of Gonzalo that evening, and was word perfect in his first scene before he went to bed.

At twenty-five minutes past eight on Monday evening Hector was on the pavement outside the apartment building where the Forresters lived. He was a little early, for he intended to make his call at half-past eight exactly. It would not do to surprise the Forresters at their evening meal, or too soon after it. He had calculated that people in the Forresters' position ate at seven o'clock. He himself ate at the Snak Shak from six to six twenty-five precisely, every evening of his life.This evening he had returned to the Y.M.C.A., re-washed his already clean face and hands, and put on the clean shirt which he would not normally have worn until Tuesday morning. He put on a new blue tie, especially purchased, and felt as he looked in the mirror that it produced a rather rich effect under his ruddy face and somewhat heavy bluish jowl. He then waited patiently, running over Gonzalo's first scene in his head, until it was time to make his call. And, as always, he reached his destination ahead of time. So he walked to a point two blocks away, walked back again, and at eight-thirty precisely he pressed the bell of the Forrester's apartment.

Nellie opened the door. "Good-evening, Mrs. Forrester,"

said Hector; "I just happened to be passing, and I remembered something I wanted to mention to you."

A surprise awaited him in the tasteful living-room. Vambrace, Valentine Rich, young Bridgetower and a person whom he still thought of as "the Webster girl" were seated there. It was not until this moment that he realized how sensitive and secretive he was about his desire to act; he could not possibly blurt out his request before these people. His dismay showed in his face.

"We were just chewing over a few problems," said Mrs. Forrester. "You sit down over there." She pointed to an empty armchair. "I'm sure you'll agree with me. Now listen: the first scene of the play is a storm at sea; the garden at St. Agnes' runs right down to the lake; why can't we have the first scene on a real ship in the lake, and then get everybody to move their chairs to the upper lawn for the rest of the play?"

"I don't think they'd like to walk all that way, carrying chairs," said Professor Vambrace. "Many members of our audience are advanced in years. As a matter of fact, they may stay away from a pastoral; the damp, you know, after sundown."

"It seems to me that Mrs. Pauldron brought that up when it was suggested that we use her lawn," said Griselda, innocently.

"It's quite a different quality of damp at her place," said Mrs. Forrester; "and the garden at St. Agnes' is on a much higher ground. The warmth of the day lingers there much longer."

This remarkable piece of sophistry was allowed to pass without further comment.

"Larry won't like it," said Solly; "in fact I don't suppose ʌe'd even talk about it. Your scheme would mean two sets of lights."

"Not a bit of it," said Mrs. Forrester; "the ship scene would be played before sundown. There would be a lovely natural light."

"It isn't really practical, Nell," said Valentine Rich. "Audiences hate hopping up and down. And anyhow, where would your storm be on a perfectly calm bay?"

"If we are going to act outdoors, why don't we make the utmost use of Nature?" said Nellie. "Surely that's the whole point of pastorals; to get away from all the artificiality of the theatre, and co-operate with the beauty of Nature?"

"No, Nell; I've done several outdoor plays, and my experience has been that Nature has to be kept firmly in check. Nature, you see, is very difficult to rehearse, and Nature has a bad trick of missing its cues. If I am to direct the play, I really must veto the ship on the lake."

"All right," said Nellie, "but if you wish later on that you had done it, don't expect any sympathy from me."

"I promise you that I won't," said Valentine.

It was at this point that Roscoe Forrester came in from the kitchen with a tray of drinks. He was a man who liked to make a commotion about refreshments. When Valentine asked for a whisky and soda he was loud in his approval; that, he said, was what he liked to hear. When Griselda asked for some soda water with a slice of lemon in it he became coy and strove to persuade her to let him put "just a little stick" in it.

"No, really," said she; "my father has promised me a bicycle if I don't drink until I'm fifty."

"But you've already got a car—," said Roscoe, and then perceiving that a mild jest was toward, he roared, and slapped his thigh, and called upon the others to enjoy it. He was the sort of man who does not expect women to make jokes.

"I don't permit Pearl to touch a drop," said Professor Vambrace, solemnly. "A matter of principle. And also, she is obliged to favour her stomach."

Roscoe hastened to agree that a girl's stomach deserved every consideration. "What about you, hon?" he asked, beaming at his wife.

"Well, just a weeny wee drinkie," said Nellie, and as he poured it she gave little gasps and smothered shrieks as evidence of her fear that it might turn into a big drinkie.

Professor Vambrace's principle was solely for his

daughter's benefit; when asked to pour for himself he was generous, though sparing with the soda which, he explained unnecessarily, was likely to cause acidity if taken in too great quantity. Hector and Solly were allowed to receive their drinks without comment.

It was then discovered that Hector had taken Roscoe's chair, and there was a polite uproar, Roscoe asserting loudly that he preferred the floor to any chair ever made, Hector saying that he could not hear of such a thing, and Professor Vambrace pointing out very sensibly that the dining-room was full of chairs, which he would be happy to move in any quantity. At last order was restored, with Roscoe on the floor smiling too happily, as people do when they seek to spread an atmosphere of ease and calm.

"There's a point which we mustn't overlook," said Nellie, turning her wee drinkie round and round in her hands and looking solemnly. "We'll have a lot of resistance to break down, doing a pastoral. People here haven't been educated to them, yet. Actually, you might say that we are pioneering the pastoral in this part of the world. So we'll need strong backing."

"I don't favour advertisement," said Professor Vambrace; "I've never found that it paid." This was true; in the quantities approved by Professor Vambrace, advertisement might just as well not have been attempted; he was a homeopath in the matter of public announcement.

"It isn't advertisement in the ordinary sense that I'm thinking about," said Nellie; "I mean, we want to get the right people behind us. I wonder if we wouldn't be wise to have a list of patrons, and put them in the programme."

"Aha, I see what you mean," said Professor Vambrace, glowering intelligently over his glass; "friends, as it were, of the production. In that case, the leading name would be that of Mr. G. A. Webster, the father of our charming young friend, here; he has lent his garden, and that is very real support—solid support, I may say." He laughed, deeply and inwardly; it was as though barrels were being rolled in the cellars of the apartment house.

"It goes without saying that Mr. Webster is a very important patron," said Nellie, in what she conceived to be a tactful tone, "and his name must be on the list along with the District Officer Commanding and both Bishops, and the Provost of Waverley and the Mayor and the president of the Chamber of Commerce. But to head the list I feel that we want a name which will mean something to everybody—the name of someone whose position is absolutely unassailable; I was rather thinking—what would you say to Mrs. Caesar Augustus Conquergood?"

In such roundabout terms as these are the secret passions of the heart brought before the world. Mrs. Caesar Augustus Conquergood was the god of Nellie's idolatry. This lady, whom she had rarely seen, was her social ideal; the late Conquergood had been associated in some highly honourable capacity with the Army, and he and his wife had been moderately intimate at Rideau Hall during the Governor-Generalship of the Duke of Devonshire; the widow Conquergood was reputed to be very wealthy, and doubtless the report was correct, for she enjoyed that most costly of all luxuries in the modern world, privacy; she was very rarely seen in Salterton society, and when she appeared, she might have been said to hold court. Nellie had met her but once. She did not seek to thrust herself upon her goddess; she wished only to love and serve Mrs. Caesar Augustus Conquergood, to support and if such a thing were possible, increase her grandeur. If Mrs. Caesar Augustus Conquergood's name might appear, alone, at the top of an otherwise double column of patrons of the Salterton Little Theatre then, in Nellie's judgment, the drama had justified its existence, Thespis had not rolled his car in vain, and Shakespeare was accorded a posthumous honour which he barely deserved.

There is a dash of pinchbeck nobility about snobbery. The true snob acknowledges the existence of something greater than himself, and it may, at some time in his life, lead him to commit a selfless act. Nellie would, under circumstances of sufficient excitement, have thrown herself in the path of runaway horses to save the life of Mrs. Caesar

Augustus Conquergood, and would have asked no reward—
no, not even an invitation to tea—if she survived the ordeal.
Such a passion is not wholly ignoble. She had schemed for
four months for this moment when she would put her adored
one's name at the head of a list of patrons for *The Tempest*,
and nothing must go wrong now.

"I don't know that I am in complete agreement with you,"
she heard tiresome Professor Vambrace saying; "if we are to
have patrons, surely they should be people who have helped
our Little Theatre in some way. I cannot recall that Mrs.
Conquergood has attended a single performance."

"Ah, but you see," said Nellie, "if we interest her, she
will become a regular supporter."

"It seems a very ostentatious method of gaining her
attention," said Vambrace, "and if we have to print her name
in the programme to get her to come, we might perhaps be
better off without her. After all, her dollar is no better than
anybody else's."

Nellie's neck flushed; sometimes she thought that Vambrace was no better than a Red. "As though it were her
dollar we were after," she said, reprovingly; and then, with
an affectation of serpent-like wisdom, "her name would draw
in a good many people of the very type who ought to be interested in the Little Theatre."

"In that case, perhaps we ought to offer her a part," said
Solly. "Now here, in Act Three, is my favourite stage
direction in the whole play: *Enter several strange Shapes,
bringing in a banquet*; she could be a Strange Shape; type-
casting. I'll put it in the form of a motion if you like."

"Solly, that isn't the least bit funny," cried Nellie.

"I didn't mean it to be," said Solly, "it's cold fact."

"If you can't do anything but sneer, the sooner you go
back to England the better."

"If you mean that you want me to retire from my job as
assistant director of this play, Nellie, I'll do so gladly. You
pushed me into directing, and then you pushed me into
assisting, and if you want to push me out altogether you have
only to say so."

"Aw, now Solly, don't let's get sore," said Roscoe; "you know how Nell gets stewed up about things."

"Roscoe, I don't," cried Nellie, near to tears.

"There is no need for anybody to retire from anything, or to go back anywhere," said Professor Vambrace. "Nor, I think, is there any need for us to head our list of patrons with the name of a person who, whatever her social eminence may be—I am not qualified to speak upon such a point—has never done anything for the Little Theatre."

"If I may offer my opinion, Professor," said Hector, "I think there is a good deal in what Mrs. Forrester has said. There is powerful rivalry in Salterton society between town and gown, military and civil service, as everybody knows. We are not supposed to have these divisions in a democracy but somehow we have them. As an outsider—a teacher who is neither town nor precisely gown—I can see this perhaps better than you. I have heard it suggested that our Little Theatre is recruited a little more heavily from the Waverley faculty than is acceptable to some quite large groups of people. Of course we know why that is so; the faculty members are perhaps more active in their support of the arts than the military or the business people. But if we hope to offset an impression which I, as treasurer, consider an unforunate one, we must be very careful about our list of patrons. I believe that we should have such a list, and I believe that it should be headed by some name not associated too closely with any of the principal groups which comprise the city. Mr. Webster's name must come very high. But I agree with Mrs. Forrester that the name of Mrs. Caesar Augustus Conquergood should come first. I do not know her, but I have heard of her, and I have always heard her spoken of in the highest terms. I don't mind saying that I think it would have a marked effect at the box-office."

His hearers were impressed. Hector had all the advantage of the man who speaks infrequently, and whose words carry special weight for that reason. Furthermore, his introduction of the word "box-office" was masterly. Professional theatrical groups occasionally take a fling and perform some work, for sheer love, which they know will not make money; amateur groups never forget the insistency of the till. The notion that Mrs. Conquergood's name might raise the takings was too much for Professor Vambrace, who gave in with an ill grace. The redness departed from Nellie's neck; she was jubilant, though she tried to conceal it. And she looked upon Hector as an oracle of wisdom.

Nellie's mind, though busy, was not complex. She had never mastered the simple principle of *quid pro quo* which was, to Hector's orderly intelligence, axiomatic. But she received a lesson in it half an hour later when Hector, with well-feigned casualness, said:

"When is the casting for the play to be completed?"

"Oh," said Nellie, "we are going to have auditions for all the parts later this week."

"Surely not for all the parts? I understood some time ago that Professor Vambrace was to play Prospero, and Miss Vambrace Miranda, and that Miss Webster was to be Ariel. And I think you told me that young Tasset was to be Ferdinand. I believe that Caliban and the two funny men are also cast?"

"Well, tentatively, but of course we are going to hold a public reading before anything is decided finally."

"But I think it unlikely that any of those parts will be alloted otherwise?"

"You know how it is," said Professor Vambrace; "the Little Theatre must give everyone a chance. Still, it is pretty plain that certain people will do certain parts better than anyone else who is likely to turn up. And, frankly, there are some debts to be paid; those who have borne the burden deserve a measure of reward."

This was an opening which Hector had not foreseen, but he took it with the skill of an experienced politician. The shyness which he felt when he first arrived had quite departed.

"I had thought of that myself," said he. "I have been treasurer of the Little Theatre for the past six years. When I took it over its books were in a mess; now they are in perfect order and we have a substantial sum in the bank. During the years when I have worked in the box office I have often wondered what it would be like to be with those of you who were enjoying the fun behind the footlights. And if there is a part which I could play in *The Tempest*, I should like to have it."

"Why not wait until next year?" said Nellie. "We're sure to be doing something which would have a part in it for you. You know, something good. A detective, or a policeman, or something."

"I may not be here next autumn," said Hector.

"Not here?" Nellie was horrified at the thought that a new treasurer would have to be found.

"No. I have been offered some work by the Department which would take me out of town. If I accept, it will mean beginning work at once. But of course, if I am offered a part in *The Tempest* I should turn down the Department's offer for the present, and would be here next season."

Even Nellie could see what that meant.

"Had you a special part in mind?" she asked.

"It had occurred to me that I might try my hand at Gonzalo. The wise old counsellor," said Hector, looking around for appreciation of this joke. But there was none. Professor Vambrace felt that in some way he had been finessed, and was trying to figure out where; Nellie was wondering if she had not been wrong, half an hour ago, to feel so warmly toward Hector; why, the man was nothing but a self-seeker and his obvious counting on her support seemed, in some inexplicable way, to dim the brightness of Mrs. Caesar Augustus Conquergood. Valentine Rich and Solly had made up their minds independently that it was plain that, whoever cast the play, they were not to be allowed to do it. The gathering had a somewhat stunned and inward-looking air as it ate the sticky buns and coffee which Nellie brought forth, aided by the faithful Roscoe.

Hector ate a bun, and took one cup of coffee, and then made his departure, well pleased with his evening's work.

When he was gone, Nellie was the first to speak.

"Well, did you ever hear anything like that?" she cried. "He simply put a pistol to our heads; he plays Gonzalo or we can get a new treasurer."

"The way I look at it, it was a kind of a deal, hon," said the artless Roscoe. "He supported you about the patrons, and then you had to support him about the part he wanted. It's nothing to worry about; happens in business and politics every day."

"This isn't business or politics, Roscoe. We've got our audiences to think about. For anything I know, this man has never acted before. Val, why didn't you step in and veto it? You could. You're director."

"Really, Nell, the casting seems to be so much in the hands of the local committee that I saw no reason to interfere."

"But he's so obviously unsuitable."

"We don't know that yet. We can always change in the early rehearsals if he's too bad."

"Val, this isn't professional theatre. You can't kick people out like that. So the only possible thing is to keep unsuitable ones from getting in."

"When once particular personal interests begin to be consulted, artistic integrity flies out at the window," said Professor Vambrace darkly.

"If that is meant to have any bearing on the arrangement of the patrons' list, I want to say here and now that I am acting only for the good of the Little Theatre." Nellie confronted him, bravely but with tears in her eyes.

The Professor lolled his large, bushy head about on the back of his chair, and made gestures with his heavy eyebrows. "In that case, there is nothing more to be said about the matter," replied he.

"Yes, there is," said Nellie, shaken with emotion; "we've got to have some fairly good-sized parts to allot among all those people who are coming to the try-out reading on Thursday night. I was counting on Gonzalo as a nice little plum for somebody—something that would stop everybody saying that the casting of all the good parts is done by the committee beforehand—and now that man has just grabbed it. It's awful!"

"I still don't see what's so awful about it, hon," said Roscoe, pacifically. "What makes you think he'll be so much worse than the others?"

This crass comment caused Professor Vambrace to close his eyes.

"That's a very good question," said Solly.

"Oh it's all very well for you all to sit around and sneer," wailed Nellie, and burst into tears. Roscoe took her hand and patted it. "Take it easy, hon," said he; "it'll all be the same in a hundred years."

There was some embarrassment, but not very much, at Nellie's breakdown; most of the people present had seen her weep before, for reasons less easily understandable. But it seemed to put a period to a dull and exasperating evening, and they took their departure.

Professor Vambrace quickly swung away into the night; he was a man who genuinely liked walking, and his feet and the heavy ash walking stick which he carried seemed to spurn the ground. Valentine and Solly climbed into Griselda's car.

"Shall we drive for a while?" asked Griselda.

"I should like that more than anything," said Valentine Rich.

It was not until they had left the city and were driving by the river that Solly spoke.

"I can't imagine what Nellie was making such a fuss about," said he.

"You were very naughty about Mrs. Conquergood," said Griselda.

"Well, damn it, I squirm at that kind of thing. Why is it that a supposedly democratic country is so eaten up with snobbery of one sort and another?"

"Everybody has their own kind of snobbery. I suspect you of being an intellectual snob, Solly."

"Well, what about you? You're rich—so rich, if you want to know, that I didn't dare call you a few nights ago because I didn't think I could entertain you suitably—and everybody that wants to know you and doesn't is sure that you're a shrieking snob."

"I am the humblest of God's little ones," said Griselda, passing another car a shade too closely.

"Anyhow, Nellie's fantod had nothing to do with me or Old Ma Conquergood. She was angry because Mackilwraith suddenly wanted to act. I don't see why he shouldn't. He's done a good job as treasurer, and I suppose he wants some of the glory of acting. He wants to be one of the gaudy folk of the theatre, weaving a tissue of enchantment for Mrs. Caesar Augustus Conquergood and your father. Poor old cow, he's stage-struck. And at his age, too!"

"I rather liked him," said Valentine. "I thought it was sweet the way he came in pretending that he was passing by, and then popping out his bid for a part so neatly. I have a soft spot for people who are stage-struck. Next autumn I shall have been in the professional theatre for eighteen years, and I'm still stage-struck."

"Heavens," said Griselda, "you must have started just when I was born. I'm sorry, that sounded rude."

"I am thirty-six," said Valentine; "I was your age when I got my first job."

"Did you have an awful struggle?" asked Griselda; "I mean with your family, and getting a job, and all that."

"No, I didn't. When I told my grandfather I wanted to be an actress he was most kind and sympathetic. And in those days there were some good stock companies, and I was able to get a job in one of them. And I've never really had much difficulty about jobs since, which is lucky, because it's chancy work. But I've always been willing to go outside New York, you see, and that makes a difference. And I've done some directing, which is helpful. So it has really been a very busy eighteen years. No, oddly enough, the only people who were discouraging were my friends. Nellie, for instance, was sure I'd never manage to get along."

"If you don't mind saying," said Solly, "how did you get sucked in for directing *The Tempest* here? I mean, you probably don't look on it as the crown of your career. What made you say yes?"

"Well you see, I'm at that funny point in my life where I'm important enough to be asked to do favours, but not important enough to be able to refuse them without giving offence. When Nell found out that I was coming back to Salterton this summer, she wrote at once."

"And you couldn't refuse an old friend?"

"I couldn't refuse someone whom I had once known, very easily. Of course, I hadn't seen her for ten or twelve years."

"Really? I rather gathered from what she said that she might have given you your start."

"No, no; we were friends as girls, though never very close."

"That's very interesting, in the light of what we have heard."

"It's fantastic to think of you and Mrs. Forrester being about the same age," said Griselda.

"We are, none the less. In fact, she is a few months younger."

"I suppose the responsibility of the Salterton Little Theatre is what has worn her down," said Solly.

"Don't be horrid," said Griselda.

"Why not? You implied that Nellie looks years older than Miss Rich."

"I know, but it's different, coming from a man."

"What has got into you, Griselda?" said Solly. "You've gone all mealy-mouthed and hypocritical."

"I'm blossoming into womanhood," said Griselda, "and I have to be very careful about what I say. Daddy was mentioning it just a day or two ago. He said that people would take it amiss if I said what I really thought; he said a woman had to be at least forty-five before she dared risk an honest expression of opinion."

When they had dropped Valentine at her hotel, Griselda said to Solly: "Would you like to come home? What about something more to eat or drink?"

"You should never ask anyone to have anything *more*," said Solly, "for it implies that they have had perceptible refreshment already, which is rude. If you are going to make such a hullabaloo about your womanhood, you must be careful of these niceties."

"Thank you for telling me," said Griselda. "I haven't really had a very good upbringing. You know what boarding-schools are. If some of the rough speech of the lacrosse field and the prefects' room still clings to me, I should be obliged if you would mention it."

"What is going to happen to you?"

"Daddy hasn't made up his mind yet. There is talk of a finishing-school, but I'd like to go to Europe and be a student."

"What of?"

"Oh, anything. It would be quite enough just to be a student. They seem to have such good times. Riots, and political action. Do you know that there is a university town in Italy where the police have not been permitted even to speak rudely to the students in centuries?"

"Don't be deceived. The university undoubtedly maintains a force of some kind which keeps the students under. Your idea of a student is about a hundred and fifty years out of date. Students today are a pretty solemn lot. One of the really notable achievements of the twentieth century has been to make the young old before their time."

They had reached the front door of St. Agnes' and Griselda opened it with her key. "Don't tiptoe, Solly," said she; "it's only half-past eleven."

"Sorry," said he; "I always tiptoe at home."

They went into the library, which was dark, smoky and smelly. Mr. Webster sat in a corner, reading the *Colnett Journals*.

"You know Solly Bridgetower, don't you, Daddy?"

"No," said Mr. Webster, "who is he?"

"He's right here."

"Oh. I'm sorry. I didn't see you in the shadow. What did you say your name was?"

"My name is Solomon Bridgetower, sir."

"Well, well. I dare say you are some relative of Professor Solomon Bridgetower, who died a few years ago."

"I am his son, sir."

"I knew your father slightly. Were you aware that your father was perhaps the finest geologist this country ever produced?"

"I have heard many people say so."

"Yes. Wasted, teaching. But he did some splendid work in his vacations."

"Very good of you to say so, sir."

"Mother still living?"

"She was very ill two months ago. I came home to look after things until she recovered."

"I remember her as a girl. She was very interested in Oriental things at that time."

"The Yellow Peril?"

"Yes, that was it. She still keeping up with it?"

"From hour to hour, sir."

"Well, well; it is our hobbies that keep us young. Do you want anything to eat or drink?"

"We thought we'd see what there was, Daddy."

"There isn't much of anything, I'm afraid. They left a few sandwiches but I ate them half an hour ago. It's a funny thing; there never seems to be enough food in this house. You could get Freddy up; she knows how to make sandwiches."

"Oh, no, please don't do that," said Solly.

"Or some breakfast food. I know for a fact that there is quite a lot of breakfast food in the pantry; several kinds. Would you like a bowl of breakfast food, Bridgetower?"

"No, really, sir."

"What we'd really like, Daddy, is a drink, and you have a big tray of things right here."

"Oh, certainly. Help yourself, Bridgetower. The ice has all melted, I'm afraid."

"I like it at room temperature, sir."

"Really? An English taste. Healthier, I suppose."

"Shall I pour anything for you, Griselda?"asked Solly.

"No. I never drink anything. I don't think it becoming in one of my years. I expect when I'm old and hardened I'll soak. Freddy drinks."

"What? Freddy drink? Nonsense!" said Mr. Webster.

"Oh nothing serious, Daddy. She's what I'd call a nipper. A nip here and a nip there. Like health salts; as much as will lie on a ten-cent piece."

"Rubbish. She's going through a religious spell. She can't have both a religious spell and a nipping spell at the same time."

"Oh Daddy, don't be provincial. It's only evangelicals who can't mix drink and religion. Freddy's madly. Anglo-Cat; they swig and pray like anything."

Griselda went on chattering to Solly, and Mr. Webster reflected, as he had done so many times, how wretchedly he missed his wife. She would have known what to say to young men that Griselda brought home. She would have dealt with Freddy's religious nonsense. She would have gone at once to the heart of the matter about Freddy drinking. But what can a father do? Can he confront a girl of fourteen and say, Do you drink? He cannot beat her, and he most certainly cannot reason with her. Why didn't those schoolmistresses do their job? He wished, sometimes, that as fate had decided to make him a widower, fate had done the job properly and made him a childless widower. He was very fond of Griselda and Freddy, but he confessed to himself that he really had no firm idea of how they should be brought up. If they had been boys, now—. But girls were such unpredictable creatures. He came of a generation to which any girl, before she is married, is a kind of unexploded bomb.

"I'd better go now," said Solly, when he had finished his drink. "My mother worries until I am home, and I don't want to distress her."

"I hope we'll see you often, Bridgetower," said Mr. Webster.

"You will, sir."

"Solly's helping with the play," explained Griselda.

"Oh God," said her father; "do you know, for the last two or three days I have quite forgotten about that play?"

"I hope you won't find it too dreadful, sir."

"Daddy's terribly jealous of his garden."

"I know it sounds ridiculous, but when I am at home I can't bear the thought of strangers trampling about just outside the house. It fusses me. But it's unreasonable, of course. I recognize that. So if you see me glowering out of windows at you, pay no attention, will you?"

"I know how you feel, sir," said Solly, and went with Griselda out of the little pool of light through the dark corridor to the door.

Instead of leading him to her car Griselda took him by the arm and headed for the garden. "Let's walk for a few minutes," said she. "Your mother won't really mind, will she?"

Solly knew how very much his mother minded lateness, and how much more she would mind it if she suspected that he was walking in the moonlight with a girl who was, in her opinion, a regular Dolly Varden. But it is not easy for a young man to suggest to a girl that her charms do not outweigh his mother's displeasure, and before Solly knew quite what was happening they were approaching the upper lawn, chosen as the scene of the play.

Griselda said nothing as they walked, which alarmed Solly. The thought flashed through his mind that perhaps Griselda had been possessed by a sudden passion for him, and that she would demand something—possibly even what novelists occasionally referred to as All—from him here among the trees. Griselda was beautiful, and he was not lacking in the attributes of a man. But there is a time and a place for everything, and Solly felt that if there were to be any scenes of passion between himself and Griselda, he would like to stage manage them in his own way. The thought which was uppermost in his mind, when at last

Griselda stopped and turned to him, was that his mother never went to sleep until he had come home and that her displeasure and concern, issuing from her rather as the haze of ectoplasm issues from a spiritualist medium, filled the house whenever he came home late.

"Solly," said Griselda, looking at him solemnly, "you said something when we were driving which worried me. You said that you wanted to take me out last week and didn't because you were afraid that you couldn't amuse me. Please, Solly, don't do that again."

"Well, all right, I won't. But what could we do?"

"Do we have to do anything? You can come and drink Daddy's whisky and talk, if you like. Or we can go out in my car. Really, Solly, it frightened me when you said that people thought I was a snob and didn't dare ask me out unless they had lakhs of rupees and big emeralds clenched in their navels. I've been awfully lonely since I came home. I don't know many people in Salterton."

"I wasn't really being serious."

"I think you were."

"Well, all right then, I was. You see how it is, Griselda. People think you expect the very best of everything—"

"Then people don't know."

"Your father is a very rich man—"

"For Salterton. I expect really rich people sneer at him and ask him to carry their bags."

"But it isn't just money. You look as if you expected a great deal."

"Can I help the way I look?"

"You'd be out of your mind if you wanted to. You know that you're beautiful, don't you?"

"I'm beautiful about on the scale that Daddy's rich—for Salterton."

"But it's more than your looks. You have the air of one who wants rather special things, and special people."

"Of course I do. But I also want all sorts of things and all sorts of people."

"Me among them? Thanks."

"You're very special."

"Oh? Well, thanks again."

"Don't be difficult, Solly. I have to be myself. I suppose that by all the rules of what people expect I should be a loud-laughing, bug-eyed, silly little mutt at eighteen, but I'm not. I feel quite calm and collected most of the time. I'm an oddity, I suppose. Like you."

"What's so odd about me?"

"You don't need to be told. It's not just that you have brains. It's that you seem to have a skin less than other people. People like Nellie Forrester abrade you. And when you snarl at them most people think it's superiority, but I know that it's because they sin against something you hold very dear. I've known you for years in a kind of way, Solly. I want to know you, really and truly. So promise me that if you feel like talking to me, you'll say so?"

"Of course I will, Griselda darling." Solly was so touched by her understanding of him that he had quite forgotten about his mother. So touched indeed, that he took Griselda in his arms and kissed her, with an admirable mixture of friendliness and gallantry.

It was at this moment that a thin and watery beam of light swept across the dewy grass and fell upon them, and Freddy's voice was heard to say "Aha!" in melodramatic accents.

"Freddy, go back to bed and stop Ahaing like Hawkshaw the Detective.

Freddy said "Aha!" again, with marked relish.

"Freddy, you are behaving like the comic kid sister in a cheap farce," cried Solly. He and Griselda, hand in hand, ran across the lawn and stood under Freddy's window.

"You keep your hooks out of Solly," said Freddy, from above. "He's for me, if I decide not to be a nun."

"You have entirely misunderstood the situation," said Solly. "I was paying a compliment to your sister's intellect and discernment, and not what you think."

"Boloney," cried Freddy; "Gristle has a gob of pink goo where her brain should be, and you know it. I'm glad I had my big flashlight. You looked just like a love-scene in a cheap movie."

"Remind me when we meet to lecture you on the proper use of coarseness in repartee," said Solly. "And now, I really must go home."

Griselda drove him home, and he kissed her again before he got out of her car, and promised to see her often.

His key seemed to make a shattering noise in the lock. And when he entered the hall, which was in darkness, maternal solicitude and pique embraced him like the smell of cooking cabbage. He crept upstairs and there, as he knew it would be, was the light coming from his mother's half-open door. There was nothing else for it, so he braced himself to be a good son.

"Still awake, mother?" he said, looking in.

"Oh, there you are, lovey. I was beginning to worry. Come in."

With her teeth out and her hair in a pigtail his mother looked much older that she did in the daytime. On the counterpane lay *The Asiatic Enigma*. Solly sat at the end of the bed, noting as he did so that she had her maternal expression on, the one which was reserved for him alone. Gone was the formality and irony of the dining-table; this was Mother, alone with her Boy.

"What kept you so long?"

"It was a long meeting. We had a lot of details to clear up."

"At this hour? Surely not."

"Well, afterward a few of us went for a short drive to clear our heads."

"That must have been very pleasant. Who drove?"

"Griselda Webster."

"I see. You weren't going too fast, I hope?"

"No, no; quite slowly."

"Who else was with you?"

"Oh, Valentine Rich was one. She's very nice."

"Yes, I'm sure all these girls you meet are very nice, but

there's always one at home, lovey, isn't there—waiting till whatever time it may be."

"Yes, of course, mother; you're the pick of the lot. But it's only half-past twelve, you know."

"Really? It seemed later. But since I've been ill, I find the nights very long."

"Then you must go to sleep at once, dear."

Solly kissed his mother, and went to the door.

"Lovey?"

"Yes, mother?"

"There's something on your mouth, dear—something that tastes rather like scent. Something you have been eating, I suppose. Wash it off, dear."

Hector's good sense and caution prevented him from any premature rejoicing on the strength of his tactical victory at Nellie Forrester's. He knew that Nellie and Vambrace and those who comprised the artistic element in the Little Theatre were not pleased that he should wish to act, although he was not aware how deep their opposition went or from what it sprang. There is always resentment when a beast of burden shows a desire to prance and paw the air in the company of horses trained in the *haute école,* and to Nellie and her friends Hector's ambition seemed no less pitiable than presumptuous. His superiority in the box office was freely admitted; his generalship in the annual drive to sell subscription tickets and memberships for the Little Theatre was the subject of a generously worded vote of thanks at every annual meeting; his insistence upon issuing a pink slip of authorization every time it was necessary to buy something for the plays was tolerated, because it saved a great deal of money and prevented Larry Pye from running up ruinous bills at lumber yards and electrical supply houses. He had the respect of the whole Little Theatre so long as he remained its business genius, and by applying some simple rules of business to an organization which was made up of unbusinesslike people he had achieved a reputation for fiscal wizardry. But when he expressed a desire to act, it suddenly appeared to those who admired him as a treasurer that he was a graceless dolt, intolerable in the world of high art in which they moved. Such sudden reverses of opinion are not uncommon when a man seeks to change his role in the world.

Hector knew that his battle was not quite won. Nevertheless he allowed himself to say to his colleague Mr. Adams, the head of the English Department, when they met in the teachers' commonroom, "I hope you'll be in town in late June?"

"Yes, I will," said Adams. "Why?"

"The Little Theatre are going to do *The Tempest*; I thought you'd be interested."

"Yes, of course. That's very ambitious. Are they going to be able to get together a strong cast?"

"Yes, I think so. Though perhaps I shouldn't say that for it looks as though I might take a part myself. I hope I won't be the weakest link in the chain."

"I'm sure you won't," said Adams, who was not really sure at all, and he went on his way reflecting that wonders would never cease, and that if Old Binomial was going to appear, he would certainly not miss the play for anything, as it was sure to yield a few good unintentional laughs. Mr. Adams had been an indifferent student of mathematics himself, and had a grudge against Hector because he gave too much homework to his pupils who might otherwise have been writing essays for Mr. Adams. But he quickly spread the news that Hector was about to blossom forth as an actor, and the following day the Principal referred to it facetiously when he met Hector in the corridor. And all of this Hector enjoyed greatly, as an old maid might enjoy being twitted about the possession of an admirer.

But he knew very well that until he had successfully passed the test of the casting reading later in the week, where, if ever, his opponents would trip him up, the part of Gonzalo was not assured to him.

Hector's life had not been of the sort which usually

brings forth actors,—even Little Theatre actors. Not, of course, that any particular circumstances can be relied upon to bring forth a particular sort of ability, but his life had been notably unfriendly toward the development of that taste for stimulating pretence which actors must possess. He had been born in a small Ontario village where his father was the Presbyterian minister. The Reverend John Mackilwraith was a failure. The reason for his insufficiency, if it could be discovered now, probably lay in his health. He never seemed to feel as well as other men, but as he had never known good health he had no standard of comparison, and accepted his lot, almost without complaint. That is to say, he never complained of feeling unwell, and he rarely complained in an open manner about anything else, but his whole way of life was a complaint and a reproach to those who came into contact with him. He was unsatisfactory to his congregation, because when they complained to him of misfortunes they were uncomfortably conscious that he had misfortunes of greater extent and longer duration. At funerals his mien of settled woe somehow robbed the chief mourners of their proper eminence. At weddings his appearance was likely to turn the nervous tears of a bride into a waterspout of genuine apprehension. Because the church which he served demands a high standard of scholarship in its clergy it is certain that at one time he must have known a reasonable amount of Hebrew and a good deal of Latin and Greek, but these classical attainments had not wrought their supposed magic of enrichment on his mind, and nothing that could be traced to them was ever to be discerned in his sermons, which were earnest, long and incomprehensible. He pursued his career, if such a spirited word may be applied to so dispirited a life, at a time when church-going was much more a social obligation than it is now, and in communities where any lapse from conventional conduct was soon noticed and sharply censured. But, even with these advantages, he quickly reduced his congregations to a determined and inveterate rump of faithful souls who felt that without Presbyterianism, even on this level, life was not worth living. When Hector was born he was in his last, and worst, charge.

The Reverend John was no doubt to be pitied, but pity is an emotion which cannot be carried on for years. He was a gloomy and depressing parson. There are parsons who make gloom an instrument of their work. They are actively and challengingly gloomy; their gloom is from a banked-down fire of wrath against the villainies of mankind which threatens at any minute to burst into roaring flame. There are parsons who are gently melancholy, as though eternal longings had brought on a mild nausea. But John Mackilwraith's gloom had none of this professional character. Ribald fellows in the village called him Misery Mackilwraith. And yet, who knows? Professional attention to his diet, injections of a few elements missing in his physical makeup, a surgical operation, or a few hours' conversation with a psychiatrist might have made a different man of him. But none of these solutions ever occurred to him. Instead, he sent up long, miserable prayers to God, with no expectation that anything would come of them. He had grown accustomed to neglect in all quarters.

Hector's tender years were passed in an atmosphere which could not be properly described as religious, though religion played a greater part in his consciousness than would have been the case if he had been the son of a butcher or a grocer. There was no deep devotion, no consciousness of hidden sources of strength, not even a rigid puritanism in that household. But weddings and funerals, the drudgery of pastoral calls, the recurrent effort of Sunday and the consequent exhaustion of Monday were familiar to him as the accompaniments of his father's profession. And he knew from his earliest days that he was a dedicated boy; he was expected to be an example not only to all Presbyterian boys in the district but a reproach to boys of lesser faiths. He knew that much was exacted of the cloth in both the spiritual and physical senses, for when his father's black trousers were cut down into knickerbockers for him he was singled out not only by his solemnity of expression, but by the startling blackness and shininess of his lower parts. And because he had been born to this lot, he accepted it without question; as children always do, and as some adults continue to do, he invented reasons why he should be as he was, instead of seeking for means by which he might be delivered from his fate.

His mother did nothing to relieve the misery of the household, though she could not justly have been said to increase it. She took colour from her husband, for she had no strong character of her own. The Reverend John had married her in the first year of his first charge. She had been a farm girl, living with an uncle and aunt, and she had thought that it would be a fine thing to be a minister's wife. She knew nothing of men, and her suitor's glumness and lack of energy appeared to her as the attributes of a being spiritually and intellectually superior to farm boys. The latter, she knew, "had thoughts" about girls; it was plain that the Reverend John had no thoughts of that kind about them at all. He wanted what he called "an helpmeet". He nominated her for this position one evening at nine o'clock in the parlour of the farmhouse; she accepted the nomination at precisely one minute after nine, and by a quarter past nine the fortunate suitor was walking back to his boarding-house, having kissed his fiancée once on the brow. They married, and she discovered that being an helpmeet to a minister was not such hard work as helping around the farm. With the man she had chosen, however, it was not enspiriting, and by the time Hector was born, twelve years later, she was as miserable and as steeped in failure as he.

She was a short, stout woman, shaped like a cottage loaf. A nubbin, with a twist of wispy hair on it, formed her head; a larger nubbin comprised her bust and upper reaches; the largest nubbin of all was formed by her spreading hips. She must have had legs, but her skirts concealed them. She had little to say, and it is doubtful if her mental processes could be called thought; they consisted of a series of dissolving views, mostly of possible disasters and misfortunes which might overtake her and her family. Because she was an unready speaker she was not able to dominate the women in the churches where her husband ministered, and because she could not dominate them she became their drudge. She always had more sewing, or baking, or money-collecting to do than any of the others, not because she did them well but because she was not alert enough to secure an organizing position whenever a bazaar or a "drive" for funds was projected.

The birth of Hector brought to her life its one lasting passion. She loved him as dearly as her inexperienced heart would allow. He was a large and solemn baby, and he throve in spite of his mother's care. Her physician assured her that he was a splendid child, and needed nothing but food and sleep for his well-being, but Mrs. Mackilwraith had lived too long with her husband to be able to believe any nonsense of that kind. She breast-fed him, and worried that he was not getting enough, or that if sufficient in quantity, her milk was deficient in quality; she could not trust herself to produce the right sustenance for her darling. She augmented his breast feedings, therefore, with patent foods, which she tried to make him drink from a cup when he was three weeks old, almost finishing him in the process. Because he was stuffed, he occasionally threw up, which convinced her that he had some malformation of his digestive fittings. She put too many frocks on him, which made him restless, and she starched them, which made him break out in rashes; she treated the restlessness by walking the floor with him, and the rashes by salves, which did no good. Kindly women tried to tell her what to do for her child, and her doctor grew almost abusive, but it was useless; she was determined that Hector was hard to raise, and with the ability to attract ill-fortune which she had caught from her husband, she made it so.

Indeed, if he had not been a sturdy child he might have succumbed to his mother's determination that he should linger close to death's door. When he grew out of babyhood she dosed him for constipation. This was a bugbear of the Reverend John's, and she was convinced that Hector had inherited it. Her husband took a large dose of castor oil every Saturday in order that his brain might be at its keenest on Sunday. But it was clear to her that such weekly dosing was not enough for a child, and Hector was plagued with syrups, pellets, suppositories and nastiness of every kind all the week through, and because his young bowels were never permitted to have a mind of their own, they behaved whimsically and he often had pains. Nor was constipation all. His mother believed that whenever a child had a white ring around its mouth, it was suffering from worms. Hector, whose inside was continually being churned with cathartics, very often had this symptom, and the worm powder was poured from its pink tissue wrapper upon his tongue, followed by a gobbet of jam which only made the dose more gritty and nauseous.

Because Hector was a growing boy, he was encouraged and indeed compelled by his mother to stuff himself, and though constipated and supposedly wormy he grew into a hearty lump of a lad, with thick, curly black hair, long eyelashes, solemn grey eyes and ruddy cheeks. When he was disturbed a dark flush crept over his face. It was this high colour, as much as anything, which made other boys dislike him. The children of Canada are not, in general, ruddy; hot summers, bitter winters and the heat of winter houses all combine to make them pale, though it is a healthy pallor. Church mothers agreed that "that young one of Reverend Mackilwraith's looked as if he was going to have apoplexy any time", and their sons resented and bullied Hector as something different from themselves.

He bore this bullying with stoicism. He felt that he was picked on because he was better than the others. There was no snobbery in this thought; it was the way of the world that a minister's son should be better than other boys. He was even good-natured about it. But once he lost his temper.

He was being baited by a rat-faced boy, a Baptist—Hector knew the religious denomination of every child in the school, as a matter of course—who had brought a gang of his companions along to see the fun.

"Say fork," said the Baptist, menacingly.

"Why?" asked Hector, backing against the wall of the school.

"Because I'll soak yuh if yuh don't," said the tormentor, squinting and twisting his face menacingly. "G'wan, say fork."

"Oh all right; fork," said Hector.

"Got a hole in yer pants as big as New York," screamed the Baptist. His admirers roared with laughter, but there was no mirth in it; under the microscope the meanness in the soul of a little boy cannot be distinguished from that in the heart of an adult fascist jailer.

"Now: say spoon."

"Spoon."

"Yah! Suck yer mother's teat all afternoon!"

This Hector could not bear. Not for himself, but for his mother, he was suddenly possessed by anger. That this rat-face should speak of her so! He had but the dimmest notions about sex, and his mind shrank from the smutty, ignorant talk of the schoolyard, but he knew that his mother had been spoken of in a way which he could not tolerate, and live. His face turned its darkest red, and he went for Rat-face with both fists flying.

"Fight! Fight!" The schoolyard cry went up and in a few seconds there was a crowd around the two boys.

Rat-face fancied himself as a fighter. He was the sort of boy who moves from group to group in a playground, dancing and striking the air, and asking in a menacing voice if anybody wants a fight. Such boys rarely find anyone who dares to take the challenge. Hector knew nothing of fighting, but he was a heavy, powerful boy and he was angry as Highlanders are angry, with blood hissing in his head, and throbbing behind his eyes. Rat-face attempted to dance and feint, but Hector rushed in upon him, caring nothing for his blows, and hammered him until the astonished Rat-face gave up any pretence of fighting and tried to run away. But Hector seized him and swung him around with his back to the wall of the school. And there he punched and pummeled him until Rat-face, who was a puny child, fell down in a faint.

Then the cry went up! Hector Mackilwraith had killed Rat-face! Hector Mackilwraith was a brutal bully who had defied the conventions of dodging and feinting and pawing the air so dear to little boys, and had unfairly hit his opponent as hard as he could! Nobody dared to touch him, but they all screamed abuse. Shortly a teacher arrived, who shrieked when she saw blood running from Rat-face's nose and mouth, and sent a boy to fetch the principal. The principal came on the run, and Hector was sent to his office to wait, while Rat-face was restored to such limited consciousness as his heredity and his fate permitted him to enjoy.

The principal was a just and mild man, who did not want to beat Hector if he could find a way out of it; Hector had never sinned before, and it was plain that there had been some unusual reason for his fury. But when he asked Hector to explain why he had beaten Rat-face into insensibility the boy would give no answer. How could he repeat, to an adult, those shameful words about his mother? How could an adult understand them? The disgrace, the filthiness of what Rat-face had said was linked with dark mysteries of which Hector had little knowledge, but an infinity of disgusted, fascinated surmise. It was clear that adults did not want children to know of these mysteries, for they never mentioned them. How, then, could Hector mention the unmentionable to the principal? How could he ever mention it to anyone who would understand? He knew that there was no way out of his predicament, and he stubbornly held his tongue.

The principal had no alternative but to beat him. Rat-face's parents would expect it, and if he could not suggest to them that there had been fault on both sides they might complain to the school trustees. As beatings go, it was a mild affair. The principal got out the special strap authorized by the provincial Department of Education for the purpose, and gave Hector four strokes on each hand. But both the principal and Hector knew what was happening; a reputation was falling to ruin; Hector Mackilwraith, a preacher's son, was Getting The Strap, and the shadow of corporal punishment had fallen across a pulpit. In such a community as that, the preachers formed a Sanhedrin, and as they were severe towards others, they were harshly judged when disgrace touched them.

It was thus that Hector, as a boy of eleven, brought his family into disgrace which lasted for perhaps a fortnight. It was agreed in the village that it had always been plain that the boy would break out, some day; it was agreed that his parents had done a poor job of bringing-up, and that if there had been more beating at home this public disgrace might have been avoided; it was agreed that preachers' young ones were always the worst. And then a dark suspicion arose that somebody's hired girl was carrying on with a married man who worked in the woodyard, and Hector's fall from virtue was forgotten. But he did not forget it. His mother had wept over him, loving him the more in his disgrace; and he, knowing that it was because of her that he had fought, and knowing the utter impossibility of ever explaining to her why he had fought, loved her and grieved with an intensity which unobservant people would have supposed to be beyond his years.

Nobody at that school ever provoked him to fight again, and Rat-face became his toady and trumpeter. Thus Hector learned about one kind of love, and a valuable lesson about the way of the world, into the bargain.

When Hector was fourteen his father died. He wet his feet at a Spring funeral, his cold in the head became a cold in the chest, and that in turn became pneumonia. He was a disappointment to the last. It was the habit of people in that district to set great store by the last words of those who died; the last words of a Presbyterian minister would be of particular interest, for he might reasonably be supposed to tarry for a moment on the brink of eternity, and make some helpful comment upon it, before breaking finally with this world. A pious boy, dying of a ruptured appendix (diagnosed as "inflammation of the bowels") earlier that same year, had distinguished himself by exclaiming "I see the light" (printed

in the local paper's obituary notice as "I see The Light!")
in his latter moments. It was confidently expected that a minister of the Gospel would better this. But the Reverend John
lay in a coma for several hours before his death, and expired
without saying anything at all.

He left his widow and son very badly off, for he had never
received more than enough for bare livelihood at any time
in his life. His estate amounted to about thirty-five dollars in
cash, which was found in a tin box in his desk, and the furnishings of the manse. His congregation, with one of those
warm impulses which restore faith in mankind, made a hasty
collection, paid for the funeral and handed over two hundred
and fifty dollars to his widow. They did more; after several
ministers had preached for the "call" in their church, they
took care to call a young man just ordained, and unmarried,
and gave him to understand that he was to have the manse,
but with Mrs. Mackilwraith as his housekeeper, and that this
arrangement was to last for at least one year.

It seemed as though the death of the Reverend John, who
attracted misfortune, released a sudden run of luck in favour
of Hector and his mother. He set out at once to find a job
which he could do after school hours and on Saturdays, and
found one quickly at a village grocery which paid him a
dollar and a half a week. And within two months an old and
forgotten aunt of the Reverend John's died, leaving six
hundred dollars which came to Mrs. Mackilwraith. Everybody in the village knew of this, and was pleased by her
good fortune. They did not even complain very much when
she immediately spent one hundred and fifty dollars of it on
a brass memorial plaque which was fastened to the wall of the
church, to the right of the pulpit, and which declared that
John Mackilwraith had been beloved not only by his wife,
but by themselves. It was ironical that the topmost ornament
on this plaque was the device IHS, with the letters so curiously interwoven that they looked like nothing so much as a
dollar sign.

Nobody ever knew whether the young minister who consented to take on Mrs. Mackilwraith as part of his manse re-

gretted his bargain. But when the year which had been agreed upon was finished another year began without any offer to leave on the part of the widow-housekeeper. She and Hector lived on at the manse, and when the old caretaker of the church died within a year of the Reverend John, Hector asked for his job, and got it by agreeing to take less money than his predecessor. This meant that he worked hard at school, ran to the grocer's and delivered parcels and moved boxes and barrels until six o'clock, and worked hard at his lessons until nine. On Saturdays he worked at the grocer's all day. On Sundays he was in the church by seven o'clock to light the stove and sweep the building. At eleven o'clock he solemnly placed the big Bible on the pulpit cushion, and held open the door of the vestry while the young minister made his solemn march to the pulpit. He then retired and pumped the organ. During the afternoon he prepared the Sunday School room for use, and cleaned it when the school was over. At seven o'clock he repeated his morning's duties, and after evening service he closed the church. On communion Sundays he was helped by his mother in cutting bread into cubes, and in washing the two hundred little wineglasses which were used in that ceremony. If the Sunday School room was wanted during the week, which usually happened two or three times, it was his work to see that it was heated and ready. He performed all these duties well and thoroughly.

The fact is that Hector was as great a success as his father had been a failure. Not only was he strong and willing; he was also intelligent. He organized his time carefully, and if any direction was given to him which lay outside the ordinary realm of duty, he made a note of it in a little book. He was solemn and silent, and the boys and girls at the continuation school called him "Saint Andrew", from the name of the church where he was beadle. But other people liked him because he was trustworthy and thriving, and because it was plain that he was capable of looking after his mother, who might otherwise have been a reproach to them.

It was in the third spring after his father's death that the young minister, the Reverend James McKinnon, asked Hector to come to see him in his study one evening after supper. The study was much as the Reverend John Mackilwraith had left it, except for some pipes and a tobacco jar, and a framed photograph of Mr. McKinnon's graduating class. When Hector went into the study his mother slipped through the door after him, and settled herself with an air of expectancy in the only chair other than the one occupied by the minister. This meant that Hector had to sit on a low leather-covered couch, with broken springs, and placed him at a psychological disadvantage.

"Hector," said the Reverend Mr. McKinnon, "your mother has asked me to speak to you on a matter of grave concern. In June you will complete your schooling here. What lies before you? It is your mother's wish, as it was the wish of your late father, that you should enter the service of God. As the son of a minister there are scholarships open to you at one or two universities. Your school record suggests that you might fittingly aspire to one of them.

"There is more to being a minister, however, than education, noble though the pursuit of learning is. The gown and bands may mark the teacher, but it is the working of God's spirit in the heart and mind which marks the minister. It is not too soon, now, to ask God what His will is for you. We need have no fear, I think, as to what His answer will be. It is not impossible that He has spoken to you already, in the watches of the night, though I doubt if you would have concealed the fact from your dear mother, or perhaps from myself, if that had been the case. Supposing, therefore, that you have not heard the call already, I offer myself, at your mother's request, as your guide and mentor in this all-important matter. Let us pray, therefore, for guidance."

Mr. McKinnon said all of this with great earnestness and sober kindness, and before he had quite finished Mrs. Mackilwraith was on her knees, with her face in the seat of her chair. The minister rose, and as Hector did not at once follow his mother's lead, he gestured to him to kneel by the couch.

But Hector remained seated, and spoke in a low, clear voice.

"Thank you sir, for your kindness," said he, "but I have already made up my mind that I am going to be a school-teacher."

"It is not for any man to say that he has made up his mind on such a matter until he has first taken some account of God's mind for him," said Mr. McKinnon.

"The call to the ministry is not the only call," said Hector. "I feel the call to teach."

"It is doubtful whether at your age you have heard the call in all its plenitude," said Mr. McKinnon. "The minister also wears the gown of the teacher, and I think that that is all of the vision that you have permitted yourself to see. The rest will come. Now let us pray."

"No," said Hector. "I'm not going to be pushed into the ministry. I've no mind for it at all."

"Are you refusing to pray with your mother and me?"

"Yes," said Hector loudly, and the dark flush spread over his face.

Mr. McKinnon sat down. He was only ten years older than Hector, and although he could keep up his ministerial dignity under most circumstances, he still, at times, suffered from a mortifying sense of insufficiency. Mrs. Mackilwraith, who had been kneeling with her head twisted around toward them during this conversation, with an expression of maternal misery on her face, now climbed painfully to her feet and sat down again, weeping softly and unbecomingly. After a few false starts she found herself able to utter.

"It's a mercy your father didn't live to see this day," she quavered. "It was his dearest wish that you should follow him in The Work."

"I never heard him say so," said Hector. Because he was young and fighting for his life, he gave unnecessary vehemence to his speech; his mother took this to mean that he thought that she was lying (which she was, for the Reverend John had never made any plan or expressed any wish for Hector's future) and wept the more. For the three years past she had been romanticising the Reverend John, and she clearly remembered his saying a good many fine things which had never, in fact, entered his mind or passed his lips.

The Reverend Mr. McKinnon decided to have another try. "Hector," said he, "it grieves me to see you being both cruel and foolish. Your mother knows what your father wished for you. She knows what she wishes for you. In a decision of this kind you must not think only of yourself. The sacrifices demanded by the ministry are numberless. But its glories, too, are numberless. To be counted among the ministers of God is to be used for the highest purpose God has designed for man. The fleshpots of this world are superficially attractive; I will confess to you that there was a period of my own life when I seemed to see the beckoning finger of pharmacy luring me toward a life of worldly ease and pleasure. But I would not retrace my steps now. Nor will you wish to do so, when once you have submitted yourself to the Will of God. His yoke is easy, and His burthen light; your father found it so, and so will you."

"You never knew my father," said Hector. "I don't think anything was easy for him. And I'm telling you now that I will not be a minister. I'll have to live my own life and make my own way, and it'll not be in the church. I told you I'd make up my mind."

"Have you no consideration whatever for your mother?"

"Yes. I'm going to support her. It is my duty, and I'll do it. But I'll do it as a schoolteacher."

"I see that it is a waste of time to argue with you while you are in this frame of mind," said Mr. McKinnon. "I shall leave you with your mother, and if you have a spark of manhood in you, her tears, if not her arguments, will prevail with you."

He left the room, and went to his bedroom, where he sat uncomfortably on the edge of his bed and thought the thoughts of a man who is not master in his own manse, and who has been worsted by a boy of seventeen.

Hector, left alone with his mother, made no attempt to comfort her. He sat for ten minutes, during which she cried softly and persistently. Then he went to her chair and put his hand on her shoulder.

"It's no good to cry any more, mother," said he. "You could have saved yourself all this if you had listened when I said I'd made up my mind. Now don't worry; I'll look after you and it'll all come out right. I've planned everything."

No more was said on the matter until the end of June, when it appeared that Hector had matriculated with honours, and he made application for a year's training at the nearest Normal School, which was thirty miles from the village in which he had grown up.

In the autumn Hector went to the Normal School, to be trained as a teacher. He had never been away from home before but he felt no uneasiness about his situation. He had five hundred dollars, all of which he had earned himself; he had a suit for every day, which he had ordered from Eaton's catalogue; he had a best suit which the Reverend James McKinnon had given him, it being a layman's suit of blue which he had improvidently bought a bare six months before he donned black forever. These material possessions were not great, but they were all his own, and he had an immaterial possession which was of immeasurably greater value; he had a plan of what he meant to do during the next ten years. He had made up his mind.

When he left home no one would have thought that his mother had ever had any ambition for him save a teacher's life. She had an ability, invaluable in a weak person, to persuade herself that whatever was inevitable had her full approval, and was in some measure her own doing. She was eager to further his plan in any way open to her.

Hector did not want money from his mother, and he did not want her to make sacrifices for him. He felt perfectly confident that he could look after himself, and her too, as soon as his year of training was over. In the years when many boys show an indecisive and unrealistic attitude toward life, Hector had grown unusually calculating and capable. The village said that he was long-headed. He had been able to detach himself from his home atmosphere enough to see that what lay at the root of many of his father's misfortunes was a lack of foresight, of planning, of common sense. In his concerns as an errand boy and beadle, Hector found that common sense could work wonders, and that planning enabled him to get through his work with no fuss. Planning and common sense became his gods in this world.

He was too much a minister's son to be without a god in some other world, and he was lucky enough to find the god which suited him in mathematics, represented in his schooling by algebra and geometry. In these studies, it seemed to him, planning and common sense were deified. There was no problem which would not yield to application and calm consideration. He took care to do well in all his school work, but in these subjects he exulted in a solemn, self-controlled fashion. The more difficult a problem was, the more Hector would smile his dark, shy smile, and the more cautiously would he ponder it until, neatly and indeed almost elegantly, he would pop down the solution. During his last two years of school he never failed to solve a problem correctly. When Hector went to the Normal School he possessed the secrets of life—planning and common sense. He planned that within ten years he would be a specialist teacher of mathematics in a High School, and common sense told him that he could do it as he solved problems, with proper preparation, caution and calm resolve.

Normal school yielded, almost without a hitch, to Hector's system. He was quickly singled out by the teachers as a student of unusual ability. These teachers, it must be explained, were not so much engaged in teaching, as in teaching how to teach. It was their task to impart to the young men and women in their care the latest and most infallible method of cramming information into the heads of children. Recognizing that few teachers have that burning enthusiasm which makes a method of instruction unnecessary, they sought to provide methods which could be depended upon when enthusiasm waned, or when it burned out, or when it had never existed. They taught how to teach; they taught when to open the windows in a classroom and when to close them; they taught how much coal and wood it takes to heat a one-room rural school where the teacher is also the fireman; they taught methods of decorating classrooms for Easter, Thanksgiving, Hallowe'en and Christmas; they taught ways of teaching children with no talent for drawing how to draw; they taught how a school choir could be formed and trained where there was no instrument but a pitchpipe; they taught how to make a teacher's chair out of a barrel, and they taught how to make hangings, somewhat resembling batik, by drawing in wax crayon on unbleached cotton, and pressing it with a hot iron. They attempted, in fact to equip their pupils in a year with skills which it had taken them many years of practical teaching, and much poring over Department manuals, to acquire. And often, after their regular hours of duty, they would ask groups of students to their homes and there, in the course of an evening's conversation, they would drop many useful hints about how to handle rural trustees, how to deal with cranky parents, how a girl-teacher of nineteen, weighing one hundred and ten pounds, might resist the amorous advances of a male pupil of seventeen, weighing one hundred and sixty pounds, how to leave a rural classroom without making it completely obvious that you were going to the privy, and how to negotiate an increase in pay at the end of your first year. Hector absorbed all these diverse pieces of information as his natural mental nutriment. There was no question about it, he was cut out for a teacher.

More clearly than in any other part of his work, this showed in his model-teaching. This was a species of practical work in which a Normal School student visited a city school, and taught a lesson to a class of living, breathing children, under the eye of an experienced teacher who made a report on the student's success to the Normal School principal. Many students who were impeccable in the theoretical side of their work broke down badly in model-teaching. One young man in Hector's year, who had almost overcome a severe case of inherited bad English, lost his nerve and addressed his first class as "youse". A girl, attempting to tell a class some apocryphal stories about the early musical development of the young Handel, lost her nerve and spoke thirty-seven times of "the harpischord", which, as she had never seen or heard the instrument in question, was not altogether surprising. Another girl burst into tears when no child volunteered to answer the first question she asked in a classroom. But not Hector. It was plain at his first model lesson that he was the captain on his quarterdeck. He was a born disciplinarian; that is to say, he never had to mention discipline. He was a born teacher, tireless in explanation, ingenious and ready in example, enthusiastic but not flighty in his approach to his work. Teachers who sent in reports on his model lessons were unstinting in their praise, and one elderly teacher, who had seen generations of neophytes pass through these early tests, was known to have sobbed a little, in professional ecstasy of joy, when describing Hector's lesson on the Lowest Common Denominator.

His year at the Normal School was a success, qualified only by his unaccountable conduct at the Annual "At Home"—conduct which amounted to public scandal, and for which he never offered any explanation. It was this incident which gave rise to the opinion among his fellow students that Mackilwraith was brilliant, but strange. Nevertheless it was agreed that the school which got him for a teacher would be lucky.

The lucky school was a rural establishment which appeared, to the casual observer, to be planted in the middle of a wilderness. To its pupils, and to people for two or three miles in each direction however, it was in the centre of a thriving and heavily populated area. There was one room, in which children from six to fourteen were gathered, and everything they learned was taught to them by Hector, who was now nineteen. He ruled firmly and well, and it never occurred to him at any time to be at a loss, or to doubt his authority, or to laugh at his own omniscience. He was not as popular as the teacher who had been there before him, because when she found that there was a little spare time at the end of the day, or half an hour to be got through on a Friday afternoon, she had read stories to the children; Hector's way was to give them arithmetic to do, or to test them in "mental arithmetic". This amusement consisted of his firing off twenty figures or so, and then demanding the total from a pupil chosen at random. A few pupils loved this; most of them dreaded and hated it. Sometimes he would show off a little; he would permit each child in the class—there were thirty-seven of them—to toss a figure, great or small, at him, and he would add them all together in his head and write the total on the blackboard in huge figures. This was better fun than when the addition was being done by the pupils, but it was not so improving, and it did not happen often.

When his second year came around, Hector had secured his increase in salary from the trustees, and was ready to begin on a vital part of his plan. He was now sending home money regularly to his mother, who continued to live at the manse. He had begun teaching at six hundred dollars a year, and now he was getting seven. His mother received half of this, and the remainder was spent for his board. He clothed himself with money which he received for a summer job of time-keeping for a road-construction company. And in this second autumn, when he was twenty, he set to work to obtain a degree of B.A. from Waverley University, working extra-murally.

Getting a degree extra-murally has certain decided disadvantages. The first of these is that the student has no one to make him work, and no companionship to lighten his work. The next is that he must take in a great deal of information in circumstances which are, as a general thing, uncongenial to such exercise. The third is that he suffers from a sense of isolation from the centre of learning which he hopes to regard as his Alma Mater, and fancies that those students who are on the spot are gaining insights which are denied to him; his position is comparable to a man who is in a house where a wedding feast is going on, but who is forced to remain in the cellars and suck his portion of the cheer through a long tube. The first and second of these troubles did not bother Hector; he liked work, and could settle down to it as well in his bedroom at the farmhouse where he boarded as anywhere else. But the third concerned him greatly, for he wanted his degree in mathematics and physics, and these are not matters which can be studied alone to best advantage. Therefore Hector got rid of all the things which could be done in isolation in three years of solitary study after school hours. Each spring he would make his way to a village six miles away, where there was a clergyman who was a graduate of Waverley, and while the clergyman snored in an arm-chair, Hector would square himself to the dining-room table, and write an examination or two. And when he had done as well as he could by this method he gave up his rural school, and went to Waverley for two years of study in the place where study is most easily and most effectively accomplished.

Money was, as always, the problem. He had saved something from his summer jobs, but not enough to carry him through two winters of university study. It was necessary, therefore, that he should find a job which he could combine with university work. He found it, working as a waiter in a restaurant which catered particularly to students, and which used students for most of its lesser staff. There were many students who were, like himself, working their way through the university, and not merely was there no discrimination against them—they were, on the contrary, regarded as especially deserving of commendation. Their courage and determination were undeniable, but it was an unfortunate fact that much of the best that a university has to offer was denied them. When students gathered for conversation, they were working. When the weekend brought a cessation of work at the restaurant, Hector had to spend Sunday deep in his books. When a lecture or a demonstration had particularly stirred his mind he could not take time to pursue that stirring; he had to go and rush orders of coffee and doughnuts to other, less needy students. The determination of the man who works his way through the university is beyond question, but it is not likely that he will get as much from his experience as the student more fortunately placed. He has not time to be young, or to invite his soul.

Nevertheless, he achieved his end, and the glorious day came when his mother saw Hector, as one of an apparently endless line of students, receive his diploma from the Chancellor, and return to the body of Convocation Hall, an indisputable B.A. He plunged at once into a summer's work which gave him the coveted specialist certificate, and with a light heart he bade farewell forever to the teaching of history, spelling, geography—all the trivial subjects which had been part of the routine of a primary school teacher. He had no trouble in finding a position in a small collegiate institute and when, four years later, the post of the head of the department of mathematics at the collegiate at Salterton fell vacant, he applied for it, and was chosen from among twenty aspirants. His cup was full. He had done all that he had meant to do, and he had done it by planning and common sense.

In his new position he received a good salary, and it was his mother's idea that she should come to Salterton and keep house for him. But Hector thought otherwise. He preferred to live at the Y.M.C.A., in a room which he had partly furnished himself and to eat at the Snak Shak. The habit of overeating which had been imposed upon him in childhood persisted, and at thirty he was already paunchy. He pointed this out to his mother as evidence that he was quite able to look after himself, far more capable of doing without her than was the Reverend James McKinnon, who had grown much older in appearance, but whether as a consequence of pastoral duties, or as the outcome of a diet of stewed beef, pie and soda crackers it was impossible to tell. Mrs. Mackilwraith had saved almost every penny that Hector had ever sent her, and it never occurred to her to move out of the manse. The unfortunate McKinnon had even given up dreaming of such a thing; he lived as a lodger in his own house, the victim of other people's thoughtfulness and generosity.

Prosperity wrought slowly but surely upon Hector. After four years as a department head, he began to feel that the social side of his life needed attention, and through acquaintances who were interested in it he was drawn into the Salterton Little Theatre. He was elected to the treasurership almost at once, and he showed to advantage in that office. He was always in the background when theatre parties were given, smiling and drinking one drink. He liked to be where people were gay, but he did not permit an uncontrolled gaiety in himself. He liked to see pretty women running about in a state of excitement, and he liked the Little Theatre lingo, copied from the professional theatre, in which "dear" and "darling" were customary forms of address; but he never made use of such endearments himself. And it was a fact, though it was of interest to no one but Hector, that he had never known any intimacy—no, not the slightest—with a woman. There had been that terrible business at the Normal School "At Home"—but he had driven that down into the cellarage of his mind, and had almost forgotten it.

He was forty when he decided that he would like to act, and planned and exercised his common sense to secure for himself the part of Gonzalo.

CHAPTER
3

ROGER TASSET glanced around the clubroom with the sure eye of a connoisseur, to see if there was anything there which was of interest to him. He had been in Salterton for six weeks and except for a couple of routine flirtations with waitresses he had had no association with women of the kind which he valued. If he couldn't start something soon, he told himself, he would go off his head with boredom. It was useless to deceive himself; he simply had to have women.

Roger was extremely careful not to deceive himself upon this point; indeed, it was a matter on which he offered himself constant reassurance. Most men, without being conscious of the fact, spend a great deal of time and effort in bringing about circumstances which will enable them to support an ideal portrait of themselves which they have created. Roger, from a very early age, had thought of himself as a devil with women, and in consequence he was continually obliged to seek women with whom he could be devilish. He was not of a reflective temperament, and thus it could not be said of him that he embraced libertinage as a philosophy or a way of life, as did Don Juan. But he had convinced himself that sex meant more to him than it did to most men, and that by attracting and seducing women he was being true to his nature and fulfilling a rather fine destiny.

Unlike as they were in external things, Roger shared Hector's faith in planning and common sense, and he had applied these principles to his career of seduction. And as many things respond well to planning and common sense, he had succeeded in seducing quite a number of women between his eighteenth year and his present age of twenty-five. He sincerely believed that women were all alike, and it was certainly true that those with whom he had been successful shared many characteristics in common. For one thing, they all showed an abandon which was foreign to Roger's nature; he never consummated a conquest without taking precautions which would make it impossible for a child to be attributed to him. With girls who might not understand this, he was careful to make it plain. He had a series of little talks, also, about the necessity for taking love lightly, as it came, and for relinquishing it with a smile when it was still in its fairest flower; this convenient attitude was calculated to make any girl who sought to detain him longer than he wished seem unsporting and stuffy. If anyone should think that Roger's attitude was somewhat calculating and joyless it must be said in his defence that he approached seduction professionally, or as a business; he believed success in that field to be a necessity, without which he would lose faith in his own reality and importance in the world. One does not take risks with the source of one's self-respect.

Roger was a soldier, good enough to be well thought of by his superiors and not so good as to cause them disquiet by flashes of originality. He had been sent to Salterton for a course of special training. Nellie's suggestion that he should give temporary assistance to the Little Theatre had come as a godsend to him. He cared nothing for the theatre, but he knew that it was a place where there were likely to be plenty of girls. He had arrived at the clubroom promptly at eight o'clock on the night set aside for the auditions for *The Tempest*, and found himself among the first half-dozen.

The clubroom was the top floor of an office building. It had been a public hall in the days when people did not mind climbing three flights of stairs in order to attend a political rally or a lantern-slide lecture. It was now a rather seedy place with a low platform at one end. The walls had originally been a disagreeable brown, but the Little Theatre had sought to cheer them by painting them bright yellow to a height of twelve feet; as the hall had a twenty-foot ceiling the effect was not altogether happy. The decorations consisted of pictures of theatrical interest: a programme signed by Sir John Martin Harvey on his last visit to Salterton, a similar memento of Sir Harry Lauder, a signed photograph of Robert B. Mantell as King Lear, another of Genevieve Hamper in *The Taming of the Shrew*, a telegram of congratulation from Margaret Anglin to the club on its tenth birthday, a printed postcard from Bernard Shaw refusing permission to perform *Candida* without payment of royalty, and several sets of photographs of past productions. Cupboards for costumes were built against one wall, and behind a screen was a small kitchen, where refreshments could be made. The objects most prominently displayed in the room were two framed certificates testifying that the Little Theatre had distinguished itself in the Dominion Drama Festival.

For the audition, chairs had been arranged in a semicircle with a table facing them. Three of these chairs were now occupied by women who had been mentally dismissed by Roger with the hard words "Total Loss". Another woman was busy behind the screen, rattling crockery. Two men were in conversation by a window; Roger knew one of them to be Larry Pye and the other was the man whom he had met briefly on that rainy day at St. Agnes'—the man who knew about seats—McNabb or some such name.

Roger was bored. It looked as though a dull evening lay before him. He cheered up a few minutes later, however, when a group of girls arrived. He had little time to appraise them, for Mrs. Forrester came up the stair, accompanied by Valentine Rich, and Roger gave his whole attention to them; he had always found it excellent policy to keep on good terms with older women; they always liked a fellow with a bit of dash, and their liking was worth having. The Rich woman seemed to be a silent piece; she was polite enough, but she did not glow when Roger gave her his special, intimate smile. Nellie glowed, however, most gratifyingly.

"Roger dear," she said: "you must meet everybody. You don't mind me calling you dear, do you dear? I'm old enough

to be your mother, or an aunt, anyhow. And in this game
you get into the way of calling people dear. You see?"

"If you're more than five years older than I am," said
Roger, "my eyes are deceiving me, and they don't. Not about
that sort of thing. And if you pretend to be older than you are
so that you can boss me, I have to teach you a lesson, Nellie
dear."

"Five years!" Nellie gave a playful shriek in which co-
quetry, indignation and regret for lost youth were prettily
blended. "How old do you thing I am?"

"About twenty-eight—a year or two either way."

"My dear boy! Don't they test your eyesight in the Army
any more?"

"Yes. I have perfect vision. I also have a wonderful instinct about such things."

"Well, your instinct is wrong this time. If you want to
know, Val here and I are just the same age, aren't we Val?"

Nellie meant this to be a surprise to Roger, and so it was.
He had taken Valentine to be many years Nellie's junior. But
he gallantly told them that he stuck to his original estimate.
Valentine did not care; she thought nothing of Roger's sort of
charm. But Nellie's heart was like a singing bird whose nest
was in a water'd shoot. She seized upon the next couple to
mount the stair. It was Professor Vambrace and his daugher.

"Pearl, dear, you haven't met Roger Tasset, have you?
He's going to play Ferdinand to your Miranda."

"Really, Nell, you must be discreet," said Professor Vambrace; "no parts have been officially allotted as yet. Good
evening Tasset."

Pearl Vambrace murmured inaudibly, extended her hand
to Roger, and then took it back again when he seemed about
to shake it. This caused her to blush. Roger eyed her professionally, reflecting that this was a little more the sort of thing
he had been expecting.

"I am very happy to meet you," he said, giving the words
just a little more significance than the situation required. But
Vambrace took his daughter by the arm and moved her on
toward the semicircle of chairs; he seemed to choose one with

special care, and place her in it, before he went to the central table, and began to unload papers and books from a large, bulgy brief-case which he carried.

"Good evening," said a voice at Roger's shoulder, and he turned to find the treasurer of the club smiling at him, his hand extended.

"Oh, good evening, Mr. McNabb," said Roger.

"Mackilwraith," said Hector. "So you've come to try your luck, have you. So have I."

Roger had not thought of his presence at the audition in quite this way. It had never occurred to him that he would not be cast as the leading juvenile of any play which he chose to act in; he was not vain, but it was unlikely that an amateur drama group would find anyone better qualified than himself for a part which demanded looks, charm and a handy way with women. But these are not thoughts which one confides to a stranger. Particularly not to a stranger who looked like this one.

Years as a successful teacher had given Hector an air of quiet authority. He was almost as tall as Roger, though he was much stouter; his hair was thick, wavy and very black; black and thick were the eyebrows above his grey eyes. His face was full—almost fat—and ruddy. He was smiling, and he had excellent teeth. His voice was low and pleasant, and three generations in Canada, and a Lowland mother, had not quite flattened all the Highland lilt out of it. But it was a quality of sincerity about the man which intimidated Roger; it was not the professional sincerity of the professional good fellow; it was the integrity of a man who has every aspect of life which is important to him under his perfect control. Roger thought it wise to be a little diffident in his reply.

"Nellie suggested that I come along and see if there was anything I could do," said he. "I've done a little acting at school, you know, and a bit since. Never tried Shakespeare though."

"Ah," said Hector, seriously, "Shakespeare will test all of us to the uttermost."

"I dare say," said Roger, somewhat dismayed by this pious approach to the matter.

"Nevertheless, we are fortunate in our director. A professional, you know. She will tell us our faults. It may be severe, but we can take it." Hector smiled darkly at the thought of the artistic travail ahead. "There will be a great deal to be learned," he continued, with sober satisfaction; he was still trying to convince himself that his desire to act was rooted in a passion for self-improvement, rather than in a simple wish to have fun.

Roger wondered how to get away from this fellow. Every man has his own set of minor hypocrisies and Roger's was extensive, but it did not include the trick of disguising pleasure as education. Luckily Solly was passing at the moment and he hailed him.

"Hello there, Ridgetower," said he; "are you going to try for a part?"

"Hello, Brasset," said Solly; "no, I'm not."

"Not Brasset; Tasset."

"How odd. Not Ridgetower; Bridgetower."

"Sorry. I'm bad at names, I'm afraid."

"But you never forget a face, I'll bet."

"Well, no; as a matter of fact I don't. How did you know?"

"It is characteristic of people who forget names that they never forget faces. At least, so I have often been told. It seems a pity. Only remembering half, I mean."

Roger had an uncomfortable feeling that he was being got at. A frowsy lot of fellows you met in clubs like this. McNabb—no, Mac-whatever-it-was—and this fellow Bridgetower, with his messy hair and his long nose. Thought himself smart, obviously; a university smart-alec. Roger squared his shoulders and looked soldierly. There was one thing he never forgot, and that was a girl's face. Neither of these fellows looked as though they had ever seen a girl at shorter range than thirty yards. He could afford to despise them.

"You have both acquainted yourselves with the play, I suppose?" said Hector, who sensed a strain in the conversation and sought dexterously to relieve it. He failed in his purpose, for Solly was affronted by the suggestion that any Shakespearean play was unfamiliar to him, and Roger, who had been in many plays and had never troubled to read more than his own part, felt that the schoolteacher was trying to be officious.

"Time enough for that when we know whether we have parts or not," said he. And Hector, who was not as self-assured in these circumstances as he pretended, took this as a suggestion that he might be passed over in the distribution of roles, and flushed.

It was at this moment, luckily, that Nellie tapped on the table for order, and the three men parted with relief, and took chairs. Nellie told the meeting what it was for, which everybody knew, and then asked Professor Vambrace to say a few words. The Professor told the meeting, in his turn, that Shakespeare had been a playright of genius, and that the Salterton Little Theatre, with its customary instinct for the best in everything, had chosen to present one of his finest comedies. In a rather long parenthesis he explained that a comedy need not be particularly funny. He touched upon the Comic Spirit, and quoted Meredith at some length and with remarkable accuracy. He then gave quite a full synopsis of the plot of *The Tempest* and quoted two or three passages which he especially admired, all of which, by coincidence, were from the role of Prospero. He moved himself visibly. In all, he spoke for twenty minutes, and when he sat down there was respectful applause.

Nellie rose again, and told the meeting how fortunate the Little Theatre was to have Miss Valentine Rich of New York and London to direct the play for them. She assured them that it would be a rare privilege to work with Miss Rich, and that nothing short of their utmost efforts would suffice under such circumstances. Miss Rich was a person of whom Salterton might well be proud. She was also an example to the Little Theatre of what might be achieved by sheer hard work. Miss Rich would now address them.

Valentine arose, not altogether pleased to be displayed as the result of a career of dogged persistence. She said that she was very happy to be in Salterton again, which was true, and that she looked forward to working with them, which wasn't. She hoped that they would not find her as hard a taskmistress as Mrs. Forrester had suggested. She was confident that they could work together to give a very satisfactory and entertaining performance. She said this briefly, and with professional assurance and charm, and when she sat down the audience applauded in a markedly more hopeful manner than before.

With a late beginning and speeches, it was now almost nine o'clock. Nellie told the meeting that they had no time to waste, and said that they would work through the cast methodically, as it appeared in books of the play. At this point there was an audible rustling, as the meeting produced its copies of *The Tempest*, in everything from neat little single copies to large quarto volumes in which all the plays of Shakespeare, with steel engravings, were included.

The first part to be allotted, said Nellie, was that of the magician Prospero. Would those who sought this role please raise their hands?

There was no immediate response, but within five seconds Miss Eva Wildfang rose to her feet, and said that after the masterly reading which Professor Vambrace had already given of some speeches from that part she felt that many of those present would agree with her that Professor Vambrace was the man to play it. She looked about her for signs of this widespread agreement, but none were apparent. Miss Wildfang's cult for the Professor was an old story to everyone but herself and Vambrace.

The Professor closed his eyes, and rolled his head once or twice upon the back of his chair. Then he said that if it was the desire of the club that he undertake the part of Prospero, he would do so, though he would retire instantly if there were any other aspirant to it.

Nellie looked about the room expectantly, and said that if there were no comment, she would tentatively pencil in the Professor's name opposite the name of Prospero.

At this point Mr. Eric Leakey rose at the back of the

group, and said that he had taken literally the President's remark that the parts would be cast as listed in the book. In his copy the first name was that of Alonso, the King of Naples. He did not wish to set himself up as a rival to Professor Vambrace in matters of learning, but he had come to the meeting in order to read for the part of Prospero.

Miss Wildfang threw a glance in Mr. Leakey's direction which suggested that he had in some way affronted her. Nellie smiled and knit her brows at the same time, as though Mr. Leakey had created a great deal of confusion by his tardiness. It was Professor Vambrace who spoke.

"By all means," he cried; "by all means! Nothing is further from my mind than any desire to seize upon a role for which another man is better qualified. You must read at once, my dear sir. Come forward; come forward!"

"No, no; there is no need for that," said Nellie, when Mr. Leakey had picked his way through a maze of chairs, and was almost in front of the committee table. "It will simply cause confusion if we all begin to move around. Just read from where you are, Mr. Leakey."

"What shall I read?" asked Mr. Leakey, retreating.

"What had he better read?" asked Nellie of Vambrace.

"I suggest the greatest speech of all," said the Professor, and in his loud bass voice he declaimed:

> *You do look, my son, in a mov'd sort,*
> *As if you were dismay'd; be cheerful, sir.*
> *Our revels now are ended. These our actors,*
> *As I foretold you, were all spirits, and*
> *Are melted into air, into thin air:*
> *And, like the baseless fabric of this vision—*

"Exquisite; exquisite," he murmured, as though to himself. Then, returning to a world where such improprieties as casting-readings existed, he said, "You'll find it in Act Four, scene one, at about line 146 if you are using the New Temple edition, Mr. Leakey. Don't rush yourself. Take your time."

This show of erudition finished Mr. Leakey. He found the passage, and read it in a strangulated tone, while his bald spot grew redder and redder. He sat down amid silence, which indicated very clearly that he would not do.

"Thank you, Mr. Leakey," said Nellie, making some marks on a piece of paper. There was a general feeling that Mr. Leakey had thrust himself forward; those who hoped for parts took warning by his shame.

After this things moved in an orderly fashion. As each part was announced by Nellie, a few people declared themselves aspirants, and usually took care to add that it was just a notion they had, and that they would be happy to do anything they were fit for. It was a long and weary business, and there were several parts which nobody seemed to want at all. Reading progressed in much the same diffident, flat, half-choked fashion for all the parts, as though the actors had but one voice among them, and that a bad one. But when the part of Ferdinand was in question, Roger read in a warm, attractive voice which roused the meeting from its embarrassment and torpor. He did not, perhaps, reveal the fullest meaning of the passage which was allotted to him by the demon memorizer Vambrace, but he brought to it qualities of masculine charm which are rarer in Little Theatres than female beauty, than dramatic instinct, than true comic insight, than tragic power. Even Miss Wildfang, the single-hearted, cast an appreciative look toward him as he sat down. Everyone, in fact, showed a lively interest in him, save one. That one was Griselda, who appeared to be asleep.

There are few proverbs so true as that which says that beauty lies in the eye of the beholder. As Solly looked at Griselda during the slow progress of the reading he thought that he had never seen her so beautiful before. How could he have overlooked such a miracle until this time?

Yet the beauty of girls of eighteen is rarely of a commanding sort. It is very easy to miss it unless one is in the mood for it. Griselda, at this moment of revelation, would not have seemed beautiful to Mrs. Bridgetower. The white skin would have seemed to that lady to reflect bad health and late nights; the red lips were very lightly touched with colour, but they were startling in so white a face; her hair, thick, waving and the colour of honey, could have been dismissed by Miss Wildfang as stringy; Mrs. Mackilwraith, observing the blue shadow on the eyelids which sheltered Griselda's cornflower-blue eyes, would have been seized with a powerful desire to give her a worm powder; and her nose, slightly more aquiline than is the present fashion, was very near to being a hook in the eyes of Nellie Forrester. If Larry Pye had been asked for his opinion of her figure he would probably have said that it would be better when she filled out. But to Solly, as he gazed, she seemed all that the world could hold of beauty and grace.

If Griselda's beauty showed to special advantage at this time it was because she was feeling a little unwell, and in consequence was relaxed and still. Quietness is a great beautifier, and in that room where there were so many tensions and expectations, so many warring ambitions and nervous cross-currents, her remoteness and her air of spiritual isolation were beautiful indeed.

Beautiful and, to Roger, irritating. He had read well; he knew it. Everybody had realized it except the pale girl. He had met her, of course. He never forgot a woman's face. But her name? Well, anyhow, her father owned that big place on the river where the play was to be done. Her indifference to his reading nettled him, and robbed him of his pleasure in the sensation he had caused. Was she asleep? Or couldn't she be bothered to open her eyes to see who was reading? There was no doubt about it, she was the best thing in the room. Those clothes meant money. Only the rich could look so elegantly underdressed. A good figure. A kid's figure, but good. Not skinny. He hated boyish figures. Sweet face. But he'd like to take that indifferent expression off it. He'd do it, too. He'd teach her not to sleep when he was doing his stuff. This was what he had come for. This, properly managed, would just about last the length of the course which he was taking. This would be a very nice little item for his collection.

Griselda was not the only girl in the room with pretensions

to beauty. Valentine Rich did not pay much attention to the reading; she knew that she could, if necessary, impose an appearance of intelligence upon an actor, but she could not give a good presence to someone who lacked it; she searched the room for people who might look well in costume. Her eye was taken by Pearl Vambrace. There, she thought, was a girl with possibilities. A distinguished, rather than a pretty, face; lots of nice dark hair, rather in need of a good vinegar rinse; not a bad figure and really beautiful eyes. But it was Pearl's expression which made her face an arresting one; she had the still, expectant look of one listening to an inner voice. This was a girl, thought Valentine, who must in some way be brought upon the stage.

There was to be no difficulty about it, seemingly. When the part of Miranda was open to contest, Pearl read the test passage very well, with intonations which suggested those of her father, though not to a farcical degree. As she read Vambrace fixed her with a steady gaze, and moved his lips in time with hers; once or twice he frowned, as though to show that she had departed in some measure from the pattern he had set for her. Valentine thought this irritating and embarrassing.

When at last the reading was over the committee retired to make its decisions; as the club had no private room they were compelled to go out on the landing, shut the door behind them, and stand at the head of the stair. Those to whom this delicate task was given were Nellie, Professor Vambrace, Solly and Valentine. The other club members remained inside, where cakes and strong tea were being served.

"This shouldn't take very long," said Nellie. "Just as I expected, no outstanding new talent showed up. Except Roger Tasset, of course. Isn't he a dream? A wonderful Ferdinand."

"The casting of Ferdinand must hang, to some extent, upon the casting of Miranda," said Professor Vambrace, weightily. "We must achieve a balance, there. Young Tasset has weight, undeniable weight. The question is, has he too much weight? We do not want him to seem—how shall I say it—too heavy for our Miranda. Whoever she may be," he added, in a tone as though the club were alive with young women capable of playing that part.

"I don't think there's any doubt that Pearl is our choice for Miranda," said Nellie.

"Do you really think so?" said Vambrace anxiously. "It is very hard for me to be objective in such a decision. In fact, I shall not take part in it."

"Your daughter read charmingly," said Valentine. A little on the rhetorical side, perhaps, but that is a fault which is easily corrected. And she looks right for the part. In fact, I want her for Miranda."

"Do you really?" said the Professor. "You think that she has the—how can I describe it—the weight, the authority for Miranda?"

"Miranda is only fifteen," said Valentine. "Authority is not really so necessary as a good appearance and a nice voice. She has both."

"You feel that her voice will suffice?" said the anxious father. "I cannot conceal from myself that it lacks sonority, particularly in the higher tones. And you must realize that she was not at her best this evening. I warned her. I warned her repeatedly. But she would go on sucking coughdrops all evening and as a result, when it came her time to read, she was cloyed. I was quite vexed with her."

"She will be very good," said Valentine; "and she will look very well with Tasset."

"Aha," said the Professor, rubbing his chin with a rasping sound. "Yes; she will play chiefly with him and with whomever we may choose for Prospero. We must strive for balance, within our limitations."

"Well, if you play Prospero," said Valentine, "the balance should be just about perfect."

"The decision must be made by the remainder of the committee without reference to me," said the Professor. "Common decency forbids that I should have any part in it. But there is just one point—not, I think, an unimportant

one—which I must make before I retire. It is this: if I play
Prospero—mark you, I say *if*—the question of a convincing
family resemblance between that character and Miranda is
adequately dealt with." The Professor bowed slightly, and
withdrew himself to a distance of five feet from the rest of
the committee, which was all the withdrawal possible on the
landing. It did not occur to him to go downstairs.

"Oh do come back, Walter," said Nellie. "We've never
seriously thought of anyone but you." It was only in
moments of the utmost emotional stress that anyone called
Professor Vambrace by his first name.

"I had imagined that it was settled some time ago," said
Valentine mildly. She was wearying of the Professor's
coyness.

"We did speak of it, sometimes, as a possibility; but when
it comes to casting we are determined to give everyone a fair
chance," said Vambrace, whose relief and pleasure at having
secured the best part for himself were wonderful to behold.

"In that case, what are we going to do with Mr. Leakey?"
said Valentine. "He wanted to be Prospero, and he didn't
read too badly."

"Oh Val, he was dreadful," said Nellie.

"Not impossibly dreadful; he was nervous, having to brave
us all, poor sweet. I'd like to cast him as one of the funnies.
Stephano, for instance."

"Why not cast him for Gonzalo?" asked Nellie.

"Because I want Mr. Mackilwraith for Gonzalo."

"But Val, he's such a stodge."

"So was Gonzalo a stodge. Anyhow Mackilwraith will
look very fine with some grey in his hair and a nice beard.
Shakespearean stodges must be made picturesque."

"I'd like to be perfectly sure that Mackilwraith in that
part wouldn't upset the balance of the play," said the
Professor.

"May I suggest, Professor Vambrace, that I shall be able
to do a good deal to give the play its proper balance?" said
Valentine.

"Oh quite, quite, quite."

"Now for Caliban, I want that rubbery-looking boy. What's his name—Shortreed."

"But Val, he hasn't been in the club long, and he's one of the stewards in the liquor store. Will he be acceptable to the rest of the cast? We have to think of that."

"You think of it," said Valentine. "I want him for Caliban."

In this fashion the casting proceeded. Valentine got her way about everything. Faced by her determination, Nellie and Professor Vambrace were ineffective. This was the first time that Valentine had shown anything but an indifferent acquiescence to their proposals, and they wondered uneasily whether she might not prove a Tartar. The fact was that in matters relating to her work, Valentine was not a theorizer and a talker, but a worker, and this was the first occasion that she had been able to get her teeth into anything solid in connection with the play. When she saw a group of possible actors, she could do her casting rapidly and without reference to Little Theatre politics. In a remarkably short time all the male parts in the play were decided upon.

"Now," said she, "what about the women? We've got Miranda. Who's to be Ariel? It'll have to be a girl; you have no man with ballet training, I suppose? You said something about Griselda Webster, Nellie; is there any special reason why she should have it, aside from the fact that she is pretty?"

"Yes. She sings quite well."

"Have you heard her?"

"Well, no; not really. But I've been told."

"I'll hear her tomorrow. Her figure isn't precisely what I would choose for an airy spirit. However, we can't have everything. Now what about these goddesses?"

"If I may make a suggestion," said Professor Vambrace, "I think that Miss Wildfang should be considered for the part of Juno. She has not thrust herself forward, but she has been a very faithful worker in the Little Theatre since its foundation, and the head of the refreshment committee for the past seven years. She has, unquestionably, a classic countenance. For 'ox-eyed Juno', as Homer describes her, I cannot think of a more fitting choice."

"I can," said Solly, speaking for the first time. "What about Torso Tompkins?"

"Solly!" cried Nellie, in a tone of despair.

The Professor's face was bleak. "In Shakespeare," said he, "a certain balance is an absolute necessity. There is a quality of modernity about Miss Tompkins which it is impossible to disguise."

"She's widely admitted to have the finest figure in Salterton," said Solly, stubbornly, "and she has a large personal following. If you want to sell tickets, put The Torso in a cheesecloth shift and chase her across the stage to slow music."

"Which was she?" asked Valentine.

"One of those girls who said they'd do anything," replied Nellie. "A bold-looking girl with black hair."

"She is called The Torso for the best of reasons," said Solly. "She has a bosom like a girl on the dust-jacket of a historical novel, as well as other agreeable features. And when it comes to being ox-eyed, The Torso begins where Miss Wildfang leaves off."

"I'll have a look at her," said Valentine. "Other goddesses?"

"I want to suggest dear little Freddy Webster for one," said Nellie. "She isn't here tonight, but as the play is to done at her father's home I think it would be a very nice thing to include her."

"Is she that dark, serious-looking child I met at St. Agnes'?"

"Yes."

"Excellent. I'll speak to her sister. Shall we go in now?"

Their reappearance in the clubroom brought an immediate silence. The hopeful readers stood about in groups, drinking the copper-coloured tea and eating the economical little cakes supplied by Miss Wildfang and her assistants. Griselda had chosen to be one of these, and was moving about with a large teapot. This made it difficult for anyone to talk to her for very long, and Roger Tasset was greatly cha-grined. He was with a knot of three girls, one of whom was Miss Bonnie-Susan Tompkins, known as The Torso. She had, indeed, a splendid figure, but the beholder was rarely permitted to see its beauties at rest. If she was not swinging one foot she was tossing back her hair; she arched her neck and heaved up her rich bosom most fetchingly, but too often; from time to time she waved her hands and snapped her fingers as though to some unheard, inner dance-tune; when she laughed, which was often, her posteriors gave a just-perceptible upward leap, in sympathy. Her face was as ani-mated as the rest of her; she was a lip-biter, an eye-roller, a sucker-in and a blower-out of breath. Her energy was de-lightful for five minutes, and exhausting after ten. As the committee came through the door, she laughed at a remark which Roger had made. It was a carrying laugh, and through her jersey dress her gluteals could be seen to contract sud-denly, and slowly relax again. When the committee passed her on their way back to the table her eyes swivelled nimbly in their sockets. Ox-eyed doesn't begin to describe it, thought Valentine.

"We have reached several decisions", said Nellie to the meeting "and I shall ask Miss Rich to announce them."

Valentine read a cast list. No hopes were dashed, for few of those present were so vain as to think that they were certain to get parts. They were, as a group, modestly willing to act if they were thought good enough, and content to be left out if they were not. The passionate egotism of Professor Vambrace by no means represented the temper of the club.

If anyone had been watching Hector when his name was read as the choice for Gonzalo they would have noticed that he flushed a little, smiled a little, and swallowed. But no one was looking.

"A few parts have not been cast," said Valentine, "but I want to allot them as soon as possible. May I see Miss Webster and Miss Tompkins for a moment, please?"

Roger was indignant. Wasn't the Webster piece to be cast,

after all? If so, why was he wasting his time? If the Tompkins girl was to take her place, he could reconcile himself to it, he supposed, but that was not what he wanted. He had quite forgotten about Pearl Vambrace.

Griselda and The Torso sought out Valentine in a corner, as the hubbub of conversation rose again.

"Hi, Griselda," said Miss Tompkins. "Long time no see."

"Hello, Bonnie-Susan," replied Griselda; "what have you been doing?"

"Better ask what I haven't been doing," replied The Torso eyes rolling, hair tossing, bosom advancing and retreating. It was her way to pretend that she lived a life of violent erotic adventure, but this was true only in a very limited sense.

"I am told that you sing, Miss Webster," said Valentine. "Now I want you to tell me quite frankly: how well do you sing?"

"I've a fairly reliable soprano voice," said Griselda, "and I've had good lessons. Not for noise, you know, but for quality."

"Do you sing, Miss Tompkins?"

"I was a wow in the Campus Frolic a couple of years ago," modestly replied The Torso, "but I don't know how I'd be on any hey-nonny stuff. But I'm a worker." Everything about her leapt, throbbed and tossed, in token of her sincerity and eagerness.

"Suppose we say, then, that you shall play Juno," said Valentine. "You have a fine appearance for the part, and if your voice is suitable we'll consider it settled."

The Torso was transported. She rushed back to her friends, hissing, "I've got a part! Listen kids, I've got a part!"

"Does your sister sing?" said Valentine, turning to Griselda.

"Well—yes, she does. But I don't know what she would say about acting. She's an odd child."

"Tell her I would be greatly obliged if she would consider it, will you?" said Valentine. "We are short of singers, and the music is going to be very important."

111

When Griselda had left her, Valentine felt Nellie's hand on her arm. "Val," said she, in a tone of gentle reproach, "you haven't really cast Bonnie-Susan Tompkins for Juno, have you?"

"Yes, why not? The Torso is just what the part wants."

"Oh, don't call her by that awful name. Val, darling! I don't want to interfere, but is she suitable? She's an awful one for the boys."

"What could be better? So was Juno, in her overbearing way."

"But in a classic, is it right?"

"Nellie darling, a lot of classics have remained classic because they have girls in them who are awful ones for the boys."

Once in the street most of the members of the Little Theatre set off toward their homes, the lucky ones with a light step, and those who had not secured parts less blithely. And yet they were not unusually depressed; they were, most of them, people to whom defeat was an accustomed feeling. A small group remained while Nellie hunted up the janitor whose job it was to lock the door behind them.

"May I give anyone a lift?" cried Griselda, from her car.

"Me. I always want a lift," said Solly, and climbed in beside her.

"Mr. Mackilwraith, may we drop you anywhere?"

"Thanks," said Hector, "I'll walk. I would like fresh air. It was very stuffy in the clubroom tonight." As he spoke he leaned through the window.

"I'm awfully glad you're going to be Gonzalo," said Griselda, and smiled.

"It's good of you to say so," replied Hector, and he returned the smile somewhat shyly. Then he went down the street in the determined manner of a man who is walking for air.

"Nice of you to say a kind word to Mackilwraith," said Solly as they drove away. "I'll bet he has a grim life, teaching wretched kids all day. That's what I face, if I can't find anything better."

"I was glad to see him chosen when Nellie and that odious Professor Vambrace didn't want him. I thought it was horrid of them to make such a fuss when he wanted a part, just because he wasn't one of their gang."

"Valentine Rich dealt them a few shrewd buffets in the hall when we were choosing. I like her more and more."

"Yes. She's even holding it over my head that I may not be cast as Ariel, to Nellie's horror. Nellie thinks that a good part for me is the price for using Daddy's garden. I like Val Rich's way much better; she makes it appear that my own ability has something to do with it. Solly, would you like to come home for awhile?"

"Really, I think I'd better get back to Mother at once, Griselda."

"I meant it quite nicely. I wasn't going to kiss you in the garden again or anything unmaidenly like that."

"You didn't kiss me. I kissed you. But you know how Mother is."

"No, I can't say that I do. I don't think I'd know your mother if I saw her. I believe I know her voice, though."

"Oh? How?"

"Somebody called up a couple of days ago, and asked if you were there. I happened to answer the phone. It was a very discreet sort of voice, but something whispered to me that it was your mother."

" 'Oh great, just, good God! Miserable me!' " said Solly.

"What?"

"Browning."

"Solly."

"Yes?"

"Doesn't your mother want you to see me?"

"Well—I don't know."

"Is it me particularly, or is it any girl?"

"Mother has been very ill," said Solly. "It makes her extremely sensitive. She's afraid that I'll forget about her. And I don't think she realizes that I'm not a child."

"A very nice, loyal speech. Well, here we are at your home, and it's still well before midnight."

"It's no good being huffy, Griselda. I have to take care of my Mother. There's nobody else to do it."

"I quite understand. But I'd hoped that you cared for me, a little, as well."

"Of course I care for you. I think I'm in love with you."

"But you can't be sure until you've asked your mother. Well, in the meantime, will you let her know where you are going when you are out? Because I don't really like having people who don't say who they are calling up to ask if you are with me."

"Don't be silly, Griselda. You're being unfair."

"That's what men always say."

"How do you know what men always say? Now listen to me: while my Mother is unwell my first duty is to her. If you don't like that we'd better drop this whole business right now."

"Neatly put. Good-night."

"Oh Griselda, darling; it's stupid to quarrel like this."

"Yes. You'd better go now."

"But I don't want to leave you until we've straightened this out."

"It's perfectly straight now. I certainly don't intend to dispute your mother's claim to all your attention and love. So what more is there to say?"

"Griselda, you're indecently ready with your tongue. You can think up nasty things to say much too fast for your own good. Please don't say things that will drive us apart just for the fun of saying them."

"I can't help it if I am not stupid enough to be good company."

"Oh, hell!" said Solly and tried to kiss her. But she turned away her face, and he was left with his neck stretched, feeling foolish. He opened the door of the car and stepped out.

"When can we meet again and talk this over reasonably?" he asked.

"I don't see much point in talking about it at all," said

Griselda. "Don't bang that door or your mother will want to know who brought you home."

Solly's face was white with anger and humiliation. But he took care not to bang the door.

As Hector walked back to the Y.M.C.A. he felt himself uplifted and renewed. He had done it! He had wanted a part in the play, and he was now assured that a part—the very part which he had chosen—was his. Of course, he had planned it, and he brought common sense to bear upon this, as upon all his ambitions. But until the cast was read out by Valentine Rich he had felt, far at the back of his mind, that this was conceivably a matter in which planning and common sense, those two invaluable secrets of life, might not work their accustomed magic. But they had done so! He reproached himself affectionately for his doubts. He would never doubt again. Anything he wanted could be brought about by a proper direction of his energies. Anything within reason, he reminded himself cautiously. It was not certain, for instance, that planning and common sense would make him Prime Minister of Canada. But then, he did not want that office. If he had chosen politics as a career, however, who could say? But the part of Gonzalo was his, and what was more, he had already memorized all his words in the first two acts. He ran over a few speeches in his mind. Poetry— even such poetry as Shakespeare has given to Gonzalo—is like wine; it is not for unseasoned heads. The rhythm and the unaccustomed richness of the words worked powerfully upon Hector's sensibilities, which had until this time been teetotallers in the matter of poetry. He was in a melting mood. How very good of the casting committee, he thought, to meet his wishes in this way. He had supposed, that night at Mrs. Forrester's, that there had been some unspoken opposition to his plan to act. But obviously they had thought better of it. Generous, large-hearted people! Well, they should not be disappointed in him. He had not reached beyond his capacities. If he had wished to play Prospero, now, or Caliban—. But he knew himself, and he knew what he could do. It was a great thing to know yourself.

It was a fine May night, and the moon shone brightly as Hector crossed the park. It had been nice of Miss Webster to congratulate him. He had not taken much notice of her before, but there was no doubt about it, she was an uncommonly nice girl. She had spoken so—he searched for the right word—well, so *nicely*. This was all the more meritorious in her because she had been educated in private schools. Boarding schools. He did not approve of private schools. It was a well-known fact that many of the teachers in them were not really qualified to teach; they had received no instruction in pedagogy; they merely had a knowledge—sometimes, he admitted, quite a thorough knowledge—of the subjects they taught. He was not a bigot in pedagogical matters. Still, if pedagogy were not a necessary study for a teacher, the Department would not lay so much stress upon it. Yet, in this expansive, unbuttoned mood, Hector was ready to admit that Miss Webster was a good advertisement for whatever school she had attended. Nevertheless, he chuckled to himself, he would like to throw a few quick problems in factoring at her, just to see what she made of them.

At some distance from the path, under the trees, was a bench, and upon it were a boy and girl in a close embrace. Ordinarily Hector would not have noticed them, for the eye sees only what the mind is prepared to comprehend. He saw them now; Hector the actor, rather than Hector the teacher of mathematics took note of what they were doing. He felt indulgent. It was a fine night; why should they not seek romance?

Romance, he realized, had been a scarce ingredient in his own life. There was, of course, romance in his steady rise from a country lad to his present position, but that was not the sort of romance he meant. There had been that awful business at the Normal School "At Home". But had he not put that behind him? He flushed at the recollection; twenty-one years since that painful evening, but it still had power to shame him. Nevertheless, that was water under the bridge, and Millicent Maude McGuckin was a married woman in a distant city, doubtless with children near to the age that he and she had been when it all happened. Down into oblivion he thrust the dismaying memory. Just before it disappeared however, he told himself that things would be different if he had that evening to live through again. If one could have the keen appetite of youth, with the experience of age! This cliché of thought rose in his mind as fresh and rosy as Venus from the sea, and he pondered delightedly upon it.

It would be different now. He was master of himself now. If he could have his chance again! And then, so suddenly and sharply that it made him catch his breath, came the thought: Why not? But no, it was out of the question. He thrust the thought from him. But again it returned: Why not? Well, was not he the head of the mathematics department of a large school, past the time for—the expression which his mother had used, when speaking of such matters —for girling? But why not? The question returned with an insistency which made him doubt that it arose in his own mind; it was as though another voice, a clear, insistent voice, spoke to him. Why not? Why not?

Had not a girl—and not just any girl, but a pretty, well-mannered girl, a girl compared with whom Millicent Maude McGuckin in her heyday seemed clumsy and countrified— addressed him in warm and friendly terms a bare fifteen minutes before? Had she not gone out of her way to do so? Had she not offered to drive him home? Had she not smiled upon him as she spoke? Had he missed something in that smile?

Music was not an interest of Hector's, but in every mind there linger a few rags and tatters of melody, and particularly of melody heard in impressionable youth. From the deeps of memory there rose a forgotton song, a song which had been played at the Normal School "At Home" on that fateful night:

> *Every little movement*
> *Has a meaning all its own*

117

It was an insinuating tune, a kind of harmonious dig in the ribs. Had there been a meaning in Griselda's smile which he (old sobersides that he was; he smiled at his stupidity) had overlooked? But the thing was ridiculous! She was a child; eighteen—nineteen, he did not know. He was talking himself into the idea that she was attracted to him. Still, it was not unknown for young women, and particularly young women of unusual character, to be drawn toward older men. And need he suppose that he was without attraction? He was wearing his best suit and his grey Homburg hat with the smart silk binding on the brim. A figure not utterly lacking in distinction, perhaps? Thus reflecting, and a little frightened by his thoughts, Hector arrived at the Y.M.C.A and went to bed.

Recurrently during the years his dreams had been plagued by the phantasmata, the hideous succubi, which visit the celibate male. This night, for the first time in his life he dreamed that a beautiful woman, lightly clad, leaned toward him tenderly and spoke his name; her smile was the smile which he had seen the night before. He woke in the night to the knowledge that for the second time in his life he was in love.

To keep pace with her father Pearl Vambrace had to take strides so long that her body was thrown forward, and she held her arms bent at the elbow.

"Don't slouch, Pearl," said the Professor.

"You're going a bit too fast for me, Father."

"No use walking unless you walk at a brisk pace. Head well up. Breathe deeply through the nose. Deep breathing refreshes the oxygen supply of the blood."

For another hundred yards nothing was heard except the rhythmical snorting of Professor Vambrace. His nose was large and finely formed, and when he breathed for his health it made a soft whistling sound, like a phantom peanut-roaster.

"Posture is more important now than ever. In this play

you will be, so to speak, on display. Acting involves severe physical discipline."

"Yes, Father."

"We must train like athletes. The Greeks did so. Of course there were no women on the Greek stage."

"No, Father."

"Nor on the Shakespearean stage, for the matter of that."

"No, Father."

"All the more reason why you should be in the pink of condition. Plenty of sleep. A light but sufficient diet. Lots of fruit. Keep your bowels open. Avoid draughts."

"Yes, Father."

"Don't suppose that there are no draughts in early summer," said the Professor, as though Pearl had contumaciously insisted upon this absurdity. "They are just as bad as in the winter. A summer cold is much the most difficult to shake."

"I suppose so."

"You may take it from me."

"Yes, Father."

Another hundred yards with the peanut-roaster going full blast.

"Some very odd casting done tonight."

"What didn't you like, Father?"

"What is the sense of putting that Tompkins girl in as Juno? Where's your balance going to be with that hoyden lolloping about the stage? Eva Wildfang was the obvious person for the part. It was nothing short of perverse for Miss Rich to overlook her."

"Maybe she thought Miss Wildfang was too old."

"What do you mean, too old? Eva Wildfang is a woman of cultivation. She knows who Juno was. I don't suppose this Tompkins creature ever heard of Juno before tonight. And Mackilwraith! Stiff as a stick. What will become of your plasticity, your fluidity of movement, with him on the stage?"

"Maybe Bonnie-Susan will be fluid enough for two."

"Who's Bonnie-Susan?"

"Bonnie-Susan Tompkins."

"Bonnie-Susan! Pah!"

Another hundred yards, during which the Professor fiercely renewed the oxygen in his bloodstream. Then—

"Pearl?"

"Father?"

"That last remark of yours, about the Tompkins girl being fluid; was that intended as a jest?"

"Only a little one, Father."

"It is not the sort of pleasantry which I like to hear from a daughter of mine. There was a smack of pertness about it."

"Sorry, Father."

"It had an overtone of indelicacy."

"Oh, I didn't mean anything like that."

"I should hope not."

After the next spurt of walking it was Pearl who began the conversation.

"Father, who is that man who is to play Ferdinand?"

"You were introduced to him, were you not? Of course you were. He is a Lieutenant Roger Tasset."

"Yes, but do you know anything about him beyond that?"

"He is here to do some special military course. I think that he comes from Halifax. Mrs. Forrester picked him up. We lack younger men."

"Do you think he will be good?"

"I sincerely hope so. He appears chiefly with us. Perhaps I can take him for some special coaching. I mean to give you all the help I can—not merely in the scenes which you play with me. Perhaps we might include him in some of our private rehearsals. We could work for balance."

"Oh, I think that would be lovely."

Pearl Vambrace lived a life which, to the casual glance, seemed unendurable. But she had gown up to it, and although she knew that it was not like the life of any other girl of her acquaintance she did not find it actively unpleasant. If the chance had been offered to her, she would not have changed her lot for that of anyone else; she would have asked, instead, that a few changes be made in the life she had.

She would have asked, for instance, that her father should not snub her so often, and so hard. She had never seen him as the casting committee had seen him, anxious and almost humble on her behalf. She saw him only as one who made constant demands on her, and was harshly displeased if those demands were not met. He insisted that she be first in all her classes during her school life, and somehow, with a few lapses from grace, she had managed it. But she was not to be a blue-stocking, he said; she was to be truly womanly, and for that reason she must have general culture, nice manners and a store of agreeable conversation. These attributes he did his best to implant in her himself, sparing no severity of tongue if she fell below the standard he had fixed. She would undoubtedly marry, he said, and she must fit herself to be the wife of the right sort of man. Neither Pearl nor her father recognized the fact, but this really meant being the sort of wife that Walter Vambrance wished he had married.

Mrs. Vambrace was a devout Roman Catholic lady, and when she had married the Professor it had been with a strong hope that he would shortly join her in her faith. It had seemed likely enough at time. The romantic side of Catholicism had appealed to the young Vambrace, and his ravenous intellect had rapidly mastered subtleties of Catholic philosophy which were beyond her understanding. When her parents urged her to wait for his conversion before marrying, she had declined to do so, for the conversion was, in her mind, a certainty. But it had not come about. For a time the Professor stuck where he was, elegantly juggling with coloured balls of belief. But then his enthusiasm had cooled, and without anything definite being said, it became clear that he had lost interest in the project. His wife was free to do as she pleased.

What she pleased to do did not strengthen the bond between her and her husband, nor did it especially endear her to her Church. She sought mystical experience. She read, reflected, meditated, fasted, did spiritual exercises, and prayed, hoping humbly that some crumb of unmistakeable manna would be vouchsafed to her. She was gentle and kind and tried to do her best for her husband and child, but her yearning for a greater enlightenment blinded her to many of their commonplace needs. Pearl, as a child, had always been oddly dressed. She had never had a party, and was rarely asked to the parties of others. Her father, after a few disputes with his wife and one really blazing row with a monsignor who called to protest, caused Pearl to be educated in Protestant schools, but made her way difficult by insisting she be entered on the school records as an agnostic. It was the Professor's contention, after his experiment in Catholicism, that a man could lead a life of Roman virtue without any religion at all, and he harangued Pearl on this theme from her fifth year. Her mother, tentatively and ineffectually, tried to soften this chilly doctrine with some odds and ends of spiritual counsel, snippets from a store of knowledge which led her daily farther from the world in which her body had its existence, which no child was capable of understanding. If Pearl had not been a girl of more than common strength of character she would have been in danger of losing her reason in that household.

Instead she was, at eighteen, a shy, dark girl with the fine eyes which Valentine had remarked, and the look of distinction which sometimes appears on the faces of those who have had to depend very much upon their own spiritual resources. Submissive to her father, loving and helpful to her mother, she was nevertheless conscious that she had a destiny apart from these unhappy creatures, and she waited patiently for the day of her deliverance.

Had it come, had the Great Experience arrived, which would free her from the loneliness which that divided household had imposed upon her? She thought with shame of her awkwardness when he had put out his hand for hers, and she had lacked courage to give it. But what had she done to deserve such luck as to have that wonderful young man to play her lover in *The Tempest*?

How beauteous mankind is!   O brave new world,
That has such people in't!

She murmured the words to herself as she sat on the side of her bed brushing her hair. Her father had always said that she would marry. Would she marry anyone half so thrilling as Roger Tasset? Her attempt to get new information about him on the way home had come to nothing. But her father meant to ask him to the house!

Was that anything to be thankful for? It was a neglected house, reasonably clean, but everything in it was threadbare, not from lack of money but from lack of desire for anything better. A Roman father, a mother who desired only to be alone with the Alone—what kind of household would such people maintain? She looked at her familiar room with new eyes; a white iron bedstead, a chest of drawers, a small mirror with a whorl in it, and a chair with weak back legs; her clothes hung behind a faded chintz curtain in a corner; the only picture was a framed postcard of Dürer's "Praying Hands", put there by her mother when she was a child, as next best thing to a crucifix; but there were many bookshelves with books of childhood, and the books of a sensitive, curious lonely girl. But to Pearl, in her present mood, it looked a pitiful room for a girl who hoped to attract the notice, and perhaps the love, of a prince among men. Such a girl should have a lovely room—the kind of room which she was convinced that Griselda Webster must have—and stocks of lovely clothes. Her father had taught her to talk, as he said, intelligently, but she was not convinced that this would be allurement enough for Roger Tasset. We always undervalue what we have never been without; Pearl thought little of intelligence and the conversation that goes with it.

She peered into the cloudy depths of the mirror, expertly avoiding the worst of the distortion caused by the whorl. In her white cotton nightdress, short-sleeved and falling only to her knees, she might have been a sibyl looking for a portent in the sacred smoke; but she was only a girl with the unfashionable sort of good looks staring at herself in a bad mirror. What right had she to be thinking of that glorious Apollo, of that planner of twenty shabby seductions?

Rye and tap water; it was to this melancholy potion that Solly turned for solace after he had called in at his mother's room, and put her mind at ease for the night. He was guiltily conscious that, as he talked to her, he was comparing her age and dilapidated face, so baggy without its teeth, to Griselda's fresh beauty; when he bent to kiss her a whiff of her medicine rose unappetizingly in his face; she mumbled his cheek and called him "lovey", a name that he detested. Then, escaping to his attic sitting-room, he was free of her.

Free? Not much more so than when he sat at her side. He sipped at his flat drink and reflected upon his condition. His loyalty to his mother was powerful. Why? Because she depended so heavily upon it. She had told him, he could not reckon how many times, that he was all that she had in the world. This was true only in an emotional sense, of course. Mrs. Bridgetower had come of a family well established in an importing business in Montreal, and when her father died, well before the days of succession duties, she and a sister had shared his considerable estate. Nor had her husband left her unprovided for. Without being positively wealthy, she was a woman of means. It requires a good deal of capital for two people to live as Mrs. Bridgetower and her son lived, when there has been no breadwinner in the family for ten years. Money, it is often said, does not bring happiness; it must be added, however, that it makes it possible to support unhappiness with exemplary fortitude.

If only his father had lived, he thought. But when Solly was twelve Professor Bridgetower had surprisingly tumbled from a small outcropping of rock, while with a group of students on a field expedition, and as they gaped at him in dismay and incomprehension, he had died of heart failure in two minutes. The eminent geologist, with his bald head and his surprised blue eyes and his big moustache, was suddenly no more. That night Solly had sat by his mother's bed until dawn, and in the coherent passages of her grief she made it plain to him that he was, henceforth, charged with the emotional responsibility toward her which his father had so unaccountably abdicated. The intellectual façade, the intricate understanding of the Yellow Peril, the sardonic manner, were a shell within which dwelt the real Mrs. Bridgetower, who feared to be alone in the world and who was determined that she should not be so long as there was a man from whom she could draw vitality.

It was not that she offered nothing in return. She told Solly, embarrassingly, at least once a year that if it were necessary she would gladly lay down her life for him. But in the sort of life they led nothing resembling such a sacrifice was ever likely to be required. He never made any corresponding declaration, but daily and hourly he was required not to die but to live for her. This had meant the sacrifice of much that would have made his schooldays happier, and when he had gone to Waverley it had made it impossible for him to share fully in the university life.

Escape to Cambridge had been a glorious break for freedom. A life of bondage had not unfitted Solly for freedom; it had served only to wet his appetite, and his first year at Cambridge had been the realization of many dreams. He had even managed to evade her wish that he should return to Canada for the long summer vacation, and had gone to Europe instead, living life as it can only be lived at twenty-two, dazzling his Canadian eyes with the rich wonders of Mediterranean lands. But toward the end of the Michaelmas Term a cablegram had brought him, literally, flying home: "Your mother seriously ill. Heart. Advise immediate return. Collins." And when he had reached Salterton three days later, Dr. Collins had informed him, with a cheerful manner which seemed offensive under the circumstances, that his mother had "turned the corner", and would be all right after six weeks in bed, if she took care of herself. By the end of the six weeks it was plain that this meant that Solly should take care of her; mention of his return to Cambridge had caused her face to fall and a gummy tear or two to creep jerkily down her cheeks; Dr. Collins had informed him, on her behalf, that she should not be left alone at present.

The young are often accused of exaggerating their troubles; they do so, very often, in the hope of making some impression upon the inertia and the immovability of the selfish old. Solly's writhings in his bonds were necessarily ineffective. A sense of duty and fear of a show-down with his mother kept him in check; it was unnecessary for her to take any countermeasures against the discontent which he could not always hide, because she held the purse-strings. His allowance was still, presumably, piling up in the bank at Cambridge, but at home he had nothing except for driblets of money which his mother handed to him now and then with the words, "You must have some little needs, lovey."

Little needs! He needed freedom. He needed a profession at which he could support himself. He needed the love and reassurance of someone other than his mother. He needed someone to whom he could talk, without reserve, about the humiliating thralldom which she had imposed upon him since his thirteenth year. As he sat in his armchair, sipping his miserable drink, a few stinging tears of self-pity mounted to his eyes. Self-pity is commonly held to be despicable; it can also be a great comfort if it does not become chronic.

Griselda's taunts had cut him sharply. It was all very well for her to imply that he was tied to his mother's apron strings. But what did she know of his mother's illness, and of the seriousness attached to it by Dr. Collins? "Your mother must take things very gently; no upsets; you're the apple of her eye, you know; you must cheer her up—try to take her out of herself." It was a duty, a work of filial piety which his conscience would not permit him to evade, however distasteful it might sometimes be. How unfair it was of a girl to make no attempt to understand a man's obligation to another woman whose very life might depend upon his tact and consideration! How hateful women were, and yet Griselda—how infinitely desirable! How could one who looked as she had looked to-night be as unreasonable and as wilfully cruel as she had been? He hated her, and even as he hated he was torn with love for her. There was only one thing for it; he must try to forget his wretchedness in some work.

It is a favourite notion of romantic young men that misery can be forgotten in work. If the work can be done late at night, all the better. And if the combination of misery and work can be brought together in an attic a very high degree of melancholy self-satisfaction may be achieved, for in spite of the supposed anti-romantic bias of our age the tradition of work, love, attics, drink and darkness is still powerful. The only real difficulty lies in balancing the level of the work against the level of the misery; at any moment the misery is likely to slop over into the work, and drown it.

This is what happened to Solly. He took up a copy of *The Tempest* in which he had already made a great many notes, and which was fat with bits of paper which he had thrust into it here and there, with what he believed to be good ideas for the production scribbled on them. But he could not read or think; the words blurred before his eyes, and he could see nothing but Griselda's face—not pinched and angry, as when she had turned away from his kiss, but as it had been in the clubroom, when she had seemed to sleep through Roger Tasset's reading. In a few minutes he gave up the struggle, and thought only of her. And as this palls upon even the most heart-sore lover, he went at last to bed.

CHAPTER
4

FOR TWO weeks after Mr. Webster had told him that the Little Theatre was going to invade his garden, nothing happened, and Tom began to deceive himself that perhaps nothing ever would happen. It is thus that a man who has been told by his physician that he has a dreadful disease seeks to persuade himself that the doctor was wrong. He feels nothing; he sees nothing amiss; little by little he thinks that there has been a mistaken diagnosis. But one day it strikes, and his agony is worse because he has cajoled himself with thought of escape. And thus it was with Tom. One morning, shortly after breakfast, a large truck drove across the upper lawn at St. Agnes', and with remarkable speed four men dug a great hole and planted a Hydro pole in it. When Tom rounded the house half an hour later they were busily setting up a transformer at the top of it.

"Who gave you leave to stick that thing up in my lawn?" roared Tom.

"Orders from the office, Pop," said a young fellow at the top of the pole.

"Nobody said nothing to me about it," shouted Tom. "Why didn't you ask me to take up the sod before you began all this?"

"Never thought of it, Pop," said the young man. "Don't get your shirt in a knot. The grass'll grow again."

"Not so much of your 'Pop', my boy," said Tom, with dignity. "When I was in the Army I took the starch out of dozens like you."

"That was cavalry days, Pop. Mechanized army now."

"You come down here and get your bloody truck off my grass."

"Who's going to make me?"

"I know how to get a monkey out of a tree," said Tom. He had a crowbar in his hand, and with this he deftly struck the base of the pole. The young man, whose climbing irons were stuck in the pole, got the full benefit of the vibration, and did not like it.

"Hey, go easy, Pop," he shouted.

"You get your truck off my lawn," said Tom.

The truck was backed away to the drive, and Tom felt that honour had been preserved. But he knew also that he was fighting a rearguard action. During the afternoon a party of soldiers arrived with another truck, which they drove on the grass, and under a corporal's direction they set up two brown tents.

"What's all this?" said Tom.

"For the Little Theayter," said the corporal. "One tent for lights; the other for odds and ends. Major Pye's orders, sergeant."

Tom liked to be recognized as a sergeant in mufti, but he knew that after those tents had been up for three weeks he would never get the grass right that summer.

That evening two cars brought Mrs. Forrester, Miss Rich, Professor Vambrace, Solly Bridgetower and Major Larry Pye to St. Agnes'. They surveyed the pole and the tents with pleasure.

"It's always a big thrill when a show begins to shape up, isn't it Tom," said Nellie.

Tom, who had been haunting the upper lawn in case new liberties should be taken with it, said that he didn't know, never having had any experience with shows, but if his opinion was asked he thought that the pole and the tents looked a fair eyesore.

"Of course they do," agreed Nellie. "But they won't when

you've planted some nice shrubs and little trees around them."

"Maybe you'd like me to camoofladge this telegraph post as a tree, ma'am," said Tom. But his sarcasm was wasted on Nellie.

"Oh, I didn't know you could do that," she said. "Of course that would be wonderful."

"We don't want to put you to extra work any more than is needful," said Professor Vambrace, "but it will be necessary to give us some sort of raised stage. Something about two feet high, fifty feet across and thirty feet deep will be wanted, I should think. Can you do that with sod?"

"Now, now, let's treat first things first," said Major Pye. "I'm going to want a pit dug right in front of the acting area—not a big thing, but a pit about four feet deep, eight feet wide and four feet across, lined with waterproof cement."

"Oh Larry, what for?" said Nellie.

"To put my controls in," said Larry. "That's where I'll be all through the show. I'll have my board down there. And every change of light—bingo! Along comes the cue and I hit it right on the nose—bingo! You can put the prompter down there with me, if she doesn't take too much room," he added, magnanimously.

"And just when am I supposed to get all this done by?" said Tom.

"You've got the better part of five weeks," said Nellie. "Of course we'll be rehearsing here a great deal, and you won't be able to work while we are busy, but you'll have your mornings to yourself as a general thing."

"Now just a minute, ma'am—" he began, but Valentine cut him short.

"I think it would be well if I made all the arrangements with Mr.—?" She paused.

"Gwalchmai's the name, miss; Thomas Gwalchmai." Rarely has the fine old Welsh name of Gwalchmai sounded less accommodating to the lazy Saxon tongue than as Tom spoke it then.

"With Mr. Gwalchmai," said Valentine, smiling pleasantly

and pronouncing it to perfection. "We shan't need a raised stage, and it would be unthinkable to dig a pit in this perfect lawn. We have done quite enough damage as it is. Shall we say then, Mr. Gwalchmai, that nothing need be done to the grounds until it has been discussed with me?"

"Well, I don't want to be a stumbling-block, miss," said Tom, much softened, "but there's a limit to what can be done, and—"

"Of course there is," said Valentine. "But it will be most helpful if we may rehearse here during the evenings and perhaps on a few afternoons, as well."

"Oh, that'll be quite all right, miss," said Tom, eager to please.

Later, when they had gone inside the house for further discussion, Professor Vambrace complimented Valentine on the skill with which she had managed Tom, whom he described as "an obstructionist—hide-bound, like all people who live close to the soil."

"He seems very nice," she replied; "we must be careful to give him his due; that's the secret of getting on with most people."

Professor Vambrace, who had a deep conviction that he himself had never received his due, assented earnestly. Larry Pye, who considered himself a born colonel who had been kept down by jealousy in high places, nodded vigorously. The world is full of people who believe that they have never had their due, and they are the slaves of anyone who seems likely to make this deferred payment. Valentine, in a few days, had assumed this character among them, and they were all convinced that she was a woman of extraordinary penetration. She never sought or demanded anything for herself, she was ready to listen to everybody, within reason, she had no interest in humiliating or thwarting anybody, and in consequence all the keys of power in the Salterton Little Theatre had been gathered into her hands.

Always excepting, of course, those widespread powers which Nellie regarded as her own. She had, as she explained to Roscoe, grown up with Valentine Rich, and although Valentine had undoubtedly made a name for herself in the theatre she, Nellie, had gained what was perhaps an even wider experience. In the Little Theatre, she always said, you got a broader grounding; she had painted scenery, made costumes, acted, directed, dealt with matters of business, done everything, really, that could be done in a theatre. What was more, she knew Salterton as Valentine did not, and she had to see that no local apple-cart was upset. Oh, she didn't deny for a moment that Valentine knew her job, but after all, Salterton was *not* New York, and there was no good pretending that it was.

When it was time to talk about music for the play, therefore, Nellie felt obliged to make her opinions known.

"You needn't worry about it at all," said she; "I arranged everything with Mr. Snairey last week. The Snairey Trio should sound lovely in the open air. And he's had experience, you know."

"Surely that isn't old Snairey who used to play in the Empire for vaudeville when we were children," said Valentine.

"I should think he played there when your grandfather was a lad," said Solly. "You don't seriously mean that you've asked him, Mrs. F.?"

"Oh course I do. He says he has some lovely music which theatre orchestras always play for Shakespeare; Sir Edward German's *Henry VIII* dances."

"I see," said Valentine, in a voice which suggested that she saw more than Nellie. "And what about the songs?"

"I mentioned them, and he said he thought he could fake something. His daughter Loura can sing offstage, and the girls onstage can fill in with mime. He hasn't any music for the songs in the play, but he said he thought we could use something pretty and Old English."

"From what I know of old Snairey, that means that they will play *William Tell* during the storm scene, and Ariel will flit across the stage to the strains of *The Farmer's Boy*. Really, Mrs. F., you've done it this time."

"Oh Solly, don't be so superior," said Nellie; "there are a

million things to be done, and I appear to be the only one ready to do them. If you know so much, why didn't you arrange about the music?"

"Because nobody asked me to," said Solly, bitterly.

"Well, it's settled now, for good or ill."

"No," said Valentine; "Mr. Snairey can be dealt with, I expect. Very likely he and his Trio can play, but someone must see that suitable music is provided. Who is the best musician in town?"

"Myrtle Swann, by long odds," said Nellie; "they say she has forty pupils."

"But we don't want a piano teacher; we want someone who can direct an orchestra and some singers," said Valentine.

"The obvious man is Humphrey Cobbler," said Solly.

"Oh heavens, you can't have him," said Nellie; "he's not right in his head."

"Who says so?" said Solly.

"Oh, lots of people at the Cathedral. And he's such an untidy dresser. And sometimes he laughs out loud at nothing. And he never gets his hair cut."

"He has many of the superficial marks of genius," said Valentine. "Who is he?"

"The organist and choirmaster at St. Nicholas'," said Solly. "I assumed he would be the first man to be asked."

"Not by me," said Nellie. "They say he's a Drinker."

"That's probably just a mannerism from being an organist," said Valentine; "they use their feet very oddly. Go and see him, Solly, and find out what can be done."

Nellie bit her lip, and said nothing. She thought of telling Valentine and Solly that Salterton was not New York, but decided to let them find it out for themselves.

Having decided that he was in love with Griselda, Hector reflected that he must devise some clever scheme to let her know it. He was not a reader of novels, and he very rarely went to the movies, but he felt that he knew enough about romance to carry out his plan in his accustomed efficient and successful manner. His problem was, he told himself, simple enough in essence: he loved Griselda; he would give gradually stronger hints that this was so until he was able to make an outright declaration; that done, she would love him, for he considered it impossible that a woman should be loved without loving in return; he had heard of such cases, but they did not involve young and inexperienced girls; he and Griselda would then love each other. Beyond that point he did not think. One thing at a time. Affection would beget affection; that, he assured himself, was what always happened.

The disparity in their ages was against him, in a way. And yet, had she not started the affair by that smile which she had given him? He did not attach too much meaning to it, but he did not discount it, either. Well, here was a field in which he had never tried planning and common sense before, but he would not desert those tried and true friends now. In the black notebook, over a period of a week, appeared a page filled thus:

PLAN OF CONDUCT

P	C
be dignified, friendly	*not too stiff*
make jokes	*not seem mere buffoon*
show still young, good	
muscles, etc.	*take off 25lb., cut pie?*
outsmart people, show	*don't overdo, seem*
trained mind	*wasteful*
spend freely	

To put his plan in action he seized a chair at the first rehearsal, and lightly threw his leg over the back of it.

"Can you fellows do that?" he asked Roger and Solly, who were talking to Griselda.

"I'd probably rupture myself if I tried," said Solly.

Roger quickly did what Hector had done, first with his right leg and then with his left.

"Let's see you do it with both legs," he said.

Hector tried it, and although his right leg, with which he had been practising, answered satisfactorily to the call of romance, the left leg knocked over the chair, and he stumbled.

"See what I mean?" said Solly, officiously seizing him by the arm, to prevent a fall. "You might easily unman yourself doing a trick like that."

What a coarse thing to say in front of a young girl, thought Hector. He would have liked to punch young Bridgetower in his loose mouth. He was humiliated. But no one appeared to notice his humiliation. The Torso had joined them, seeing that kicking was toward, and was demonstrating how she could hold her right foot above her head with her right hand, and spin on her left leg. This showed a good deal of her drawers, which were pink and short and had lace on them. Nobody had eyes for the red-faced Hector.

As for cutting out pie, he had read in the *Reader's Digest* that slimming exercises and abstinences should not be embarked upon hastily. And so for a couple of weeks he cut out his usual piece of pie with his lunch on Tuesdays and Fridays, but did not tamper with his dinner menu.

During those two weeks he found no opportunity to address Griselda directly, but he watched her closely, and the feeling for her which he had decided to call love, a feeling in which worship and the yearning to champion and serve her were untainted by any fleshly aspiration, deepened and took hold of him as no feeling had done since he had made up his mind to get a university degree.

Solly's expedition in search of Humphrey Cobbler took him to a part of Salterton which was new to him. He walked slowly down one of those roads which are to be found in the new sections of all Canadian cities; rows of small houses lined both sides of the street, and although these little houses were alike in every important respect a miserable attempt had been made to differentiate them by a trifle of leaded glass here, a veneer of imitation stonework there, a curiously fashioned front door in another place, by all the cheap and tasteless shifts of the speculative builder. A glance at one was enough to lay bare the plan of all. Even that last modesty of a dwelling—the location of the water closet—was rudely derided by the short ventilation pipes which broke through each roof at identically the same spot. These were not houses, thought Solly, in which anyone could be greatly happy, or see a vision; no ghost would dream of haunting one of them; the pale babies being aired in their perambulators on the small verandahs did not look to him as though they had been begotten in passion; the dogs which ran from one twig-like tree (fresh from the nursery) to another, did not seem to be of any determinable breed; he could not imagine anyone at all like Griselda living in one of these dreadful boxes.

He was surprised, therefore, as he drew near the house which bore Humphrey Cobbler's number, to hear a burst of cheerful singing, accompanied with great liveliness on the piano. When he rapped at the door it was quickly answered by a red-cheeked, rather stout young woman with very black hair; her feet were bare, and her crumpled cotton frock somehow gave the impression that she wore very little beneath it. She bade Solly come in, and he found himself in a barely furnished and rather dirty room, where a shock-headed man was seated at a grand piano, and four barefoot, tousled children were singing at the tops of their pleasant voices.

"Hello!" roared the pianist. "Sit down; we'll be with you in a minute."

"Sweet nymph, come to thy lover," sang the children.

"Words! Words!" shouted the man. "Spit it out!"

Obligingly, the children spat it out, with such clarity that when they had finished their song the man cried "Good!" and chased them away.

"We have a little workout twice a day," he said to Solly. "Lay the foundation of a good voice before puberty; that's the whole secret. Train them gently over the break, and then they've a voice that will last them fifty or sixty years."

"Have you many child pupils?" Solly enquired.

"Oh, those aren't pupils; they're my own. People won't pay to have children taught to sing. What can I do for you?"

"You are Humphrey Cobbler, I suppose?"

"Yes. You're Solomon Bridgetower. I've seen you about."

As he explained what he wanted, Solly was able to take a good look at his host. Humphrey Cobbler was the kind of Englishman who has a high complexion and black, curly hair; his nose was aquiline, his build slight. He might have been taken for a Jew, if it had not been for his bright, restless eye, like a robin's, which leaped constantly from Solly's face to his feet, from his feet to his hands, from his hands to his ears, and from his ears to something curious and amusing which apparently was hovering above his head. Cobbler, like his wife, was not overdressed; his trousers were held up by an old tie knotted around his waist, his shirt lacked most of its buttons, and his bare feet were thrust into trodden-down slippers. His hair, to which Nellie had referred, was saved from complete disorder by its curls, but there was a great deal of it, and from time to time he gave a portion of it a powerful tug, as though to brighten his wits, much as some people take pinches of snuff.

When Solly had made his suggestion Cobbler seized upon it with enthusiasm. "Of course I'll do it," said he; "we can make a very complete thing of it. There's plenty of lovely music for *The Tempest*, but we'll use all Purcell, I think. I don't suppose you'd like to revise your plans and do Shadwell's version of the play, would you? A much tidier bit of playwrighting, really. No? I feared not. Wonderful music there." Darting to the piano he burst into song:

Arise, arise, ye subterranean winds!

"Doesn't that stir you? Marvellous stuff! However, if you insist on sticking to the old Shakespeare thing we can do something very tasty. Your people can sing, I suppose?"

"They say so," said Solly. "I'm not sure about all of them.

Perhaps you have met Miss Griselda Webster? She is to play Ariel, and she sings charmingly."

"Let's hope so," said Cobbler.

"I'm afraid we can't offer you any fee," said Solly, with some hesitation.

"I didn't expect you could," said Cobbler. "Odd how so few really interesting jobs have any fee attached. Ah, well. You don't mind if I work Molly and the kids in for a bit of backstage singing, do you? They'd love it."

Solly had not liked bringing up the matter of the fee, and in his relief he replied as though the presence of Molly and the little Cobblers backstage were all that was needed to make life perfect. He then brought up the matter of Mr. Snairey. Cobbler opened his mouth very wide, so that Solly was able to see the pillars of his throat, and laughed in a wild and hollow manner.

"I know it's a nuisance," said Solly, "but Mrs. Forrester has asked him, and he has accepted, and it was only with some difficulty that we persuaded her that Snairey's choice of music might be, well, undistinguished. You don't think you could get along with him, I suppose, just for the sake of peace?"

"My dear fellow," said Cobbler, "my whole life is moved by the principle that the one thing which is more important than peace is music. It is because I believe that that I am poor. It is because I believe that that many people suppose that I am crazy. It is because I believe that that I have just said that I will take care of the music for your play. I shall get no money out of it, and my experience of theatre groups leads me to think that I shall get little thanks for it. If, as you suggest, I get along with old Snairey for the sake of peace, it will be your peace, and not mine. I have not often heard him attack anything which I would dignify with the name of music, but when I have done so, that music has been royally —indeed imperially and even papally—bitched. I shall have nothing to do with him, in any circumstances whatever."

"That creates rather a situation," said Solly.

"If I'm to be captain of music I must be allowed to pick my own team."

"Yes; I see that, of course."

"And you also see, if I mistake not, that you will have a terrible row with Mrs. Forrester, and another with old Snairey. Let me give you a piece of advice, Bridgetower; don't borrow trouble. To a surprising extent trouble is a thing one can allow other people to have, if one doesn't throw oneself in its path. You have already the harried look of a man who regards himself as the Lamb of God who takes upon him the sins of the whole world. That's silly. Now let me tell you what to do: go back to Mrs. Forrester and tell her—in front of witnesses, mind—that I'll do it, but I won't have Snairey. Then let her deal with Snairey. He's senile, anyhow. Promise him a couple of seats for the play and he'll be all right. Pass the buck. It's the secret of life. You can't fight every battle and dry every tear. Whenever you're dealing with something that you don't really care about, pass the buck. You've got me to do your music; that's what you wanted, isn't it? Very well then, let Mrs. Forrester clean up the mess."

He turned again to the keyboard, and began to improvise very rapidly in the manner of Handel, singing the words "Pass the buck" in a bewildering variety of rhythms and intonations. Solly, sensing that the interview was over, left the house, and for some distance down the street he could hear the extemporaneous cantata, for piano and solo voice, on the theme "Pass the buck".

Solly gave Nellie Cobbler's message, in front of witnesses as he had been told to do, at the very next rehearsal; he chose a moment when she was already distracted by other worries, said his say, and hurried off to attend to something else. He felt that he was behaving meanly, but comforted himself with the assurance that in certain complex situations perfect honour and fair dealing were out of the question. And he had, indeed, enough to worry him. Larry Pye, who had not read *The Tempest*, was discovering from the rehearsals which he occasionally overheard that there were magical devices in the play which he was expected to supply. His technique in meeting this problem was in the best Cobbler tradition of passing the buck. "You plan 'em, and I'll make 'em," said he, and Valentine had asked Solly, as her assistant, to see what he could do.

Solly's first move when confronted with a problem was to seek help from books. The Waverley Library, he discovered, was fairly well stocked with books about magic as anthropologists understand the word, and it could provide him with plenty of material about medieval sorcery; it also contained books by Aleister Crowley and the Rev. Montague Summers which assured him feverishly that there was plenty of magic in the world today. But of practical illusion it yielded only *The Boy's Book of Magic* and two books by Professor Louis Hoffmann, who wrote about card tricks in an intolerably facetious style and obscured his already obscure explanations still further with Latin quotations and badly drawn diagrams. After two days of poring over these works Solly reported to Valentine that Shakespeare's blithe direction "with a quaint device the table vanishes" was still impossible of realization by any means which he could discover.

"Oh, never mind then," said she; "we'll just use the old pantomime tipover trick. It is really the simplest when it's well done. I merely thought you might find something better."

So she had known a way of doing it all the time! For five minutes Solly was convinced that he hated Valentine.

He could not hate her for long, however. He was compelled, many times at each rehearsal, to admire the firmness, the good humour, the speed without haste, the practical knowledge of the stage, and the imagination which she applied to the task of training the actors of the Salterton Theatre to do what they had never done, or dreamed of doing, before in their lives. She very soon discovered what each actor might reasonably be expected to give, and then set to work to make sure that he gave it all. It was she who revealed to the world, and to Mr. Leakey himself, that Mr.

Leakey could be quite funny if he didn't try to be his very funniest. It was she who found out that Mr. Shortreed had a large bass voice, and could outroar Professor Vambrace. It was she who demonstrated that The Torso, having once been made to cry, could stand perfectly still on the stage and look unexpectedly distinguished as well as merely pretty. And it was she who allowed it to be seen, tactlessly, in Nellie's opinion, that Griselda Webster was a slacker, unwilling to make a sustained effort.

It was she, moreover, who dealt with the difficult problem created by Mrs. Crundale. This lady might have been an artist of some attainment if she had not married Mr. Crundale, and devoted her best efforts to furthering his career as a bank manager. The costumes which she designed for *The Tempest* were charming and imaginative. It was true that all the Reapers were expected to reveal a great deal more muscular shoulder and leg than they were likely to possess, and that costumes which she had designed for emaciated people seven feet tall had to be adapted for plump people considerably shorter after the casting had been done. But this was not the crux of the problem presented by Mrs. Crundale. The crux was simply that she had designed costumes for Ariel, all the goddesses and the Nymphs which required that their bosoms be bare, not partly or fleetingly, but completely and indeed aggressively. She had shown these designs to almost everyone connected with the play and everyone had obediently admired them, while wondering what was to be done.

Mrs. Crundale's position was clear, and had been clear for years. She was an Artist, and to her the human body was simply a Mass, with a variety of Planes; twelve years ago she had explained this thoroughly after a nice-looking rugby player from Waverley had spiritedly declined her invitation to pose for a portrait in the nude. Nobody connected with the Little Theatre quite liked to explain to Mrs. Crundale that the breasts of several well-known young ladies of Salterton, though undoubtedly Planes, had other connotations,

141

and could not fittingly be unveiled at a public performance. But Valentine did so.

"These dresses will look charming when they are standing still, Mrs. Crundale," said she, "but when the girls dance your line will be completely spoiled. I suggest that you revise these slightly, giving some concealment for a strapless brassiere underneath."

And Mrs. Crundale, who had really only wanted to make the point that the human body was nothing to her but an arrangement of planes, agreed without a murmur. Devoted, tireless little Mrs. Hawes, who was head of the costume-making committee, assured Valentine that because of this backing-up on the part of Mrs. Crundale, she was able to breathe easily for the first time in many weeks. She had, she explained, dreaded the fittings.

Valentine showed herself no less able in her handling of intangible problems than in her swift settlement of the question of Mrs. Crundale's unworldly designs. Solly was deputed, like assistant directors everywhere, to deal with a variety of matters of bothersome detail, and he revealed a genius for complicating and fantasticating all details. Instructed to look after the furnishing and decoration of the vanishing banquet table he worked busily with a group of assistants, and created a pleasant but confusing mass of gilded ewers, plates of exotic fruits, flasks of wine in colours no vintner would have recognized, and monstrous edibles which suggested that every guest was to be served with a whole wedding cake; this feast, spread upon a cloth which had been painted and gilded to the last inch, was widely admired by all except the actors who had to carry it. They were wearing fantastic masks, made by a young woman whom Solly had encouraged to do her uttermost, and they complained that they could not see. One of them, a Waverley lecturer in economics whose devotion to the drama was limited to murder plays and farces, declared that if he were expected to wear a lion mask, and carry a peacock in its pride at the same time, he would withdraw from the whole affair. Solly was aggrieved.

"But you can't achieve a big effect by niggling methods," said he; "of course it could all be made simpler, but this isn't a simple play."

It was at this point that Professor Vambrace chose to explain that all works of genius were essentially simple, and were best interpreted by simple methods. In such a play as *The Tempest*, said he, it was vital that the magnificence of the words should not be lessened by too great a show of costumes and accoutrements. Simplicity, he told Solly, and the world in general, was the keynote of greatness. What was the use, he asked, of an actor like himself bringing the fullest power of his intellect to bear on the proper interpretation of his role, if the audience was to be perpetually distracted by shows of petty magnificence which had nothing to do with the play?

What followed was a full-dress row, in which wounding and bitter things were said on both sides. The Professor nobly led the forces of Simplicity, without any very useful backing, for the economics lecturer carried few guns as an aesthetic disputant, and lost his temper when Solly made an unwise reference to disgruntled accountants. Solly was not much better off, for his followers were all young women of artistic aspirations, whose idea of argument was to huff and flounce, except for the mask-maker, who wept—the difficult, lemony tears of a handicrafter whose all has been scorned. It was a moment for generalship, and Valentine acquitted herself with brilliance. Both sides, she said, were right. She hoped that they would attach some weight to her judgment, for although she did not attempt to rival them in scholarship (this went down very well with Professor Vambrace) she had had a good deal of practical experience. What was to be sought in a Shakespearean production was a large, simple, overall plan; within that plan it was possible to elaborate many details, and to enrich anything that seemed to call for enrichment. The establishment of the basic simple plan she felt that they might safely leave to her; working with men of the intellectual stamp of Professor Vambrace she was certain that she would not go far astray. She was grateful to Solly and his assistants for the care which they had lavished upon the appurtenances of the play; such attention to detail in the professional theatre would only be obtained by spending very large sums of money. She begged them all to work together for the good of the Salterton Little Theatre. In unity there was strength. People of talent were bound to have these clashes of temperament. She had no misgivings about the production. And so on, in a gentle, but firm voice until the forces of Simplicity and the forces of Superfluity each received, in some mysterious fashion, an impression that they had slightly gotten the better of the other.

Particularly noteworthy in this instance was Valentine's use of the magical word "temperament". This is a quality which many people pretend to despise, but which they rather like to have attributed to themselves in a kindly fashion. Even the economist, hearing it, was mysteriously soothed; he felt that he was a good deal more high-strung than anyone supposed, and as Valentine had cleverly discovered this secret of his, he would gladly wear a lion's head mask and carry anything at all, for her sake.

The only breast which was not calmed was that of Miss Wildfang. Arriving a little late for the quarrel, and not fully understanding it, she knew only that Professor Vambrace's intellectual, moral and aesthetic authority had been challenged. She did not re-open the issue at once, but for a day or two afterward she went from group to group at rehearsal, spreading the Vambrace theory of utter simplicity. Finally the Professor himself had to ask her to desist. Theatrical people, he suggested, must be allowed their theatrical love of finery and display. A thrice-refined soul like her own needed no gaudy trappings to help it to the appreciation of a masterwork, but there were other, lesser creatures whose needs must be considered. Miss Wildfang assented, and was plunged into an even more pitiful state of mental concubinage toward Professor Vambrace than before.

It must not be supposed that rehearsals moved forward in an atmosphere of quarreling, or that Valentine's method was always that of the oil-can. Her action in the matter of the swords was brisk. It was Roger Tasset who asked her if, when he first entered on the scene in Prospero's enchanted island, he should wear a sword. Valentine, who had not thought about the matter, said that she supposed he must, as it was wanted in the action. But then there arose a clamour among the other actors who played courtiers; they all wanted swords, and broke up the rehearsal in order to demonstrate their ideas of what they should do with them. It would be very pleasant and authentic, they thought, if they frequently drew their swords and saluted each other with them. They then began to haggle about the proper method of saluting with a sword, and Larry Pye, who was working near at hand, walked good-naturedly upon the stage and said that whatever might have been the method in the old days, this was the way it was done now. Soon half a dozen actors were stamping, frowning and brandishing imaginary swords. Valentine announced abruptly that there would be no swords in the play which were not specifically called for in the action, and that she wanted no manners from the modern parade ground; she would demonstrate the use of swords herself.

This gave offence to Roger. He felt that some slight had been made upon the profession of soldiering. He was also heard to say that he did not think that he needed to learn anything about the use of a sword from a woman. All of which was illogical and silly, but Roger's strongly masculine personality made up in emotion for anything which his words might lack in good sense.

Roger's conduct at rehearsals was unsatisfactory. An engineer by profession, he had not long been able to resist a project of Larry Pye's to put a public address system in the grounds at St. Agnes'. Valentine had expressly forbidden Larry to wire the stage for sound, and to hide microphones in the bushes, which was what he wanted to do. She would make herself responsible for the audibility of the actors without any such doubtful aids, she had said. Larry had found it difficult at first to take this seriously; after all, he said, a P.A. system was part of the modern set-up and if it were not in evidence the audience would think that the Little Theatre was doing the thing on the cheap. But when he found that she meant what she said, he agreed to compromise on what he named a calling-system. This was an apparatus which enabled the actors who were not wanted on the stage to linger in The Shed, where a large amplifier was installed; the Stage Manager, behind the scenes, would have a microphone by means of which he might summon them to him in plenty of time for their cues. In addition, Larry said that he would rig up a talk-back between himself, in his pit in the front of the stage, the Stage Manager and Humphrey Cobbler's musicians. This arrangement, which sounded comparatively innocent to Valentine, proved to mean a great deal of wiring which Larry chose to do during rehearsal time. Roger elected to help him, which meant that he was not often ready when his cues came, that he appeared on the stage with the patronizing manner of a man who has left important work for lesser employment, and that he was sometimes to be found during scenes in which he was not concerned, crawling about the stage with a coil of wire, with the air of a man who believes himself to be invisible. It was when confronted with such situations as this that Valentine realized, more sharply than Nellie ever knew, that Salterton was not New York.

A worse thorn in her flesh than Roger, however, was Mr. Shortreed. George, or as he preferred to be called, Geordie Shortreed, was a steward in the government liquor store and in that capacity was acquainted with all the gentle and simple of Salterton. He knew who drank wine, who drank imported Scotch, who drank the cheaper liquors, and who bought good stuff for themselves and what he called belly-vengeance for their guests. He had a large bass voice and a monkey-like physique which had persuaded Valentine to cast him as Caliban. Because Caliban is a large and important part, and one which was coveted by several other actors in the Little Theatre, it was thought that in casting a man who was, in essence, a bartender for it the Little Theatre had behaved in a commendably democratic way. Canadians are, of course, naturally democratic, but when they give some signal evi-

dence of this quality in the social life they like to get full
marks for it. Everybody had, therefore, been a little nicer
to Geordie than was strictly required, nicer, that is to say,
than they would have been to someone who was an unques-
tioned social equal. Geordie, however, refused to play this
game according to the rules. Instead of being quietly grateful for the friendliness of professors and business men who
always bought the best Scotch, he was rather noisily familiar
with them, and revealed himself as a practical joker. A great
patron of joke-shops, he had a large collection of ice-cubes
in which a fly was imprisoned, of cigarette-cases with spring-
ing surprises in them, of rubber snakes, of cameras which
squirted when they were supposed to be taking pictures. He
proved to be the kind of actor whose delight it was to dis-
compose those who were on the stage with him; to make
them laugh, if possible. Valentine rebuked him for this twice
and each time he allowed his great voice to drop to a
rumbling whisper as he said: "I know, Miss Rich; I oughtn't
to do it, and that's a fact; don't imagine I don't realize what
a privilege it is for the bunch and I to work with a real artist
of the theatre like yourself; I guess it's just that it's so wonderful that makes me carry on like that; but it won't happen
again, I assure you." But it did happen again.

It could not be denied that Mr. Shortreed's knowledge of
the text of the play was richer and more curious than that of
anyone else. Like Professor Vambrace, he knew it by heart
from start to finish. But whereas the Professor showed off his
knowledge only by prompting a little ahead of the official
prompter, Geordie delighted in perverting lines to unexpected uses in private conversation. Like many great wits of
the past, he planned his effects carefully at home, and then
sprang them as impromptus at rehearsals. He was the kind
of actor, too, who loved to address people offstage by the
name of the character which they played on. Thus he never
approached Hector Mackilwraith without roaring "Holy
Gonzalo, honourable man!" except on the day when Hector,
hoping to show himself youthful in the eyes of Griselda,
appeared in a new and too gay sports shirt, when Geordie

struck his brow and cried "What a pied ninny's this!"

Hector did not like this last sally, but upon the whole he admired Shortreed's wit and envied it, for it often raised a laugh. If only he could be distinguished in that way! Something deep inside him told him that Shortreed's jokes were stupid and overstrained, but his new craving to be a social success was silencing that inner voice which had kept him, for forty years, from making the more obvious kind of fool of himself. He too studied his text of the play in private, seeking lines which he might twist into a retort upon Shortreed, but his mind was ill-suited to such work, and he found little. He had to content himself with pretending to shrink from Shortreed, saying, "Don't you come near me; you're a demi-devil," but he knew that this was pitiful. Indeed, he became conscious for the first time of a certain thinness in his intellectual equipment which he had not noticed before.

Hector had a certain reputation as a wit, among the students of the Salterton Collegiate Institute and Vocational School. This was founded upon his occasional sarcasms and upon one joke, which he had brought to birth eight years before, and which had become a tradition in the institution. It had happend thus: one warm June afternoon Hector was supervising a gymnasium filled with students who were writing an examination; a boy had raised his hand, and said, in an offhand voice, "Sir, do you know the time?"; Hector, with his dark smile, took out his watch, looked at it, returned it to his pocket and said, "Yes." What a shout of laughter there had been! And how the tale flew around the school! Young Porson, you see, had asked Mackilwraith if he knew the time; not if he'd tell him the time, you see; just if he *knew* it. And Mackilwraith had just said Yes, you see, with a perfectly straight face, because he did, you see, but he didn't say what the time was, because that wasn't what he'd been asked, you see?

In the great days of the Italian Comedy certain gifted actors prepared and polished special monologues, or acrobatic feats, or passages of mime, which became peculiarly their own, and these specialties were called *lazzi*. This witty interchange about the time became Hector's *lazzo*, and at least once a year some boy would play straight man, or stooge, to him, in order that this masterstroke of wit should be demonstrated anew. Time did not appear to wither, nor custom stale it. Thus when Hector found himself pitted against a man like Shortreed, whose jokes changed from day to day, he found himself at an unexpected disadvantage.

Geordie's career as a humorist, though meteoric, was short-lived. Like many another man before him, his fall was brought about by the sheer, inexplicable malignancy of fate.

There lived at St. Agnes', under Tom's special care an ancient horse called Old Bill, whose work it was to pull the large lawn-mower. Both Tom and Mr. Webster were agreed that motor-mowers were instruments of Satan, designed to chew up and deface fine turf; the lawns, therefore were mowed by a simple but very sharp mechanism which Old Bill dragged slowly behind him; for this work Old Bill wore a straw hat to protect his head from the sun, and curious leathern goloshes over his steel shoes, so that he would not cut the lawns. Dressed for work Old Bill was a venerable and endearing sight, and during rehearsals he became a favourite with the cast. They petted him and brought him sugar.

One afternoon Tom was cutting grass at some distance from the stage, when he became dissatisfied with the edge on one of the blades of the mower, and decided to touch it up. He left Old Bill under a tree and went off to The Shed for a file. Mr. Shortreed, observing this, had a really great comic inspiration; he had a cue coming soon, and he would enter on Old Bill. Miss Rich wouldn't like it, of course, but surely when she saw what a laugh the bunch got out of it she wouldn't mind too much. Anyway, he hadn't time to worry about that, and he would chance his luck. Yes, there was old Vambrace yelling out his cue—

> *Thou poisonous slave, got by the devil himself*
> *Upon thy wicked dam, came forth!*

With a roar he leapt upon Old Bill, kicked the startled animal in the belly, and headed for the stage. Bill, who had never been used so in his life, bolted, and as he ran two of his leather shoes dropped off, so that he was steel-shod. As he burst through the bushes, bearing Geordie on his back, the effect was all a humorist could desire. Women shrieked; men roared; Professor Vambrace and Pearl, who were in the middle of the stage, took to their heels. It was Geordie's instant of utter triumph, the apotheosis of a practical joker. Then, bewilderingly, Old Bill gave a frightful scream, reared upon his hind legs, and dropped upon the ground. There he lay, screaming piteously for perhaps ten seconds; then he was still, his teeth bared, his eyes bulging.

Tom arrived on the run. "Dead as a nit," said he.

The cause of death was established by Larry Pye. "He's gouged up the ground with his hooves, you see," he explained. "Here's the main cable not three inches down, in this steel conduit; Tom just put the sod over that this morning. Here's a poor join in the conduit, and he's hit the cable with his shoe. That's what did for him. Wouldn't happen once in a million years. But it happened this time. Thanks to you, you god-damned stupid bastard," he said, regarding Geordie with an officer's eye. Geordie walked away and was noisily and copiously sick under a bush, but nobody pitied him.

Old Bill, venerable and loveable in life, was a disagreeable sight in death. His belly swelled shockingly, within a few minutes, which caused him to move a little from time to time, and to creak as though in an uneasy slumber. The actors did not want to look at him, but they could not take their eyes off him. At last Mr. Leakey, moved by who can say what motives of delicacy, fetched a tweed jacket (it happened to be Larry Pye's) and draped it over Old Bill's face.

"We shan't rehearse any more this afternoon," said Valentine. "But I should like to see the committee for a few moments."

It is enough to say that Mr. Webster refused to allow the Little Theatre to replace Old Bill, saying without much real conviction that he supposed accidents would happen. Valentine had a frank talk with Geordie, in which she permitted herself to forget that Salterton was not New York; she was seconded by Major Larry Pye, who spoke with great restraint, all things considered. Geordie wrote a letter to Mr. Webster in which the shrieking figure of Apology was hounded through a labyrinth of agonized syntax. Old Bill was hauled away to the knacker's, sincerely mourned by Tom and Freddy.

In the production of every play there comes a low point of rehearsal, after which the piece climbs to whatever climax it is destined to reach. There could be no doubt about it, the day Geordie killed the horse marked that point for *The Tempest*, as produced by the Salterton Little Theatre.

Leonardo Da Vinci asserted that the human eye not only received, but gave forth rays of light; Hector's eye, at any time before he fell in love with Griselda, might have served as a proof of this theory. But now it was dulled. In the late springtime, when he should have been deep in that exhaustive revision of the year's work which was so much a feature of his teaching, he would spend as long as five minutes at a time staring out of the window, twiddling the cord of the blind, while his pupils wondered what had come over him. His particular brand of classroom humour no longer held any charm for him. There had been a time when, during such a spring revision, he had sent two or three of the more backward pupils to the blackboard every day, to work out problems under his direct gaze; as they blundered, he had goaded them, not angrily, with a mingling of humour, pity and a little contempt. If it is true, as is so often asserted, that the greatest humour is near to pathos, Hector qualified on these occasions as a great humorist: although few of the stupid ones learned much about mathematics during these ordeals, some of them learned lessons of fortitude which were invaluable to them in later life. But this spring all the ardour of the born teacher was gone from him. He was like a sick man, but his pupils did not guess the cause of his sickness.

Spring had been his chief season for detentions. Every

afternoon he had collected a group of boys and girls in his classroom after school was over, in order to make sure that they finished the work which they had not done during the lesson period. But this spring he was noticeably ill at ease for the last hour of the school day, and left as soon as the last bell had rung. He made his way at once to St. Agnes' and if no rehearsal was called he would do little jobs for Larry Pye, or measure the area which had been set aside for seats, or do something to make it decent for him to linger there. Rehearsals usually began at five o'clock and ended at eight, when the light began to fail; Hector was the first to come and the last to go.

He had, in the course of a few weeks, learned much about himself. He had learned that he had no talent as a joker. But then, he was comforted to notice, Griselda did not seem to care for jokes, and never smiled at Shortreed's finest strokes, though she often laughed at young Bridgetower's nonsense, which meant nothing to Hector. He learned that his youth was gone, and that his attempts to dress youthfully made him ridiculous. Larry Pye, who was over fifty, could wear anything he liked, including very old Army shorts, and no one laughed; but when Hector wore a sports shirt he felt naked and looked foolish. He had learned that it was possible for him to throw himself in Griselda's way constantly, without her taking any notice of him. She, who had smiled so meaningly at him, did not even heed his presence now. And yet when it was necessary to the action of the play that she, as Ariel, should sing softly into his ear as he pretended to be asleep, he knew that his face reddened, that his breathing was hard and that the blood beat in his ears and eyes; he thought "I love you, I love you," as she knelt by him, and was hurt and dismayed that in some way the message was not plain to her. Wild schemes, as they appeared to him, kept coming into his mind by which he would make his love known. He would write a letter—but he knew his limitations as a writer. He would ask to see her privately some evening, ask for an hour uninterrupted; but would he be able to speak? No, he could not face such an ordeal; the old gods of planning and common sense had deserted him. He would wait until some lucky chance brought them together, and then, on the spur of the moment, he would speak. But chance never did bring them together. He did not know what to do.

His love for Griselda had undergone a change which frightened him. When he had awakened that morning, sure that he loved her, he had enjoyed the happiness of the sensation. For perhaps a week he had thought of his attachment chiefly as an appurtenance to himself. In his little mental drama he was the principal figure, and Griselda was a supporting player. But as time wore on the emphasis shifted, and Griselda became the chief person of the drama, and he was a minor character, a mere bit player, aching for a scene with her. For the first time in his life Hector discovered that it was possible for someone to be more important to him than himself.

He had no need now to look ruefully at the item in his Plan of Conduct which urged him to give up pie. His appetite waned, and his accustomed waitress at the Snak Shak commented on it. He did not lose any of his bulk, but he looked puffy and distressed. One day he tore the Plan of Conduct out of his book and burned it; it seemed to him to be stupid and worthless, an insult to what he felt. Indeed his whole concept of life as something which could be governed by schemes in pocketbooks appeared to him suddenly to be trivial and contemptible.

He wanted to talk to somebody about his love, but he knew no one to whom he could even hint of such a thing. He engaged Mr. Adams in conversation about *The Tempest*, and led up to the character of Ariel. "I think you'll like that in our production," said he; "we have a very clever girl playing Ariel, a Miss Webster."

"She'll have to be clever," said Adams; "Shakespeare wrote that part for a boy, and it's always a mistake to cast a woman for it. I don't know that I care to see some great lolloping girl attempt it." This last remark was pure spite, and Adams did not really know why he made it. But there is a spirit of Malignance which makes people say offensive things to lovers about those they love, even when that love is hidden, and Mr. Adams was, for the moment, the instrument of it. Hector was wounded, but he could say nothing, for fear of revealing what might, he knew, bring him into derision.

Sexual desire played no conscious part in what he felt for Griselda. Indeed, it had never entered his life since that incident at the Normal School Conversazione. He did not long to possess her physically; he wanted to dominate her mentally. He wanted her to think of him as he thought of her, as of someone who stood high above and apart from the rest of mankind. He wanted to defend her from dangers; he wanted to bring her great gifts of courage and wisdom; he wanted to take her from the world and keep her to himself, and to know that she was blissfully happy to renounce the world for him. He thought that once he had declared his love, she might permit him to kiss her, but his imagination shrank quickly from that kiss; it would, he was sure, be a thing of such pain and joy that it might rob him of his senses. He had never, in all his forty years, kissed any woman but his mother.

Nevertheless, he was strongly conscious that Griselda was a woman, and was subject to the disabilities which he believed to be a special and unjust burden to her sex. When, at rehearsals, she seemed to be a little out of sorts, or flung herself on the grass to rest, or wore the look of weary beauty which had worked so powerfully upon Solly at the casting meeting, Hector grieved that she might be in the throes of those "illnesses peculiar to women" of which, as a boy, he had read in patent medicine almanacs. Thinking this, he could become quite maudlin on her account, and once remarked to the astonished Mr. Leakey, out of the blue, that woman had a great deal to bear which men could only guess at.

If only he could tell someone about his love! The urge to talk about it was mastered, but only just, by his fear of making himself foolish, or of destroying the magic of his feelings by giving them a voice. Once he thought seriously of seeking an interview with Mr. Webster, and telling that gentleman that he, Hector, loved his daughter and wanted her father's consent to seek her hand. This was, he realized, no longer the custom, but what he felt for Griselda demanded the fullest measure of formality. Besides, he was nearer in age to Mr. Webster than to his daughter; an older man, and the father of such a girl, would surely understand the frankness and nobility which prompted such an action. Fortunately better sense prevailed, and Mr. Webster was spared an interview which he would have found embarrassing and depressing.

Freddy was not so fortunate. Hector found her in the grounds at St. Agnes' one afternoon when he had, as usual, arrived early for rehearsal; she lay on the grass, memorizing her words as the goddess Ceres. Hector had no fear of adolescent girls, for he had taught hundreds of them. Here, he thought, was someone he could pump about Griselda.

"I see you are getting your words by heart," said he.

"Yes," said Freddy.

"That's right. We won't make much progress until we are all perfect in our words."

"I suppose not."

"Do you find memorizing hard?"

"Not when I'm allowed to concentrate on it."

"You should memorize each night, the last thing before you go to sleep. That is the best way to memorize formulae, or anything like that."

"Really?"

"Why are you not at school?"

"I've been ill; I'm taking a term off."

"Pity, pity; you shouldn't break the flow of your education until it is complete. That is, if you can afford to keep up the continuity, which not everyone is able to do."

"The doctor told my father to keep me at home. I've nothing to say about it."

"Ah. Pity, pity."

A pause, during which Freddy and Hector regarded one another solemnly.

"A very fine old house you have here."

155

"Thank you."

"How old, now?"

"Oh, about a hundred and thirty years, I suppose. Prebendary Bedlam built most of it."

"Who?"

"You aren't a native of Salterton, are you?"

"No."

"Then it's not likely you'd have heard of him."

"You have a lovely big room, I expect."

"No, quite small."

"But your sister has a lovely big room, I expect?"

"She has two rooms; a sitting-room and a bedroom with the biggest bed in it you ever saw, with a crimson silk bedspread," said Freddy, who was getting tired of this and decided to give the pryer some well-deserved mis-information. "She has a marvellous bathroom, with a sunken tub, and a peach basin, and a black john and a toilet roll which plays *The Lass of Richmond Hill* when you pull it," she continued, beginning to enjoy herself.

Hector was not sure how he should take this. Long experience of girls of Freddy's age told him that she was lying. Nevertheless, she was Griselda's sister, and to that extent sacred. He decided to give her the benefit of the doubt.

"That's very interesting," said he. "And which would be her window, now?"

"Those big ones there," said Freddy, pointing to her father's windows. Was he a Peeping Tom, she wondered.

"Has your sister finished school?"

"Yes."

"Ah, she didn't lose terms like you. She'll have been very clever at school?"

"Not very," said Freddy.

"Really? But she was a leader, I suppose? I expect she was very much admired?"

So that's it, thought Freddy. This silly old clown is stuck on Gristle. The dirty old man, chasing a girl less than half his age. Just another John Knox. With the concentrated spite of the eunuch, or the sexless, she said:

"No, she wasn't liked, really, except by a few. But she was the champion burper of the school. She can swallow an awful lot of air, you know, and belch the first few bars of *God Save the King*, while saluting. She was always begged to do it on stunt nights."

Hector walked away, saddened. The child was a liar, and perhaps not quite right in the head, but her blasphemy had wounded him, none the less.

Hector was wrong in supposing that Griselda did not notice him. She noticed that he seemed often to be in the way, that he changed colour and breathed heavily when she sang her little piece into his ear, and that he seemed to be physically timid and fearful of accidents. This last observation was unjust, and was the outcome of Hector's solicitude for her; as Ariel she had to climb about on some platforms which Tom had put up at the back of the stage and disguised with greenery; it never entered her head to be frightened of these trivial heights, but whenever she had to get down from them, she was likely to find Hector there, with a hand outstretched, and a look of apprehension on his face; he would assist her to the ground, gingerly, and walk away, as though embarrassed. Larry Pye sometimes wanted to do the same thing, but she knew Larry; he wanted to squeeze her legs as he lifted her, and she usually jumped straight at him, causing him to skip ungallantly out of danger. But she assumed that Hector was a fusspot who thought that she could not jump six or eight feet without breaking something.

Hector, like everyone else in the company, came into the game which she played with Roger, as well. That young man had not fallen under the spell of Valentine Rich's personality, as everyone else connected with the production had done in some degree. There was between them one of those unaccountable antipathies which occasionally occur, and which nothing can be done to remedy. Roger admitted that Valentine was an unusually capable director, but he did not like her; he set her down as a Bossy Woman; perhaps this was because he knew that she could never be influenced by his sort of charm. Valentine considered Roger a godsend as a juvenile lead in an amateur play, but she did not like him; he was a type which she had met many times in the theatre, and which, except for theatrical purposes, she could not endure. And although she was fully as tactful in her dealings with him as with the rest of the company, he sensed her dislike beneath her courtesy, just as she sensed his dislike beneath his compliance. Shut out from the group which was warmed and enspirited by Valentine, he made fun of it to Griselda.

She was quickly attracted by anything which savoured of sophistication, and to the young the easy, ill-founded cynicism which finds everybody and everything just a little second-rate is a kind of fool's gold. It was flattering that Roger should make fun of the others to her; to be chosen as the confidante of a superior spirit is always flattering. Griselda was very far from being a fool; she had what Dr. Johnson called "a bottom of good sense", but she was not quite nineteen, and she had never met anyone like Roger before.

He, in his turn, was delighted that he had so quickly found a way to attract her. She was not, he recognized, like any girl upon whom he had tried his skill before. She was wealthy, which meant that he must be very careful, for one does not lightly seduce rich girls; they have too many powerful relatives, and are too much accustomed to getting the better of all things. He seriously questioned whether he could proceed to the usual conclusion of his plan with Griselda. Indeed, he marvelled dimly that gold, which could make an attractive girl so much more attractive, should also protect her so thoroughly. And as well as money, Griselda had the manners and the conversation of a well-bred girl who has read a great many books of the easier sort, and these qualities Roger mistook for worldly wisdom and unusual intelligence. For the first time in his life Roger had met a girl with whom he felt that a "nice"—well, fairly nice—relationship was worth cultivating. Griselda was capable of giving him something which he valued even more than physical satisfaction; she could give him class. The other thing he could find elsewhere when he wanted it. Never any shortage of that.

Thus they struck up an amused conspiracy against the rest of the company. Nobody cared except Valentine, who thought it bad for the play; except Hector, who did not understand it but who saw that Griselda was too often laughing in a corner with Tasset; except Pearl Vambrace, who had fallen as much in love with Roger as it is possible to fall in love with a man who never speaks to you except in lines written by Shakespeare, lines charged with a noble love which is nothing but play-acting.

Bad for the play—yes, Valentine thought that. But she knew that she was nettled by anything which gave Roger satisfaction, and she was angry with herself for being so petty. She could not keep up her accustomed tact one day at rehearsal when Roger repeatedly fluffed his lines in a scene with Pearl.

"Roger, it's far past the time when you should know this scene," said she.

"Sorry," said Roger, in a tone which suggested that he thought she was being wearisome and must be humoured.

"It's useless to say that you are sorry if you have no intention of improving," she said; "you have said 'Sorry' in very much that tone at the last four rehearsals. I am growing tired of it."

Pearl, moved by the desire for self-sacrifice which is one of the most dangerous characteristics of unwanted lovers, spoke:

"It's really my fault, Miss Rich," said she; "I make a move there which puts him off, I think."

"No, you don't do anything of the kind," said Valentine crossly; "you are perfectly all right and you would be much better if you had something to act against."

"If I am really such a nuisance, Miss Rich," said Roger, "perhaps it isn't too late to reconsider the casting."

"Oh, don't talk like an idiot," said Valentine, angrily conscious that she was growing red in the face. "You are the best

159

person for the part, and you know it. You can do it very well, and you will do it very well. If you drop out now you will make all sorts of difficulties for everybody. But I want you to work at rehearsals, and spend less time giggling in the background with Griselda. You are both of you behaving like children. A production like this depends on everybody's good work and good will. It simply is not fair to behave as you are doing."

Roger was very angry. That he, a man who had got the better of so many women should be spoken to in that tone by a woman, and in front of a lot of nincompoops! He turned to leave the stage.

"Go back to your place, Roger, and finish your scene," said Valentine in the voice which had caused two London critics to call her the best Lady Macbeth among the younger generation of actresses.

To Roger's intense astonishment, he did so, and under the stress of anger, he acted quite well. But as he looked into Pearl's eyes he saw pity and love there, and he hated her for it until the rehearsal was over, when he promptly forgot her.

At eleven o'clock that night Griselda sat at her window, studying her lines. She had been alarmed and shamed by Valentine's words; she was also angry. If that was the way Valentine thought about her, she would show that she could behave in any way she pleased, and act Ariel too. She looked out of her window at the upper lawn; there was the spot, there by that tree, where Solly had kissed her. She remembered it with pleasure. But what a mess he had turned out to be! Afraid of his mother! Griselda, who had forgotten what it was like to have a mother, and who could not know what the relationship between a man and his mother can be, was scornful. Roger wasn't such a softy. It was only since she had met Roger that she had really known how silly most people are.

Was she in love with Roger? She didn't really know, but she half suspected that she was. Anyhow, she knew who did love Roger, and that was that stupid Pearl Vambrace, whose hems were always uneven, and whose hair looked as if it needed a good wash. But Pearl wasn't going to get Roger until Griselda had quite made up her mind about him. Yes, very likely she was in love with Roger.

The fact was that Griselda's notions about love, allowing for differences of sex, were no more clear-cut than those of Hector Mackilwraith. But as she leaned out of her window and took a long breath of the warm spring night, she felt that it was a very fine thing to be eighteen and in love.

On the other side of the house Freddy crept to the window of a darkened closet and looked out. Yes; there it was; just what she had expected to see. A dark shape standing among the trees, not easy to make out, but apparently with its head thrown back and its eyes raised, undoubtedly in worship, toward the windows of her father's bedroom.

Putting half a walnut shell in her mouth she popped her head out of the window and shouted in her deepest voice: "Who's that down there?"

There was a wild trampling of shrubbery, and a thickset figure rushed toward the road.

CHAPTER
5

AS THE time of the opening performance drew nearer there were rehearsals in the grounds of St. Agnes' three or four times a week, and after many of these Griselda offered the actors what she liked to call "a bite". Roger said that he could not understand why she did it, and it seemed to herself that it was not in her new character as an amused observer of the human comedy. But although the flame of hospitality within her was not a bonfire, it was steady and bright, and it appeared to her to be wrong that people should come to her home and go away again without having received food or drink. Therefore she worked out a plan for giving the Little Theatre bread and cheese and fruit and coffee; she even insisted upon paying for these things herself and serving them herself, so as not to put her father to expense or to make extra work for the servants. The facts that her father did not care about such expenses and that the servants had not enough to do did not enter into the matter; she felt that the Little Theatre was at St. Agnes' because of her doing and that she ought to take care of at least some of their wants. So contradictory is human nature that she could think sneeringly of her fellow-actors while taking considerable pains on their behalf. As Freddy said in her more sentimental moments, Griselda was not a half-bad old boob in her way.

The Little Theatre loved it. Acting is a great provoker of hunger and conviviality, and the bread and the cheese, the fruit and the coffee were consumed in great quantities. Professor Vambrace complimented Griselda upon the classical simplicity of this refreshment; it put him in mind of the meals in Homer, he said. Pearl and he ate heartily upon these occasions, not knowing what Spartan nastiness the pre-occupied Mrs. Vambrace might have left in the refrigerator for them at home. But Griselda's hospitality begot hospitality in others, and soon the actors were vying with one another to entertain the cast after a rehearsal; simplicity was forgotten, and hospitality raged unchecked. Some of these affairs were very pleasant; others were markedly less agreeable. Mrs. Leakey's after-rehearsal soirée came well down in the latter category.

What Mrs. Leakey felt when she discovered that Leakey was going to other people's houses to eat and drink, without her, four times a week, was simple jealousy. But it was not Mrs. Leakey's way to admit to base emotions; she sublimated them. So she addressed Leakey thus:

"You can't very well go on eating everywhere and anywhere, week in and week out, without Repaying Hospitality. We don't want people to think we're cheapskates. I don't know that we're exactly in a position to entertain. Goodness knows we have little enough in the way of cups and saucers. But if other people are having the cast in after rehearsal, we'll do it too. So you'd better invite the whole tribe for next Friday night, and get it over with."

When Mrs. Leakey heard that the fare at St. Agnes' was of the simplest, she smiled a superior smile. Beginning at ten o'clock in the morning on the Friday in question, she worked the greater part of the day on the food which she would serve that night. She baked a chocolate cake and a white cake; she iced the former in the difficult and lumpy Log Cabin style, and the latter she covered with a deep layer of sticky stuff resembling marshmallow. She imprisoned little sausages in pastry and baked them. She made an elaborate ice cream, and coloured it green. She made sandwiches of the utmost difficulty, possible only to a thirty-third degree sandwich-maker, in which bananas were tongued and grooved with celery; sandwiches loaded with cream cheese, or encrusted with nuts and olives; sandwiches in which lengths of chilly asparagus were entombed in two kinds of bread; sandwiches in which fish, mayonnaise and onion were forced into uneasy union. She produced pickles of her own making from the cellar cupboard, and created a jelly from which the imbedded bits of fruit stared forth, like fish from a ruby bowl. By evening she was, to use her own phrase, "all in", and let Mr. Leakey know it before he went to rehearsal.

"Don't be later than nine getting back here with them," she said; "we don't want them hanging around till all hours. Some of us have to get up in the morning if others don't."

This was enough to make Mr. Leakey nervous all through the rehearsal, which began at half-past six, and to put him into a state of real apprehension from half-past eight onward. But when the cast arrived in a body at the Leakey home at half-past nine, who could have been a more gracious chatelaine than Mrs. Leakey?

"I'm glad you came just in whatever you stood up in," said she, taking in Griselda, who was in slacks, the Torso, who was in shorts, and Valentine, who wore a suit but the tail of whose blouse kept popping out. Mrs. Leakey wore a creation of scratchy lace which showed off her large, strong collar bones to great advantage.

She had invited a few ladies of her acquaintance to help her in serving the refreshments. Some hostesses might have felt that this was a mistake, for these ladies knew nothing about the play, were not members of the Little Theatre, and wanted to talk about other things. Now a theatrical company, however ill-assorted or however amateur, is bound together by ties which are incomprehensible to outsiders. They want to talk about their play, or if they talk of other things, they are likely to talk about them in a manner which does not readily take in strangers. Even a determined hostess like Mrs. Leakey may find herself bested by this exclusiveness. She decided to make small-talk with Solly on the one topic which seemed to interest him.

"I've been hearing Eric his lines," said she, offering him a pickle; "I must say they don't mean much to me."

"Oh," said Solly, who was tired and not in a mood to encourage this line of conversation.

"I think some of Shakespeare's characters are awfully

overdrawn," said Mrs. Leakey, firmly.

"Really?" said Solly, looking curiously into a sandwich.

"As a matter of fact, I've said to Eric that it seems to me that more people would like Shakespeare if he had written in prose."

"Very likely."

"Still, that's just one person's opinion."

"Quite."

The party took on a strongly Ontario character. That is to say, all the ladies gathered in the drawing room, and all the gentlemen gathered in a small room behind it, which Mr. Leakey used as his "den". In the dining-room, enthroned behind the silver service, one of Mrs. Leakey's female friends poured out coffee, and the other female friends came to the table from time to time to load up with fresh consignments of food. Roger wanted to talk to Griselda; Valentine wanted to talk to Solly; the Torso yearned in a generous and all-embracing fashion to be at the men. But the power of the hostess at such affairs is very great, and Mrs. Leakey liked to run her parties on tried-and-true pioneer lines. So the sexes ate in decent segregation, and were so cowed that they obediently gobbled some of everything which was offered to them, regardless of how little they wanted it. And promptly at half-past ten the ladies rose, almost as one, and the guests departed.

"Well," said Mrs. Leakey; "thank Heaven they didn't stay till all hours. Now we'd better get these dishes washed; I don't want them staring at me when I come down in the morning. It's been a hard day, but I don't want it to stretch over into another."

By midnight the Leakeys had washed everything and put it away, and were in bed, having shown themselves hospitable.

It was not long before Mrs. Bridgetower, who had a knack of knowing what was going on even when she was most secluded and ailing, heard about this round of hospitality.

"You know how it grieves me not to be able to do my

part," she said to Solly. "When your Father was alive this house was a rendezvous—a regular rendezvous. But I simply couldn't see so many people at once in my present condition. I might manage a few, but I couldn't manage all."

"Please don't worry about it, Mother," said he. "Nobody minds."

"Oh, don't they?" said his Mother. "I didn't know that I'd been forgotten quite so quickly. There was a time, I can tell you, when people looked to this house for hospitality. And you know, lovey, that there is nothing I like so much as to see your friends here."

Solly had often been assured of this by his mother, but the evidence pointed in a different direction. What his mother liked was to see his friends come to the house, fail in some direction or other to measure up to the standard which she set for companions of her only son, and depart in disgrace. It was still remembered against one miserable youth that five years before he had crumbled a piece of cake on the drawing-room carpet, and had then nervously trodden in it and tracked it into the dining-room; Mrs. Bridgetower could still point out exactly where his crumby spoor had lain. Solly hoped to let the matter drop, but his mother detected this and continued:

"Perhaps the best thing would be to have them in in small groups of three or four, one group each week, for tea. If you will give me a list of their names I shall make up the groups, and telephone them as their time comes."

"I'm afraid they wouldn't be able to come to tea, Mother," said Solly; "most of these affairs are rather late in the evening."

"Oh, I could never manage that; the anxiety of waiting all evening for them to come would be too much for me."

"Of course it would, Mother. They understand."

"Oh, so they've been discussing it, have they? Well, I don't want them to understand anything that isn't so. I am quite capable of offering hospitality on my own terms. When I was a girl and we got up any private theatricals, we usually made rehearsals an excuse for very charming little teas, and sometimes eggnogg parties."

"I know Mother, but this is different. Much more professional in spirit."

"Hmph, the world seems to be advancing in everything except amenity."

"Would you be happy if I invited a few people in, just for a chat in my room, after a rehearsal, now and again? You wouldn't need to bother with them then."

"You could hardly invite girls to come here under those circumstances."

"Of course not. Just a few of the men. And then we should have shown ourselves hospitable, and you wouldn't have been troubled."

"Well, perhaps so. I shall write a note to Mrs. Forrester, explaining why I have not undertaken to entertain the group as a whole, and then you shall have the men in by twos and threes."

Mrs. Bridgetower wrote the note that same day, and at the next rehearsal Nellie said:

"Oh Solly, how sweet of your mother to write to me like that! I don't know of anyone else in Salterton who would have done it. Really she's wonderful! So hospitable, and so gracious. It must be a terrible hardship to her that she can't entertain as she wants to! Of course we all understand. I'm sending her a little bouquet and a note from me and Val."

It was not a happy inspiration which persuaded Solly to arrange the first of these masculine gatherings on a night when Miss Cora Fielding was also entertaining the company. The Fieldings were jolly people, and unlike Mrs. Bridgetower they really liked to see their children's friends in their house.

Not only was there chicken and ham and potato salad and olives and anchovies and fruit salad and several sorts of sweetmeats; there was also rather a lot of liquor, and as Mr. Fielding was more hospitable than discreet the party, at the end of an hour was lively and noisy. At the end of the second hour, square dances were being performed in a room which was much too small for them, and Valentine had danced a hornpipe with great success. The party broke up at midnight; several people kissed Miss Cora Fielding goodnight, and everybody assured the older Fieldings in merry shouts that they had had a wonderful time.

Solly, who was wondering what he would say to his mother if she happened to be awake, was walking purposefully toward the gate when Humphrey Cobbler hailed him:

"Not so fast, Bridgetower; let us adjourn to your select masculine gathering at a dignified pace."

"Oh, well, really I hadn't quite realized that Cora was throwing a party tonight. Must have got my dates mixed. Probably it would be better if you came to me another time."

"Nonsense. There is no time like the present. Procrastination is a vice I hate. Now, who's coming with us? Tasset? Hey, Roger Tasset! You're coming on to Bridgetower's party aren't you?"

"Oh yes, I remember now that I said I would," said Roger, without enthusiasm.

"Who else? Mackilwraith? Ahoy, there, Mackilwraith; come along with us."

"Isn't it rather late?" said Hector.

"Not a bit of it. Barely midnight. Come on. We're going to make the welkin ring at Bridgetower's."

"The what ring?" said Hector.

"The welkin. It's a thing you make ring when you get drunk. Bridgetower has a lovely fresh welkin, just waiting to be rung. Come on!"

The half mile walk to Solly's home was not enlivened by much conversation. Why, Solly wondered, had he asked this ill-assorted group? Tasset was a man he wanted to know better, for Tasset was plainly attractive to Griselda, and Solly told himself that he wanted to study his rival. Heine, he felt, would have done so. To cast himself in the role of Heine somehow lessened the ignominy of being a rejected lover; he might be nothing to Griselda, but in his Heine role he was certainly an interesting figure to that dim, invisible, but rapt audience which, since his childhood, had watched his every move. Tasset was the crass, successful soldier—the unworthy object upon whom the Adored One chose to squander her affection: he was the scorned, melancholy poet, capable of examining and distilling his emotions even while his heart was wrung.

That explained Tasset most satisfactorily. But why Mackilwraith? Hector plodded at his side in silence, setting down his feet so hard on the pavement that his jowls gave a little quiver at every step. Why, out of all the men in the cast, had he thought of asking this dullard? He raked his mind for a romantic or even for a reasonable explanation, but he could find none.

Cobbler he had asked because he liked him. Cobbler was a man so alive, and so apparently happy, that the air for two or three feet around him seemed charged with his delight in life. But the Cobbler who was so lively a companion by daylight, in the midst of a rehearsal, seemed a little too exuberant, a little too noisy, in the stillness of the night, when one was growing nearer to Mother with every step. He had not the air of a man who would be really considerate about making a noise on the stairs. And the drinks which he had accepted from the hospitable Mr. Fielding had made him noisier than usual.

As though to bear out his fears, Cobbler began to dance along the pavement and sing:

> *The master, the swabber, the bos'n and I,*
> *The gunner, and his mate,*
> *Loved Moll, Meg and Marian, and Margery,*
> *But none of us cared for Kate.*

"For God's sake, don't make such a row," said Solly. "You'll wake the whole neighbourhood."

"I am full of holy joy and free booze," said Cobbler. "I feel moved to sing. It is very wrong to resist an impluse to sing; to hold back a natural evacuation of joy is as injurious as to hold back any other natural issue. It makes a man spiritually costive, and plugs him up with hard, caked, thwarted merriment. This, in the course of time, poisons his whole system and is likely to turn him into that most detestable of beings, a Dry Wit. God grant that I may never be a Dry Wit. Let me ever be a Wet Wit! Let me pour forth what mirth I have until I am utterly empty—a Nit Wit." He sang again:

> *For she had a tongue with a tang,*
> *Would cry to a sailor 'Go hang!'*
> *She loved not the savour of tar nor of pitch*
> *Yet a tailor might scratch her where'er she did itch.*
> *Then to sea, boys, and let her go hang!*

"Please be quiet," said Solly desperately. "We're near my home now. My Mother is unwell, and she will be asleep." (Fat chance, he thought, inwardly.) "We'll go right up to my room; I wouldn't like to disturb her."

"Sir, you are talking to a Fellow of the Royal College of Organists," said Cobbler, with immense solemnity. "You can rely utterly upon my good behaviour. *Floreat Diapason!*" He began to tiptoe exaggeratedly on the pavement, and turned to whisper Ssh! at Hector, whose feet were making a good deal of noise.

Roger thought fleetingly of excusing himself. This was going to be a miserable affair. Bridgetower was afraid of his mother, and Cobbler was playing the fool. Why had he ever allowed himself to be mixed up with such a pack?

The Bridgetower house was in darkness and the front door was locked. Solly was suddenly angry. She knew that he was bringing friends home. This was intolerable. As he rattled his key in the lock Cobbler gave another conspiratorial Ssh! Why, Solly demanded of himself, does she xpose me to this kind of thing? To be shushed entering my own home! Angry, he made a good deal of noise in the hall, and led the procession upstairs. At the first landing, as he had expected, was the ray of light from his mother's door.

"Is that you lovey?"

"Yes, Mother. I've brought some friends home."

"Oh, I did not think that you would, now that it's so late."

"It's just a little after midnight, Mother."

"You won't be too late, will you lovey?"

"I can't possibly tell, Mother. Did you leave some sandwiches?"

"When you didn't come home by ten I told Violet to put them away."

"I'll find them. Good-night, Mother."

"Good-night, lovey."

Half an hour later they had eaten a good many sandwiches and drunk some of Solly's rye, which for the occasion he had diluted with soda water instead of the lukewarm drizzle from the tap. Humphrey Cobbler had established himself as the leader of the conversation and was holding forth on music.

"If there is one gang of nincompoops that I despise more than another," said he, champing on a chicken sandwich, "it is the gang which insists that you cannot reach any useful or interesting conclusion by discussing one art in terms of another. Now there is nothing I enjoy more than talking about music in terms of painting. It's nonsense, of course, and at worst it's dull nonsense. But if you get somebody who knows a lot about music and a lot about painting, it is just possible that he will have an intuition, or a stroke of superlative common sense which will put you on a good scent. If you ask me, we're too solemn about the arts nowadays. Too solemn, and not half serious enough. And who's at the root of most of the phoney solemnity? The critics. Leeches, every last one of them. Hateful parasites, feeding upon the blood of artists! Do I bore you?"

"You don't bore me," said Hector. "Not that I know anything about the arts. Though I have had some musical experience." He smiled shyly. "I used to pump the organ in my father's church."

"Did you now?" said Cobbler. "Do you know, that's the first really interesting thing I've heard you say. It humanizes you, somehow. Can you sing?"

"Very little. I've never had much of a chance."

"You ought to try it. You've got quite a nice speaking voice. You ought to join the singers in the play. Now there's music that you can get your teeth into. Purcell! What a genius! And lucky, too. Nobody has ever thought to blow him up into a God-like Genius, like poor old Bach, or a Misunderstood Genius, like poor old Mozart, or a Wicked and Immoral Genius, like poor old Wagner. Purcell is just a nice, simple Genius, rollicking happily through Eternity. The boobs and the gramophone salesmen and the music hucksters haven't discovered him yet and please God they never will. Kids don't peck and mess at little scraps of Purcell for examinations. Arthritic organists don't torture Purcell in chapels and tin Bethels all over the country on Sundays, while the middle classes are pretending to be holy. Purcell is still left for people who really like music."

"I like the music you have chosen for the play," said Hector; "what we heard tonight was very pretty."

"Thank you," said Cobbler. "Pretty isn't just the word I would have chosen myself for Purcell's elegant numbers, but I discern that your heart is in the right place."

"A pretty girl is like a melody," hummed Roger.

"Excuse me," said Cobbler, turning toward him, "but I must contradict you. A pretty girl is nothing of the kind. A melody, if it is any good, has a discernible logic; a pretty girl can exist without the frailest vestige of sense. Do you know that that great cow of a girl they call The Torso— a pretty girl if ever there was one—came to me the other day and told me that she was musical, indeed surpassingly musical, because she often heard melodies in her head. Her proposal was that she should hum these gifts of God to me, and that I should write them down. She then hummed the scrambled fragments of two or three nugacities from last year's movies. There were two courses open to me: as a musician I could have struck her; as a man I could have dragged her into the shrubbery and worked my wicked will upon her."

"As a matter of curiosity, which did you do?" asked Solly.

"Curiosity killed the cat," said Hector, who was a little

embarrassed by the turn the conversation had taken; never-theless, he wanted to show himself a man's man, and something witty seemed called for.

"I deny that," said Cobbler; "the cat probably died a happy martyr to research. In this case I was spared the necessity for decision; Mrs. Forrester called me away at the critical moment to ask if it would be necessary for the musicians to have any light, or whether they could get along with the few rays which might spill from the stage. When Nellie is in one of her efficient moods all passions are stilled in her presence."

"She's a damned efficient woman," said Roger. "There wouldn't be any show without her."

"I'd like her better if she hadn't such an insufferably cosy mind," said Solly.

"What do you mean by that?" said Roger.

"Oh, you know; she makes everything seem so snug and homey; she wants to be a dear little Wendy-mother to us all. Not being a Peter Pan myself, I don't like it."

"Peter Pan, the boy who never grew up," said Hector, to show that he was following the conversation, and also that he was as keen in his appreciation of a literary reference as anybody.

"Funny, I would have thought that Peter Pan was a pretty good name for you," said Roger.

"Would you," said Solly; "and just why would you think that?"

"Take my advice and don't answer that question," said Cobbler. "You two are bound to quarrel eventually, but if you take my advice you won't do it here."

"And why are we bound to quarrel, may I ask?" said Roger, very much on his dignity.

"Because, as everybody knows, you are both after the Impatient Griselda. It's the talk of the company. At the moment, Tasset, you are well in the lead, but Solly may leave you behind at any moment. Your fascination—I speak merely as an impartial but keen observer, mind you, and mean nothing personal—is beginning to wane. At any moment Griselda may weary of your second-rate man-of-the-world manner, and turn toward our host's particular brand of devitalized charm."

This was sheer mischief-making, but Cobbler liked mischief and had had enough to drink to make him indulgent toward his weakness.

"I had not realized that we were so closely watched," said Solly. He and Roger were both caught off their guard by Cobbler's words. But they were not so startled as Hector. So intensely had he concentrated on his own passion that he had not observed anything unusual in the attentions which Roger had been paying to Griselda; nor was he acute enough to have noticed anything significant about the way in which Solly avoided her. And here he was, confronted with two unsuspected rivals, both younger and more attractive than he, whose presence had been unknown to him! He had not drunk much, but his stomach heaved, and he felt cold within. He had no time to consider his plight, however, for Roger turned to him.

"That's a lie, isn't it, Mackintosh?" said he.

"What? What's a lie?" said Hector, startled.

"A lie that everybody is watching Griselda and me. I've been giving her a mild buzz, of course. Got to pass the time somehow. But nobody's been talking about it."

"I don't know," said Hector.

"Of course you don't know. Nobody's been talking and nobody cares. You're lying, Cobbler."

"Nobody says that with impunity to a Fellow of the Royal College of Organists," said Humphrey. *"Floreat Vox Humana!"*

"And exactly what do you intend to do about it?"

"Nothing at present. But I'll embarrass you some time in public, and make you sorry."

"I never heard such nonsense in my life," said Solly. "I couldn't be less interested in Griselda Webster. I've known her, man and boy, for years. She has a heart like an artichoke; one man pulls off a leaf, dips it in melted butter, and consumes it with relish; another does the same. Anybody can have a leaf, but nobody gets them all, and nobody touches the core. I've had a leaf or two; why should I grudge Tasset his turn?"

"Perhaps that's the way you talk about women in the universities," said Roger. "In the Army we're a little more particular."

"In the great shrines of humanism we don't need arbitrary rules to keep our manners in order," said Solly, bowing rather drunkenly over his glass.

"Come, come, gentlemen," said Cobbler. "Don't go all grand on us. You must admit, whatever you say about Miss Webster's character, that she is an unusually personable young woman."

"Handsome is as handsome does," said Solly owlishly. "Griselda is attractive—damnably attractive. But it's all on the surface. If I may so express it, she is like a fraudulent bank which advertises a capital of several millions, and has perhaps five hundred dollars in actual cash. She is lovely; I repeat it, lovely. Because I am peculiarly sensitive to beauty I admit to a certain tenderness for her on that account; but her heart is cold and empty."

"Horse feathers," said Roger, with heat. "She's just a kid —a damned nice kid. She has to be taught what life's all about, and what love is; just because you couldn't get to first base with her you say her heart is cold and empty. I know better."

"Ah, I knew that we could rely upon you, Lieutenant," said Cobbler. "Our host is a man of theory, you, a man of action. From your remarks I deduce that you have already bruised the teats of her virginity?"

This was greeted with a moment of silence. Then—

"What the hell do you mean by that?" demanded Roger.

"Three guesses," said Humphrey, smiling. "It is a rather delicate phrase from the Prophet Ezekiel—one of the nicer-minded prophets. In my capacity as an organist I hear a lot of Scripture; it's an education in itself."

"Listen, Cobbler," said Roger, "I've lived a rough life— a soldier's life— but I have no use for raw language, particularly when applied to women. Just be careful, will you?"

"But I was careful," said Humphrey, smiling; "I could have put it plainly, but I chose a Biblical phrase to suit the solemnity of the occasion. And from what I know of your past history, Lieutenant, your objection to raw language has never stood in the way of your fondness for what fussy people might consider raw conduct."

"I've been around," said Roger; "and I've known a lot of girls."

"It was said of that great and good monarch Henry VIII," said Cobbler, "that his eye lighted upon few women whom he did not desire, and he desired few whom he did not enjoy. Would you consider that a fair description of yourself?"

"I don't say that I haven't taken my pleasure where I found it," said Roger, "but it was usually a fifty-fifty deal. Girls don't get laid against their will. But don't get any wrong ideas about Griselda. She's different."

"Aha, then you are in love!" cried Humphrey. "There is nothing men like so much as generalizing about women; all women are alike, except the one they love. She is the exception to all rules. And there is no lover so pure and holy in his adoration as a reformed voluptuary. You love her, Tasset!"

"Very well then, I love her. I'm man enough to admit it," said Roger and was startled and somewhat alarmed to hear himself.

"Spoken like a man!" cried Humphrey.

"I don't believe you," said Solly, heatedly. "Just a few minutes ago you described your attentions to her as a mild buzz."

"Well, did you expect me to blab out my private feelings?" said Roger.

"That's what you've just pretended to do," said Solly, "but I don't believe you love her. How could you love her? You haven't got it in you to love anybody. The only thing that a crass, ill-conditioned yahoo like you could want with a girl like Griselda is-is-is her body." He finished weakly, for he had wanted a strong word, and could not immediately think of one which was not also too coarse for the occasion. "You just want to seduce her," he said, and sat back in his chair looking hot and rumpled and somewhat wet about the eyes.

Roger stood up. "By God, Bridgetower, there are some things I won't stand," said he. "Get up on your feet."

So it was to be a fight! Solly was no fighter, but he did not lack courage; he would let Tasset hammer him to a pulp before he would take back a word of what he had said. He stood up, throwing off his coat as he did so, and confronted Roger. Humphrey Cobbler skipped nimbly behind a table, and Hector, his heart in his mouth, followed him.

The ceiling was low, and dipped at the corners of the room, for it took the shape of the roof of the house; the light was bad, for it came from a single lamp which threw a patch of brilliance on the ceiling and a poor light everywhere else. There was a small rug on the slippery floor, and a good deal of furniture everywhere. It was not an ideal battleground.

Roger was in good condition, and knew how to box. But when he took a boxing posture he found that Solly had placed himself just out of reach, and was holding his fists at waist level, and clearly intended to do nothing. Who was to strike the first blow?

They might have stood glaring at one another until good sense took hold of them if Solly had not been so frightened. But he was convinced that Roger would do him desperate harm—might indeed kill him—and he was determined to make one gesture, one final Heine-like act of defiance, before the slaughter began. So he drew up his lip in a sneer, and laughed in Roger's face.

This had the desired effect. Roger stepped lightly toward him, and hit him on the nose, twice in the ribs and once on the jaw, with such speed that it seemed to Solly that the blows all landed at once. But with a great effort he struck at Roger's diaphragm, having some dim notion that a blow there would be very telling. The treacherous rug slipped, and as he fell he jerked up his head and struck his adversary under the chin with it, causing Roger to bite his tongue painfully. They fell to the ground with a crash, and lay there, moaning from their injuries.

As the noise subsided a sound from below made itself heard; it was not loud, but it was persistent; it was the tapping of a stick.

"Oh God," said Solly, getting up; "it's Mother." He hurried to the door. "It's all right, Mother," he called; "something fell down; nothing wrong." And then, foolishly inspired, he added, "I hope we didn't wake you?"

His mother's voice came tremulously up the stairs. "Oh, lovey, I'm so frightened. I thought the whole roof was coming down."

"No, no, Mother; no trouble at all. You'd better go back to bed."

Even more tremulously came the reply. "I can't; I'm on the sofa in the hall. I feel so weak. I think I need one of my white tablets."

"I'll have to go to her," said Solly.

"Better clean the blood off your face, first," said Humphrey.

It was Hector who acted. He dipped his handkerchief in the cold water in the bottom of the bowl which held ice for the drinks, and cleaned away the jammy ooze which had gathered under Solly's nostrils.

"We had better go home now," he said.

"No, no, that would convince Mother that something dreadful had happened. Anyhow it will take me some time to get her to her room if she has one of her weak spells. Stay here and keep quiet till I come back." Solly hurried down the stairs on tiptoe.

Roger had risen from the floor and was sitting with his tongue held between two cubes of ice, like the meat in a sandwich. Humphrey made as though to prepare him another drink, but Roger shook his head; a man who has bitten his tongue shrewdly feels a sickness all through his body which demands rest and quietness, not drinks. So Humphrey made a drink for himself and one for Hector, and sat down. Although they could not see it, all three were oppressively conscious of the pill-taking, the laboured breathing, the mute reproach, and the mordant old comedy of mother-and-son which was being played out at the foot of the stairs.

For some time nobody spoke. After perhaps five minutes Roger rose and went into Solly's bedroom, which was behind the room in which they were, and finding a washbasin there he set to work to relieve his swollen tongue by holding it under the cold tap.

Hector and Humphrey looked at each other.

"I don't like this," said Hector.

"No. Bad business,"said Humphrey. "But probably we'll be able to talk some sense into them when they come back." He had had the fun of provoking a quarrel; he now looked forward with appetite to the fun of patching it up.

"I don't mean these two fellows," said Hector; "I mean that I don't like Miss Webster to be mixed up in a thing like this—rough talk and fighting."

"Oh, heavens, don't worry about that. She'll probably never hear of it. Not that she would mind, I suppose; girls rather like to be fought over. Not that this was a fight a girl could take much pride in. But don't worry. Nothing will come of it."

"How do you know that something has not come of it already?"

"Meaning—?"

"They talked—they talked quite cold-bloodedly of—well, of intimacy with her."

"Oh well, that's just talk, you know. You know how lads are."

"Yes, I think I do. But that sort of talk disgusts me, and makes me angry, too. I wanted to knock their heads together."

"I don't know that I'd try that, if I were you."

"But we are older than they are. Surely one of us should take a stand?"

"What about? I don't see what you are getting at."

"Well," said Hector patiently, as though explaining the binomial theorem to a pupil, "they shouldn't talk that way about a girl's honour. A girl's honour is like a man's reputation for honesty—probably more easily destroyed. It is sacred. Men should treat it with reverence."

"Aha, so that's your notion, is it? Well, if I recall correctly, I was the first one to suggest that Griselda's honour might have been a little blown upon. Now, in point of fact, I don't believe that. But I wanted to find out what Tasset was up to, and I thought maybe I could goad him into an admission or a display of some kind. And I did."

"Well, then I think you ought to be ashamed of yourself."

"I'm not, though. You're not what could be called an original moralist, are you?"

"I know the difference between right and wrong, I hope."

"How nice for you. I don't."

"I suppose it is nothing to you that a beautiful and innocent young girl might lose her honour?"

"Listen, Mackilwraith; do me a favour, will you; stop calling it her honour. You give me the creeps. Tasset has rather a reputation; I just wanted to find out what he was up to, if I could."

"He leads an immoral life, does he?"

"By your standards, I suppose he does."

"Are there other standards for decent people?"

"That depends on the part of the world the decent people find themselves in, and the education they have had, and the place in society they occupy. Does Tasset strike you as an immoral fellow?"

"If he is loose with women I don't see that there can be any argument about it."

"Strictly between ourselves, I don't like him either. Still, if it's his nature to chase women, should we judge him?"

"There is such a thing as self-control."

"You certainly ought to know. You look as though you had controlled yourself, I must say."

"Certainly. In my profession anything else would be unthinkable."

"The unthinkable has always been rather in my line. You don't appear to have controlled yourself at the table, by the way. Quite a lad with the knife and fork, aren't you?"

"That is different. It harms nobody."

"I see. You don't think this control business can be over-done, do you?"

"How could it be?"

"Well, you know what Galen says: If natural seed be over-long kept, it turns to poison."

"Who was Galen?"

"Never heard of Galen? Claudius Galen? The father of medical practice?"

"Is he dead?"

"A small matter of seventeen hundred years."

"Ah. Well I dare say his opinion has been contradicted since then. Medical opinion is always changing. Do you see *The Reader's Digest*?"

"Galen wasn't just a pill-roller. He was a first-rate psycho-logist. The remark I have quoted to you is really a philo-sophical opinion phrased as a medical maxim."

"But it is out-dated."

"Damn it, wisdom is never out-dated."

"But how can the opinions of a doctor who died so long ago be any good today? In religion, of course, age is a good thing. But not in medicine."

"All right, Mackilwraith, you win. I feel myself to be an angel, beating my ineffectual wings in vain against the gran-ite fortress of your obtuse self-righteousness."

"You're not an angel. I think you're rather silly. Why do you clutter your mind with what a dead doctor said?"

"Galen isn't just a dead doctor, man; he was a great spirit. Probably a lot of his ideas are fantastic now. But he had flashes of insight which we can't discount. That's what makes a man great; his flashes of insight, when he pierces through the nonsense of his time, and gets at something that really matters."

"You are a lucky man to have room to spare in your head for truck of that sort."

"Truck?"

"Most of us find it hard enough to keep track of the things that we really need to know."

"Oho, now I know what you are. You are an advocate of Useful Knowledge."

"Certainly."

"You say that a man's first job is to earn a living, and that the first task of education is to equip him for that job?"

"Of course."

"Well, allow me to introduce myself to you as an advocate of Ornamental Knowledge. You like the mind to be a neat machine, equipped to work efficiently, if narrowly, and with no extra bits or useless parts. I like the mind to be a dustbin of scraps of brilliant fabric, odd gems, worthless but fascinating curiosities, tinsel, quaint bits of carving, and a reasonable amount of healthy dirt. Shake the machine and it goes out of order; shake the dustbin and it adjusts itself beautifully to its new position."

"As a mathematician I can hardly agree with you that disorder is preferable to order."

"Mathematician my foot! Do you know anything about linear algebra? How are you on diophantine equations? Could you tell me, in a few words, what Bertrand Russell has added to modern mathematical concepts? You are a mathematician in the way that a teacher of beginners on the piano is a musician!"

"I know what I know," said Hector, "and it is sufficient for my needs."

"But you don't begin to realize how much you don't know," said Humphrey, "and I shrewdly suspect that that is the source of your remarkable strength of character. For you are strong, you know; you talk like a fool, but you have amazing personal impact."

It was at this moment that Roger returned, and sat heavily down in his chair.

"How's the tongue?" asked Humphrey.

"Thwobs," said Roger.

"Aha. Swollen too, eh?"

Roger nodded. There was a gloomy silence. Humphrey slipped down into his chair and closed his eyes.

Hector looked at Roger long and closely. It was his duty,

he knew, to speak to him about Griselda. He ought to tell this man to stop annoying Griselda with his dishonourable attentions. But how could he do so? It was not that he lacked moral authority; he knew what was right, and he knew what he should do about it. But how could he rebuke Roger without giving away the fact that he, Hector, loved Griselda? The shock of finding that he had two young rivals had shaken him severely. He thought deeply, and the longer he thought the harder it was to speak. But at last he found a form of words which seemed to him to meet the needs of the occasion, and he spoke, so hollowly that Roger started a little in his chair.

"Do you consider yourself a suitor for the hand of Miss Webster?"

"Eh!"

"Do you want to marry Miss Griselda Webster?"

"I don't know. I haven't thought that far."

"Then you ought to leave her alone."

Roger regarded him with surprise. He was not a sensitive young man, and Hector's earnest, flushed face held no message for him.

"Listen, Mackintosh, how would it be if you mind your own business?" he said, at last.

Hector could not think of a suitable reply, and silence fell again.

At last Solly returned; his face was white and drawn, except for his swollen nose and a lump on his jaw. When Hector said that it would be well for them to leave he insisted that they stay.

"No, no" said he; "I've given Mother a sedative, and soon she will be in a deep sleep. But if you go downstairs now you may waken her. And I'd like you to stay. I need company."

"Listen, Bridgetower," said Roger, "I'm sorry about this. About disturbing your mother, I mean. And I didn't mean to hit you so hard."

"Quite all right," said Solly.

"You're not a type I like, if you know what I mean. But as

your type goes, you're not too bad."

"I understand you," said Solly. "As a matter of fact, I don't like your kind, either. Judged by any decent standard you are a pismire, an emmet, but it shouldn't be impossible for us to get along."

"Yes, it takes all kinds to make a world, as they say. Shake hands?"

"Certainly."

Humphrey stirred in his chair, and then started up, wide awake.

" 'Deeply have I slept, as one who hath gone down into the springs of his existence, and there bathed.' " said he. "Bit of useless knowledge for you, Mackilwraith; a poet you've never heard of and wouldn't like."

"Beddoes," said Solly.

"Neatly spotted," said Humphrey. "Full marks to Master Bridgetower for identifying the quotation. A great man, Beddoes and, like Purcell, still unmauled by the mob. Did I see you fellows shaking hands? Ah, the manly press of flesh! What a wonderful device it is for bringing insoluble quarrels to an apparent end! I take it that you've slipped Mum a Mickey Finn? How wise; sedatives to the sedate. Well, well, who's got the bottle?"

"No more for me," said Hector.

"Nonsense. You haven't got any way of providing us with some hot water, have you, Bridgetower?"

"There's an electric kettle downstairs."

"Fetch it, like a good fellow, will you? And you might as well bring a lemon and some sugar when you come."

When Solly had returned with the necessaries Humphrey quickly prepared four strong hot toddies.

"Now," said he, "while you were otherwise engaged, Mackilwraith drew it to my attention that he and I, as older men, should help you two to straighten out your affairs. This fighting over Griselda Webster won't do. If you want my frank opinion, the girl isn't worth it. A pretty little voice, but nothing out of the way. Take my advice: marry a woman with a good big mezzo range, plenty of power, and perfect pitch. Besides, neither of you really cares much about her; you just imagine that you do. 'Esteem and quiet friendship oft bear love's semblance for a while.' Beddoes again, Mackilwraith. Esteem and quiet friendship; that's what you feel for Griselda. So no rough stuff, with her or with each other. Agreed?"

"I'm taking her to the Ball," said Roger.

"I shall see you there," said Solly, who had not until that moment had any intention of going to the Ball.

An hour later two further rounds of toddy had made a great difference to Solly's party. On the floor below Mrs. Bridgetower was in such a sleep as only one of her white tablets, washed down with hot milk, could give her. Upstairs in the attic sitting-room three of the four men were talking animatedly and Humphrey Cobbler was holding forth to Hector on education.

"Of formal education," said he, "I have had but little. When I was a lad I was sent to a choir school. I had, if I may be permitted to say so, an exceptional soprano voice. They needed me, Mackilwraith; they needed me. And if there is one thing which utterly destroys a boy's character, it is to be needed. Boys are unendurable unless they are wholly expendable."

"Funny thing, when you flushed your closet just now," said Roger to Solly, "it put me in mind of a wonderful Dominion Day celebration we put on a couple of years ago when I was stationed out on the West Coast."

"All celebrations should be wonderful," said Solly, putting more sugar in his drink. "And that is one of the big troubles with Canada; we have very little ceremonial sense. What have we to compare with the Mardi Gras, or the Battle of Flowers? Nothing. Not a bloody thing."

"Because I was needed, I was impossible. I never worked at my school lessons, but I worked like a black at my music. And whenever I had to sing in Service, I put on a superb show. Well—what could they do? The Dean was headmaster of the school; was he going to boot his best soprano boy out into a cold world because he didn't do his sums? You see the situation?"

"Well, now, we had to parade on Dominion Day of course, and it was a hot day and we were all pretty well browned off. And we were worse than browned off—in fact you could pretty well say we were completely cheesed off—when an order came round that the O.C. wanted all the junior officers to remain in barracks that night—Dominion Day night, you see—because some bigwig from Ottawa wanted to have a look around, you see?"

"Our national dislike for doing things on a really big and spectacular scale, shows up in this play. You heard that row a couple of weeks ago when old Vambrace and Eva Wildfang were carrying on about the beauty of simplicity? They think Shakespeare can be run entirely under his own steam. He can't. You've got to have as much lavishness in costume and setting as you can, or your play will be a flop. The day of Shakespeare in cheesecloth costumes and a few tatty drapes is done."

"Of course I knew that I had the Dean right where I wanted him. Well, suddenly some American impresario got a notion that he wanted to take part of our choir to the States for a tour. The Dean said that only boys who had achieved a scholarly record of such-and-such could go. But ha! The impresario had been to Service. 'Of course I've got to have that solo boy,' says he. 'That boy isn't eligible to go,' says the Dean. 'Then I'll have to think again,' says the impresario. You know, I've always thought that fellow must have been a bit of a pansy. I was good, but I couldn't have been that good."

"There we were, you understand, cooped up in barracks, on a holiday, after a heavy afternoon in the sun. I suppose they thought we gave the damn place a lived-in look, or something. So we thought up a scheme. Or really—give the devil his due—it was a fellow named O'Carroll worked it out and when the evening came we were ready."

"Taste is at the bottom of everything. Given taste, you can go to any lengths. For instance, you remember the row about

those costumes that old Ma Crundale designed? The ones
with no fronts in them? They were tossed out because the
girls couldn't wear them. But given enough taste, it could be
done, and it would be a knockout! In fact, if I were given a
completely free hand, I think I could work a completely
naked Ariel painted gold into *The Tempest* and there
wouldn't be a word of complaint. Just breathless admiration!
But it would all be done with taste, you see?"

"The upshot was that the Dean gave way; he didn't want
to lose the publicity or the big fee, either. So away we went
to the States for six months. You should have seen us, Mackilwraith! For the first part of the programme we wore our
blue cassocks and our ruffs, and sang Byrd and Tallis and all
that. Then for the secular stuff in Part Two we switched into
evening dress, with Eton suits for us boys. Ah, Mackilwraith,
if you could but once have seen me in a bumfreezer and a
clean collar, singing 'Love was once a little boy', it would
have made a better man of you!"

"As soon as dinner was over we made our excuses and got
out of the mess as fast as we could. It was easy, because the
O.C. was dining with the bigwig. We got over to the men's
quarters, which were empty; everybody was out on the town.
Some of us who were engineers arranged wires on the
handles of all the water closets on each floor. Then we did
the same in every other building where there were any. Then
we established a central control in the administration building in the dark, and waited."

"Given taste, you can then go as far as you like with your
big stage effects. Hundreds of people milling about if you
like. Fill the stage with horses and dogs. Pageantry in a big
way. Make it complex! Let it fill the eye! Let it be enriched,
bejewelled, Byzantine! The parrot-cry that simplicity is one
with good taste comes from people who cannot trust their
taste in anything which is not simple. Shakespeare demands
all the opulence that we can give him!"

"The man who had charge of us boys was one of the
counter-tenors, a dear little chap named Thickpenny—
Roland Thickpenny. You know what a counter-tenor is?

No, I thought not. You've lived a dreadfully meagre life, Mackilwraith. A counter-tenor is a male alto. He is a tenor who has trained and enriched his falsetto register so that he can sing in a lovely, clear voice, and fill in the alto part in the male choir in a cathedral. You can't have women in Church choirs; they sour the Communion wine, or something. They're damned nuisances, anyhow. Well, Thickpenny was a dear—a chubby, red-faced little fellow, with a lovely voice. Women in the States went wild over him. Wanted to see what made him sing like that. Thought he was a eunuch, or something. Dear old Thickers was always being chased by some orgulous hag. But he was true to Mrs. Thickpenny and all the little Thickpennies at home."

"At last the great moment came. The O.C. walked out into the barrack yard with the bigwig. Every window in every building was open. We pulled all the wire controls. There was a perfect Niagara of flushing closets. We did it again. And again. It was a *feu de joie* of w.c.'s. The O.C. and the bigwig scampered inside again. We never heard a word about it. That taught him to keep us in on Dominion Day."

"Tasset, I'm going to make a life's work out of it! If it kills me I'm going to squelch this notion that there is anything meritorious about simplicity on the stage. I proclaim the Baroque, Tasset! I laud the daedal!"

"But if Thickpenny was a man of iron, Mackilwraith, I was not. For you must know that I, too, had my following. 'That dear little boy,' ladies would exclaim, and want to kiss me. Now, Mackilwraith, it was in a place in Montana called Butte, that a very beautiful woman, a superb creature of about thirty-five, I suppose, caught me at a party and kissed me to such purpose that my voice broke on the voyage home. And that is why I refuse to get stewed up about any woman's honour. What about my honour, such as it was at the age of eleven? Worse still, what about my voice? For once it was gone the Dean made my life a perfect misery. But you can't say my American tour wasn't educative."

Catch as catch can, and every man for himself, the conversation spun on through the night. Only Hector was silent, nodding from time to time and allowing his glass to be filled almost without protest. At five o'clock they went home, Roger to appear at a lecture at nine, Humphrey to sleep till noon, and Hector to greet a class which found him pale, inattentive and apt to desert them while he sought the drinking fountain.

CHAPTER
6

EIGHT DAYS before the first night of *The Tempest* the following advertisement appeared in the Salterton evening paper for the last of five successive publications;

And for this fifth appearance the following note was appended to the advertisement:

190

This addition to the auction notice was printed in no larger type than the rest of the advertisement, but it caught a surprising number of eyes on the Tuesday when it appeared. Anything which concerns a subject dear to us seems to leap from a large page of print. Freddy Webster, who was no careful reader of newspapers, saw it, and snorted like a young warhorse.

"Giving away books!" said she. "But only to preachers! Damn!"

Later that evening she met Solly, who was in the garden wondering, as all directors of outdoor performances of *The Tempest* must, whether the arrangements for the storm-tossed ship in the first scene of the play would provoke the audience to such derisive laughter that they would rise in a body and demand the return of their money at the gate.

"Yes, I saw it," he said in answer to her question. "Pretty rotten, confining it to the clergy. Not that I care about Philosophy, or Theology, or even Superior Fiction. But there might just be something tucked away in Miscellaneous which would be lost on the gentlemen of the cloth."

"Whatever made Valentine do it?"

"Apparently, two or three years ago, the old chap said something, just in passing, about wanting his books dealt with that way. And they're quite unsaleable, you know. A bookseller wouldn't give five cents apiece for the lot."

"Have you seen them, Solly?"

"No; but you know how hard it is to get rid of books. Especially Theology. Nothing changes fashion so quickly as Theology."

"But there might just be a treasure or two among them."

"I know."

"Still, I don't suppose a preacher would know a really valuable book if he saw one. They'll go for the concordances and commentaries on the Gospels. Do you suppose Val would let us look through what's left?"

"Freddy, my innocent poppet, there won't be anything left. They'll strip the shelves. Anything free has an irresistible fascination. Free books to preachers will be like free booze to politicians; they'll scoop the lot, without regard for quality. You mark my words."

Freddy recognized the truth of what he said. She herself was a victim of that lust for books which rages in the breast like a demon, and which cannot be stilled save by the frequent and plentiful acquistion of books. This passion is more common, and more powerful, than most people suppose. Book lovers are thought by unbookish people to be gentle and unworldly, and perhaps a few of them are so. But there are others who will lie and scheme and steal to get books as wildly and unconscionably as the dope-taker in pursuit of his drug. They may not want the books to read immediately, or at all; they want them to possess, to range on their shelves, to have at command. They want books as a Turk is thought to want concubines—not to be hastily deflowered, but to be kept at their master's call, and enjoyed more often in thought than in reality. Solly was in a measure a victim of this unscrupulous passion, but Freddy was wholly in the grip of it.

Still, she had her pride. She would not beg Valentine to regard her as a member of the clergy for a day; she would not even hang about the house in a hinting manner. She would just drop in, and if the conversation happened to turn upon books, as some scholarly rural dean fingered a rare volume, she would let it be known, subtly, that she was deeply interested in them, and then—well, and then she would see what happened.

With this plan in view she was at the residence of the late Dr. Adam Savage at five minutes to ten on the following morning, dismayed to find that an astounding total of two hundred and seventeen clergymen were there before her, waiting impatiently on the lawn. They ranged from canons of the cathedral, in shovel hats and the grey flannels which the more worldly Anglicans affect in summer, through Presbyterians and ministers of the United Church in black coats and Roman collars, to the popes and miracle workers of back-street sects, dressed in everything under the sun. There was a young priest, a little aloof from the others, who had been instructed by his bishop to bespeak a copy of *The Catholic Encyclopaedia* which was known to be in the house, for a school library. There were two rabbis, one with a beard and one without, chatting with the uneasy geniality of men who expect shortly to compete in a race for a shelf of books on the Pentateuch. There were High Anglicans with crosses on their watch chains, and low Anglicans with moustaches. There were sixteen Divinity students, not yet ordained, but trying to look sanctified in dark suits. There was a stout man in a hot brown suit, wearing a clerical stock with a wing collar; upon his head sat a jaunty grey hat, in the band of which was fixed a small metal aeroplane; it was impossible to say what he was, but he wore a look of confidence which bespoke an early training in salesmanship. There was a mild man with a pince-nez, who was whispered to be a Chistian Science practitioner. There was no representative of the Greek Orthodox, the Syrian or Coptic Churches; otherwise Chistianity in its utmost variety was assembled on that lawn.

It was never discovered how clergymen for a radius of fifty miles around Salterton got wind of Dr. Savage's post-humous bounty. The local newspaper took the great assembly of holy men as a tribute to the power of its advertising columns; indeed, as Freddy approached, a press photographer was climbing into a tree to take a picture of the extraordinary sight. However, the orgulous pride of newspapers is widely understood. The gossips of Salterton decided, after several weeks of discussion, that the matter was beyond any rational explanation, but that the Christian Church must be better organized, and more at one on certain matters, than they had thought.

At five minutes past ten, when the clergy were beginning to buzz like bees, a car stopped in front of the lawn and young Mr. Maybee and Valentine climbed out of it. They were a good deal surprised and discomposed to find a crowd waiting for them, and hurried to open the front door. It had been their intention to sit quietly in the library at a table, arranging some final details of the sale and welcoming the occasional clergyman who might drop in for a book. Instead they were closely followed up the steps, not rudely, but as cattle follow a farmer with a pail of hot mash. When the door was opened the clergy increased their pace, still without rudeness, but with a kind of hungry fervour, and Valentine and young Mr. Maybee found that they were entering the library at a brisk trot. It was a room of moderate size, and might perhaps have held fifty people when full. Seventy rushed into it in sixty seconds, and the remainder crowded as close to the entry as they could.

One does not describe the activity of clergymen in a library as looting. They were, in the main, quiet and well-bred men, and it was in a quiet and well-bred manner that they went to work. The pushing was of a moderate order, and the phrase "Excuse me" was often heard. Natural advantages, such as long arms, superior height, and good eyesight were given rein, but there was no actual snatching nor were the old intentionally trodden upon. No very wide choice, no thoughtful ranging of the shelves, was possible in such a crush, and with good-humoured philosophy the visitors seized whatever was nearest. There were a few friendly disagreements; a shovel hat and the brown suit had each got hold of five volumes of a nicely bound ten-volume set of the works of a Scottish metaphysician, and neither could see why the other should not yield his portion. The rabbis, pushed into a corner where there was little but New Testament material, struggled feebly to reach their Promised Land, without knowing precisely where it was to be found. The young priest found his encyclopaedia, but it was too bulky to be moved at one time, and he knew that it would be fatal to leave any part of it behind him, in the hope of making a second trip. An elderly Presbyterian fainted, and young Mr. Maybee had to appeal in a loud voice for help to lift him through the window into the open air; Valentine took her chance to crawl out to the lawn, in the wake of the invalid.

"What shall we do?" she asked the auctioneer, who was a nice young man, and supposedly accustomed to dominating crowds.

"God knows," said Mr. Maybee; "I've never seen anything like it."

"You must cope," said Valentine, firmly.

Mr. Maybee climbed back upon the windowsill. "Gentlemen," he called in loud voice, "will those who have chosen their books please leave as quickly as possible and allow the others to come in? There is no need to crowd; the library will be open all day."

This was no more effective than a bus-driver's request to "Step right down to the rear, please." The clergy at the door would not budge, and the clergy in the library would not attempt to leave until they had filled their pockets and heaped their arms impossibly high. Young Mr. Maybee at last climbed down from the windowsill, and confessed defeat to Valentine.

There are times when every woman is disgusted by the bonelessness of men. Valentine had, in her time, directed outdoor pageants with as many as five hundred supernumeraries in the crowd scenes. She quickly climbed upon the window-ledge herself.

"This won't do," she cried in a loud, fierce voice. "You must follow my directions to the letter, or I shall have to call the police. Or perhaps the Fire Department," she added, noticing that the magical word "police" had done its work upon these ministers of peace. "All those in the hall go to the lawn at once." With some muttering, the brethren in the hall did as they were bid. "Now," she cried, to the crowd in the library, "you must take the books you have chosen and leave by the back door." In three minutes the library was empty.

By half-past eleven two hundred and thirty-six clergymen had passed through the library, some of them three and four times, and the shelves were bare. Dr. Savage's bequest had been somewhat liberally interpreted, for an inkwell, a pen tray, two letter files, two paperweights, a small bust of Homer, a packet of blotters and an air-cushion which had been in the swivel chair were gone, as well. The widest interpretation had been placed on the word "library" in the advertisement, for some of the visitors had invaded the upstairs regions and made off with two or three hundred detective novels which had been in the old scholars's bedroom. Even a heap of magazines in the cellarway had been removed.

"I don't think there is a scrap of printed matter left in the house," said young Mr. Maybee.

He was mistaken. After the rehearsal that night Valentine sat on the lawn with several of the cast of the play who wanted to hear about the adventures of the morning. A picture and an account of the distribution of Dr. Savage's library had appeared in the newspaper, but rumours were abroad that clergy had come to blows, that a Presbyterian had been struck down with thrombosis while taking *Calvin on the Evangelists* from a high shelf, that a book of photographs called *Nudes of All Nations*, which had appeared unexpectedly at the back of a shelf of exegesis, had been whisked away under the coat of a bachelor curate, that *Voltaire's Works* in twenty-four octavo volumes had been seized by a Baptist fundamentalist and thrown from an upstairs window to his wife, who was waiting on the lawn with a sack—the range of speculation was limited only by the fancy of the people of Salterton. Valentine was able to set their minds at rest, though in doing so she lowered the spirits of several anti-clericals and Antinomians among her hearers.

"Nothing really wild happened," said she; "it was all quite orderly, after the beginning, though it was amazingly quick and a bit dishevelled at times."

"But every book went?" said Freddy.

"Not even that. Every book that could be seen went, but when Mr. Maybee and I began a complete clear-out of grandfather's vault we found about ten or twelve more books. They were stored away very neatly in a wooden box; somebody had even wrapped them in brown paper. I can't imagine why; they looked like the most awful junk. Victorian novels in three volumes, and that sort of thing."

"They sound fascinating," said Griselda. "I love Victorian novels."

"These aren't really good ones," said Valentine. "Nothing, I mean, that anybody would want to read. I looked at one or two. We've put them in the sale, as a single lot."

The conversation had passed to other things. But Hector had heard. If Griselda liked Victorian novels he would get these for her. It would be a distinguished gift—not expensive, but a sign of his attentiveness to her tastes. Besides, books were always a safe gift; in his journey through the world Hector had somewhere picked up the information that only books, candy and flowers might be given to a lady without seriously compromising her honour.

Freddy had heard, also. If Dr. Savage thought enough of a handful of books to keep them in his vault, they were worth her investigation. Imagine Valentine putting them in the sale without so much as a thought! What ignoramuses theatre people were! Before Freddy went to bed that night she carefully counted her money. She did not expect to have to pay a big price, but she wanted to know just where she stood. Reading a favourite chapter of *Life Through the Neck of a Bottle* before she went to sleep, she was conscious of a warm glow—a book-collector's glow when he thinks he may be on the track of a good thing. Old books, old wine—how few of us there are, she reflected, who really appreciate these things.

The following day, the Thursday before the sale, was an anxious and difficult one for Hector. At lunchtime he hurried to Dr. Savage's house, feeling guiltily conspicuous, as some men do when they are upon an errand connected in their minds (but in nobody else's) with love. There were few people about, and he quickly found what he was looking for; it was a box which had, long ago in the past, served for shipping of a small typewriter; the maker's name was painted on its sides. Within it were several books, neatly wrapped in brown paper; Hector lifted one out and began to unwrap it.

"Mus' ast yuh not t' handle the stuff," said a voice behind him. It was an employee of Elliot and Maybee, a seedy man who smelled of beer.

"I merely want to see what these books are," said Hector.

"Tha's all right. My instructions are, mus' ast yuh not t' handle the stuff."

"But how can I tell what this is unless I look?"

"T'ain't nothing. Just books."

"But what books?"

"Dunno. Mus' jus' ast yuh not t'handle the stuff."

"Is there anyone in charge here?"

"Eh?"

"Who is in charge here?"

"Me. Now lookit, Joe, we don't want no trouble. You jus' slip away, see, like you was never here. Don't want yuh handlin' the stuff."

Hector was not an expert in the management of men, but occasionally he had an inspiration. He reached into his pocket and took out a dollar.

"Let me see what these books are, and it's yours," said he.

"Okay, Joe. But we don't want no trouble, see?"

Hector unwrapped several of the books. They were old, undoubtedly, and they had a musty smell. He had a notion that really old books were bound in leather; these were bound in dingy cloth, and the gold on their bindings was faded. Still, if Griselda wanted them, he would see that she got them. He gave the beery attendant the dollar, and an extra twenty-five cents.

"May I use the telephone?" said he. He was shown that instrument, which Dr. Savage, after the custom of his generation, had kept decently out of sight in a low, dark cupboard under the stairs. The mouthpiece looked as though it had not been cleaned in the twenty years of its installation. After a long and rather complicaed conversation with a girl in the office of Elliot and Maybee, he extracted a promise that she would ask old Mr. Elliot not to put the box of books up for sale until at least a quarter past four on the following day; she could make no promises; she could not say exactly when Mr. Elliot himself was likely to be in the office; Mr. Maybee had gone to the country on business; he could try to talk to Mr. Elliot after four o'clock, but she could promise nothing.

Hot and annoyed and frustrated, Hector escaped from the black hole under the stairs just in time to hurry back to school for the afternoon session. His stomach was upset. He had still to make his arrangements with Pimples Buckle.

Under ordinary circumstances nothing would have persuaded Hector to visit such a person as Pimples Buckle, who was Salterton's nearest approach to a gangster. But Pimples was reputed to be able to provide what Hector, at this moment in his life, wanted more than anything else in the world —a card of admission to the June Ball.

The June Ball was the glory of Salterton's social year. Given by the cadets of the great military College which lay at the eastern entrance to the city, it had for many years been surrounded in the highest degree by that atmosphere of smartness and social distinction with which the military so cleverly invest their merry-makings. In Salterton, to be asked to it was to be a person of social consequence; not to be asked to it was to be a nobody. The invitations sent out by the cadets themselves were, of course, to young ladies who had entertained them, in one way or another, during the year; there were cadets so dead to all decent feeling that they invited girls from other cities, but the majority were properly sensible of the great cubic footage of cake and the vast gallonage of tea which they had consumed on Sunday afternoons, and they did their duty—often an extremely pleasant duty. Other guests, distinguished persons from out-of-town and the nobility and gentry of Salterton, were asked by the Commandant and his staff. There were those who said it was easy to get an invitation; there were others, and Hector was one of them, who found it the hardest thing in the world.

He wanted to go, of course, because Griselda would be there. Had not Roger declared, during that memorable night at Solly's, that he was taking her? The Ball, indeed, had split the cast of *The Tempest* into sheep and goats: most of them were going, and The Torso had received a choice of five escorts; Valentine had been asked, as a distinguished visitor to the town, and anyhow, as Dr. Savage's grand-daughter, she had a prescriptive right to an invitation; all the girls in the cast had been asked, and even Miss Wildfang was to be present as the partner of a professor who liked well-matured women; even Geordie was to be there, through some miscarriage of social justice, for he announced with a wink that he had drag in a certain quarter. The Leakeys had had no invitation, and expected none; indeed, Mrs. Leakey made this a point of perverse pride, telling the world that she was no high-flyer, whatever other people might be. Professor Vambrace had received an invitation for himself and his wife and daughter, and had refused it without consulting either of them, assuming that they would not wish to be present. Everybody who wanted an invitation, it appeared, had received one. Several of Hector's colleagues at the school had been invited, and it was to the head of the English department, Mr. Adams, that he first turned for advice.

"Just suppose," he said in a falsely jocular tone, "that I wanted a bid to the Ball; where could I get one?" He thought that "bid" was rather good; just the right note of casualness.

"Well," said Mr. Adams, who was not at all deceived; "you might be able to get a card from somebody who had one and decided not to use it. That's sometimes done."

"Oh? As a matter of fact, I had thought of going, just to see what it's like. You don't know anybody who has a spare card, I suppose?"

"Not a soul. There's one thing you have to be careful about, of course; if they spot you at the door with somebody else's card, they'll ask you to leave at once."

"Oh? As stiff as that, eh?"

"Oh, very stiff. You know how these military people are. Why, I once saw a man tapped on the shoulder and asked to leave just as he was making his bow to the Commandant's wife. He turned as red as a beet, and slipped away. Several people laughed as he passed. I'd hate to put myself in that position."

"Yes; yes indeed," said Hector, reflecting sombrely on this disgrace, which was entirely Mr. Adams' invention. If Griselda were to see, or even hear, that he had been attempting to get to the Ball on false pretences! He would never be able to explain it.

Still, there must be some way. He turned next to Geordie.

"Of course, my card is strictly legitimate," said Geordie.

"Of course," said Hector.

"Still, I've heard of people getting to the Ball in all sorts of funny ways. Some are smuggled in in the rumble seats of cars. I knew a fellow once who drove over in a truck, with a white coat on; said he was taking ice-cream to the caterer; drove round to the back, took off the white coat and tripped the light fantastic till three, laid a girl from Montreal in the shrubbery, and was in the group photo at five, having had a swell time. And sometimes people row across the harbour in boats; they haven't any guards along the shore, you know; just beach the boat and walk in."

Hector did not think that any of these bold ruses would suit him.

"Of course, there are always a few invitations to be had, if you want them bad enough," said Geordie, with the air of rectitude which becomes a man whose invitation is strictly legitimate.

"How do you get them?" said Hector.

"It's entirely a matter of money."

"Yes; I expected that. Who has them?"

"Well, don't tell anybody I told you, but Pimples Buckle always has a few."

Hector had not been permitted, at his first visit, to see Pimples himself. He had talked with a dark, greasy young man, who wore sidewhiskers and a dirty sweatshirt, in the office of Uneeda Taxi, which was the legitimate part of Pimples' business. Unwillingly he had revealed to the young man what he wanted, and the young man had chewed a match and looked at him with scorn.

"Ain't no use talkin' to Pimples now," he had said. "Come back the day before the dance."

"You'll tell him what I want?"

"Yeah."

"Shall I 'phone him before I come in?"

"Naw. Pimples don't like the 'phone. Don't be a dope. And bring cash."

"How much?"

"Dunno. Better bring plenty."

At half past four on the day before the ball Hector stood in the inner office of Uneeda Taxi, and Pimples Buckle sat with his feet on a rolltop desk.

"Well prof," said he, "so you want a ticket to the Big Ball."

"Yes," said Hector.

"What's the matter? Did yours get lost in the mail?"

"I have no invitation. That's why I'm here."

"Oh, so that's why you're here, eh? Funny, I was wondering what brought you."

"I supposed you knew. I left a message with your man outside."

"Wop? Yeah, he told me you'd been in. But what I want to know is this: what makes you think I've got any tickets, eh?"

"Somebody said you usually had a few."

"Jeeze, the stories that get around. Why, prof, don't you know I could get into a lotta trouble selling tickets to the Ball? And you'd get in trouble too; you'd be an accessory after the fact, and you'd be compounding a felony, and Jeeze knows what else."

"Have you any tickets?"

"Not so fast, prof. You remember me, don't you?"

"Yes, I remember you."

"Yeah, you was new at the school the last year I was there. I was in one of your classes. Algebra. And you remember what you used to tell us? Take it easy, you used to say; just take it easy. Well, prof, you take it easy now. Would you like to sit down?"

"Thank you, I would."

"Well, you can't because there ain't no chair." Pimples chuckled with enjoyment. "Now, prof, why do you want to go to this Ball?"

"Is that any affair of yours?"

"I'll say it is. You don't look the type, somehow. Who's the broad?"

"The —?"

"The dame. What's a guy like you want to go to the Ball for if it ain't to take some dame? You want to romance her under the stars, prof?"

"If you will sell me a ticket, let's do it now."

"Jeeze, you're touchy. Most fellows your age would be complimented to think somebody thought they was after a dame. Are you getting plenty of what she's got?"

"What is your price?"

"Very special to you prof. Fifty bucks. I always treat my old teachers right."

"Fifty!"

"Sure. This ain't no two-bit belly-rub you're going to, y'know."

Sick with humiliation and outraged prudence, Hector counted out five ten-dollar notes. Pimples reached into an inner pocket and produced an envelope, from which he drew an engraved and crested card in the upper left-hand corner of which was written, in an official hand, "Hector Mackilwraith, Esq."

"Make sure you get your fifty bucks worth outa the broad," he said, winking cheerily, as Hector hurried from the room.

There was a very good crowd at the auction, which was gratifying to young Mr. Maybee, for he had worked hard to persuade old Mr. Elliot that the day of the Ball was a good day to hold it. Mr. Elliot, product of a more leisurely age, had insisted that every woman of the sort who might be expected to attend the sale of a professor's effects would be at home on such an afternoon, lying in a darkened room with pads of cotton soaked in ice-water upon her eyes. Mr. Maybee had assured his partner that, on the contrary, all of Salterton would be keyed up and eager for amusement, and what was more amusing than an auction in June? He had carried his point, and here was the crowd to prove it.

The morning sale, when the bedroom furnishings and kitchen effects had been sold, had been successful; the goods had brought within fifty dollars of what he had privately estimated, and he congratulated himself on good selling and good reckoning. This afternoon he hoped to do a little better than his estimate. Like an actor, or a concert performer, he put out his feelers—his sensitive auctioneer's antennae—to receive intuitions from his audience. It was a good audience, alert, receptive to suggestion, and sufficiently excited by the thought of the approaching Ball to be ready to bid freely. After a few deep breaths to refresh his voice, Mr. Maybee stepped upon his auctioneer's rostrum, and looked out over the lawn at the bidders, the curiosity seekers, the amateurs of auctions, some standing, some perched on shooting sticks. He rapped upon the table with his pencil, and promptly at two o'clock the afternoon sale began.

It was not, Mr. Maybee recognized, a great sale. Old Dr. Savage had owned no treasures. His furniture had been very good in its time, but like many people who live to a great age, the old scholar had become indifferent to his household belongings; Mr. Maybee's trained eye told him that nothing of consequence in the house had been bought after 1925; most of the furnishing had been done about 1905. The leather chairs had scuffed, scabby surfaces; a velvet-covered sofa, upon which the Doctor had taken his afternoon nap for many years, showed all too plainly at one end that he had done so with his boots on, and at the other that he had drooled as he slept. The furniture seemed to have died with its owner; chairs which had looked well enough in the house showed weak legs when held up for sale; water-colours which had looked inoffensive on the walls seemed, on this sunny day, to be all of weak and ill-defined blues and greys, like old men's eyes. But Mr. Maybee was not discouraged. He knew what people would buy.

To the surprise of everyone except Mr. Maybee, the large pieces of furniture went cheap, and the trinkets went dear. A large and ugly oak dining table, with ten chairs and a hideous sideboard, went for forty-five dollars; a tea-wagon brought forty-two. A couple of lustre jugs, which Valentine could not remember seeing before, fetched the astonishing sum of thirty-six dollars for the pair. The silver sold well, for though it was ugly, it was sterling. A mantel clock, presented to Dr. Savage thirty years before by the Waverley Philosophical Society, brought a staggering initial bid of fifty dollars, and went at last for eighty, though it had never been known to keep time. A kitchen clock, which Mr. Maybee waggishly announced would keep either Standard or Daylight Saving Time, was sold to an Indian from a nearby reservation for six dollars, which was four dollars more than it was worth. A bundle of walking-sticks was sold to a sentimentalist who had learned a little elementary philosophy from the Doctor many years before, for five dollars. A Bechstein piano which had belonged to Valentine's grandmother was bid for briskly after Mr. Maybee had played a spirited polka on it, and brought three hundred dollars. A teak workbox, described by Mr. Maybee as the life's work of a life prisoner in the nearby penitentiary, brought a beggarly four dollars, which the auctioneer mentally estimated to be about ten cents for every pound of its weight.

Freddy enjoyed the sale thoroughly. She wondered, however, how long it would be before the wooden box of books would be offered. But Hector's message had been received by Mr. Elliot, who had passed it on to Mr. Maybee, and it was not until half-past four that it appeared. By that time Hector was standing at the back of the crowd.

"A box of books, ladies and gentlemen. I cannot offer you a more exact description. As you know, Dr. Savage's library was given away yesterday, according to his own wish, to the clergy of Salterton. (There was some laughter here, which Mr. Maybee rebuked with his eye.) "These few remaining books were discovered in the Doctor's vault after that disposal. Anyone who wishes a sentimental souvenir of a great scholar and gentleman cannot do better than acquire this lot. What am I bid?. . . Come along, there's a spice of mystery about this box; you don't know what you'll get. . . . What do I hear? Who'll say a dollar for a starter? A dollar, a dollar, a dollar—do I hear a dollar?"

"Fifty cents," said Freddy, and blushed fiercely as people turned to look at her.

"I have fifty. Who'll say a dollar? A dollar for the mystery box. Come on, you can't lose. At least ten books here, each one worth a dollar apiece. A dollar, a dollar, a dollar. Aha, I have a dollar. Thank you sir."

Freddy turned towards the bidder. Old Mackilwraith! What did he want books for? He didn't look as though he ever read anything but examination papers. Except menus, she thought spitefully. She caught Mr. Maybee's eye, and nodded firmly.

"Two; two, two. I have two dollars for the mystery box."

Hey, thought Freddy; I meant another fifty cents.

"Three; three; three. The gentleman at the back offers me three."

Freddy nodded again.

Hector was quite as much annoyed as Freddy. What did she want with those books? Should he hurry to her and tell her that he was buying them for her sister? But the bidding was moving too quickly. The box was now at ten dollars, and the bid was Freddy's. He nodded again. Eleven dollars! It was ridiculous.

Mr. Maybee was delighted. It was such odd contests at this time which made his life a pleasure, and picked up the sums which he could not realize from old-fashioned dining-room sets and scabrous old couches. The bidding proceeded briskly, and he knew that he had two stubborn people on his hook.

The box now stood at eighteen dollars. As Hector raised it to nineteen, Freddy made a great decision. She had only twenty dollars, but she could not be beaten; she had to have the box, now. She would simply go on, and explain to Daddy how matters had stood. Surely he would understand. He wouldn't want her to be beaten in public, like this. And even if he didn't understand he would have to pay up; he couldn't let her go to jail. People would say he had neglected her, and make a delinquent of her.

"Twenty," said she, boldly.

"Twenty-one," said Hector, and his face was flushed so deeply that it seemed in danger of going quite black.

On the bidding went until Freddy was at twenty-eight. She faltered. Thirty dollars was a terrible sum of money to pay for a box of—what? It might be old hymn-books for all she knew. Her eyeballs were very hot, and she was afraid that she might cry. But she wouldn't. She closed her lips firmly and looked down at the grass.

"I have twenty-nine. Twenty-nine dollars in this epic contest between two people who really know their literature! Do I hear thirty? All through at twenty-nine? Another dollar may do the trick! Am I all through at twenty-nine?"

Hector hated Freddy with the deadly hate of a man who had been made a fool of by a petty gangster, and who was now, twenty-four hours later, being made a fool of by a child. Hector was not mean, but the circumstances of his life had made him careful with money; it was the sinew of every success he had ever known. Fifty dollars to Pimples Buckle and now, twenty-nine dollars for these books! Even the children of the Webster family, it appeared, had long purses. But he had beaten her!

"Ah, I have thirty! Thank you sir. Thirty; thirty; thirty. Will you say thirty-one?"

Hector said thirty-one almost without thinking, as he sought the new bidder. There he was. A Jew! Hector became anti-Semitic in a fraction of a second.

The new bidder was, quite plainly, a Jew. A calm, bold man with a cigar, he had been unnoticed in the crowd until this moment.

The bidding rose, dollar by dollar, as Hector sweat nervous drops which seemed to draw his strength from him. The books were with the stranger, at forty. On Hector plunged, and a dreadful headache seized him. The crowd was delighted. Mr. Maybee almost sang.

The books were with Hector at forty-nine. The stranger bobbed his head. Hector could bear no more. He was beset by fiends. In a blasphemous moment he permitted himself not to care whether Griselda had Victorian novels to read or not.

"Sold at fifty, to the gentleman with the cigar!"

There was a flutter of applause, mingled with some sounds of disapproval. The contest for the books had been enlivening, but a Salterton audience was not sure that it was suitable that the victory should go to a stranger. It was widely felt that the Jew, though a bold bidder, had shown himself a little too pushing. There were few things to be sold after the box of books, and by five o'clock most of the crowd had gone.

When the unknown bidder sought out the clerk after the sale, to pay his money and claim his books, he found Hector and Freddy waiting for him.

"Do you mind telling me why you wanted that box?" said Hector, more angrily than was wise.

"Surely you know why," said the stranger, coolly.

"No, I don't."

"Then why did you bid on it yourself?"

"I wanted those books for a special purpose."

"And so do I," said the stranger. It was at this moment that Valentine joined them. She too wanted to know why so much had been bid for a box to which she had given no thought.

"Oh, surely you know," said the stranger. It took the three of them a few minutes to convince him that they knew nothing at all about it, and had not given the box more than a cursory examination. His eyelids drooped a little, and he smiled.

"You really ought to be more careful," he said to Valentine. "Let me show you what I mean."

He reached into the box and pulled out a package, which he unwrapped.

"You see," said he; "*Under Two Flags,* in three volumes, published by Chapman and Hall in 1867; in very good condition. Doesn't that mean anything to you?"

"Not a thing," said Valentine. "It's by Ouida, isn't it?"

"Yes. It is quite a valuable book. Now look at this: *East Lynne*, by Mrs. Henry Wood; published by Tinsley in 1861. Very nice."

"Valuable?" asked Freddy.

"Not so valuable as the other, by a long shot. But worth about a hundred and fifty dollars."

There was a heavy silence. Young Mr. Maybee had joined the group, and his nice blue eyes opened very wide at the mention of this sum.

"But you really should have been careful of this," said the stranger, unwrapping three more volumes. "You see: *Lady Audley's Secret*; the author's name is not given, but it was M. E. Braddon; published by Skeet in 1862. This really is a treasure."

"How much?" It was Valentine who spoke this time.

"Hard to say. At a rough guess I would put it at about twenty-five hundred dollars. I spotted them at once when I was looking around yesterday. Pure luck, or perhaps flair; I'm here for a brief holiday, but I never take complete holidays. I am sorry about this, but if you had wanted to keep it you should not have put it up at auction, should you?"

Neither Valentine nor Mr. Maybee had anything to say. The stranger transferred the books to a briefcase which he carried, and in doing so revealed an envelope which lay at the bottom of the box. It was addressed to Valentine in her grandfather's hand. She read it at once.

My dear—

As I fear that you will find little among my things that you may wish to keep, I leave you these books, which I have had by me for some time. You can easily take them back to the States with you, and if you take them to a good bookseller—a really good one—he will give you a price for them which may surprise you. Look upon this as a special bequest from me, and one upon

which you will not have to pay inheritance tax.
                                    With my fondest love
                                                          A.S.

"Well, I shall say good-bye," said the stranger. "If you ever happen to be in New York, and are interested in rare books, I shall be happy to show you what I have in my shop. Here is my card."

Only Mr. Maybee had the presence of mind to take it. The group broke up, and four of them went their different ways with painful and conflicting thoughts buzzing in their heads.

Long before the light began to fade on this beautiful June day the ladies of Salterton were dressing themselves for the dinner parties which came before the Ball. Already in the composing room of the local newspaper the long galleys of type were ranged in which their gowns were described, for the Society Editor had been busy on the telephone for three days past. Every lady who was to be present at the great affair had been called, and asked for a description of what she would wear; in some cases this call was inspired by courtesy rather than curiosity, for particularly among the older ladies it was not unknown for a gown to make several annual appearances, and the Society Editor could have done much of her work by simply consulting the back files. The descriptions which appeared were very brief; they conveyed nothing, to the stranger, of the real appearance of some of these remarkable garments; but to the informed reader they were rich in information. The briefest extract will suffice:

Mrs. A. M. Mangin: lilac crepe, with lamé panel to tone. Miss Dymphna M'Dumphy: rust satin, with scarf in the M'Dumphy tartan, and a parure of cairngorms. Mrs. Shakerley Marmion: wine velvet. Mrs. M. Medbourne: écru shantung, with panels of self-coloured lace. Mrs. E. P. Moubray: amethyst cut velvet. Mrs. James Mylne: pleated puce crepe, with inserts of Paddy green moire . . . etc., etc.

The persistent reader, seeking information about the ladies associated with the Little Theatre's forthcoming production, might have compiled his own paragraph, thus:

Mrs. Roscoe Forrester: champagne lace. Miss Valentine Rich: flame taffeta. Miss Bonnie-Susan Tompkins: a strapless peach satin, with slit skirt. Miss Pearl Vambrace: pink organdie with puff sleeves. Miss Griselda Webster: white silk jersey, with Greek drapery.

The newspaper never made any mention of what the escorts of the ladies wore; it went without saying that they wore evening dress of every cut known during the past fifty years, and that the military wore dress uniforms, some of which had been made during their slimmer days, so that the trousers had been augmented at the back with gussets which were not always a perfect match.

Since half-past five Pearl Vambrace had been in her bedroom with the door locked. At three o'clock she had taken a long and elaborate bath, in the course of which she made a violent assault upon her armpits with her father's razor. She had then composed herself for a nap, for she had read in a magazine that in order to look radiant at night, it was necessary to rest in the afternoon; such rest delayed the onset of crow's feet, the article said, and Pearl, at nineteen, was determined to show no crow's feet when she appeared at the Ball with Solly.

As she lay on her bed, trying to relax completely, she thought how astonishing it had been that Solly had asked her to go to the Ball with him. She had never, even in dreams, expected that Roger would ask her. He never seemed to pay any attention to her at all. At rehearsals he took her in his arms, and kissed her in the manner prescribed by Valentine, and although this experience terrified and ravished her it did nothing to make Roger less of a stranger: so must some maiden of the ancient world have felt when Jove descended and absent-mindedly made her his own. Even in the two private rehearsals, in her home, which Professor Vambrace had been able to impose upon the reluctant Roger, he had paid little attention to her. No, it was beyond the range of belief that Roger would ask her to go to the Ball with him, and when Pearl heard that Griselda was to be his partner she was too miserable even to be jealous. And then, astonishingly, Solly had asked her to go to the Ball with him, and shortly afterward a note had arrived from his mother, inviting her to dinner beforehand.

Relaxing completely was hard work. Try as she might to make herself heavy, and pretend that she was sinking through the bed, as the magazine had directed, she continued to twitch and jump unexpectedly. She would look dreadful at the Ball, she was sure—a mass of wrinkles, hollows and haggard shadows. And breath! Gargle as she might before going to the Bridgetowers', how would she make sure afterward that her breath was—how did the advertisements put it?—"free of offence"? Could she slip her toothbrush and a tube of paste into her evening bag? She must sleep! She had a long and doubtless gay evening before her, in the company of a young man whom she scarcely knew. And even before the Ball began she had a dinner party! She had never been to a dinner party in her life, and she had heard that Mrs. Bridgetower was a lady who demanded a high standard of elegant behaviour from her guests. She must relax! She must! In her efforts to relax Pearl twisted herself into a ball, and closed her eyes so tightly that the red darkness behind her eyelids seemed to writhe and surge.

Her misgivings would have been greater if she had had any idea of what had been in progress at the Bridgetower home during the past week. Solly had no particular desire to go to the Ball, but his mother had accepted their joint invitation on his behalf as well as her own. He felt that, if Griselda were to be there with Roger, he might as well be there himself, to keep an eye on her. But with whom? He must have a partner. His mother, in a fit of unaccustomed perverseness, had declared that it was impossible that he should go with her alone. He must have a suitable girl, and she would accompany them in the role of dowager and chaperone. But what girl? Cora Fielding was bespoken. Any other girl whose name he suggested was for one reason or another black-balled by his mother. Finally, in a fit of rebellion, he asked Pearl, whom he hardly knew, and when she regained her powers of speech she said, very politely, that she would be delighted.

Then the fat was in the fire! His mother had risen to new and, to her, refreshing heights of satire when he told her who his partner was to be. She had then decided that, whatever impossible social situations her son might prepare for her, she would comport herself with dignity and according to the rules of etiquette which she recognized. It was out of the question that the Vambraces should invite Solly to dinner before the Ball: therefore she would give a dinner party, and invite Pearl. It would not be a large party; her health would not permit of such a thing. But she would invite young Lieutenant Swackhammer, an officer in the Royal Canadian Navy who was the son of a cousin of her husband's, and whoever he was taking to the Ball with him. This was, she later learned, a Miss Tompkins, to whom she sent a note of invitation.

Cruel things were said of Pearl Vambrace. Mrs. Bridgetower insinuated that she had ugly legs, although her legs were graceful enough. Griselda had told her father that Pearl had a moustache, which was untrue, although there was a suggestion on her lip of something which might, in forty years or so, be a small and ladylike moustache. Mrs. Forrester thought that her hair was greasy, but it was not uncommonly so. There was something about Pearl which attracted the malignity of most women; only Valentine Rich had seen that, under proper guidance, she had a quality which was close to beauty. Pearl herself was unconscious of anything of the kind; she had washed the offending hair the night before and rinsed it in water which contained so much lemon juice that it was now rather brittle, and flew about unaccountably. She had invested most of her small savings, painfully gleaned from the sums which her parents occasionally gave her, in some cosmetics, the first that she had ever bought. And by efforts which had been humiliating and exhausting, she had acquired a dress which she thought was suitable for the Ball.

Her parents had not been interested when she told them Solly had asked her to be his partner. Professor Vambrace, who had taken such pains to make his daughter a good talker, did not appear to show this talent. He had come to life, however, when Pearl said that she had nothing which was fit to wear on such an occasion. She had a garment of dark corduroy, with a short skirt, which had been her ceremonial garb since she was fifteen, but she had no ball gown. The Professor had announced that he himself would take this matter in hand, and Mrs. Vambrace was content that it should be so. Therefore the Professor, had marched Pearl into a shop, and had told a salesgirl, firmly, that he wanted a gown suitable for the Ball, and that it must be pink and of a modest design, and must not cost more than thirty-five dollars. There was only one gown answering to these specifications in the shop. Pearl tried it on. Her father stared at her long and hard.

"The straps of your chemise show," said he.

"She'll have to wear a strapless bra," said the salesgirl.

"A what?" asked the Professor.

"I'll fix her up with one," said the girl.

"Don't trouble," said the Professor; "she can tie some ribbons on her under-garment and it will look well enough. It will look better when you are wearing the right shoes," he said.

"These are the best ones I have, Father," said Pearl, who was now thoroughly miserable. Unskilled in matters of dress she knew enough to see that the gown was of a very unpleasant pink, suggestive of measles, and made her dark skin look yellowish.

"Is there to be no end to expense?" asked the Professor, rhetorically. "Have you any slippers in pink satin?"

"Nobody has worn satin slippers for about twenty years," said the girl, who felt for Pearl. But to Pearl it seemed that the whole world of fashion had weighed the Vambrace family, and found it wanting.

At last a pair of slippers had been found which met with the Professor's approval. But they had no toes in them, and that meant a pair of new stockings. They marched home at top speed, and the Professor renewed the oxygen in his blood in a very angry manner. He had quite a lot of money, chiefly because he never spent any of it on his wife and daughter, but Pearl's outfit had run to almost fifty dollars, and he felt himself to be on the verge of bankruptcy. That evening, as they ate a rather nasty potato salad and some sour canned cherries, he had raged like a Savonarola against the vanities of female dress. Pearl, who loved her father, felt that she had ruined him, that she had behaved in a selfish and unworthy fashion, and that she was a sorrow to her parents. It was not until two days later that she could feel any pleasure in the prospect of going to the Ball.

At half-past five she began to dress. Normally she could dress herself for any occasion in three minutes, but she believed that her toilette for her first Ball should be a ceremony, and she was determined to make a ceremony of it. Her sleep had not been a success; indeed, she had never really slept at all, but had lain in a reverie compounded of all the social mishaps and miseries which could befall her in the evening to come. She was glad when it was time to dress.

Everything must be clean. She therefore put on clean underthings, and reflected that they were not very inspiring. She then put on the new stockings, in which her legs looked so well that even Mrs. Bridgetower would have been hard pressed to find fault with them; it was too bad that she had to hitch these glories to a garter-belt which age and many washings had brought to a sad pass. She then put on the pink organdie dress itself, and in her excitement thought that it looked better than it had done in the shop.

It is a measure of Pearl's inexperience in such matters that she put on her dress before she began to make up her face, and set to work without protecting that garment in any way. She laid out her purchases on her chest of drawers, before the mirror with the whorl in it. What should she do first? Cream, was it? She rubbed her face with a medicated sub-

stance which she had economically purchased, and which
was said to improve the complexion, keep away mosquitoes,
and relieve soreness after shaving. There: her face looked
shiny, but you toned that down with powder. She patted a
great deal of powder into the grease; she had chosen a light
shade, to relieve the darkness of her complexion, and the
transformation, she felt, was remarkable. Now what? Rouge,
probably. She had purchased dry rouge, and she patted a
firm spot of it on each of her well-marked cheek-bones. It
was surprising what this did to her eyes; they looked quite
brilliant, almost wild, in fact. Now the eyes themselves. The
girl in the shop had recommended a light eye-shadow, but
Pearl had preferred a rich green, with flecks of gold in it;
she applied this liberally to the sockets of her eyes, below as
well as above. She had read somewhere that makeup, to be
effective, must be put on with boldness as well as subtlety, or
it was of no avail; certainly the eye-shadow made a difference, but no doubt it was designed to look its best under
artificial light. Now eyebrows: the eyebrow pencil which she
had was new, and it took her some time to sharpen it, for the
point kept breaking; her own brows were full, though not
heavy, and had never been plucked; she drew some lines over
them which gave them solidity. Now lipstick, and she would
be finished. She had bought a purplish lipstick, thinking that
it would form a pleasant contrast with the rather chalky pink
of her rouge. She had seen girls put it on; they lathered their
lips generously with the colour, and then bit them. She did
this, and immediately her mouth was a messy wound. With a
soiled handkerchief she scrubbed it off and tried again. The
very light down on her lip—so cruelly referred to by Griselda
as a moustache—caught the colour, and made her look ridiculous. In all, Pearl put on five mouths before she achieved
one which she decided would have to do.

Now hair. She could not dress it neatly, for washing had
taken all the oil out of it, but she had a plan. She had a
piece of ribbon which nearly matched her dress, and she tied
this in a bow on one side of her head, and let her hair hang
down behind it. This showed her ears, which were neat.

She knew now why ladies of high fashion took so long to dress. It was nearly seven o'clock, the hour when Solly had promised to call for her. Ah, there he was below, talking to Father. She seized her coat—her only coat, a much worn garment in light brown, of a vaguely sporting character—and pulled it round her shoulders, hoping that it would look as though she were the casual sort who always wore a sports coat with evening dress. She took up her bag—a rather too capacious bag of dingy red velvet, with a tassel hanging from the bottom, which had belonged to her mother—and ran downstairs. Solly seemed startled to see her, but Professor and Mrs. Vambrace appeared to notice nothing amiss. Professor Vambrace was prepared to act the Fond Father, and Mrs. Vambrace was not a woman who paid much attention to externals.

"Take care of her, Bridgetower; take care of our little one," said the Professor in a voice half jocular, half tearful. "It is the father's heart which is broken at his daughter's first ball." This notion, he thought, was worthy of Barrie, and he was proud of it. He kissed Pearl, with his eyes shut, which may have been as well, and shortly afterward she was with Solly in his mother's car. He said very little, and seemed to Pearl to be strangely apprehensive, but as she shared this feeling she decided that he, like herself, was worried about the evening before them.

"Good evening, my dear. You look sweetly pretty," said Mrs. Bridgetower, as she greeted Pearl in the hall. But Pearl could scarcely answer; she caught sight of herself in a full-length mirror. She looked ill and slightly crazed, with a pink bow on one side of her head, and her eyes aglare. The flush of tuberculosis was on her cheeks, and her mouth looked as though she had eaten untidily of the insane root which takes the reason prisoner.

And her gown! It looked like one of the crepe paper costumes while children wear at Hallowe'en. What should she do? What could she possibly do?

"Hello, Pearl! Gosh, anything for a laugh, eh? That's the

spirit!" The speaker was Bonnie-Susan Tompkins, the partner of Lieutenant Swackhammer; they had followed Mrs. Bridgetower into the hall.

Pearl was stricken. When her hostess suggested that she leave her coat upstairs, she darted upward in unmistakable flight, without waiting for Ada, the elderly maid, to show her the way.

The Torso was a silly girl, and a hoyden, and unseemly in her desire for the attentions of the male. But like many silly, hoydenish, man-crazy girls, she had a great charity within her. One of her admirers had said that she had "a heart as big as a bull", and if this special enlargement carries with it a certain sweetness and generosity of nature, the phrase may be allowed to stand. She ran up the stairs after Pearl. What she did cannot be related here, but in ten minutes they were both in the drawing-room, drinking sherry, and Pearl looked better than she had ever looked in her life; if there was any makeup on her face, it had been applied with The Torso's artful hand. And the relaxation which she had sought earlier in sleep had come now, by this great purgation through self-knowledge and terror.

Mrs. Bridgetower's dinner party was an unforeseen success. She had expected nothing from it, for she disapproved strongly of Pearl Vambrace, whom she had not seen in three years, and she knew nothing of Lieutenant Swackhammer's partner, but feared the worst. And when the Lieutenant had appeared in her drawing-room with The Torso, it seemed to her that matters had gone beyond the limits even of her generous pessimism. Bonnie-Susan wore a gown of peach satin from which her beautiful shoulders emerged in startling nakedness; the creation was held in place, presumably, by some concealed armature, for it had no straps, and although it was impossible to peep down the front of it, the impression which it gave was to the contrary. And as if this were not enough, the skirt was split to the knee in such a way that very little of her left leg was visible at a time, but there was a tantalizing promise of infinite riches. It was a beautiful gown, and had cost her father a lot of money, but it was not a gown to win the approval of the anxious mother of a susceptible son. Mrs. Bridgetower's first words to The Torso were to bid her to come close to the fire, lest she be cold.

The Torso, however, was a girl of a great resource. She knew that the mothers of young men rarely liked her on sight, though she was not sure why this was so, and she had developed a manner which disarmed and often won these natural enemies. She was so frank, so pleasant, that mothers usually decided that they had misjudged her; she impressed them by her common sense in agreeing with their opinions; she charmed them by taking sides with them against their sons in matters relating to the wearing of overshoes and warm scarves. She laughed at their jokes and, in her own phrase, she "jollied" them. She jollied Mrs. Bridgetower so successfully that after half an hour that lady felt that there might be some hope for the younger generation after all.

Lieutenant Swackhammer, too, was a success. He had a fund of small talk, and although he had lived inland for the first eighteen years of his life, he had subsequently developed a bluff, sailorly, salt-water manner, which went very well with his somewhat extreme deference to age and grey hairs. He laughed a good deal at nothing in particular, and had a splendid grip of whatever was obvious and indisputable.

With such guests as these, Mrs. Bridgetower blossomed. The Torso laughed at all her ironies, and whenever The Torso laughed, Lieutenant Swackhammer laughed too. Pearl Vambrace, though apt to be silent, was respectful and behaved nicely, and when she did speak, she said something sensible, and said it in a neatly rounded sentence, of which her hostess approved. In the atmosphere of success, Solly brightened up, and poured out the wine with a generosity begotten of relief.

The meal was a long and heavy one, and concluded with special glasses of ice-cream, into which a spoonful of crême de menthe had been injected, like a venom; with this, chocolate peppermint patties were served and Pearl, who was unaccustomed to rich food, began to feel a little unwell and sleepy. It was at this point that Ada announced that Master

Solly was wanted on the telephone.

"The telephone is the curse of the age," said Mrs. Bridgetower; "even our after-dinner coffee is not safe from it."

"Oh, how right you are," said Bonnie-Susan; "you know, Mrs. Bridgetower, I often think things were really better when you were a girl. No 'phone, and no boys calling up all the time, and all those lovely horses and carriages and everything."

"Absolutely right," said the Lieutenant, champing a third peppermint patty.

"I do not quite ante-date the telephone," said Mrs. Bridgetower, "but in my youth it was employed with a keener discretion than is the case today."

Meanwhile Solly, with the receiver at his ear, was listening to Humphrey Cobbler.

"Hello there, Bridgetower, what about coming to see me tonight?"

"Can't. It's the night of the Ball, you know."

"What Ball? Oh, that thing. Well, you don't want to go to that, do you?"

"Oh course I do."

"You amaze me. Oh, I suppose you're protecting your interests, eh?"

"I do not understand you."

"The hell you say. She's going with Tasset, isn't she?"

"I believe so."

"And who, if I may ask, are you escorting to this dreary brawl?"

"Miss Vambrace."

"Who's she?"

"Miranda in the play."

"Oh, her. Can't say I know her. She doesn't sing, does she?"

"I don't know."

"Well, find out before you do anything silly. Remember my advice; take a woman with a good big mezzo range every time. Listen, how would it be if I came with you?"

"No."

"I've got a dress suit."

"You have no invitation."

"A formality. We artists are welcome at all doors."

"No; it wouldn't do."

"I could carry a fiddle case; pretend I belonged to the orchestra."

"No."

"Don't you think you're being just a teeny-weeny tidge snobbish and class-conscious?"

"No."

"Very well, then; sweep on in your fine carriage over the faces of the humble poor. There'll come a day. . . . You don't want to reconsider?"

"No."

"Can't you say anything but no?"

"No."

"Very well then. Go ahead; plunge into a maelstrom of gaiety. And God forbid that, when the revel is at its height, your merriment should be dampened by thought of me, crouched over a dead fire in my sordid home, drinking gin out of a cracked cup."

"God forbid, indeed."

"In poverty, hunger and dirt."

"As you say."

"Well—good-bye."

"Good-bye."

The cards of invitation specified that the Ball would begin at nine o'clock. To Hector's precise mind, unattuned to elegant delay, it was therefore important that he should appear upon the stroke of nine, and he was dressed in his hired evening suit by half-past eight. He was not happy about the suit. It was not the cut or the fit that bothered him, for he was not pernickety about such things; it was, rather, the material of which the suit was made; this was a face-cloth, which time had rendered not merely smooth, but slippery. The way in which the coat cut away to the tails, and the shortness of the tails themselves, seemed to him to be not quite right, but he assumed that there were many styles in evening coats. The old man from whom he had rented the suit had assured him that it was a splendid fit, and that he looked like a prince in it. There had been no white waistcoat to go with the suit, so Hector had purchased a smart one for himself, as well as a collar, a stiff shirt and a tie which was conveniently tied already, and fastened at the back with a secret hook. The obvious newness of his linen, he hoped, would take the eye of society from the curious shininess of his suit.

By a quarter to nine he was in the hall of the Y.M.C.A., waiting for his taxi. It was prompt to the minute, and at precisely five minutes to nine he found himself at the Ball.

Nobody was on hand to receive him. Nobody asked for his card of invitation. On a dais at one end of the room the band was chatting, and a couple of orderlies in the gallery were arranging chairs. There was no one else to be seen. Turning from the hushed splendour of the empty ballroom Hector sought and found a door marked "Gentlemen"; it was dark, quiet and comforting in there, and he settled himself to wait.

It was not a happy choice of a hiding place, for although nothing could be more natural than his presence there, and nothing less likely than that any official person, finding him, would ask to see his card of invitation, it was a retreat with humiliating associations for him. Was it not behind a similar door, similarly marked, that he had taken refuge so many years ago, at the Normal School "At Home"?

Here, in the darkness, he could not escape that recollection. Time had somewhat blunted the edge of it, and he had got into the habit of pushing it down into the depths of his mind whenever it troubled him, but tonight he was without defence. Sweating slightly, he faced the fact that he had made a fool of himself at the "At Home", and that it was possible that he might make a fool of himself again at the Ball, and for a similar reason.

Hector had been a prominent figure in his year at the Normal School. By the time the annual "At Home" was due he was easily the leader among the young men of the class.

Had he not been chosen by popular vote as "Student Most Likely to Become Deputy Minister of Education"? And as such he was the obvious person to invite Millicent Maude McGuckin to be his partner at the "At Home". For in the atmosphere of the Normal School the cleverest boy and the cleverest girl were expected to appear together at this function; like crowned heads when a royal marriage is in prospect, they had little personal choice in the matter; their academic position determined their relationship to one another, and if either happened to have a morganatic attachment to some less brilliant member of the class, that unworthy affection had to be suppressed for the evening of the "At Home".

Of those girls of Hector's generation whom the chaste goddess of Primary Education called to her shrine, Millicent Maude McGuckin was the fairest and most proud. She wore glasses, it is true, but behind them her eyes were brown as the waters of a Highland stream. Her upper teeth were, perhaps, more prominent than those of the insipid stars of Hollywood, but they gave a swelling pride to her upper lip, and formed her mouth into a pout which fairly ached for kisses. Her curly hair was chestnut brown; her skin was dark and sweetly flushed over her cheeks. It was a time when the female bosom was rising again from the flatness to which the 'twenties had condemned it, and Millicent Maude McGuckin's bosom, swelling gently under the stimulus of a good mark on a test in Classroom Management, or heaving proudly in a debate on "Resolved: That Country Children Are Culturally Handicapped In Comparision With City Children" was a thing to make tears of ecstasy sting the eyeballs. The bosom was coming in, but the stress upon the female leg which was so characteristic of the 'twenties had not diminished, and in this department of womanly beauty, too, Millicent Maude McGuckin was richly dowered.

> *Is she that way,*
> *Lovable—and sweet?*

ran a song popular at the time. The answer in her case was

a breathless affirmative from all the young men of her year at the Normal School.

It was never doubted that Hector would escort her to the "At Home". It would be his duty to call for her at her boarding house, walk her to the school, dance the first and last dances with her, squire her at supper and assist the Principal and staff in greeting the guests. But Hector boasted that he would do more. It must be remembered that he had never mixed on easy terms with boys and girls of his own age before he went to the Normal School, and his quick success there went a little to his head. He boasted to a group of other male students that in the Moonlight Waltz he would kiss Millicent Maude McGuckin. They expressed vehement and brassy doubt that he would do any such thing. He reaffirmed his intention; indeed, he took bets on it. It was the only time in his life that he bet on anything, and as it was himself, he considered it a certainty.

The night of the "At Home" came. Hector's courage was shaky when he called for Miss McGuckin, for he scarcely knew her, and when she tripped down the stairs of her boarding house in a blue frock, looking more lovely than would be thought possible in the light of the ruby lamp which hung there, he wondered if he had not dared too much. This was not a girl to Get Fresh with, he thought. This girl was a Sweet Girl now, and the only change in her condition which was at all thinkable was the change to Wife and Mother. That he should debauch her, by so much as a single kiss, was an unnerving thought. To Hector a kiss was no trivial matter. He had never kissed anyone but his mother, and he had an unformed but insistent notion that a kiss was, among honest people, as binding as a proposal of marriage. And in his scheme of planning and common sense, marriage had as yet no place. Yet he ached to kiss her. He wanted to kiss her without being prepared to marry her. He was shocked and at the same time sneakingly proud of this voluptuousness in himself.

Millicent Maude McGuckin did nothing to allay his fears. A spirited girl, with a turn for debating, she had thoughts of a parliamentary career, and of asserting the right of women to take over everything, in a large and general way. Her attitude toward Hector, therefore, was one of mettlesome raillery. When he made as though to help her on with her coat, she said, "Thanks, I'm still quite capable of putting on my own coat," and when he took her arm to help her down the icy steps of the boarding house she said, "What's the matter? Are you afraid you'll fall?" When he became silent under these witty rebuffs, she said, "You certainly aren't very conversational tonight, are you?" And when he haltingly tried to make amends she said, airily, "Oh don't talk if you have to make an effort; I dare say you are wishing I was some person else." By the time they reached the Normal School, Hector was completely cowed by Miss McGuckin's bantering social manner.

Standing in the "receiving line" was no ordeal. It was Hector's task to introduce each couple as they arrived to the Principal, who had not seen most of them since four o'clock that afternoon. The Principal then passed on these introductions to his wife, who repeated them to old Dr. Moss, the principal emeritus. Miss McGuckin was on the other side of this venerable pedagogue, so that both her maddening charms and her wounding wit were spared him, for half an hour or so. But he had to join her again for the Grand Promenade which opened the "At Home". This ceremony probably derived from some Grand Polonaise, or other European court ceremony; nothing quite like it is traceable among the customs of the British peoples. The older guests disposed themselves in knots about the broad corridors of the Normal School, and the students, in couples, arranged themselves in processional formation in the entrance hall. Then, as the band on the third floor, where the assembly room was, played a spirited march, the pupils, arm in arm, paraded through the school and up the stairs, bowing to their guests and being bowed to in return. It was rather a pretty and pleasing custom and one which the students enjoyed, but for Hector it was a humiliation. Miss McGuckin kept whispering "Left, left . . . you know your left foot, don't you? . . . Bow; don't just

225

duck your head. . . . Don't hold my arm so tightly." And as she badgered him, the more he was enthralled by her, and the more eagerly he wished to dominate her, win her, hear her say "Oh, Hector!" as he covered her full lips with kisses.

Nobody could say of Hector that he was not persistent. He danced with Millicent Maude McGuckin, as custom demanded, and made no reply to her criticism of his dancing save a sheepish smile. He endured it when she took him into a corridor to demonstrate a step. Under her direction he opened and closed windows, fetched chairs, and harried the band leader to play her favourite tunes. For although her conversation, baldly recorded here, may suggest that Miss McGuckin was censorious and demanding, it must be remembered that she was only eighteen, and the charm of youth clouded the sharp outlines of her essential character. The other girls—charming girls, destined to be capable schoolteachers and agreeable women—seemed to him insipid beside this paragon. A worshipper of planning and common sense himself, Hector adored these characteristics in Miss McGuckin, and never thought that a woman might possess more pleasant attributes. But she made him nervous, and when he was nervous his stomach, in his own phrase "went back on him".

This trouble was not too inconvenient until the supper interval. He felt secret stirrings in his bowels, but had no time to consider them. But a supper of eight sandwiches, two pieces of cake, six cookies, and a plate of ice cream, washed down with two cups of coffee, gave his revolting stomach something to work on.

He took supper with Miss McGuckin, of course, and also with old Dr. Moss and Miss Ternan, the instructor in Art. Dr. Moss described his trip to the Holy Land in considerable detail, while the others listened. The old gentleman carried in his pocket a New Testament, bound in wood from the Mount of Olives, which he showed for their admiration. Millicent Maude McGuckin was full of pretty curiosity, asking for information about the diet of the Holy Land, and demanding in particular to know whether Our Lord had subsisted chiefly on dates, pomegranates and figs; it appeared extremely probable to her that He was a vegetarian. It was not necessary for Hector to say anything, so he ate stolidly, and poured hot coffee down upon cold ice cream with the recklessness of youth. And then, all of a sudden, his stomach squealed.

The borborygmy, or rumbling of the stomach, has not received the attention from either art or science which it deserves. It is as characteristic of each individual as the tone of the voice. It can be vehement, plaintive, ejaculatory, conversational, humorous—its variety is boundless. But there are few who are prepared to give it an understanding ear; it is dismissed too often with embarrassment or low wit. When Hector's stomach squealed it was as though someone had begun to blow into a bagpipe, and had thought better of it. His neighbours pretended not to notice.

A rumbling stomach may be ignored once, but if it persists it will shake the aplomb of the most accomplished. Hector's stomach persisted, and Millicent Maude McGuckin began to raise her eyebrows and speak with special clarity, as though above the noise of a passing train. Miss Ternan flushed a little. Old Dr. Moss unhooked the receiver of his hearing-aid from the front of his waistcoat and shook it and blew suspiciously into its inside, as though he feared that a scratchy biscuit crumb had lodged there. The stomach squealed loud and long, and then the squeal would drop chromatically in tone until it became a low, hollow rumble. It was as though, nearby, an avalanche of boulders was plunging down a mountainside toward a valley, in which a spring torrent raged and foamed. And then, inexplicably and in defiance of nature, the boulders would rush back up the hill, to be greeted with screams and bagpipe flourishes by the stricken mountaineers.

After an eternity of this, Hector rose. "Got to see if the orchestra are getting any supper," said he, and left the room, his face its darkest red.

In the men's washroom he had taken stock of himself. A fine fellow he was, to be partner to Millicent Maude McGuckin, and then carry on like that! What about the

Moonlight Waltz now, and his boast that he would kiss her!
Was this—the theological explanation came pat to his mind
—a Judgement on him for his sinful boast that he would
Take Advantage of a sweet and innocent girl, before every-
body—before the Principal and his wife, before old Dr.
Moss, who carried a Testament bound in wood from the
Mount of Olives? Like many young people, Hector was con-
vinced that his elders were the implacable foes of Eros.

No! He had to go through with it! He had bet two dollars
and fifty cents that he would do it! But the fiends in his
stomach, like an offstage chorus, mocked his determination
with snarling laughter. Suppose the stomach howled aloud
as he danced the Moonlight Waltz? Suppose—oh, horror
inconceivable!—the winds within him could not be contained as he danced! There was nothing, nothing in the world
—not money, not pride, not love of Millicent Maude Mc-
Guckin—which would make him risk such shame.

So he remained where he was. Faintly he could hear the
Midnight Waltz begin. For this special dance, all the lights
save a few which had been covered with blue gelatine were
turned off, and it was deemed to be the epitome of languorous
romance, and the crowning glory of the "At Home". With
this special dance in mind, Millicent Maude McGuckin's
mother had made her a new gown of electric blue satin,
wonderfully gathered so that it shimmered and crinkled as
she moved, making her, as the instructor in Nature Study
remarked admiringly, look just like an electric eel. Whether
she danced this dance, or whether she sat it out, Hector
never knew. The next day he was eyed curiously by the
student body, and those with whom he had laid bets made no
attempt to collect them. It was known that Mackilwraith had
reached some sort of crisis at the "At Home", but whether
it was drink, or whether, as one boy suggested, he had suddenly Had the Call to the Ministry in the midst of the gaiety,
no one knew, and no one liked to ask. As for Millicent
Maude McGuckin, she never spoke to him again.

Nobody suspected that Hector had sat in a booth in the

men's washroom through the Midnight Waltz, weeping bitterly.

Griselda was not in the best of tempers when she arrived at the Ball. Roger had called for her without a car, and had calmly said that he had supposed that they would drive in her car. He had offered to drive it for her, but she had said that she preferred to drive herself, and had hinted that he had had too much to drink. He had taken this quietly, but there was a look on his face as she parked the car, wrestling with it in a difficult place, which suggested mockery. To punish him, she kept him waiting twenty-five minutes while she left her coat and attended to her face. When they passed the receiving line and entered the ballroom, neither was in a good temper. The first couple to dance past them were Solly and Pearl.

"Good Heavens, I thought Solly was bringing his mother," said Griselda.

"Who is that girl with him?" said Roger.

"You should know. You've kissed her at every rehearsal for the past week. That's Pearl Vambrace."

"Really? I didn't know she could look like that."

"She looks much as usual to me," said Griselda, though she knew that Pearl was looking uncommonly well.

Roger danced near to Solly and touched him on the shoulder.

"May I?" said he, and danced away with Pearl, leaving Solly with the furious Griselda.

"Awfully good band," he began.

"Don't be fatuous."

"Dreadful band."

"Don't try to be clever."

"You are looking particularly lovely."

"Thank you. So is Pearl, it seems."

"Yes, she has brightened up, hasn't she?"

"They say that admiration is the greatest beautifier; you should feel complimented at the change you have made in her."

"Thanks; it's nice to be appreciated."

"Oh, she appreciates you, does she?"

"It would be immodest to reply to that one. You should ask her."

"How does she get on with your mother?"

"Like a house on fire. Practically twin souls."

"It looks like the hand of fate, Solly dear."

"It does, doesn't it."

Pearl was enjoying her first taste of social success. She did not dance well, but she followed Roger's leads adequately, and listened tremulously to his small talk. He complimented her deftly in a dozen different ways; he said what a pity it was that his work and the rehearsals had not permitted him to see more of her, and hoped that they would repair this in the future; he played his favourite trick, suggesting that they were both a little superior to the others at the Ball, and inviting her to join him in making fun of the couples who came near them. Pearl answered all that he said quietly and sensibly, but such flattery was intoxicating to her. What did it matter now that in her first attempts at making up she had dropped powder on the front of her gown, and could not get it out? The Torso had arranged her face, and dealt with the troublesome straps of her underthings by cutting them off with Mrs. Bridgetower's nail scissors and doing some neat work with safety pins. She was being admired. She was dancing. She had caught the attention of the god-like Roger. As they danced past Griselda and Solly, Pearl, filled with charity toward all God's creatures, gave Griselda a beautiful smile. Griselda saw it as a smile of triumph, of mean exultation, and she ground her beautiful teeth so hard that Solly remarked upon it.

All balls are much alike. They are wonderful; they are dull. They inspire high hopes; they bring bitter regrets. The young wish that they might never end; the old fidget for the time to come when they may decently go home to bed. They are all great successes; to some of the guests they are always failures. The guests take with them to the Ball almost everything they find when they arrive there.

Hector had taken his misgivings, his sense of defeat, his fears for Griselda, his mistrust of Roger, and all the burden of a life which had never been touched by the spirit of merry-making. When he returned through the door marked "Gentlemen" he carried with him his failure at the Normal School "At Home", fresh and painful after twenty-one years. He mingled with the guests as a man who has no notion of where he is to go, or what he will do when he gets there.

Almost at once somebody spoke to him. To his dismay it was a member of the School Board. Now Hector, like all schoolteachers, both mocked and feared School Boards; he resented their layman's interference in the mighty mystery of education, and scoffed at it, but at the same time he dreaded their power to dismiss him. It may be said that School Boards have a similar contradiction in their attitude toward teachers: they despise them as persons who have sought a cloistered life (this being the construction which they put on daily association with noisy and demanding young barbarians) and yet they reverence them as valuable properties, not easily replaced in the case of death or resignation. This makes for some uneasiness in the relationship between Board and teacher.

This member of the Board, however, was full of affability.

"Say," he said, buttonholing Hector, "that was a pretty smart thing you did this afternoon."

"What do you mean?" said Hector.

"About those books. I heard they just slipped through your fingers. Pretty smart."

"Oh—oh yes," said Hector, bewildered.

"Want you to meet Colonel Pascoe. Colonel, this is Mr. Mackilwraith, our mathematical wizard from the Collegiate. Do you know, this afternoon he went to old Dr. Savage's sale, and spotted the only valuable thing in the place. Some books. Bid up to twenty-four hundred dollars on them, and just missed them by a whisker. I'm told they're worth a cool fifteen thousand in New York."

"Is that a fact?" said Colonel Pascoe. "Well, well; let's have a drink on that."

In the refreshment room Hector quickly became a hero. The Board member showed him off as a prodigy for whom he was himself indirectly responsible. The Board member explained that he hadn't had much education himself; he was, in fact, a graduate of the University of Hard Knocks, but he respected education, particularly when it could be turned into hard cash. Hector found that he was credited with remarkable astuteness in almost having bought the books. He was introduced to the Bishop in this new character of astute bibliophile, and the Bishop invited him to drop in at the Palace some day and look at an old Prayer Book which he had; it was well over a hundred years old, and sure to be valuable, but the Bishop would like to have Hector's expert opinion on it. By the time Hector left the refreshment room he had had three drinks, and was in a happier frame of mind.

His reputation as a shrewd collector of rare books seemed to precede him wherever he went. The figures which he was reported to have bid varied from a few hundreds to a few thousands, but they were all impressive. He was represented as a knowledgeable Canadian, determined to protect his country's literary treasure from a crafty American dealer. It was said that he was trying to buy the books in order to give them to the library at Waverley. There was some suggestion that Waverley ought to give him an honorary degree, as a reward for his patriotism and knowledge of books. Wisely, Hector said nothing; he smiled and let them think as they pleased. But as he walked through the card room, and as he moved through the gallery of the ballroom, where the mothers of the dancing young people sat, he was greeted with that stir which accompanies a person of distinction, and his curious dress suit was taken as an expression of the eccentricity which is inseparable from profound knowledge. But although this unforeseen notoriety was balm to Hector, he did not lose sight of the reason which had brought him to the Ball. Griselda was never long out of his sight.

It occurred to Roger that he was being a fool. It was all very well to revenge himself upon Griselda for her slights to his masculine dignity; it was all very well to dance with Pearl Vambrace and reflect that it was possible even for an expert like himself to have a good thing under his eyes for weeks and never notice it; but these pleasures were mere self-indulgence. Griselda, in her costly gown of Greek design, gave him a cachet which was far beyond the range of Pearl, in her pink organdie; Griselda was a Webster, an heiress; Pearl was just another girl, and girls were aways in plentiful supply. Therefore Roger took an early opportunity to return to Griselda, and found her repentant. That was fine, he thought. He would make capital of that repentance later on. He left Pearl with a vague suggestion that they should have another dance together later in the evening, and except when he did his duty by dancing with Nellie Forrester and with Valentine, he did not leave Griselda again.

Pearl was painfully overset by what she decided was a sudden coldness on his part. What had she done that was wrong? Was it breath, which she could amend by recourse to her toothbrush in the ladies' room, or was it dullness, or lack of sex appeal which nothing in the world could ever put right? She moped so pitifully that Solly could bear it no more, and asked her what was wrong. And then poor Pearl, who was too wretched to be anything but honest, told him that she thought that Roger disliked her, and that she wanted Roger to like her more than she wanted anything else in the world.

This sort of confession is complimentary to a man of middle age, but to a contemporary it is a dismaying bore. Solly said all the words of comfort he could think of, which were pitifully few, and leaving Pearl in the hands of his mother he sought the refreshment room, and drank whisky and soda. As he did so he found himself unaccountably wishing that Cobbler were with him; Cobbler would know what to do with a girl who had begun to moult in the middle of a party. And if anybody was to be offered medicine against the pangs of despised love, what about himself? He applied the only medicine at hand, freely.

Mrs. Bridgetower was not an ideal companion for a girl in Pearl's position. She did her best to be entertaining, telling of Balls which she had attended in her youth, and deploring the fact that few men wore white gloves any more. Of modern dancing she held a low opinion. Of modern dance music she could not trust herself to speak. She approved of the wisdom of Pearl's mother in keeping her daughter Sweet; so many modern girls, she said, ceased to be Sweet almost before they began to think about Balls. She was pleased that Pearl was ready to leave the dancing and sit for a while with a boring old woman like herself. No, no, Pearl must not protest; she was fully aware that she had little to say which could be of interest to a young girl.

Suitable replies to such conversation as this demand the utmost ingenuity, even in one trained by Professor Vambrace. Pearl was glad when The Torso and Lieutenant Swackhammer came along, and asked her to join them.

"Honey, you look like a poisoned pup," said Bonnie-Susan, frankly, when Mrs. Bridgetower was out of earshot. "You'd better come into the john with me and let down your hair."

In a quiet corner of the ladies' lounge, Pearl told her story to The Torso's sympathetic ear, and received that experienced young woman's advice.

"Listen, Pearl, you're just wasting your time. Roger hasn't got anything that you want. I get around, and I know. He's just a heel—a smooth, good-looking heel."

"But for a few minutes he seemed really interested in me."

"Yes, but Roger plays for keeps. And you haven't got anything that he wants. Griselda has."

"I know she's prettier than I am."

"And richer, and classier."

"Well, why don't you tell her what you think of him?"

"Because she doesn't need advice and you do. Griselda can look after herself—I think. And if she can't her Daddy can get the smartest lawyers in the country to look after her."

"Oh, Bonnie-Susan, don't you believe there's anything at all in love?"

"I certainly do, honey, but there's no love where Roger is for anybody but Roger."

It was after the supper interval that Roger took Griselda outside, and across the barrack square toward the lake. On the shore was an old stone redoubt, built to defend Canada against the assaults of the U.S.A., and it was on the outworks of this redoubt that he spread his coat, and they sat down.

"I'm sorry if I annoyed you earlier this evening," said he.

"It was nothing," said Griselda; "I was in a bad temper anyhow."

"Why? Or may I know?"

"Oh, Freddy kept nattering all the time I was getting dressed about some old books that were sold this afternoon."

"Ah, yes. The purchase of the great Mackilwraith."

"No, he didn't get them."

"Why did that make you angry?"

"Oh I don't really know. But it did. I wished I had gone to the sale, and I wished I knew a lot about old books—or anything else. Just discontentment, I suppose."

"Boredom, probably."

"Probably."

"You want something to wake you up."

"Yes, and I know what you think it is."

"What?"

"A love affair with you. You've said so before."

"Well—don't you think I'm right?"

"How do I know? One can't love somebody in cold blood."

"I wasn't thinking of it in terms of cold blood."

"I think I'd rather get a job."

"Why?"

"Why not?"

"Jobs are for people who need them. You don't need one. You'd be taking it from somebody else who did."

"Well, maybe I'd like to go on a long journey."

"You couldn't go alone. But you could go on a honey-moon tour."

"That would mean that I would have to marry a very rich man, doesn't it?"

"I don't think I like that remark."

"Why not?"

"Are you suggesting that I'm interested in you because of your money?"

"I've had money dinned into me ever since I can remember. Not at home, but by other people. When some people look at me I can see dollar signs forming in their eyes. Girls of well-to-do families become rather touchy about such things."

"I've never talked to you about money."

"No, but whenever you talk about a possible future for us, you always talk in terms that mean money. And you have your Army pay. Would you be surprised to know that I have looked it up, and know how much it is?"

"You've inherited your father's business sense, haven't you?"

"Perhaps."

"I didn't know you were so money-minded."

"Under the circumstances, that's rather funny."

"You know, you're a damned insulting girl."

"You were advising me a few weeks ago to see people clearly—as they really are. What have you to complain of?"

"I don't know whether to kiss you or slap you."

"I have always been a lover of comfort. Perhaps you'd better kiss me."

Roger kissed her, and staked a possible future as a rich woman's husband on that kiss. It was a miracle of technique. The way in which he took Griselda in his arms, and kissed her warmly upon the lips; the way in which he followed this with a tighter embrace, as though passion raged in him like a fire, and pressed his mouth upon hers until the pressure was pain; the way in which, with a quick intake of breath he laid his hand upon her breast, and kissed her throat again and again, her ears, her hair, and at last her lips; the way in

which his tongue met hers, and caressed it within her mouth
—these things could not have been bettered for neatness of
timing and execution. It would be useless to pretend that
Griselda was not moved; such address in the art of love
would have stirred an anchoress. But when at last he released
her she drew away from him, and pulling her coat about
her, sat silent for awhile, looking out at the lake.

"Well?" said Roger, at last.

"Well what?"

"Is that to be all? Suppose we do it again?"

"No, suppose we don't," said Griselda, moving a little
farther away.

"Was it unpleasant?"

"Not in the least."

"Well then—why not?"

"Just because I think not."

"You're not going to give me a talk about chastity, are
you?"

"Well, Roger, since you bring it up, I suppose I might.
Do you know what chastity is? Not the denial of passion,
surely. Somebody wise—I forget who it was—said that
chastity meant to have the body in the soul's keeping."

Roger pondered upon this for a while.

"I get it," he said at last; "I don't measure up to the demands of your soul, is that it?"

"I know it couldn't possibly sound more priggish and
foul, but that's it."

"Well God damn it, I've been given the bird for some
funny reasons, but that's the funniest."

"I know. Shall I take you home now?"

"Take me—?"

"It's my car, you know."

"Then you can damn well take yourself home. I'll walk."

Furiously Roger leapt up and rushed back to the refreshment room, where he caused comment by demanding and
drinking a tumbler of neat Scotch.

Neither Griselda nor Roger had noticed a bulky figure

following them down to the redoubt. It was Hector. Beneath the earthworks, as a communication between the trench around the tower and the lakeshore, was a passage lined with stone, damp, chilly and unwelcoming. It was in this that he stationed himself, for here he could see the two figures, but was in no danger of being seen. He could not hear their soft conversation. But he saw the kiss. It was such a kiss as he had never conceived possible. It pierced his bowels like a spear, and a historic disquiet began therein. His stomach gave a warning squeal, and then the avalanche-like roar. There, in the passage, it seemed to him that it must be audible to the couple on the lakeshore, although they were twenty feet away. With tears in his eyes, and a sick horror in his heart, and with forty wildcats shrieking their rage in his entrails, Hector turned and ran back toward the military college.

He did not return to the ball, but neither had he the power of will to go home. Instead he paced a long avenue of trees, flanked on one side by the lake and on the other by the gardens of the college, until dawn. His head was bursting; he had, he was certain, seen the first horrible move in the seduction of the girl he loved, and what had he done? He had run away. Was this because he too, long ago, had boasted that he would smirch a girl's honour at another, humbler Ball? His agony was incoherent and fearsome. But when the sun was already high he realized that he must get his coat and go home, so he returned to the square in the centre of the college.

There was a crowd there, and his appearance was greeted with a shout. This was the undefeated army of merrymakers who had remained until the very end of the Ball, while poorer spirits had driven home along the very avenue where Hector had walked away the weary night. Nothing would satisfy them except that Hector, now known as the hero of the greatest near-miss in the history of book-buying in Canada, should pose with them in a group photograph. And that was why, in the newspaper which appeared later that day,

Hector was to be seen in the centre of the merry throng, between two girls with their arms around his neck, and a third saucily perched upon his knee. It was a splendid likeness, and the fact that he was described in the caption as Professor MacElroy did nothing to diminish the prestige which his pupils accorded him as a result of this publicity.

CHAPTER
7

THE DRESS rehearsal was over, and Valentine was near the end of her director's harangue to the cast. The actors sat around her in their costumes, some upon the lawn and some on the properties of the play. Larry Pye had given them the light from a single large flood, and far above the moon rode proudly.

"I think that's everything," said Valentine. "Oh, no; I have a few personal notes on this page. Mr. Leakey, you must not wear your Masonic ring on the stage. And Mr. Shortreed, I know you took off your wrist-watch before your second entrance, but be very careful about that, won't you? Will you two men check on each other tomorrow night five minutes before curtain time? And Professor Vambrace—"

"Mea culpa, mea culpa!" cried the Professor, with scholarly waggishness, burying his face in his hands.

"Yes; your spectacles in the vision scene. It's very easy to forget. Can you find someone to keep an eye on you about that?"

"I'll be very happy to," cried Miss Wildfang.

"There are one or two of you whom I should like to see privately for a moment before you go home. Mr.—hm, no; Miss Vambrace is the only one, I think. Oh, yes, here's a note I'd overlooked: there was some awfully odd makeup, particularly on you girls in the dance of Nymphs and Reapers. What have you been doing to yourselves?"

There was an uneasy silence.

"Who put that stuff on your faces?"

"Auntie Puss," said a Nymph, faintly.

"Who?"

Valentine was conscious of someone tugging her skirt from behind. It was Mrs. Forrester. "Shut up, Val," she whispered.

"See me about it later," said Valentine. "Now I want you all to feel happy and confident. It was a very good dress rehearsal. Nothing was seriously wrong and everything that was out of order can be corrected before tomorrow night. Don't believe that old nonsense about a good dress rehearsal making a bad first night. Get some rest tomorrow if you can, and please be here by seven o'clock; if you are late you worry the Stage Manager, and that is inexcusable. Thank you all very much. Now your President wants to say something to you."

Nellie rose, and her face was drawn into what she believed to be an expression of whimsical concern.

"Well," she said; "I'm sure you'll all agree with me that Miss Rich has done marvels, simply marvels, with the material she had. I've never seen you do better, in an experience of this club which goes back more years than I care to count. And I sincerely hope she's right about a good dress rehearsal not meaning a bad first night. Some of us can remember occasions when the old saying was only too true. There's a lot in some of these old beliefs. But we'll hope for the best. It's a pity that three names have been left off the programme, and that Mr. Smith's initials are wrong; there are two thousand programmes, and if we can get enough volunteer help the corrections can be made by hand tomorrow. Will anyone offer to help with corrections? I'd do it myself, but my day will be a very full one."

There were no volunteers, except Mr. Smith, one of Larry Pye's assistants, who was determined that he should appear before the world as J. K. Smith and not A. K. Smith, as had wrongly been printed. Nellie continued.

"As you all know this is our first attempt at a Pastoral. It's an experiment, and we are breaking new ground. Whether the public will like it remains to be seen. What the critics will say we simply won't know until we see the papers. But whatever happens, we can say that we pioneered the Pastoral in Salterton, and when you try something new you have to take the rough with the smooth. And now I have a surprise for you; our good friend Mr. Webster, to whom we owe so much for the use of his beautiful grounds, invites you to supper before you go home."

This speech was greeted with great applause, for nothing appeals so strongly to the heart of the amateur actor as a thoroughly depressing estimate of his work, followed by a promise of food. As the group in the floodlight broke up, it was agreed that Miss Rich, though she undoubtedly knew her business, was too optimistic; after all, they knew enough about Theatre to be certain of one thing only, and that was that you could Never Tell. Even Professor Vambrace, so ardent a rationalist in the other affairs of life, clung to the superstition that a good dress rehearsal made a bad performance; everybody likes to be superstitious about something, and the stage provided the Professor with a holiday from the gritty scepticism which scoured the gloss off everything else he did. They moved away to take off their costumes somewhat disappointed that Valentine had not scarified them, told them that they were the worst actors in the world, regretted that she had ever consented to work with them. Nellie's speech, though a good try, was not sufficiently gloomy to slake their masochistic thirst.

A few remained in the area of lawn which formed the stage, waiting to catch Valentine's eye. But Nellie was lecturing her.

"Val, you'll have to be terribly tactful about makeup. Dear old Auntie Puss just loves to do it, and if you criticize it you'll break her heart."

At this moment they were joined by the artist in question. Miss Puss Pottinger was very small, very old, but nimble in a rickety fashion, and when she moved she jiggled all over, like a mechanical toy. For a woman considerably over eighty she was smartly dressed.

"I believe you had some criticism of the makeup on the girls, Miss Rich," said she, and her voice, like her walk, was brisk but quavery, as though it proceeded from a gramophone which was being dragged over rough ground. "If you will tell me what the matter is, I shall be very happy to correct it, very happy indeed."

"I think it was a little over-bold, Miss Pottinger," said Valentine.

"Aha, yes, but I don't think you make allowance for the lights, my dear. Stage light, you see, is much brighter than ordinary light. I try to make full allowance for that, and of course the effect looks overdone when you stand near it."

"I quite understand that, Miss Pottinger, but I watched the girls from considerable distance away, and they looked very strange."

"Aha, yes, but I gave them what I call a Ballet Makeup. Don't worry, when the lights are fully turned on, you will see the effect I intend."

"But my dear Miss Pottinger, we had all the lights on tonight that we are ever going to use."

"Aha, yes, but Shakespeare requires an exaggeration which you are probably not accustomed to. I have been doing this sort of work—as an amateur, of course—for a great many years. Indeed, when they used to have regular amateur theatricals at Rideau Hall, in the Earl of Minto's time, I always looked after the makeup. His Excellency was once kind enough to say that I was a real artist at the job, and as you know, he painted china beautifully himself. Am I to understand that my ability is being called into question?"

"Oh no, dear Auntie Puss, of course not," said Nellie, bending over and speaking sweetly into the fierce old face. "You know that we just couldn't get along without you. Auntie Puss has made up at least somebody in every play our group has ever done," she said to Valentine, in a voice which warned that respect for the aged must come before every other consideration. "We'd be just broken-hearted without her."

"I can't be expected to do everybody, as I used to," said Auntie Puss, somewhat mollified. "And of course I don't see quite as well as I did. I have to use this, now." She hauled in the slack of a black silk ribbon which hung around her neck, and held up a large and powerful magnifying glass. "I don't need anything for ordinary use, but for reading and makeup I find now that I need this."

Feeling, apparently, that she had won the day, Auntie Puss rattled nimbly away, stumbling over a root as she left the lighted area.

"Gallant, gallant," sighed Nellie watching her.

"Her makeup's bloody, and that's all that matters," began Valentine, but Professor Vambrace moved forward from the group which lurked, ready to pounce upon her.

"I don't want to cause any extra trouble," said he, in the voice of a man who is going to do precisely that, "but could the stage management contrive to give me a stem of grapes with exactly seven grapes on it; to have it concealed, I mean, in the basket on the banquet table, so that I can get it before my Big Speech? I mean

The cloud-capp'd towers, the gorgeous palaces—

of course. Then I could eat seven grapes, during that speech, and at the end—

> *We are such stuff*
> *As dreams are made on, and our little life*
> *Is rounded with a sleep.—*

I could toss away the stem. You take me? Rather fine, eh?"

"I'm afraid I don't fully grasp the point, Professor," said Valentine.

"Oh, come, Miss Rich. Surely? Seven grapes—what does that put you in mind of? The Seven Ages of Man, eh? From *As You Like It*. It is pretty clearly understood that the Melancholy Jaques is an early study for the character of Prospero. Now here we have a chance to make a synthesis— to draw Jaques and Prospero together, with this piece of business with the grapes. That's why I came on the stage with my glasses on; I had been scanning *As You Like It* in the wings. As a matter of fact, I have felt some big thing moving within me all day, but it wasn't until half-past nine that I knew what it was. Will you speak to the stage management, or shall I?"

"I do not think that we should introduce anything new into the production at this point," said Valentine. The Professor was astonished, but as the palaver appeared to be at an end, he moved away, giving place to Geordie Shortreed, who was next in line. Geordie spoke in a low voice, as though ashamed and fearful of being overheard.

"Miss Rich," said he; "will it be all right if I slip a hot-water bottle under my costume for that scene where I have to lie on the ground so long? I got awful trouble with my kidneys, and if I get a chill they'll seize right up. I got a pension for sixty per cent. disability."

"You may have your hot-water bottle if you give me a solemn promise that you won't play any tricks during the run of the show," said Valentine, severely. She had received private information that Geordie had been seen in the joke shop the day before, buying a large squirt and several feet of rubber tubing.

"Cross my heart and hope to spit myself to death," said Geordie, and went away smiling.

The last to approach was Pearl Vambrace.

"Falsies for you, my girl," said Valentine.

"I don't understand you, Miss Rich."

"Pads for the bosom. Ask Bonnie-Susan; she probably has some she would lend you. Though what she would need them for," Valentine reflected, "is beyond me."

"Oh, but won't I look terribly big? I mean, I shouldn't be gross, should I?"

"You're a long way from grossness now. And you must make allowance for stage light; it's brighter than ordinary light," said Valentine, borrowing a leaf from Auntie Puss's book.

The refreshment provided by the domestic staff of St. Agnes' consisted chiefly of a very large supply of chicken chow mein. A June night in Salterton is chilly enough to make a hot dish grateful to tired pioneers of the Pastoral. They gathered in knots upon the lawn and champed and worried about the play with great satisfaction.

"I'd be happy if I could just get enough light to kill those shadows," said Larry Pye; "but do what I will, everywhere an actor goes, he casts a shadow."

"And why not?" said Solly. "What could be more natural? Here we are in bright moonlight, and every one of us has a shadow. Larry wants us all to be like Peter Schlemihl, who sold his shadow to the Devil. I never knew a stage manager yet who didn't believe that people cast no shadows."

"It's not one shadow I complain of," said Larry. "It's four or five, mostly on other people's faces."

"Never mind, Larry," said Valentine; "your light is charming. But I do wish you could tone down that intercommunication system; every time you speak backstage, we hear your voice from The Shed, roaring behind the audience. It's confusing and often blasphemous."

"Got to keep it sharp," said Larry. "Suppose you want somebody in a hurry?"

"Do the best you can," said Valentine.

"Oh Miss Rich," sighed Miss Wildfang, who was prompter, "you have the patience of a saint! Too much patience, perhaps, if such a thing is possible. Tonight we were braced for really severe criticism; we expected it, and I may almost say that we wanted it. We cannot improve if we are not told about our faults."

"I told you about your faults," said Valentine. "All those, that's to say, about which anything can be done. I really don't believe that people thrive on harsh criticism. I've had a good deal of experience, and I've always found that you get the best out of people by being decent to them."

"Ah, yes—professionals," said Professor Vambrace. "But we are spirits of another sort—if I may quote another of the Immortal's works. Most of us are university people, or professional people. We can accept criticism of a type which would be unacceptable to the more—how shall I put it—the more—well, the more elementary intelligences of professional players."

Valentine was a little nettled. "Sir Henry Irving said that the best of amateurs were but children in art; one must teach children by kindness, and not expect everything from them which one might demand from adults. Irving also said that the hardest thing for an amateur to do was to get over the habit of stressing personal pronouns. I refuse to minister to the perverse desire of any amateur actor to be abused in public."

This was hard hitting, for the matter of personal pronouns had been mentioned before, and to the Professor himself. He turned away, and was heard to say to Miss Wildfang that the limitations of the professional stage were easily understood, in the light of his recent experience. A small matter of seven grapes, which could, nevertheless, awaken an echo of *As You Like It*, had been denied to him. Was a a really evocative theatre possible if such lack of perception were to prevail? Yes, he agreed with Miss Wildfang that the sooner a university theatre was established, the better. Then, with long rehearsal and ripe scholarship—not all of it from the Department of English, of course—the essential oneness, the great overall unity of Shakespeare's plays could be revealed.

Much as they might wish to be abused by Valentine at a dress rehearsal, it was plain that the actors were distressed at the thought of being criticized in print.

"Whatever the papers say," said Nellie, "I shall always think that we have done the right thing. But I can't answer for the others. A bad press may hit them very hard."

"What press will there be?" asked Valentine.

"The local paper, of course, and probably something in the *Waverley Review*, when it next appears, sometime in November," said Solly.

"No out-of-town papers?"

"One or two, perhaps. Your name will draw them."

"Well, what have you to worry about?"

"I'm worried about the out-of-towners; there might even

be one of those radio critics, and they are so patronizing, even when they're favourable. And if other drama groups hear that we've been panned, they'll gloat so."

"I think you are just worrying because you think you should, Nell," said Valentine. "Criticism can't possibly hurt the show; you've sold enough tickets already to assure success. Stop fussing."

"Spoken like a professional," said Cobbler, who had joined them. "I never pay any attention to criticism. Most critics of anything are frauds. Worse, most of them are bachelors or spinsters. Their opinions of what other people create are firmly hitched to their own sexual cycle. Show me a bachelor critic in whom desire burns like a furance, and I'll show you a fellow who will boost your show to the skies or damn it to the pit, according to the way the leading lady strikes his fancy. Show me the same critic at the bottom of his twenty-eight day round, and I'll show you a fellow who will give you faint praise. Every critic carries a twenty-eight day clock in his gizzard, and what he says about you depends on whether he is ready to strike twelve or one. Rule out the few critics who truly love the arts, and who would be critics even if they weren't paid for it, and the rest are needy riffraff, laughed at by all serious artists."

"What is a spinster director supposed to make of that?" said Valentine.

"If you refer to yourself," said Cobbler, "I am forced to reveal that I do not consider it possible that a lady of your charm can be a spinster in anything except the most technical sense. Furthermore, you are a true artist—a creator. Such people are not twenty-eight day clocks; they are towers in which the carillon peals whenever God chooses to stir it with his mighty breath."

"Thank you," said Valentine, who possessed the rarest of female graces, in that she knew how to receive a compliment. She blushed delightfully.

"Don't thank me; thank God," said Humphrey. "I said that you spoke like a professional. You and I are two of the three professionals involved with this show. We must stand together."

"Who is the other?" asked Larry Pye, hoping for a compliment.

"That gardener," said Humphrey. "I don't think any of you realize what a wonderful job he has done for you in making his garden look like an enchanted island."

"Oh, yes; Gawky," said Larry. "That reminds me, I want a word with him. Hey, Gawky!" He shouted at Tom, who was walking around the lawn with a pointed stick and a bag, picking up bits of paper.

"Not Gawky. The man's name is Golky," said Professor Vambrace, who stood nearby, eating a third dish of chow mein in an abstracted manner. He despised food, but he always ate a great deal at affairs of this kind where it was good and plentiful.

Tom, however, was ready to answer to almost any Saxon assault upon his name, and he came near.

"We've worn away some grass on the stage already," said Larry. "Can you do anything about that?"

"I'll cut the lower lawn tomorrow, sir," said Tom, "and sprinkle the cuttings about seven o'clock. I'll do that every night, just to keep the place looking fresh."

"That's very kind of you, Mr. Gwalchmai," said Valentine.

"Not at all miss. It's my show, too, in a way. And the cuttings will do no harm. I believe in returning everything to nature that comes from nature. But," he said, angrily spearing the glass-paper casing of a cigarette box which Larry had just thrown down, "nobody'll ever convince me that this-here cellophane ever came from nature, and nature'll never absorb it again. So I'll thank you, sir, not to throw it on my grass, unless you want your enchanted island to look like a rubbish-tip." He moved away.

"Let me get you another plate of that stuff," said Solly to Valentine.

"I'll come with you," said she, and they broke away from their group.

"I wanted to get away," said she; "everybody wants to plague and worry me about nothing. They'll all be all right tomorrow. What's worrying them?"

"They are sacrificing to our Canadian God," said Solly. "We all believe that if we fret and abuse ourselves sufficiently, Providence will take pity and smile upon anything we attempt. A light heart, or a consciousness of desert, attracts ill luck. You have been away from your native land too long. You have forgotten our folkways. Listen to that gang over there; they are scanning the heavens and hoping aloud that it won't rain tomorrow. That is to placate the Mean Old Man in the Sky, and persuade him to be kind to us. We are devil-worshippers, we Canadians, half in love with easeful Death. We flog ourselves endlessly, as a kind of spiritual purification. Now, what about some chow mein?"

They replenished their plates, and withdrew to a quiet spot where bushes half-screened them from the others.

"There's one man I must speak to before tomorrow," said Valentine. "And that's Mackilwraith. I didn't want to shame him before the others, but he was quite dreadful. He was never very good, but during this past week he's been impossible. He comes as near to fading completely into the background, leaving a gaping hole where Gonzalo should be, as any actor I've ever seen. His lines mean nothing; if I didn't know them I doubt if I'd ever distinguish them."

"Shocking," agreed Solly. "I wondered what you would do."

"I suppose I'd better get it over. Will you hunt him up and tell him I'd like to see him here? This is private enough; I'll just keep out of the way of the others."

Sated with food, the actors showed no signs of going home. Cobbler and his wife and children were sitting on the lawn, singing for a large audience. The treble voices and the one bass were sweet upon the moonlit air.

> *Come again,*
> *Sweet love doth now invite—*

they sang, and other voices were stilled to hear them.

Not all voices, however. Mr. Webster, who had been somewhat shyly circulating among his guests, most of whom were strangers to him, found that he was being shadowed by a small, monkey-like man, whose face bore traces still of the elaborate makeup of Caliban. What the devil does he want, thought Mr. Webster. Perhaps he is worshipping me because I am rich; there are such people. Maybe he hates me because I am rich; that's far more likely. I wish he wouldn't dart behind trees like that. But now he was confronted by the creature, and it was necessary to speak.

"I suppose you've had something to eat?"

"Yes, indeed, Mr. Webster; as a matter of fact, yes."

"Enough?"

"Oh yes, indeed. An ample sufficiency, as the fellow says. Ha ha."

"What fellow?"

"Eh? Oh, I guess it was some fellow in a story. Or maybe a movie."

"I see. I'm very interested in history. I like to find out what fellow said everything, whenever I can."

"Ha ha. Yes, I guess that's right."

"Coffee?"

"Uh? No, no, I've had lots of coffee, thank you very much."

"Cigarette?"

"Oh, thanks very much. But here, you have one of mine."

"No, thank you. I always smoke cigars."

"Very wise. A more wholesome smoke, as you might say."

"I've never heard anybody say that."

"Oh, yes. It's a well-known thing. Unless somebody happens to give you an exploding cigar. Ha ha."

"Why would anybody give me an exploding cigar?"

"Oh, just as a joke."

"I don't think I've even seen an exploding cigar."

"Oh, haven't you? Well I've got one in my pocket. Here."

"But I don't want an exploding cigar."

"Oh not for yourself, of course. Give it to somebody for a joke."

"No, no, you keep it."

"All right. And I certainly wouldn't offer one to you, Mr. Webster. Not after what's passed between us, I mean."

"What's that? Has anything passed between us?"

"Well, there was that matter of the horse."

"What horse?"

"Well, of course a horse wouldn't mean much to a man in your position, but a horse could be a very serious item to me. I mean, with my sixty per cent. disability because of my kidneys, you see. Frankly, Mr. Webster, I wanted to say it to your face; you were white about the horse."

"What the hell are you talking about? I haven't got a horse."

"I know. And I take the full blame. You were a prince about it. I hope my letter cleared it all up?"

"Oh! You're the fellow who killed Old Bill?"

"I did, and I tell you frankly, it shook me up as nothing has shaken me up since the Battle of the Bulge."

"You're the fellow who wrote that extraordinary letter?"

"I'm not much of a man with the pen, but I put everything I had into that letter."

"Oh. Well—you won't have any more coffee?"

"No sir. Permit me to shake you by the hand."

"Oh—ah."

"You're a white man, G.A."

"Uh."

"Maybe some day I'll be able to do as much for you."

"Ah."

"The lion and the mouse, you know."

"Mf."

His conscience freed of its burden, Geordie walked away toward the group who were listening to the music, and his host scuttled inside to the privacy of his library. To be perfectly sure that no one else could find him and tell him that he was white, he locked the door.

"Well, have you made a new man of him?" Solly had been watching from a distance, and when Hector came from behind the shrubbery where Valentine was, he joined her.

"I doubt it very much," said she. "He was sorry, and all that, but he didn't really seem to be listening to me. He said something about private trouble, and a weight on his mind, but all actors do that when they've been making a mess of a part."

"You do him too much honour when you describe him as an actor."

"No, poor sweet, he'll never be an actor if he lives to be a thousand. I've done my best for him, but only a new heart and a new soul could make an actor of him."

"You might as well add a new body to the list of requirements. Did you ever see such legs?"

"I know. Beef to the heels. I wanted the costume people to give him a long gown, but they insisted on tights. Long experience has taught me to judge pretty accurately what men are hiding under their trousers."

"You fill me with apprehension. But I know what you mean. The male leg is rarely a thing of beauty."

"Yes. I wonder why."

"It's very simple. Just an example of evolution, or natural selection, or something. In the periods when women wore long skirts they had awful legs; look at the nudes painted during those periods if you don't believe me. But when they had to show their legs, they willed fine legs into existence. And when men wore tights they had fine legs too, because they needed them. But modern man conceals his legs, and what have they become? Stovepipes."

"Or, as in your own case, toothpicks."

"That X-ray eye of yours makes me uncomfortable. As a matter of fact I possesss what I like to define as the Scholarly, or Intellectual Leg. Vambrace has toothpicks, if you talk of toothpicks. I popped into the men's dressing-room just now to call Mackilwraith, and Vambrace was changing. Do you know that he wears a species of bone-coloured long underwear, even in weather like this? A shocking sight. I felt like the sons of Noah when they had uncovered their father's nakedness."

"It's a mistake to see people dressing. One should see them either dressed or naked; those are the only two decent states. All else is shame and disillusion."

"Just for curiosity's sake, why did you refer to Mackilwraith as 'poor sweet', just now?"

"He is rather sweet, don't you think? So serious, and at heart such a really decent, nice man."

"His pupils don't think so. He's a classroom tyrant."

"Yes, that seems very probable."

"Then why sweet?"

"Well, he just seems that way to me. I hated to speak hardly to him. What do you care about whether he's sweet or not?"

"Jealousy, really. I bet you don't think I'm sweet. Not, upon reflection, that I would care to be so described."

"Oh, Solly, you've far too much intelligence for anything like that, but you're a darling, all the same, and I do thank you for the help you've given me with this show."

"Val, I love you."

"What?"

"Oh, don't be alarmed. I don't want to marry you, or tag around after you, or monopolize you. I just mean that I love you. You're a wonderful person and so much like a woman. That sounds silly, of course, but you know what I mean. So many women, even the young and pretty ones, aren't like women at all. They haven't got that wonderful, magical quality that real women have—like you. What you are explains what all the really first-rate poets are talking about. You're the first one I've known well who has it, and I love you, and I'll go on loving you. But it's nothing for you to worry about—just something for me to enjoy. Do you know what I mean?"

"Yes, Solly dear, I do. And I'm very grateful. At my age, you see, it's very flattering to hear that sort of talk from somebody as young as you. But you mustn't be foolish about me; you should look for someone younger than yourself."

"Oh, I certainly will. But I'll try to find somebody as much as possible like you. And that won't be easy. Shall we join the others?"

"Yes. And don't think I shall forget what you have said."

Solly took Valentine in his arms and kissed her. Then they joined the company on the lawn.

Ever since she had parted with Roger at the Ball, Griselda had been ill at ease. She had wanted to be rid of him. Of that she was perfectly sure. But she had not wanted to lecture him on morality. She had not wanted to pop out that pious little saw about the body being in the soul's keeping. That was what she meant, of course, but she wished that she had expressed it differently. Still, if she had not done so, what would have happened? Roger had made it plain enough that he wanted her to be his mistress. What a silly expression that was! She didn't want to be a mistress, and especially not the mistress of somebody like Roger. He hinted too much about his prowess with women. What was it he had said? That a woman's body should be played upon and made to sing like a musical instrument. He had got that out of Balzac. She had read Balzac on that subject herself, and thought it nonsense. If anybody was going to make her sing like a musical instrument it would have to be somebody who had first of all made her happy as a human being, and Roger had never done that. He was flattering, and amusing, but somehow not very likeable.

Still, she wished that she had not spoken to him like that. He would think she was just a Pill. He would probably tell other people that she was a Pill. Not that she cared what other people thought. Daddy always said that you could never be happy so long as you gave a damn what other people thought. But of course Daddy wasn't a girl, and besides, he was always worrying about what somebody thought himself, so it didn't count.

She was, she decided with some shame, much simpler than she had imagined. She was like the girls in Trollope; she wanted to be loved, and to love, and when these conditions were met, there was nothing she would not do. But she did not want to mess around with Roger, even though it might be fun while it was going on. She was, she decided after a depressing session with herself, inclined to be Pure. But she wanted it to be quite clear that she was Pure without being a Pill.

And imagine saying that she had looked up his income! Of course she had done so. He talked so much about money that she wanted to know how much he really had. It was the kind of thing girls did that girls should never admit to. But he had talked about marriage, and who wants to marry a girl of eighteen, unless she has money? Griselda was as sensitive on the subject of money as her father.

She was glad to be rid of Roger, but sorry that she had been nasty to him. Well, if that was the case, she would find an opportunity to show him that she was ready to be friendly, but not too friendly. Definitely not a mistress. On the contrary, a Trollope. Not a bad joke that. She would tell it to Freddy if the kid were not so utterly idiotic and likely to blab everything she knew out of sheer childish irresponsibility.

The opportunity came at the party after the dress rehearsal. Griselda was standing by the serving-table on the lawn, eating a plate of chow mein, while most of the company were at some distance, listening to the Cobbler family sing. Roger approached.

"Hello, Roger," said she. "Have some of this. It's good."

"Thanks, I've eaten," said he, in a tone which he believed to be one of distant politeness, but which was really rather surly. "I want a cup of coffee for The Torso. You're still stuffing, I see."

"Not still. Just. I've been hostessing. Roger?"

"Yes?"

"Don't be cross about the Ball. I didn't mean to be horrid."

"I don't understand you."

"Oh yes you do! I was a pig, and I'm sorry."

"You mean you've changed your mind?"

"No, I don't mean that. But I was a pious pig. Will you let me explain?"

"Certainly."

"Let's walk."

"All right."

"What about The Torso's coffee?"

"Oh she's probably forgotten she wanted it by now. Anyway, too much coffee isn't good for her. I'll drink it."

They set off toward the lower lawn. Hector, watching from a distance, saw them pass into shadow, then into a patch of moonlight, and then into shadow again. How should he know that Griselda was industriously eating chow mein as she explained herself, somewhat incoherently, to Roger? He saw only that Roger had put his arm around her shoulders, and then they disappeared into shadow again, and he turned away, heartsick, toward the shrubbery. It was there that he narrowly escaped walking into Solly and Valentine, who at that moment were in each other's arms. It was a bad night for Hector.

A bad night, and the latest of many such nights. Since the Ball he could think of nothing but Griselda, and of what he supposed to be her intrigue with Roger. He could not sleep. During the daytime he was supposed to be watching over pupils who were writing summer examinations, but he brought no vigilance to this task, in which he had once delighted. In former years he had kept up an incessant prowling in the examination room. Soft-footed, he had paced slowly up and down between the rows of desks, his eyes alert for talkers, peepers, cheats. But this year he had sat slumped at his desk, his eyes fixed on space, and examinees who wanted extra paper or ink were sometimes forced to snap their fingers three times before he took it to them.

His appetite had deserted him. Only habit took him to the Snak Shak at regular intervals; once there he ordered food, but he ate little of it. His skin sagged, and it seemed to him that his hair was turning white. In strict fact, grey hairs had been appearing at his temples for five years, but he had not noticed them or paid heed to them before. In these terrible days they appeared to him to be symbols of the conflict which was going on in his heart.

He loved Griselda, and it seemed to him that in that love there was no room for thought of himself. His longing for her was a pain which filled his whole body. And she was, he felt certain, the creature of that vile thing Tasset; he had persuaded her, by his villainous arts, to give her body to him. She was ruined. A soul so delicate as hers, once in contact with sin, would most certainly be shattered beyond any recovery.

At night he lay in his bed, his body rigid under the stress of the painful thoughts which would not be banished from his mind. She was a harlot. No, no! Not a harlot; not that lovely child, so new to the world and so fresh in her womanhood! She might still be reclaimed, and oh! how grateful she would be to the one who drew her back from the abyss of shame and threw the mantle of a great, understanding, world-defying love around her! After one of these bouts of self-torture, Hector would weep, and his Y.M.C.A. bed creaked under the violence of his sobs. His mother's early attempts to purge him had given him a horror of drugs, but under this stress he began to take aspirin tablets, sometimes two at a time, so reckless was he, and they helped him to get a little sleep.

It was curious that during this dreadful week, when Hector's sufferings were real and intense, he found time to regret that he had not had a more literary education. His passions were too big for his vocabulary, and he could not put all that he felt into words, even to himself. As for planning and common sense, he saw them for the extremely limited servants that they were, and the foundations of his whole scheme of life were shaken.

He knew that he was wretchedly insufficient in the part of Gonzalo. He accepted the rather mild rebuke which Valentine gave him without rancour, and almost without hearing it. He was numbed by his pain, and all that he could do was to stand as much out of sight as possible, and watch

Griselda. The sight of her eased his heart. But when she went off to the lower lawn with Roger, he turned into the shrubbery like a sick animal, to be alone. The sight of Solly and Valentine was bitter to him, but only as a blow on the back hurts a man who has been stabbed to the heart. He thought of the chow mein, or a cup of coffee, but suddenly all food was repugnant to him. He found a bench hidden among the fragrantly flowering shrubs, and sat upon it. From the lawn came the song of the Cobbler family, light and free on the summer air:

> *Gentle Love,*
> *Draw forth thy wounding dart;*
> *Thou canst not pierce her heart;*
> *For I, that do approve,*
> *By sighs and tears*
> *More hot than are thy shafts,*
> *Did tempt, while she*
> *For triumph laughs.*

He broke into a cold sweat and a horrible nausea seized him. Not far away was Griselda, and Roger with her. What were they doing? He clung to the back of the bench, his eyes shut, retching horribly.

Hector slept not at all that night. As a general thing, when that expression is used, people mean that they slept five hours instead of their accustomed eight. But Hector went to bed at one o'clock and lay awake until seven, when he rose and tried to rouse himself with a shower. The pelting of cold water on his weary flesh brought him some refreshment of body, but none of mind. In his room he tried to beguile the time with a batch of examination papers. Mechanically he spotted errors; mechanically he wrote TOSASM when that comment was justified, but he was like a man with a mortal sickness, and no temporary distraction could make him forget Griselda. At last he rose and went to the Snak Shak, where he could take nothing but a glass of orange juice—a small glass, not the Mammoth Jumbo Special.

He had no school work that morning, for examinations were nearly over, and he intended to correct papers in the Men Teachers' Room for the greater part of the day. He was free, therefore, to go to a florist's, where he ordered a large bunch of flowers.

"To whom shall we send it?" asked the clerk.

He could not speak her name. A flush spread over his face and his head ached.

"I'll write the address for you," said he.

"You'll find a nice selection of cards on the desk."

A nice selection of cards. The first one he saw said "In deepest Sympathy"; the next, "For a Joyous Occasion"; a third, bearing the picture of what might have been a baboon, but was perhaps intended for an Irishman, said "May good luck go wid ye. And throuble forgit ye". He chose a plain white card, and pondered long over his message. Dared he make a declaration of love in this way? No, no; the florist's men might read it, and know what was for her eye alone. But could he not say something which would mean nothing to the idly curious, but which would carry his meaning to her? He wrote:

> Whatever you may have been, you can count on me for anything, even Death itself.
>
> HECTOR MACKILWRAITH

He read it several times. He could not put his finger on what was wrong with it, but somehow it would not do. When he tried to crush the immensities of his emotions into words, he could not get his meaning clear. At last he wrote:

> You can count on me for anything.
>
> HECTOR MACKILWRAITH

He addressed the envelope and hurried out of the shop before the florist should learn his secret.

"Half an hour. This is your half hour call. You will receive a call at the quarter hour, and another at five minutes before curtain time. The beginners will then assemble backstage." Larry Pye's voice, vastly amplified, rang through The Shed. He spoke solemnly, as befitted a man using a public address system of his own devising, and his enunciation was pedantically clear.

Roger Tasset leapt from the chair in which he was being made up, and seized a small microphone which hung near the loud-speaker.

"Stage Management? Stage Management? Message received. Wilco."

Larry's voice was heard again, excited and quite normal in tone.

"How's it coming in, Rodge?"

"Fine, Larry; couldn't be better."

Delighted, Roger submitted himself again to the hands of the makeup artist.

What babies men are, thought Valentine. All this fuss about messages that could be much better done by a call-girl.

The Shed was filled with people. Tom had cleared if for the use of the Little Theatre, and tables and chairs for makeup had been brought in. Several experienced hands were at work on the faces of the actors, under Valentine's watchful eye, and in a corner Auntie Puss laboured over Hector Mackilwraith. She treated his face as though it were a blackboard; if an effect did not please her, she roughly scrubbed it off with a towel and tried another. She would examine him intently through her magnifying glass, and then go to work without its aid.

"A little white at the temples, I think," said she. "What we call a Distinguished Gray. Very becoming."

"Miss Pottinger, why are you putting yellow in Mr. Mackilwraith's hair?" said Valentine.

"Dear dear; I must have picked up the wrong stick in error. Ah, well; a little powder will mend that; it's a very neutral sort of yellow."

"Perhaps one of the others will put on Mr. Mackilwraith's beard, Miss Pottinger. You must not tire yourself."

"Please do not worry about me, Miss Rich. I understand all about beards."

"I am sure you do. But I do not want to impose on your good nature."

"Miss Rich, the Earl of Minto once told me that he considered me to be a real artist at this work. And as you know, he painted china beautifully. Give me time, and I shall finish Mr. Mackilwraith and put touches on all the others."

Not if I know it, thought Valentine. She had contrived to have all the girls made up elsewhere, in a room which Griselda had offered inside the house, and she felt that she could protect the men against Auntie Puss. Great God! Look at her! With a black lining-stick she was drawing what appeared to be comic spectacles around Mackilwraith's eyes. Oh well, he's so bad anyway that it doesn't matter too much what he looks like. We'll just have to write him off as a total loss; every amateur show has at least one.

The door opened and Freddy bounced in, dressed as the goddess Ceres.

"Miss Rich," said she, "Mr. Cobbler wants to know whether you want *God Save the King* played at the beginning or end of the performance."

"At the beginning," said Valentine; "we decided that days ago."

"He said you had, but Mrs. Forrester told him to play it at the end."

"I'll talk to them about it," said Valentine, and hurried out.

"You're quite a cute kid, painted up like that," said Roger to Freddy.

"I object very much to being called a cute kid," she replied. "If it is God's will that I should be pretty, I'll be pretty; if I am to be plain, I shall be plain without complaint. But come what will, I shall never be vulgar. Only vulgar people are cute kids."

"You're going to be pretty, like your sister," said Geordie Shortreed, hideously made up as Caliban.

"Griselda is very pretty," said Freddy. "It's a shame she

has no brains. If brains ever came back into fashion for girls, it would be a bad day for her. The Torso's a bit squiffed. I can't stand people who don't know how to hold their drink."

"The old Torso squiffed?" said Roger. "Why?"

"She says she took just a nip to give her courage for the performance. That nip went to her head, so she had another to straighten her out, and they both went to her legs."

"As who wouldn't?" said Geordie, and was crushed by an austere look from Professor Vambrace, who now had a beard two feet long.

"She's been nipping at intervals ever since," Freddy continued. "She has a flask in the girl's dressing-room. She may have to be put down with a strong hand."

Solly had come in. "Talking about The Torso?" said he. "Juno has certainly been hitting the jug. When I last saw her Griselda was holding an ice-bag on her head, and Cora Fielding was laying hot-water bottles to her feet. A gay girl, lovable and undependable."

The door opened and an elderly man with two teeth, carrying a violin case, entered The Shed, followed by a colourless thin woman, and a dark and greasy man with a piano accordion hanging around his neck on a leather strap.

"This where we come?" asked the old man. He then caught sight of Solly.

"Oh, hello there," said he. "Glad to see you, Mr. Bridgetower. Can we just have a little run over the play before we start? You tell me where you want the music to come, and we'll fit it in somehow."

Solly turned white. "Good evening, Mr. Snairey," said he, and fled through the door.

"It is useless to appeal to me in this matter," said Humphrey Cobbler when, a few mintues later, he, Valentine, Mrs. Forrester, Solly and the Snairey Trio gathered on the lawn outside The Shed. "I am a musician, and as such I have come here to provide music for this play. I have devoted approximately twenty hours of rehearsal to it. I have assembled a choir of ten and an orchestra of eight, and they are all in readiness at this moment. We have rehearsed the music with the full company six times. Now, if you want me to go away, I shall do so. If you want me to stay, I shall be delighted. But what I positively will not do is wrangle with Mr. Snairey."

"Solly, I told you to tell Mr. Snairey that we had changed our plans," said Nellie, close to tears.

"You told me to get Mr. Cobbler, which I did," said Solly. "You distinctly said that you would see Mr. Snairey yourself."

"You were the fella come to see me first," said Mr. Snairey. "I'm a reasonable man, but I got my living to make, same's anybody else. Joe here coulda had two other jobs tonight, but he come here to oblige me. Either we play or we sit out, and we get paid either way. Don't know's I ever seen you before, young fella," he said, turning toward Cobbler with what he probably intended as a look of menace.

"I don't suppose you have," said Humphrey; "I've only been in Salterton about five years."

"Oh, what shall we do?" moaned Nellie. "Val, do something."

"I don't altogether see why I should," said Valentine. "You and Solly have created this situation. I suppose you must pay Mr. Snairey; I don't imagine his rates can be very high."

"Union scale," said Joe the accordionist. "You got a big show here. Musicals come high."

"It's not the money so much as my feelings," said Mr. Snairey. "Fella my age doesn't like to get pushed around like he was some young punk. We come here to play, and I guess we better play."

From inside The Shed Larry's voice boomed through the loud-speaker, announcing that it was five mintues till curtain time.

"Oh, what shall we do?" cried Nellie, weeping openly. "I must get to Larry. We can't possibly begin till all the people are in their seats. He may want to start before some really important people have come. Oh, I wish we'd never attempted this damned play!"

"What's the trouble, hon?" said a bland voice behind them. It was Roscoe Forrester. In a rush, Nellie explained, assisted by Valentine and Solly.

"I'll handle this," said Roscoe. "The rest of you just get on with what you have to do. Now, Snairey, you listen to me."

Oh, sweet relief! Oh, miraculous lightening of hearts! How they thanked God for Roscoe, the man of business, accustomed to dealing with difficult situations. Valentine could subdue a group of hostile actors or dominate an unfriendly audience, but the Snaireys of this world, the pushing incompetents, daunted her. Solly and Nellie hurried away, blaming each other in their hearts. And after three brisk minutes with Roscoe the Snairey Trio climbed into its Ford and struggled down the drive of St. Agnes', against the steady stream of cars bringing people to the play.

Behind the scenes Nellie bustled up to Larry. "It's all right," she said. "We can begin at once. They're all here. Mrs. Caesar Augustus Conquergood has just taken her seat."

Larry pressed a button. In the shrubbery where Humphrey Cobbler was established a red light flashed on his music desk, and then a green. The National Anthem burst forth, somewhat blurred by the sound of eight hundred people rising to their feet. *The Tempest* had begun.

Sending flowers to Griselda in June was carrying coals to Newcastle indeed. The gardens at St. Agnes' were filled with flowers, and Hector's two dozen roses could add nothing to the splendour of the arrangements which Mr. Webster's housekeeper placed at every advantageous spot in the house. Further, Hector's card disturbed Griselda. So she could count on him for anything, could she? But she didn't want to count on him. He was a bore, and he had a dreadful habit of staring at her. Griselda knew that she was well worth looking at, but she hated to be followed by what appeared to her to be a fixed and baleful glare. After a moment of brief annoyance at his card, she decided to put Hector's roses in the girls' dressing room, and if necessary to explain that they were a tribute from Mr. Mackilwraith to the female members of the cast.

It was from the window of that dressing-room that she leaned out as the actors trooped along a garden path from The Shed to the back of the stage, immediately after Larry's five-minutes call. Roger looked up and caught sight of her.

"You'd better hurry up," he called, "or Larry will be in a stew." He looked more intently at her, and blew a kiss. "You look like the Blessed Damozel, leaning down from the golden bar of Heaven," he said.

How nice he looks as Ferdinand, thought Griselda. And he's obviously not angry any more. I must have made myself quite clear last night. He doesn't think I'm a Pill. From the dressing-table nearby she took one of Hector's roses from its vase, kissed it, and tossed it down to Roger, who fielded it expertly, fastened it to his doublet and hurried on toward the stage.

"Who was that for?" asked The Torso, who was sitting miserably in a chair, with her head almost between her knees. Pearl Vambrace was putting cold compresses on the back of her neck.

"For Roger," said Griselda.

"Pearl, honey," said Bonnie-Susan in a controlled voice. "Don't squeeze that damned cold water down my back."

"I'm sorry, Bonnie-Susan," said Pearl. "My hand jerked."

"A likely story," said The Torso. "Just leave me alone and run down there and fascinate the open-mouthed throng. With that makeup and my falsies you should get yourself a beau or two. They just dote on us painted creatures of the theayter."

Exhausted by this flight of irony she dropped her head between her knees again, and moaned softly. Moaning seemed to ease her pain.

Hector had seen the rose thrown from the window; there were roses everywhere, but he was sure that it was one of his. However, he had no time to brood deeply about it, for he was needed in the first scene. To simulate the rolling and pitching of a ship at sea Larry Pye had devised an ingenious contraption upon which the actors stood, partly screened by shrubbery, while they were tossed and heaved hither and thither by the tempest, the sound of which was simulated by Cobbler's orchestra and a variety of wind-machines and thunder-strips backstage. It was a taxing scene and Hector, who had never been good at doing two things at once, had to exert all his wits in order to keep his balance and recognize his cues when they came. When this ordeal was over, and the audience was applauding heartily (as audiences always do when they see actors being put to great inconvenience and indignity) Hector was just able to roll seasickly to a bench and close his eyes, trying to calm his queasy stomach; he had had virtually nothing to eat for the past forty-eight hours, and the world swam giddily about him while the great voice of Professor Vambrace was heard from the stage, in Prospero's seemingly interminable narrative of misfortune.

It was a long wait until Act Two, when he appeared again, and Hector sat lonely on his bench, with bustle all about him. Griselda, lovely in the costume of Ariel, seemed once about to approach him, and he raised his eyes to hers, but then she knit her brows and turned away. Wherever she was, he was conscious of her. He was by no means sensitive to music, but when she sang "Come unto these yellow sands" and "Full fathom five" his soul was ravished because it was Griselda who was singing. When she stood ready to run onto the stage in the costume of a water-nymph, which Mrs. Crundale conceived as the merest wisp of sea-green gauze, his bowels yearned at her beauty, and his heart ached because so much of it was to be seen by any member of the audience who had paid his dollar for a seat. But most of all he grieved because the rose which she had thrown to Roger —one of his own roses—was conclusive proof to him that she was frail, that she was no better than those hired girls, taken in sin, whom it had been the Reverend John Mackilwraith's duty to scold, exhort and pray over in the manse parlour in the days of his childhood.

At the beginning of Act Two of *The Tempest* Gonzalo is required to appear as a rather jolly and witty old gentleman. Hector had never fully succeeded in rising to the demands of this scene, though he never failed in it with such thorough-going dismalness as on the first night. But one thing happened which puzzled sharp-sighted members of the audience: when Ariel bent over the form of the sleeping Gonzalo and sang in his ear

> *While you here do snoring lie,*
> *Open-eyed conspiracy*
>   *His time doth take.*
> *If of life you keep a care,*
> *Shake off slumber and beware:*
>   *Awake, awake!*

it was observable that Gonzalo stirred in his rest like a tortured man, and a single, unmistakable tear crept down his left cheek. Fortunately he had little to do in the Third Act, for what he said was inaudible and when he moved he seemed to stumble more often than a simulation of old age could excuse.

She had seen him, of course. The throwing of that rose to Roger was coldly calculated; it was a sign to him that she had received his message, understood it, and scorned it. Well, let it be so. He had had no solid food that day; his head ached and buzzed, and often dizziness overcame him so that he stumbled. But it would not be for long.

The single interval which Valentine had decreed for the play was over, and Act Four was about to begin. Gonzalo was not wanted in Act Four. Gonzalo was not wanted any-where, it appeared. Very well. When you weren't wanted there was only one thing to do, and that was to get out.

Hector hurried quietly along the path to The Shed. Good, it was empty. He did not need long. No necessity to rule his black book into *Pro* and *Contra*. He knew exactly what he wanted to do, and it would not take much time to do it.

Would she be sorry? Would she ever know? There were his roses, and their message, to speak for him. Perhaps she would be sorry that she had not accepted the help which he had offered. Would she ever know that behind that offer of help there lay a great love, everything that a man of forty, who had made his own way in the world and risen in a difficult profession, could offer? Surely she would realize it. And, realizing it, would she not sicken of the hateful Roger, reject him and live a good life—a life beautiful and sad— ever after? Or might it not be that in the course of time she would meet some kind and understanding man whom she would marry, and with whom she would bring up a family in which the name of Hector Mackilwraith would be honoured? Undoubtedly that would be it. Indeed, in this terrible hour he was certainly gifted with prophecy; that *was* what would happen. But as every good thing must spring from sacrifice and atonement, he must not falter now.

Plenty of cord here; good, heavy stuff; a superior sort of sashcord. He unfastened one of the many ropes which controlled the glasswork in the roof of The Shed, and sought to tie a noose in it. But one cannot tie a good noose without some training and previous experience, and after ten minutes all that Hector had achieved was a loop, contrived with clumsy granny-knots. The knot which his purpose demanded had, he had been told, thirteen turns in it; however, this would serve. He was ready. After a few unsuccessful throws he managed to get the noose over one of the iron supports in the ceiling, and it hung above some boxes which were hidden behind a screen. Good. He estimated the drop at about eight feet; in that, at least, he could be sure of accuracy.

Before climbing on the boxes he looked at himself in one of the make-up mirrors. His face was hideous with Auntie Puss's handiwork, and his hair was streaked with yellow paint. He tore off the false beard, and mopped his face with a towel. He was calm now, though he felt deathly ill.

With the aid of a chair he climbed upon the boxes, and

settled the noose about his neck.

Well, this was it. But before he left the world forever, should he not say some word of committal? It was many years since he had prayed, but he had always thought of himself as a religious sort of man, and he believed firmly in God. Would God understand this sudden abandonment of a decreed existence? Yes, undoubtedly Hector's God would understand Hector; there would be no TOSASM scribbled across his final record. God would know that it was an atonement, a sacrifice that another might be cleansed, indeed the only way to save the soul of Griselda Webster. God would know why he had done it.

Nevertheless, something seemed to be called for. He groped in his mind for prayer, but nothing came. A favourite phrase of his father's, used often when the Reverend John was gravelled for lack of matter in an extemporary prayer, came back to him. "O Lord, take Thou a live coal from off Thine altar and touch our lips." Yes. Then what? By now Hector was weeping desperately, and all that he could think of was "O God, here I come!" It seemed unworthy of the moment, but it was the best he could do.

Sobbing, hardly conscious, Hector leaped from his platform into the unknown. There was a jerk, a crash, a sound of artillery fire, and oblivion.

CHAPTER

8

INTO HECTOR's consciousness swam a fearful eye, a blue iris rolling upon what might have been a mound of bloodshot blancmange. Sometimes it was horribly clear; sometimes it retreated into nauseating deliquescence. A huge, accusing eye, set, no doubt, in the Head of the Supreme Being. The eye seemed to melt, growing larger as it did so; then it suddenly became very clear again, and from far away he heard a voice.

"Whatever made you do such a wicked thing?"

At the sound he experienced that sensation of falling swiftly which is so common after the first few minutes of sleep. Sensations rushed upon him. He was wet and miserable; has head ached dreadfully; he had a pain in his neck; he was cold. And there, kneeling beside him on the floor of The Shed, was Auntie Puss, staring intently into his face through her magnifying glass.

"You poor, wretched, sinful man," she said. "Are you all right?"

"My head aches," he said. And immediately: "My throat hurts."

"You may think yourself lucky that your head is still on your shoulders," said Auntie Puss. "Can you get up?"

Hector tried to raise himself, but sank back dizzily, squelching in a pool of whatever it was he was lying in.

"Is it blood?" he asked, his eyes closed.

"No; I presume it is whatever you were drinking before you attempted this rash act. You appear to have had plenty of it, I must say."

Under this unjust accusation Hector stirred a little, and the liquid foamed and seethed all about him.

"I must get help," said Auntie Puss, and added unnecessarily, "you stay where you are."

She went out, locked the door of The Shed and carried away the key in her pocket. Backstage she found Valentine, and plucked her by the sleeve. Then she whispered in her ear.

"You must come with me at once. Most important."

But Valentine was in an extremely bad temper. Professor Vambrace, disregarding her opinion in the matter, had sneaked a stem of seven grapes upon the stage, and had attempted to eat them during the most famous speech in the play. It is not simple to eat seven grapes while speaking thirteen lines. Three grapes had undone him, and five made him sound like a man talking under water; he had desperately gulped his mouthful, and pushed in the last two grapes, but he was badly rattled by his experience, and as he tossed away the empty stem— the crown of his ingenious bit of byplay—a loud and prolonged belch had burst from the depths of his beard. There had been laughter and some ironical applause. Valentine was waiting for the Professor to come off the stage. She had something to say to him.

Auntie Puss tugged at her sleeve again, and drew Valentine down so that she might whisper in her ear. A moment later they were hurrying toward The Shed.

Valentine was, as Cobbler had said, a thorough professional, and her first remarks to Hector proved it.

"What the hell do you mean by trying to kill yourself in the middle of a performance?" said she. "Before a performance, perhaps: after a performance, possibly. But what in the name of common sense possessed you to do it while you still have an entrance to make? Do you realize that there are eight hundred and thirty-two people out there, of whom seven hundred and ninety have paid admission, whose pleasure you have imperilled? Do you realize that you have very nearly ruined the effect of seven weeks' rehearsal? Get up at once, and pull yourself together."

Hector was startled by this display of heartlessness and bad temper, and he tried to do as he was told. But he could not rise beyond a kneeling posture, and fell down again. Valentine was contrite at once.

"I'm sorry, Mr. Mackilwraith, but I'm terribly angry at that fool of a Vambrace, and I'm taking it out on you. What's the matter? Do you feel very dreadful? What can I get for you?"

The kindness in her voice was too much for Hector, and he sobbed.

"What made you do it? Can you tell me? I'll help you if I can."

He tried to speak, but the only word he could say was "Griselda", and then he wept again, hiding his face in his arm.

That was enough for Valentine, however. So the poor, silly man loved Griselda Webster, and it had brought him to this! There he lay, in a pale frothing liquid which she had, for a dreadful moment, believed to be some eccentric vital fluid of his own, but which issued from a case of broken bottles which lay near him. He was drenched, his face was smeared with makeup, and there was yellow paint in his hair. All pity for him, she dragged him to drier ground, and sat upon the floor, with his head in her lap. She wiped his face with a handkerchief.

"Poor Hector," said she; "was it very bad?"

He nodded, and she could feel his body relax a little. Her comfort had started him back on the road to self-possession. It was for the best part wordless comfort—the warm, cherishing, unquestioning feminine sympathy which he had not known (and then, how meagrely) since his childhood—which Valentine gave him, but it drew him gently back from Death and the longing for Death. And so they sat for perhaps ten minutes, during which she said little, and he said nothing, but his face, which had been shapeless and hideous with grief, began to take on a more human look. His spirit was returning.

Larry's voice boomed from the loud-speaker: "Every body for Act Five please. Act Five in three minutes. Has any body seen Gonzalo? Act Five."

All the healing stillness left Valentine in an instant. "Oh, God!" she cried; "what do I do now?"

But almost as she spoke she had leaped to her feet. Hector's beard was upon the table; she quickly dabbed her face with spirit gum and fastened it on. He had removed his cloak and cap before he had climbed upon the boxes. She put them upon herself. "If Sybil Thorndike could play Lear, I don't see why I can't play Gonzalo," she said to Hector, and in her voice the actress had wholly supplanted the divinely tender creature who had seemed to coax him back from the realm of the dead. "Stay here; I'll be back as soon as I can."

Transformed into a somewhat odd old gentleman, she rushed through the door. Auntie Puss was keeping faithful guard there.

"Is he all right?"

"He will be, Miss Pottinger. Don't let anybody in."

"You may rely on me."

"I'm sure I may."

"Did he say anything to you about why he tried it?"

"Yes. To you, too?"

"He was unconscious, but he mentioned a name, more than once."

"We'd better keep that quiet, don't you think?"

"Miss Rich, nothing could make me divulge it."

Auntie Puss had need of all the resolution which an old-fashioned upbringing had given her, in order to keep her word. As soon as Valentine appeared upon the stage as Gonzalo, the whole cast seemed to know, magically, that Mackilwraith was ill, that there was some mystery about his illness, and that Auntie Puss had the key to the mystery. The audience suspected nothing, for they had paid little heed to Gonzalo before, and idly noted that he appeared to have come to life in the last act, although he played most of it with his back to them. But the audience did know that Roscoe Forrester had beckoned Dr. Bliss from his seat, and that Dr. Bliss had tiptoed out with that stealth peculiar to doctors, which is so much more noticeable than a frank exit. The play came to its end, and the cast was recalled for six bows, but Valentine did not remain with them. She ran at once to The Shed and was locked within with Hector and the doctor, while Auntie Puss stood guard at the door, and refused to say anything to anybody.

The general opinion was that Hector had had a fit. Some said it was apoplexy; others said it was heart. Geordie Shortreed, for no reason that anybody could discover, thought that it was a scandal of some kind; those quiet ones were the worst, he said with relish; perhaps it was something about a boy. The cast would not go to their dressing-rooms and change; they stood about behind the stage, chattering and gossiping and speculating, big with the mystery of The Shed. There were those, however, who had other concerns. Nellie Forrester, near to tears, rushed to Professor Vambrace.

"Oh Walter, wasn't it awful?"

"Distressing, certainly, but it will be all right tomorrow night."

"But how can it be?"

"I shall rehearse it all day tomorrow."

"What are you talking about?"

"My business with the seven grapes: I shouldn't have called it 'awful', myself. I'm sure the audience didn't notice. It just needs touching up."

"I don't know what you mean."

"Indeed? I suppose you are engrossed in this nonsense about Mackilwraith."

"I don't know anything about him. But didn't you see her go?"

"Who?"

"Mrs. Caesar Augustus Conquergood. She left before the beginning of the fifth act. I felt so humiliated."

"Probably she found the night air a little chilly. But don't be distressed; there are still four performances. I'll buy a pound of grapes tomorrow and make Pearl work with me all afternoon. I shall have my business with the grapes perfect by tomorrow night."

"I don't think it was cold at all. She left because she was bored. I just knew it. Do you suppose we ought to have put her name on the programme in bigger type? She was as big as Val and bigger than Shakespeare. It was a mistake ever to do this play out of doors. I'll never have anything to do with a Pastoral again."

It was impossible to keep everyone in the dark. When Dr. Bliss had assured himself that there was nothing wrong with Hector except shock, hunger, and a wetting, he suggested that he be moved to a place where he might rest, and that meant that Mr. Webster had to be let into part of the secret. Both guestrooms at St. Agnes' were occupied, one by the Nymphs and the other by the girls who had speaking parts in the play, for at the last minute Griselda had decided that it would be inhospitable to make the girls use makeshift dressing rooms. Mr. Webster was a humane man, but something within him powerfully resisted the idea that an unsuccessful suicide should curl up in his bed, and therefore he led the way to his daughter Griselda's pretty room, and Roscoe and Dr. Bliss helped the feeble Hector to slip off his wet clothes, put on a pair of Mr. Webster's pyjamas, and crawl into the bed there. As they passed the Nymphs' dressing room the door was opened a crack, and a bright eye appeared for a moment, and within a few minutes the Nymphs, and the girls in the other dressing room, and all their friends, knew that Hector Mackilwraith had attempted to drown himself, and had been taken upstairs in St. Agnes', soaking wet.

Fortunately The Shed had not been used as a dressing room for the men of the cast, but only as a makeup room and a greenroom. But even so, there were a variety of personal articles in it which had to be restored to their owners, and it was not Valentine's wish to have everyone snooping around The Shed, guessing at what had happened. Therefore she sought out Solly and Cobbler, told them that she wanted to keep The Shed closed, and asked them to see that the men's property was taken back to the men's dressing room, which was in the basement of the house. They went to The Shed and found the way barred by Auntie Puss.

"No one may go in here at present," said she.

"But Miss Pottinger," said Solly, "we have special orders from Miss Rich."

"Perhaps, then, Miss Rich will be good enough to come here and tell me so."

"My dear lady," said Cobbler; "it is needless to dissemble; we are privy to the dark secret of The Shed. We are going in to mop up the blood."

"I don't understand what you are talking about," said Auntie Puss.

"It's really quite all right," said Solly; "we know what happened."

"If that is so, you have no right to speak of it in that flippant tone."

"And why not, if I may ask?" said Cobbler, argumentatively. "Why should we go all solemn because Mackilwraith has hashed up his attempt at suicide?"

"Hush!" said Auntie Puss, fiercely. "Don't you dare to use that word."

"It's the right word, isn't it?"

"It will provoke a scandal if it gets around. Do you want to ruin the man's life?"

"He's just done his best to ruin it himself."

"That has nothing to do with it. He has been spared, doubtless for some purpose beyond our understanding. If you so much as hint at it again, Mr. Cobbler, I'll speak to the Dean about you, and you will have to find yourself another position."

"Blackmail!" said Cobbler.

"Call it what you like," said Auntie Puss. "This man deserves his chance, and I shall do whatever I can to see that he gets it. I do not approve of the modern custom of babbling disgraceful secrets to anybody and everybody. I do not know Mr. Mackilwraith well, and what I do know about him I do not care for, but I will not be a party to his ruin. Do you understand me, Mr. Cobbler?"

"I hear you, Miss Pottinger, but I shall never understand you. The world is full of people who have tried to kill themselves, or who have at least thought about it. It's as natural as falling in love or getting one's heart broken. I don't see what's so disgraceful about it. It's the first interesting thing Mackilwraith has ever done, so far as I know."

Valentine appeared around the corner of the house.

"Thank you so much, Miss Pottinger," said she. "Will you let me have the key now? Mr. Webster is offering some refreshment in his library. Perhaps you had better have a hot drink. You've been wonderful, keeping watch for so long."

"I am glad to do whatever I can," said Auntie Puss, who had been shivering a little in the night air. "And I advise you to remember, Mr. Cobbler, that I can do more." She rattled off toward the house, her head erect.

"My respect for Mackilwraith was never very high, and it is dropping every minute," said Solly, as they went into The Shed. "Can you imagine a man of any gumption at all thinking that he could hang himself with a rotten old rope like that? I'll bet it's fifty years old. What a boob."

"I don't suppose he thought about it very clearly," said Valentine.

"Oh yes he did," said Cobbler. "He probably imagined he was wrapped up in his sorrows, but we all have keener perception than we know. The superficial Mackilwraith, the despairing lover, thought the rope would do, but the true, essential, deep-down Mackilwraith knew damn well that it wouldn't. You don't play safe for forty years and then cut loose. Our Hector was looking for pity, not death."

"Why do you call him the despairing lover?" asked Valentine, who had thought that this was a secret between herself and Auntie Puss.

"Because it's obvious that's why he did it. He's been mooning after the Impatient Griselda for weeks. Surely you noticed? Anyway, he told me so—or as good as admitted it—at that awful brawl of yours, Bridgetower. I had a notion that he'd do something silly, though I never thought it would be anything as silly as this."

"Well, do keep it quiet, won't you, Humphrey," said Valentine. "We don't want to make trouble for him—more trouble than he has now, that's to say."

"I don't know why everybody imagines that I am going to run around town blatting everything I know. That old poll-parrot at the door said exactly the same thing to me, though much less nicely. I'm not going to blab. On the honour of a Fellow of the Royal College of Organists. But I don't see why I can't discuss it with you two; you know all about it anyway."

"It would be rather hard on Griselda. People might think she had driven him to it."

"That would merely enhance her reputation as a charmer. But really I don't suppose she had anything to do with it."

"What, then?" asked Solly.

"She was just a hook on which Mackilwraith hung a middle-aged man's nerve-storm. Do you know what I think ails Mackilwraith? Male menopause. This is his last fling at romance before he goes out of business entirely as a male creature."

"He can't be much over forty," said Valentine.

"Spiritually—if one may use the word of Hector— he's been seventy for years. No, it's the male climacteric. The last gutterings of the candle—the gurgle of the last pint of suds in the drain."

"Well, I don't agree," said Solly. "I think its the logical outcome of his education and the sort of life he has led. He's vulgar. I don't mean just that he wears awful suits and probably eats awful food: I mean that he has a crass soul. He thinks that when his belly is full and his job safe, he's got the world by the tail. He has never found out anything about himself, so how can he ever know anything about other people? The condition of a vulgarian is that he never expects anything good or bad that happens to him to be the result of his own personality; he always thinks it's Fate, especially if it's bad. The only people who make any sense in the world are those who know that whatever happens to them has its roots in what they are."

"I think you are both hard on him," said Valentine. "When I found him he was really very touching. You're both away off the track."

"Dear Val," said Solly; "if I were in a mess like that I would pray to be found by somebody like you. Somebody that pities, and doesn't natter and theorize."

"I'm happy to theorize," said Cobbler; "I keep my feelings for musical purposes."

"I'm going to see if I can get Griselda to talk to him for a little," said Valentine.

"That's brilliant," said Solly; "maybe that will put him on his feet."

"A wonderful idea, but do you think they should be alone together?" said Cobbler. "I mean, there ought to be somebody there, just to see that he doesn't get maudlin and embarrass the girl. I'd be happy to do it, if nobody else wants to."

"You're aching to snoop," said Valentine.

"Of course I am. Curiosity is the mainspring of my life. If I weren't curious I'd probably be an egocentric pinhead like Mackilwraith."

The door of The Shed opened, and Freddy came in, dressed in slacks and a shirt, followed by Tom.

"We came to clean up," said Freddy. "I suppose you'll want this room again tomorrow night?"

"Tomorrow afternoon," said Valentine. "Hadn't you heard that we are doing a special matinee for school children?"

"A brutish auditory, at half-price, but we artists must bear it in the sacred name of education," interjected Cobbler.

"No; I hadn't heard a thing about it," said Freddy.

"Heavens, I thought I had told all the cast. It was a last-minute decision of Nellie's; it appears that a few hundred kids are still confined to school, and they can all be roped in at fifty cents a head. I must go at once and make sure everybody knows," said Valentine, and ran out of The Shed.

"We'll help you clear things away," said Solly.

"Oh don't bother. Daddy's giving drinks to a few favoured souls in the library. I'm sure you would count as favoured souls if you went along."

"We'll go when we've helped you," said Cobbler. "I'm anxious to know what this stuff is that Mackilwraith knocked over. It has a vinous smell. In fact, Roscoe told me that Mackilwraith smelt like a big pickle as he was hoisting him up your stairs."

"That's my champagne cider," said Freddy, sadly. "Tom hid it away so nicely. It looks as though the old fool had contrived to break every bottle, and even at that he couldn't finish himself off."

"Not every bottle," said Cobbler. "Here are a couple with the corks in under this table. Shall we try it?"

"Please do," said Freddy. "There's not much point in keeping two. But we'll have to drink out of the necks, turn about." Two corks popped merrily, and they sat down to sample Freddy's vintage.

"Not bad," said Tom.

"Thanks, Tom, you're a big encouragement to me," said Freddy. "You know, Tom and I have figured out why Mackilwraith tried to kill himself."

"How did you learn that?"

"Oh, everybody knows it, except Nellie and Walter Vambrace and a few of the stupider sort."

"Well, why did he do it?" said Cobbler.

"Cheap religion," said Freddy.

"The way we see it, sir," said Tom, after taking a second long draught of the champagne cider, "is like this. Too many people today are like this fellow Mackilwraith. They don't believe, and they haven't got the strength of mind to disbelieve. They won't get rid of religion, and they won't go after a religion that means anything. They just mess with religion. Now if this fellow Mackilwraith had been a believer —and I don't mind saying that I'm thinking of the C. of E.—

he would have known that suicide is a sin, and his belief would have held him up in his trouble. And if he'd been an unbeliever he'd either have had too much guts to do it, or guts enough to finish it off proper. See?"

"If he'd been a strong believer or a strong unbeliever he wouldn't have been pushed off his trolley just because he couldn't get to first base with Gristle," said Freddy. "Do you know, Tom, this isn't bad at all; just as soon as the apples come in, I'm going to get busy on a bigger and better batch."

"Not bad," said Cobbler, "but not champagne. Just good cider with ideas above its station."

"I know," said Freddy, a little sadly, "but you can't make something wonderful unless you start with the right stuff."

"Like making a romantic lover out of Hector Mackil-wraith," said Solly.

The second bottle clutched in his hand, Cobbler launched into a lecture on religion, speaking as one who had been in the service of Holy Church since his ninth year.

Hector was not quite asleep. He lay happily in the bed, the softest he had ever known, with a hot-water bottle at his feet, and a cup of beef-tea and brandy working magically in his stomach. He had no thoughts beyond the moment, and a general thankfulness that he was not dead.

Outside the door someone seemed to be moving, very quietly, as though standing first upon one foot and then the other. The room was wonderfully peaceful in the light of a single lamp, and Hector could not summon up enough interest even to wonder who it might be. But at last the door opened, and Griselda came in, wearing her dressing gown.

"Are you asleep?"

"No."

"Valentine said she thought I'd better come and say good-night."

She stood by the foot of the bed, saying nothing, looking lovelier than Hector had ever seen her. Now, mysteriously, he was no longer afraid of her.

"I'm glad you came."

"Thanks. Sorry you're feeling mouldy."

"I'm all right."

"The doctor says you can't go home tonight, of course."

"I hope I'm not putting anyone out of this bed."

"Oh that's all right; I can sleep in one of the other rooms."

"It's yours?"

A dark flush spread over Hector's face. He was in Griselda's bed! But he was too tired, too blissfully at rest, to be deeply embarrassed. Griselda seemed to be trying to say something; she was blushing, and dug into the carpet with one foot. For the first time Hector saw that she was not much more than a child. At last she spoke.

"You shouldn't have done it, you know."

"No, I shouldn't."

"You must promise not to do it again."

"I won't."

Another pause, and Griselda was now very red. She suddenly sat down on the bed and took his hand.

"I'd feel dreadful if you did, you know. Because of me."

So she knew. Well, he didn't care. He was too happy.

"What made you think it would help?"

"I can't really remember, now."

She said no more. He felt that he must say something.

"Griselda."

"Yes?"

"You're too good for Tasset. Don't let him spoil you."

"I don't care for him at all. Did you think I did?"

"Yes."

"And it was because of that?"

"Yes."

"I never knew that you cared about me at all."

"I did."

"But you don't any more?"

"Not the same way; now that I know you're safe."

"What are you going to do?"

"I'm going away from Salterton. I've had an offer of a job in the Department. A very good job, really; quite a step up."

"How wonderful."

Another pause. At last Griselda spoke.

"I'd better go now. But I don't want you to think I don't know what a lot of trouble I've made for you."

"It was nothing."

"But I couldn't know, you see."

"Of course not. You couldn't know."

"And it wouldn't really have done, would it?"

"No: I see that now. It wouldn't have done at all."

"Well, good-night, Mr. Mackilwraith."

Hector looked up into her serious face, and for the first time in weeks, he laughed. After a puzzled moment, Griselda smiled.

"Good-night, Hector."

She leaned forward as she had done in that first dream, and kissed him. Then she turned out the lamp, and closed the door behind her.

Hector slept.